SON OF THE BLACK SWORD

LARRY CORREIA

A Baen Books Original

Baen Publishing Enterprises
P.O. Box 1403
Riverdale, NY 10471
www.baen.com

ISBN: 978-1-4767-8086-3

Cover art and frontispiece by Larry Elmore
Map by Isaac Stewart

First printing, November 2015

Distributed by Simon & Schuster
1230 Avenue of the Americas
New York, NY 10020

Library of Congress Cataloging-in-Publication Data

Correia, Larry.
  Son of the black sword / Larry Correia.
      pages ; cm. — (Saga of the forgotten warrior ; 1)
   ISBN 978-1-4767-8086-3 (hardcover)
   I. Title.
   PS3603.O7723S63 2015
   813'.6—dc23
                                                        2015025741

10 9 8 7 6 5 4 3 2 1

Pages by Joy Freeman (www.pagesbyjoy.com)
Printed in the United States of America

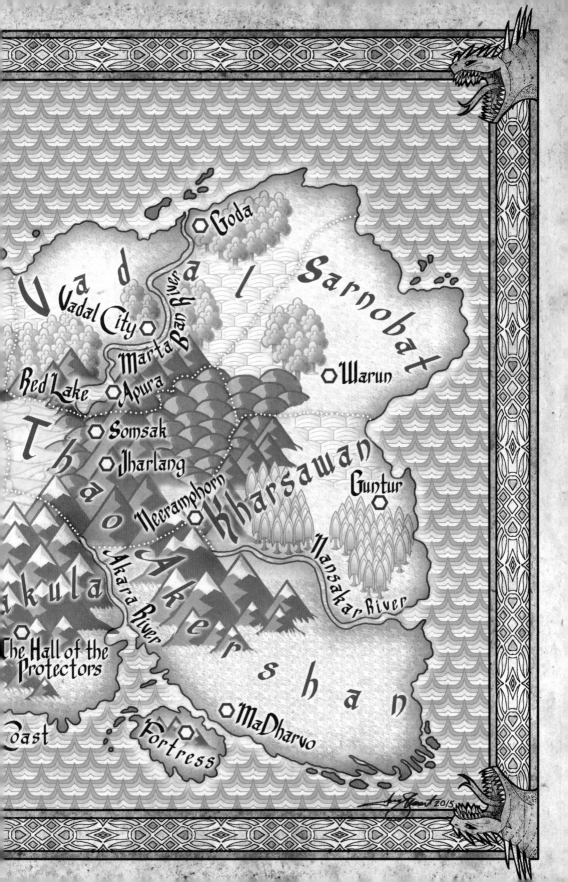

SON OF THE BLACK SWORD

BAEN BOOKS by LARRY CORREIA

THE SAGA OF THE FORGOTTEN WARRIOR SERIES
Son of the Black Sword

THE MONSTER HUNTER INTERNATIONAL SERIES
Monster Hunter International
Monster Hunter Vendetta
Monster Hunter Alpha
The Monster Hunters (compilation)
Monster Hunter Legion
Monster Hunter Nemesis

THE GRIMNOIR CHRONICLES
Hard Magic: Book 1 of the Grimnoir Chronicles
Spellbound: Book 2 of the Grimnoir Chronicles
Warbound: Book 3 of the Grimnoir Chronicles

WITH MIKE KUPARI:
Dead Six
Swords of Exodus

To Lawrence

SON
OF THE
BLACK
SWORD

Chapter 1

The familiar dream was always the same. He was on his knees, wiping a stone floor clean. The rag soaked up the red puddle, a mixture of soapy water and blood. When he wrung the tattered cloth out over his washbucket it ran in pink rivulets across his hands, a child's hands.

A noise intruded on the dream, waking him.

Footsteps.

He moved one hand to his sword, and in the hazy moment between sleep and reality, it still seemed to be a child's hand, dripping with watered-down blood, but the dream faded and reality returned. Now it was a man's hand, callused by training and scarred by battle. That hand belonged to Protector of the Law, twenty-year senior Ashok Vadal, and he did not clean blood. He spilled it.

Listening carefully, Ashok decided that the noise had come from just outside his tent. A warrior had approached, then stopped there probably to gather up his courage before waking their honored guest. Ashok relaxed and released Angruvadal's grip. Reaching for it first was an old habit. If the sword needed to be drawn, it would have told him.

The blood scrubbing dream had come to him many times before, but as usual it held no wisdom, no revelations. It meant

1

nothing. After all, it was only a dream. It was a fabrication of the mind, not a memory. It was not real. The stifling heat was real. The moist, clinging air was real. He'd been sleeping beneath hanging silks because the stinging flies that infested this region were all too real. The sweaty discomfort reminded him that he was in the wretched northern jungles of Great House Gujara, and that he'd been ordered here to kill a demon. The waking noises of the temporary camp and the unusual silence of the jungle suggested that the demon had shown itself.

The messenger hadn't announced himself yet. Ashok was used to low-status members of the warrior caste behaving this way around him, either out of respect for his office or fear of his reputation. He'd been listening to their whispered rumors for two decades now, half of which weren't true, and the other half exaggerated, but it was no wonder messengers were always so nervous around him. It was always best to cut through the awkward pause. "Is it time?" Ashok asked through the canvas.

"The demon has been sighted, Protector."

"Where?" He rolled out from beneath the silks and found his clothing in the dark.

"It's raiding a village on the coast right now." The warrior was trying to keep the fear out of his voice, and mostly succeeding. "The messenger said it's already slaughtered dozens!"

"So it's close then?"

"Yes, Protector. The demon is *very* close."

Good. It was too damned hot to have to chase it.

Ashok sprinted along the darkened path toward the sounds of screaming. His appointed escorts—a paltan of fifty warriors—were behind him, struggling and failing to keep up. The soldiers were on foot because horses didn't survive for long in the humid, muddy, vine-choked, insect-infested northern peninsula of House Gujara, so their warrior caste had no cavalry tradition here. However, when it came to fighting a demon, being on foot was not a disadvantage. Horses were terrified by demons, and no matter how well trained, could not be relied upon.

Besides, for short distances such as this, Ashok could outrun a horse.

He began to encounter fleeing villagers along the path. There were a few men, women, and children of the worker caste, but most of the refugees were casteless non-people. It made sense, because only the lowest of the low would be condemned to live close to the seashore. Many of those he passed were wounded, mostly from crashing through the thorny brush, but a few were showing the blackened, bloody patches that came from simply brushing against a demon's hide. Rub a hand against a demon one direction, it was smooth, almost soft, but run it the opposite and leave your palm behind.

There had been no time for the villagers to gather their possessions. Since the demon had struck in the middle of the night, most of the villagers weren't even clothed, but a few of the casteless were carrying squealing pigs or squawking chickens. Nonpeople were pragmatic that way. As he drew closer to the village the fleeing crowd became thicker and he had to dodge between them. They were terrified, desperate to escape, but he moved through the crushing mob effortlessly, like a raindrop falling from the sky and rolling between the leaves of a tree, seeking its inevitable path. Behind him there was a great deal of shouting as the warrior caste crashed into and roughly shoved their inferiors out of their way, off the path, and into the stabbing thorn vines.

The village was close now. The breaking of wood and the crack and pop of fire could be heard over the panicked cries. The demon itself would make no sound. They never did. Ashok could smell smoke and blood and spilled bowels, but the demon itself would have no scent. It would be a swift black shadow, with claws harder than steel, a mouth full of razor teeth, and the strength of an elephant.

The orange light from several burning huts cast wild shadows through the trees. The thick jungle parted. There wasn't much open space between the jungle and the high tide, so the ramshackle buildings had been packed tightly, practically on top of each other, and built on stilts to keep them dry above the rocky beach. Bridges constructed of wood and hemp connected the structures, and they were swaying violently as people ran across, trying to escape the spreading fires and the demon's hunger. Beyond the village was the vast dark ocean. Nothing came from the sea except for regret, fish, and demons.

There was no sign of the demon yet, but Ashok knew it was in there somewhere. His sword could sense it as well, and Angruvadal was demanding to be drawn in order to dispense death. *Not yet.* Demons seemed to sense black steel, and he didn't want to frighten the creature away. If it returned to the sea, there would be no way to follow, and he'd have to wait for another chance to catch it.

As he caught his breath, he noticed several warriors stationed at the end of the jungle path, shouting at the villagers to flee for their lives, as if the encouragement was needed. The soldiers were armed with spears and wearing the simple cloth and hide armor preferred by House Gujara, where rust was a greater enemy than actual enemies. Despite being equipped for battle and raised their entire lives to do nothing but fight, they were in no hurry to enter that burning maze to take on a demon.

"Go back the way you came! There's a sea demon here!" a very young soldier warned when he saw Ashok emerge from the jungle. "Run away while you can."

The firelight was flickering and unreliable, so the junior nayak had probably not realized who he was ordering around. Ashok didn't take his warning as an insult against his courage. He entered the circle of torchlight, and when they saw his armor they shut their mouths. "Which one of you is in command?"

The soldier realized what manner of man he's been speaking to. "Apologies, Protector! Our havildar is Virata!" It was part explanation, part summons, and then he realized that, demon incursion or not, he'd better bow to someone of such high station, so he dipped his head so fast that his padded helmet fell off into the sand. "I'll fetch him. *Havildar!* A Protector is here!"

"A Protector? Impossible." Another warrior, gone a bit fat, came jogging up. He was too old to hold the low rank of havildar—a leader of ten—but of course, a great house would only send the dim and disgraced from among its warrior caste to protect a cursed holding such as this. "Our house has abandoned us. We're all going to die here. There's no—"

The ornate armor of the Protector Order should have been a giveaway, but Ashok showed him the token of his office so there could be no question about who was now in charge. The officer's eyes widened when he saw the gold flash in the firelight. "Take me to the sea demon," Ashok said.

"I can't!" the officer wailed.

Ashok couldn't believe his ears. The Law was clear about both of their duties in this situation. "Are you disobeying my order?" His tone was cold. "Calm yourself and speak carefully before you answer."

"No, Protector. It was...I don't know...I saw it reach through old Ravna's stomach, take hold of his spine, and pull his head right through his shoulders. Such a thing can't be real! I ordered a retreat because we had to run. I had no choice."

That babbling didn't answer Ashok's question. The havildar was stupid with fear. Demons could shatter even a great warrior's courage, and he was fairly certain this man had never been counted among House Gujara's great to begin with. "Calm yourself and tell me, where is the demon?"

The havildar cowered. "Too strong...Too much blood. I can't...Won't go back..."

In a time of crisis, some men might shirk their duties, but to a Protector, obedience was everything, and the Law required him to punish this demon for trespassing. He couldn't do it if they were lollygagging around while it swam back to sea, so Ashok backhanded the warrior in the mouth hard enough to loosen a few teeth from his jaw. The officer fell in the sand, whimpering.

"*Where?*"

"We saw it in the storehouse!" interjected the young soldier before Ashok could put his boot to the havildar. He was pointing into one of the larger fires. "Past that big building there. Last I saw, the demon was heading toward the casteless quarter, that direction."

The casteless were not people, they were property, but they looked enough like real men that the sea demon probably wouldn't be able to tell the difference. Ashok could only assume that non-people tasted the same as real people to a demon.

"It was huge! It had to duck to get through the big storehouse door." The junior soldier lifted one hand as high as possible, stretching it over his head, and even stood on his toes.

The nayak was tall, nearly as tall as Ashok, in fact. Even allowing for some exaggeration from the terror of seeing such a thing, that meant this demon was a big one. The larger demons that bothered to come up on shore were particularly bloodthirsty, and their raiding period could often last an entire season. If it wasn't stopped tonight, then its rampage would continue, night after night, until it was killed or sated. It would take a few minutes for his fifty-man escort to catch up, and when they did they would be too out of breath to be immediately useful. The demon would surely sense the arrival of that many soldiers and might decide to leave. It couldn't be allowed to escape.

"Reinforcements are coming. Tell the risaldar in charge that I've gone after it."

"Alone?"

Ashok drew the ancestor blade of Great House Vadal from the sheath on his belt. Angruvadal was eager. The sword retained the collected martial instincts of every man who had ever carried it into battle, all in a length of metal so black that it absorbed the light around it, and so sharp that it could even pierce the hide of a demon. The nayak realized what it was and took a fearful step back.

I am never alone.

The heat was so intense that it was difficult to even approach the growing fire. A black shape shot between the storehouse and a burning shack. Ashok would have followed directly, but his skin was not nearly as impervious as that of his prey. Despite the fact that they lived their lives beneath the waves, fire didn't seem to harm demons. Ashok ran along the shore, leaping from rock to rock, looking for a path through the flames. Unclean saltwater soaked his boots, and he cursed the fools who would build a village in such a tainted place.

Most of the residents had fled or died. Now the demon was just toying with the stragglers, feasting before it returned to the depths. They'd always struck him as spiteful that way. He spotted the demon again as it leapt over a rope bridge, but then he lost it in the smoke. The air scorched his eyes as he started up a narrow ramp after it. Ashok paused to tie a scarf over the lower half of his face in a vain attempt to strain the air. It made sense that the creature would have the advantage here. Demons could breathe air or water, and in comparison to that, what trouble was smoke?

Ashok selected a path and pushed on through the maze of connected huts and scaffolding. The bridge was flimsy and rocked wildly as he ran across. He reached a solid platform, and a lucky shift of the wind granted him a lungful of decent air and a clear view. A few coughing survivors pushed past him to climb down the ladders. One desperately leapt over the side to fall into the black waves. It was foolhardy to ever touch Hell, but it was shallow enough here that nothing immediately tried to devour that worker. Tonight the ocean's nightmares were on dry land.

He had been taught that the best way to track a demon was to follow the signs of chaos. Wherever demons went, they left carnage in their wake. They were the living embodiment of destruction. Sword in hand, Ashok moved down the platform, following the trail of blood and discarded body parts. Demons never stopped moving, and they liked to carry their victims' bodies as they bounded from place to place, gnawing on them until they found someone else to rip into. Once they'd gorged themselves, and their bellies were stuffed full, they would usually pause long enough to vomit up what they'd just eaten in order to make room for more. There was a foot, still wearing a sandal. There were several severed fingers on top of a pile of unidentifiable organs. He was on the right path.

The trail led down another narrow bridge. The cracks between the boards revealed crashing surf below. The only thing separating his body from the evil sea was some rickety stilts and rotting wood. It was strange enough to make even a man without fear pause. How could anyone, even the lowest of the low, live like this? Then the wave retreated, revealing shining sand, and his confidence returned.

This largest group of platforms was kept purposefully separate from the rest. This was the oldest and most confusing part of the village, with huts and structures haphazardly built in layers on top of each other for generations. It didn't matter which house's territory he was in. Casteless quarters always felt similar, giving off an air of disintegrating shoddy construction and a general filthiness. The Law mandated that the living area of the untouchables be kept separate from that of the whole men. Bits of glowing ash were falling from the dark sky, and several buildings in the casteless quarter had caught fire. Ashok took cover behind the corner of a hut and listened. Something was screeching. It was a horrible, bloodcurdling sound. He hoped the demon had attacked a piglet because that sound should not ever come out of a human throat, no matter how low in status the human might be.

Keeping Angruvadal low at his side, Ashok stalked toward the darkened barracks where the cry came from. There was a sickening crack and the noise abruptly stopped. Ashok froze.

The demon knew he was here.

The huge hut was big enough to house dozens of casteless. Ashok's eyes couldn't quite pierce the shadows inside, but he knew that it was watching him. He knew the demon would look upon him and see a tall man, lean and hard, dressed in lamellar armor, plates lacquered gray and inlaid with silver, held together with leather and silk, not so different from some of the humans it had killed before, and hardly intimidating to something as strong as an elephant. Only unlike the others, this man was completely devoid of fear.

Something smooth and vast slid along the floor of the hut, blacker than its surroundings. There was a shimmer as a bit of firelight reflected off of its nearly impenetrable hide. It didn't immediately barge into the open to try and eat him as he had hoped. He'd surprised the last demon he'd fought by side-stepping its charge and opening its guts with Angruvadal. This demon was not so stupid. No... This demon recognized that this particular human was somehow different than the others. It understood that this human wasn't prey.

Both of them had magic in their blood.

Curious, the black shape slowly lifted itself from the floor and slid forward into the light. The demon flowed so smoothly that its movements were like pouring oil. It had to twist its wide shoulders to fit through the door. The soft wood crumbled to bits as the demon's razor hide rubbed against it. Once on the platform, the demon no longer had to slouch. It rose to its full height, towering over Ashok. The young nayak at the jungle's edge hadn't been exaggerating its size at all. Sighting a demon on dry land at all was a rare experience. Most men would go their entire lives without seeing one. Ashok had seen four, and this was the biggest by far.

Demons came in many shapes and sizes, and it was whispered that truly vast beings had been seen amid the waves, but the ones he'd fought had been shaped like men... mostly... though each of them had been distorted in a different way. This one was too tall, its limbs too long, its fingers longer still, and each ended in a black point. There were three fingers, splayed wide, with a translucent webbing between them. Its legs were too short, too squat. Its head was a lump, nearly featureless except for a horizontal line that divided the lump in half.

"The ocean belongs to demons. Land belongs to man. So says the Law." Ashok slowly lifted his arm, revealing his black steel blade.

The line across its otherwise blank face split open, revealing teeth, black and shiny and sharp as the rest of its body. It let out a hiss of air that sounded surprisingly dry and raspy. That was the first sound he had ever heard a demon make. It must have recognized the sword that had been dispatching its kind since the Age of Kings.

"The penalty for trespass, for either side, is death."

Now they understood each other.

The demon bolted.

Ashok went after it.

Demons were faster than men, but a Protector was no longer just a man. He caught it before it could get around the side of the casteless barracks and struck. Nothing in the world was sharper than an ancestor blade, and it cut smoothly through the demon's back. Their blood was thin and milky, and it shot out as if it was kept under a great deal of pressure. That wound was deep enough to fell any normal being, but it only stung the demon.

It spun, swinging at him, but Ashok dodged aside as its claws obliterated the barrack's wall.

Moving as fast as lightning, the demon lashed out over and over again. Ashok moved back, placing his body to avoid the blows and turning aside the rest with his sword. The demon's claws and bones were grown from a material harder than steel, nearly as hard as the ancient sword, and glowing sparks rose whenever they met. Ashok was not concerned for his sword. The chips were from the demon's bones, because nothing could harm this sword except dishonor.

He had fought and defeated three demons, but combined, the many bearers of Angruvadal had killed nearly a hundred, and though their memories were not perfectly clear, their instincts remained, and they belonged to him now. The demon's erratic movements were expected, almost predictable.

Ashok dodged a mighty blow and ran the edge of his sword up the demon's arm in response. White blood hit him in the face. Demons didn't have veins and arteries like a man. Instead the interior of their limbs was a solid slab of dense meat, white as snow, all of it soaked in their thin blood. But like a man, let the blood out and they began to weaken. The Protector attacked, lunging forward to drive several inches of black steel between its flexible ribs. Their vitals were hard to reach, and even when pierced, they didn't die quickly. The creature flowed back, out of reach of the sword.

If demons felt pain, they never showed it. They were like Protectors that way.

It leapt to the side, crashing through a railing to fall to the next level. He thought about letting it go. No one really knew how demons' bodies worked, so maybe he'd wounded it enough that it would slink off and die... But the Law was clear. The penalty was death, so he had to be certain. If the demon couldn't dive directly into the depths, it would head for the surf. Where the two worlds met was no man's land, but in anything not shallow enough for a man to see his feet, evil lurked, and then *Ashok* would be the trespasser. He had to catch it before then.

Without hesitation, Ashok leapt over the side after it. His boots hit solid wood. He could still feel the vibrations of the fleeing demon. This level was darker, damper, covered in hanging ropes and moist nets and the stink of fish. Only the casteless ate the unclean animals of the ocean. Catwalks stretched between the stilts and scaffolds. There were beds of flea-ridden straw in every corner. This place was nastier than the foul huts above. Even among the casteless there was rank, so how low did one have to sink to be the lowest amongst them?

There was a crash and a shout just ahead. Ashok ran down the catwalk, through a rain of smoke and ash from above and a mist of saltwater from below. A shack had been constructed of discarded garbage, using the stilts of a real building as a frame. There was a hole in the wall where the demon had smashed through.

Inside the shack were several women and children, filthy, ragged, and thin. The untouchables had been hiding, hoping the demon would pass them by, but instead they had wound up right in its path. A male casteless, old, defiant, and tiny, was the only thing between the monster and its victims. Ashok had never known that one of the non-people could be capable of real bravery, but this casteless dreg was defending the shack like he was a warrior defending the Capitol.

Only Ashok noted that the old casteless was holding the demon back with a *spear*. That was a severe violation of the Law.

The demon swatted the spear aside and the old man with it. It would crush the cowering humans just out of spite before leaping to the surf below. Only Ashok reached it first and drove Angruvadal through its back and out its stomach.

"You shouldn't have come here, demon," he said as he wrenched his sword free, spilling the demon's dinner of partially digested villagers.

It twisted around and swung at him, but he ducked, and the blow shattered several of the stilts instead. He stabbed upward, through its armpit, deep into the meat of its chest cavity. At this rate, the hut was going to collapse on top of them, and it was not his place to needlessly kill the property of House Gujara. "Get out of here," Ashok ordered the casteless as he pushed the demon back against the other supports.

But rather than flee, the non-people were jabbering and squealing at him in their rough, mangled dialect. "There's two of them!"

"Behind you!" A child pointed back the way he'd come.

The sword warned him as well, a sudden rush of instincts and a desire for self-preservation, and Ashok threw himself aside. Even then, a black blur of demon flesh rubbed against him. The interlocked plates protected his chest, but where the hot hide brushed against his face, blood came welling up through his lacerated skin.

Two demons!

Both of the huge creatures were on him then, clawing and snapping. They were identical in size, shape, and viciousness. He'd never faced such a challenge before, but the sword had, and it told him exactly what to do. Ashok slashed and danced between the limbs, painting with blood and bone-shard sparks. He hit them each with a dozen clean strikes, each sufficient to kill a man, but it barely slowed the demons' onslaught.

A claw broke mail and sliced into his left arm. Another claw cut a gash through his cheek. The fresh pain merely kept Ashok focused. He was unable to feel fear, only a cold calculation of the odds, and it wasn't looking good. At least the first demon was no longer trying to escape.

The demons were bigger and stronger, but Ashok was moving constantly, trying to keep one of the savage creatures in front of the other so he only had to respond to one set of attacks at a time. There was no room to maneuver here. The casteless were running or clambering down the hanging nets like monkeys. There was a loud thump overhead as a burning beam landed on their improvised roof. Instinct whispered to Ashok, and he swung upwards, smashing through the thin boards and spilling flames onto the demons' heads.

They had no visible eyes, but the burning roof support seemed to blind them. Ashok stabbed, taking one through its pelvis, then he lowered his shoulder plate and crashed into the other, driving it off balance. The demon flesh scraped the paint from the ornate carvings of his armor, then grated across his now exposed arm. For a beast of the depths, the demon felt remarkably dry and hot. His ploy worked, and creature was put off balance and sent crashing through the ramshackle wall, over the edge, where it struck the hanging nets, thrashing about and entangling itself.

Seeing where it was suspended, Ashok leapt across, caught hold of the netting above the demon, and hung there, swinging in the fiery wind, dangling from the rough hemp with one hand. There was still a demon on the platform behind him, and the one thrashing below him, but that was only for a split second, because then Ashok struck at the ropes, cut them all in one swing, and dropped the entangled demon to the shore below.

It hit the rocks with a thud. Ashok glanced down and saw that fallen demon was twitching, its thick skull cracked open and leaking white. Hopefully that one was finished.

He scrambled up the ropes and rolled onto the top platform. The fire had spread quickly. There was a thump as the other demon leapt up and landed next to him. He attacked, but the demon intercepted his arm with a blow that would have killed an ox. Bones cracked and Ashok's sacred sword went bouncing across the floor.

Damned blood loss...He must have been injured worse than he thought. He'd never lost hold of his sword before. He called upon the Heart of the Mountain to seal his wounds as he lurched to his feet, but the demon struck him hard enough to deform steel plates and knock him through the wall of a shed.

The Protector landed in a cloud of splinters. The shed was burning around him. Flames were licking up the walls as Ashok crawled in the direction of his sword. There was still air to breathe near the floor, but his chest was so wracked with pain that it hardly mattered. The second demon followed him, webbed toes gliding soundlessly across the wood, its lump of a head clanking through the dangling chains and hooks, sending them swinging.

The demon would reach him before he could reach his sword.

It bent down and claws slid through his armor, clothing, and skin, hoisting him from the ground, up into the smoke and toward black teeth. Blood poured from the lacerations on his back, but he ignored the pain, and fought, striking with his elbow against the beast's thick skull. All he did was lose more skin. It lifted Ashok up, then smashed him back down, through a support beam, and hard onto the floor.

Angruvadal was just out of reach. Ashok lay there, the air driven from his body, flat on his back, glaring at his impending death.

The old casteless appeared through the smoke, bellowing incoherently, and jabbed his illegal spear into the demon's back. Even the finest steel had a difficult time piercing demon hide, so the blade bounced off harmlessly. The demon swiveled its eyeless lump of a head toward the casteless, not realizing in time that this non-person was no threat, only a momentary distraction, but it was enough for Ashok to roll over and lunge for his sword.

His fingers closed around Angruvadal's grip as the demon turned back to finish him. The angle was awkward, but Ashok had desperate strength and the sharpest sword ever forged. Black hide parted, hardened bone shattered, and the demon toppled as its leg came off in a spray of shimmering white.

The Protector struggled back to his feet. Now it was the demon's turn to crawl. One arm was hanging useless at his side, but Ashok could fight with either, and he went about methodically hacking the demon to pieces.

The demon rolled over and raised one of its claws, almost as if it were begging for mercy. The line opened in its lump of a head, and alien sounds poured out, a series of incomprehensible hisses and gurgles. Ashok paused for a moment. He'd never known demons had language. There was no way to know what it was trying to say, but it didn't matter, the Law was very clear on this matter.

"You are guilty of trespass." Then Ashok swung and hacked a massive chunk of flesh from the top of its head.

There was a crack as more supports gave way. The floor shifted hard to the side. He could withstand unbelievable pain and recover from injuries which would instantly kill a normal man, but that didn't mean he could breathe smoke or survive being in a collapsing stilt house as it was consumed by fire. It was time to take this fight elsewhere. Ashok put his boot on the dying demon and shoved it over the edge of the platform.

Chapter 2

Protector of the Law, twenty-year senior, Ashok Vadal stood on the damp rocks watching the burning village slide into the sea. The two demons were lying in the sand where they'd finally died. They were unclean, so he would leave them for House Gujara's wizards and alchemists to pick over. Every part of a demon's body was incredibly valuable for the magic stored within. The profit to be found in those two bodies was worth far more than the loss of a single poor village.

His body ached, a few bones had cracked, but the bleeding from his many wounds had slowed to a trickle. Ashok would need to rest for a few hours in order to let the Heart of the Mountain do its work. The Heart was the source of the Order's power and their greatest secret. The covenant was simple; it kept them alive and made them strong. In exchange they protected the Law. Within a day he'd be ready to fight again. When the Heart was done with him, he would die, but until then he would serve.

Someone was stumbling along the beach in the first light of the dawn. At first Ashok thought it might have been one of the Gujaran warriors since he was carrying a spear, but it was the old casteless instead. The untouchable was a tenacious one, but he'd been born into the wrong caste.

"The monsters are dead, but how are you still alive?" the casteless asked him.

Ashok did not immediately respond, first because the casteless's dialect was thick, uneducated, and difficult to understand, and secondly, because he wasn't used to being spoken to so directly by someone of such low station. The further one got from proper civilization, the more the legal divisions between the castes became blurry, but still, he was of the elite, the first caste of governors, and this wasn't even a real person. Living by all this saltwater must have driven the old casteless mad.

"I was stronger than they were."

"You are bleeding." The casteless was right, but his wounds would heal as they always did. It was very hard to end a Protector's life. It was kill them quick, or not at all. "And your face..." the old casteless made a scraping noise.

No one would ever accuse Ashok of being pretty, even without any new scars, but this old fool was giving him more important things to be concerned about. "Your overseers are failing. It's against the Law for a non-person to possess a weapon."

It was as if the casteless had somehow not expected the challenge, but they weren't very bright. He held the shaft close to his chest protectively and shouted, "It's mine!"

"No... It is not." Ashok scowled. The Law demanded that he go over there and cut the casteless down for this violation, but Ashok was wounded and very tired. He quoted the statute from memory, "A non-person may only possess the tools granted to it necessary to fulfill its assigned duties. Casteless are never allowed to take up arms."

"I didn't steal it. I found it washed up on the beach."

"Good." If he'd stolen it from a warrior, then regardless of how exhausted Ashok was, he'd have to execute him on the spot. A member of the first caste didn't *thank* a casteless for anything, but this creature had saved his life, so Ashok had no desire to harm him. "Then you may live."

The area was being secured by the paltan. Several warriors had spotted him and a shout went up that the Protector was still alive. Then they saw the first dead demon and began to cheer. That noise turned into a stunned silence when they saw the second demon. No one had expected that. Word spread quickly and more warriors came running. Soon he had a crowd on the beach, all staring at him and the two huge, lifeless bodies. Even in the stillness of death, they were still sleek and intimidating.

Some of them ran off to alert their wizards, so that the bodies could be butchered before the magic spoiled, but the rest of the warriors of House Gujara went on cheering Ashok. He didn't particularly care, but they had never heard of anyone defeating two demons, so he allowed it. Some were bowing their thanks. The fat havildar he'd smacked some sense into had put his forehead clear into the sand, probably hoping that a sufficient sign of deference now might save him from a flogging for his earlier cowardice.

Ashok was too tired and injured to care about the honors. The dents in the armor over his ribs was annoying and needed to be hammered out so he could breathe freely again. He began untying the many straps, when he realized that he'd almost forgotten his earlier distraction. The fool with the spear was still there. Turning to the old casteless, he waved his hand dismissively. "This transgression will be overlooked due to your circumstances. Throw down that spear and return to your overseer."

It was a remarkably merciful act for a Protector.

"No!" the old casteless shouted. He slammed the butt into the rocks for emphasis. "It is *mine!*"

Ashok was stunned by the outburst. The assembled warriors looked up in surprise.

"It is forbidden." He should have acted decisively already, to do otherwise was to make the Law appear weak before these witnesses, and the Law held no leeway for the lowest showing any disrespect to their superiors.

"I'm the one who took it out of the water. I'm the one who cleaned off the rust and sharpened the edge on a rock. I used this to protect my family!"

Casteless didn't have family. They were all property, to be organized according to their overseer's will. Was this imbecile trying to provoke him? "Fighting isn't your duty," Ashok nodded toward the warrior caste. "It's theirs."

"Where were they when the demon came? No duty for them. No. The warriors supposed to guard this village, they ran! They ran away and left us to die!"

"That is true," Ashok agreed. The assembled warriors began to mutter to each other at this terrible insult against their caste, but Ashok cared about their opinions about as much as he cared about the casteless's. "Only truth doesn't change the Law."

"Who will protect us from the warriors?"

"The fish-eater speaks of revolt!" exclaimed one of the soldiers as another nocked an arrow.

This had gone too far. Insolence could not be tolerated. *Why am I wasting my time?* It was like reasoning with a pig. He should have just taken the casteless's head and been done with it, but Ashok lowered his voice and tried one last time. The warriors wouldn't be able to hear him over the crashing surf. What he was about to admit would bring shame to the Order. "You helped me. You probably saved my life, so I do not wish to kill you."

"Then don't!"

"I have to obey the Law like everyone else."

"The Law is wrong," the old casteless snarled as he lowered the spear and aimed the point at Ashok's face.

"The Law is everything," Ashok whispered.

And then one of the warriors casually shot the disobedient casteless through the chest with an arrow. He was so thin that the arrow sped clean through his torso and skipped down the beach. The casteless's eyes widened in surprise. He managed to turn and take a few halting steps before falling on his face, where he twitched a few times and then lay still. His precious spear rolled free and clattered down the rocks.

At least the man didn't suffer.

That was curious...Ashok had never thought of a casteless as a *man* before.

The Protector lifted his hand in front of his face. Rivulets of blood had dried between his fingers, and for just a second, it was as if he was looking at the small hand of a child. Then the moment was gone. The water on his hands was unclean saltwater and the blood was only his own. This was not a dream. This was real. The warrior who had released the arrow had already gone back to marveling at the mighty demons. No one remarked on what had just transpired. There was nothing noteworthy about putting down a disobedient dog.

More warriors joined him as he stood over the corpse, including the risaldar, the experienced leader of fifty who had escorted him on the long hunt. "Excellent work, Protector. I will convey word of your great victory to our Thakoor. Your unmatched skills have brought incredible honor to your order. House Gujara will remember this deed forever. You have saved us from this menace."

"It was only a casteless..." Ashok muttered.

"I meant the pair of sea demons."

"Oh." The sand beneath the untouchable's body was slowly turning red. "Of course."

"Are you all right, Lord Protector? Do you need to rest? You appear to be hurt. We must clean your injuries. Wounds fester quickly in this jungle."

Distracted, Ashok shook his head. "I can't get sick." In Vadal, they used cremation. Ashok had no idea what the traditions of House Gujara were. "How do you dispose of your dead?"

"For the villagers? The worker caste will tend to their own." The risaldar said, before realizing that Ashok was still looking at the body. "For this? It's a casteless. I don't know what they do for non-people. Let the gulls and the crabs eat him. Please, come along, sir. You look like you need to sit down."

"What would you do for one of your own men?"

The risaldar seemed confused by this. "Gujaran warriors bury our own dead. The labor is performed by those whom he has served with."

That made a sort of sense. Ashok glanced around. The ground at the edge of the jungle didn't seem too rocky. "We will require a shovel."

"What?" the risaldar was incredulous. He looked at the blood drying on Ashok's scalp as if searching for signs of a head injury. "Why would you have us bury this wretch?"

"Because he showed more heart than any of your caste did tonight."

It hadn't been meant as an insult, but the risaldar certainly took it that way. His face darkened with rage, but no matter how skilled he was, or how injured Ashok might be, he wasn't fool enough to risk a duel with a man carrying an ancestor blade.

"Has offense been given?" Ashok asked quietly.

"No, Lord Protector. Offense has not been taken," the risaldar replied in a legally acceptable manner for avoiding a duel.

The warriors were too distracted to notice that the discarded spear was being carried back out to sea by the tide. Ashok sighed. "Forgive me, Risaldar. I'm weary and have misspoken. You and your men may attend to your master's village. I release you from your obligations to my Order. Your responsibility to escort me has been fulfilled. I will make my own way from here."

The officer gave him a stiff bow, and then stormed off.

Ashok needed to rest for a bit, and then he would find a shovel.

Chapter 3

Five years ago

The massive funeral pyre burned so hot that they could feel the warmth even from their distant vantage point. The orange pillar lit the night sky. The tower of smoke blotted out the moons and stars. Their duty satisfied, the small group of Protectors stood on the hillside and watched the bodies burn. It was rare to have so many members of the Order in a single place at the same time, but the Capitol saw full-blown house wars as serious events, requiring a swift, merciless dispensation of justice. Their battle had lasted a few hours of the morning. It had taken a huge crew of untouchables the rest of the afternoon to gather up all the dead the Protectors had left in their wake in order to build that fire.

Of course, their instructor took this moment as a teaching opportunity. "Since there is nothing beyond this life, why are we required to give respect to the remains of our dead?" Mindarin asked his students.

It was a rhetorical question, but the inexperienced members of the Order were used to Mindarin constantly asking them questions. Mindarin was known as the philosophical, scholarly leader. Questions and reasoning were his method of teaching. He applied logic to the Law so that there could be no misunderstanding its principles. Most of the acolytes found his way preferable to Master Ratul's method of severe beatings and long runs in full armor.

Ashok listened, distracted, as the young men rattled off the expected answers, it was tradition to appease the houses, or it was to prevent enemies from defiling the corpses as an insult which would lead to more strife between families, or even such practical matters as preventing the spread of disease, but *because the Law requires it* was the primary response. Within the Order, *because the Law requires it* was a safe answer to nearly every question.

The Law had required him to kill a lot of people today.

"Your answers are acceptable, as was your performance here." Mindarin told the students. It was as close to a compliment as most of them had ever received from someone of his status. "Return to camp and rest, for tomorrow will bring new duties for us all."

Ashok watched them walk down the hill, heads held high, because today they had made war on behalf of the Capitol, brought justice to a lawless family, and ended an unapproved house war. They'd fought hard, striking so fast and so efficiently that only a few hundred of their warrior escorts, and not a single member of the Order, had died in the battle. Tonight they would celebrate, unaware that this process would never end.

"Ah, the hero of the day has decided to keep his old teacher company." Mindarin stopped next to Ashok and gestured at the fire. "It is quite the sight, it is not? We taught a valuable lesson today, one that the great houses will not soon forget. They will tremble at the idea of violating the Law, and it is all thanks to you."

"It was nothing."

"On the contrary, Ashok. Your legend grows with every mission. Our obligations have increased tenfold since you joined us." Mindarin looked around. "Where is your brother?"

"Devedas took a spear thrust through the stomach and will need time to recover." The last time Ashok had seen him, he'd been in the healer's tent, vomiting up coagulated blood. "He should be ready to travel in a few days."

"That's what he gets for trying to keep up with you, lad. I saw you fling yourself into their lines. Impressive work. I'm thankful every day that your house obligated you to our Order. If we hadn't had you and that sword today, I have no doubt some of my boys would be on that fire."

"I was only doing my duty, the same as everyone else."

"You are too humble."

"I had a teacher who said that all great swordsmen need humility, because humility leads to awareness, and awareness leads to victory."

"Don't use my own words against me. You may not seek praise, so I should know by now not to waste my time giving you any, but we both know your value to the Order," the old master said. "When I was your age, the Order was a shadow of what it is today. We were fading, shrinking. You made us important again, effective and vital! You are a weapon, Ashok, a tool of justice. Your very existence has become a warning to all that they must comply with the Law. Your reputation is worth more than a legion of Inquisitors."

Ashok nodded. After the way today's conflict ended, it would be a long time before any other great houses grew so ambitious. "All must know their place."

Mindarin smiled. It was usually him quoting the Law, not the other way around. "Adherence to the Law is the only thing that keeps the world from descending into madness. It was the Law which lifted man out of superstitious barbarity and brought us into an age of reason, yet the Law is always vulnerable. The Law is a dam, and on the other side is an ocean of chaos. If a chip isn't repaired, the dam will crack. Today we simply plugged a leak."

The only thing he'd seen leaking today had been blood from thousands of bodies. "I'm not one of the newly obligated children, Mindarin. Spare me the allegories. I do what I must, that's all."

"My dam example is a metaphor, not an allegory. Sometimes, though, it is good to repeat the lessons learned in our youth. It helps us keep our minds focused the same way a whetstone keeps an edge on our steel..."

"You truly can't help yourself, can you?"

Mindarin chuckled. "Only some of us carry swords that never need to be sharpened." He looked pointedly at sheathed Angruvadal. "Tell me, fifteen-year senior, how many men did you strike down today?"

Regulations required him to be as exact as possible in his

reports, so he'd trained himself to remember every blow, every cut, every *face*. "Twenty-six violators killed and thirty-four injured during the battle itself. I estimate half of those may survive their injuries. After House Makao surrendered, I executed another five specific officers as per the Judges' sentence for fomenting rebellion, as well as their wives, and their firstborn sons."

"That is a terrible burden."

"It was just another day."

The two of them watched the great bonfire in silence for a time.

"What troubles you, Ashok?"

"Absolutely nothing," he answered truthfully.

The old master thought that over before speaking. He was no longer using his instructor's voice, but rather sounded like any other tired old man. "The acolytes' answers were acceptable, but wrong. We know there's nothing beyond life. The fire doesn't go somewhere else when the candle is extinguished. We are meat with a spark of life inside, nothing more. Yet still, something compels us to treat a corpse with the dignity we'd reserve for a whole man. They are wrong because the Law doesn't command us to respect the dead, but rather the Law *allows* us to do something we would be compelled to do regardless, something ingrained into us since ancient times. We honor the dead so the survivors remember to live."

Ashok had never been one for Mindarin's philosophical contemplations. "If you say so."

"With all the weight we have put upon you, don't forget how to live, Ashok. At times I fear our people have forgotten too much as it is." The master's words verged on the subversive, but thankfully he did not continue with that thought. "Forgive an old man his ramblings."

Ashok nodded after the young Protectors. They had taken up one of Ratul's marching chants on their way back to the camp. "Was I ever that idealistic?"

"Was?" Mindarin put one hand on his shoulder. "Lad, you still are."

Chapter 4

―――――✺―――――

"You know, Ashok, I've seen you fill a lot of graves over the years, but I do believe this is the first time I've ever seen you dig one."

Ashok glanced up and saw a familiar scarred face. He'd been too focused on his labor to notice the other Protector sitting on the rocks above. His old friend could be quiet as a demon when he felt like it.

"Hello, Devedas." Ashok had barely finished pushing the last of the dirt into the hole and stomping it down. It was said that the jungle scavengers were very persistent here, so he'd dug the hole deep. "What brings you to this muggy hell?"

"Looking for *you*, among other things. Who's in the hole?"

"Someone who didn't deserve to be eaten by crabs."

"We don't dig graves where I come from. The ground's always frozen. Why are you digging anyway? Doesn't this province have any slaves?"

"I felt like digging. That's not illegal. How long have you been sitting there?"

"Long enough to be glad I wasn't born in the worker caste. Can you imagine toiling under this miserable sun every day?"

Ashok stuck the shovel in the dirt so it would stand upright. "Do you think digging endless holes would be so much worse than endless fighting?"

"Spoken like a man who has nearly completed his house's obligation. Twenty years is a lot of service for the Order to wring out of one man." That was meant to goad him. Devedas had been doing this a bit longer than he had. "No wonder you're curious to see how the other castes live."

"There were two demons." Ashok gestured toward where the alchemists and wizards were butchering the demon carcasses further down the beach. "Big ones too. If they're getting into the habit of working in pairs, then I look forward to my retirement."

"Two?" Devedas tried not to let his concern show, but he failed. "I didn't say digging holes would be worse than what we do, but it would be terribly dull." Devedas slid down the rock, hopped the last six feet, and landed effortlessly next to him. "Good to see you, brother."

The men obligated to the Order were sons from each of the great houses, and they all brought some traditions with them. It was one of the small, allowable ways each Protector could maintain some of their history. Devedas was a southerner, so he preferred to shake hands rather than bow in greeting. It was probably because in the cold lands you had to wear such a pile of furs to live that nobody could tell if you were bowing or not, or as Devedas liked to joke, southerners didn't like to look down because that's when the bears ate you. Devedas' grip was as firm as his own.

"If I'd known you were in Gujara I would have sent for you. I could have used the help last night. I'm not too proud to admit that I only survived by luck."

"I'll say you did. Two? I hope this doesn't mean the ocean is acting up again." Devedas scanned the surf, but the waters were their normal, unclean blue. Not the agitated red that often warned of a larger raid.

It had been two full seasons since the last time their duties had put them in the same province at the same time, but they'd both grown up in the brutal confines of the Order's program. They'd survived the harshest training in the world together and fought at each other's side so many times that it was like no time had passed at all. They didn't look alike at all, with Ashok being taller and darker in both temperament and features, but they had often been mistaken for real brothers of the same house. They might not have had the same father, but they had the same swordmaster, and to a Protector that was nearly the same thing.

"A pair is an anomaly, but it's not unheard of."

"Looking at your face, those demons must have beaten you like a practice dummy." It was the sort of blunt assessment that could only come from an equal in station. An inferior would not have been so honest and a superior probably wouldn't have cared. "You look awful."

And that was with having most of the morning to allow the Heart to help him recover. It took a long time to dig a hole when one arm was so battered that the elbow didn't want to bend. "It was a good fight."

"You're not usually one to put comfort over presentation. These Gujarans are going to think the Order's gone sloppy. Why are you out of uniform?" All of them were hard as nails, but Devedas was a southerner, and he'd still arrived in this awful sweltering, chafing jungle dressed in the full regalia and armor of the Order. "Where's your armor?"

Ashok pointed toward the pile of steel and leather resting in the shade. His ancestor blade was sheathed and lying across the top of his damaged armor. Devedas' eyes lingered on the mighty sword just a moment too long.

"I still can't believe you just put that sword on the ground like that," Devedas said incredulously.

"Sometimes you need to. It isn't welded to my hand."

"But still... What if someone tries to pick it up?"

"They'd immediately regret it. Angruvadal is easily displeased."

"If I possessed such a thing I would never put it down. It seems disrespectful."

"But practical. If it feels dishonored, it'll abandon me, I'll die in battle, and then it will pick a new bearer. I didn't choose Angruvadal. It chose me," Ashok explained for the thousandth time. Devedas might have been jealous of the sword's power, but Ashok was the only one who understood the particular burden that came from bearing an ancestor blade. "It's mighty, but it is still only a sword, Devedas. Religion is false and illegal, so don't start worshipping it."

"Coveting a holy relic is a serious offense..." Devedas snorted. "I'd have to arrest myself... Sorry."

He knew exactly what Devedas was thinking about, and experience had taught him it was best to change to a lighter subject before his brother fell into one of his dark moods. "I don't know how whole men live in this place. I was dying inside my armor. Remember Pratosh from the program?"

"The kid with the lazy eye?"

"He was obligated to the Order by House Gujara. He grew up in this very jungle. I remember he used to say that you got used to the heat. Now I know why he never liked to wear a proper amount of clothes."

"And also why he was always complaining about how cold the barracks were." Devedas chuckled. Not that the acolytes' barracks hadn't been miserably cold, but complaining only made the other acolytes meaner. "Whatever happened to him anyway?"

"Dead." Ashok had to stop and think about it for a moment. Protectors died so often, usually alone and in the most forsaken corners of the world, that sometimes it was hard to keep every story straight. "He finally made senior at eight years, went to Zarger to stop an uprising, and ended up getting his throat slit on the way by desert raiders."

"Well, at least he died where it was warm...But considering it was Pratosh, his last words were probably complaining that it was a dry heat."

"He was a good man."

"More than I can say for most of us. Hold on," Devedas glanced around. "I've been running since dawn. Nobody spotted me, so I wasn't even properly announced. What does a man have to do to get food in this swine hold?"

"Forgive the inhospitality. In their defense, half the place burned down last night."

"That's no excuse for incivility." Devedas spotted a worker carrying a wrapped bundle of demon parts to a nearby wagon and shouted at him, "You there! I am Devedas, Protector of the Law, twenty-*two*-year senior." He added that last part for Ashok's benefit, because no one outside of the Order gave a damn about their relative experience or the fact that Devedas technically outranked him. In this backwater province, either of them was of far higher status than just about anyone they were likely to run into. "Fetch us some wine and something to eat. The wine had better be good. None of that watered-down swill."

The worker dropped the heavy package in the wagon and then ran as if the demons had returned. He didn't know Devedas. A demon was less dangerous. "You shouldn't have announced yourself. Now the local warriors will descend on you with great ceremony and ass-kissing."

Devedas sat on the grass in the shade a big tree. "I don't know about ass-kissing, but I could certainly use a foot rub. It's a long run from the great house to here. What do Gujaran pleasure women look like?"

"I don't know. I've been too busy following a demon raider up and down the coast for the last few weeks to request any." Ashok sat next to Devedas. The ache of his stiff muscles warned him that if he stayed still too long he would have a hard time getting back up, but it beat being dead. "So why were you looking for me?"

"I was sent here because the Inquisition requested a Protector in Gurjat. It's a stinkhole of a city a few days from here. Smugglers found some old temple to the Forgotten out in the jungle and have been digging up artifacts to sell to wizards without papers. I'm to execute them all."

"Do you need help?"

Devedas shook his head. "There's only supposed to be twenty of them, worker caste so they won't know how to fight, and they've got no useful magic to speak of. The only reason they requested a Protector is politics. Some Thakoor's firstborn has been taking bribes, and you can't have the locals disgracing each other and starting blood feuds when an outsider is more convenient. If one of us lops off his head, nobody will say a word. We're impartial like that. If you hadn't been busy chasing demons they probably wouldn't have sent me. Anyways, I encountered a herald on the road to Gurjat. He saw my uniform and thought I was you. The man must have been half blind to mistake Devedas the Magnificent for some glorified northern cow herder with a magic sword."

"I swear, you're not going to be happy until I agree to duel you again, will you?"

"Someday, I'll get my rematch," Devedas said as he traced his thumb down the white scar that ran from his right eye to his chin. Even a Protector couldn't fully heal from a wound inflicted by the black steel of an ancestor blade.

"I still feel bad about the scar."

"No, you don't. And even with it I'm still far better looking than you are. Regardless, I said I would deliver his message personally." Devedas opened a pouch on his belt and pulled out a folded piece of paper. "It gave me an excuse to visit."

Sure enough, Ashok's name was on it, though the humidity had caused the ink to bleed. Ashok took the letter. It bore the seal of the Order and had come all the way from the Capitol, but he didn't break the wax.

"What are you waiting for?"

The letter probably contained his next assignment. "In a moment."

"Ah, the great Ashok and his legendary sense of commitment. You can't read it yet because the moment you do you'll be obligated to leap up and rush off to wherever the Order requires you next. The fiercest beasts, the harshest duties, the worst violators, all fall before the unflinching judgment of Black-Hearted Ashok. You make the rest of us look lazy."

"You don't need my help for that."

Devedas laughed. "I know you better than anyone. You've reached your twenty. You can leave the Order whenever you want and return to your house with honor. Vadal women are gorgeous, and no doubt they'll pick the best-looking one to be your wife. Retire and that woman can start providing you with sons. Come on, man! You just defeated a pair of demons at the same time. That's the stuff of legends! When was the last time one of us did that?"

"Kantelin Vokkan, twenty-eight-year master, in the year 540," Ashok said absently.

"Of course, you'd remember the history lessons... You know how rare it is for a Protector to actually retire? Your house will name you to Thakoor for sure. They've probably already built a castle for you. Neighboring houses will cower at the mention of your name."

Ashok just shook his head. "You've served your obligation, but you're still here."

"That's because I'm far better at dispensing justice than you are. I'll do this until I die," Devedas grinned. "Besides, what do I have to go back to?"

He believed the real reason was because Devedas wanted to be the next master, but it would have been impolite to suggest such a thing. The Law declared its Protectors were not allowed to have personal ambition. Ambition got in the way of following orders. Ashok tried to change the subject. "So, do you have any news of the civilized world?"

"By civilized, you mean your house?"

Ashok had only been a small child when he'd been obligated, and Protectors were never dispatched to deal with lawbreakers in their own house so as to prevent bias, so it had been a long time since he'd been to his ancestral lands. "I barely remember it at all. The sword probably remembers more about Vadal than I do."

"Ah, mighty Vadal, jewel of the houses. I was there last season when House Vokkan got uppity and tested your western borders. You didn't miss much. It was a rout. Your aunt Bidaya still rules. Your cousin Harta is said to be the finest orator in the Capitol and has the judges dancing like puppets on a string. The women are pretty, the sun shines every day, crops grow year-round, and everyone is fat and happy, awaiting the return of their legendary son so he can bring home the family sword. What else do you want to know? Open the damned letter."

"What of your house?"

"Devakula is snow, volcanos, and walruses." Devedas grew somber. "Seriously, Ashok, open the letter or I'll do it for you. Master Mindarin has been ill."

"*Ill?*" Protectors didn't get sick, unless... "Why didn't you tell me?" Ashok snapped as he broke the seal.

"I only just heard myself from the messenger."

Ashok read in silence. A cold feeling settled in his guts.

"And?"

"I'm to return to the Capitol immediately and present myself before the master." Ignoring the protests of his sore muscles, Ashok got up, and went to his belongings.

"Did it say why?" Devedas asked suspiciously.

"No." He put the sword belt around his waist and cinched it tight. In this heat, fifty pounds of armor would travel faster in a pack on his back than on his body. He'd make much better time that way. It was about a hundred miles to get out of the jungle and to the Gujaran's next real town. On foot, through this terrain, if he called on the Heart of the Mountain and pushed himself to exhaustion he could be there tomorrow afternoon. If they didn't gift him with a team of swift horses there, he'd confiscate some. Riding them nearly to death and switching mounts at every settlement along the interior, this time of year with dry roads, he could be at the Capitol in less than three weeks.

"I recognize that face. As is said, when duty calls, Ashok does not hesitate." Devedas didn't seem inclined to get off the grass or leave the shade. "Mindarin is dying, isn't he?"

"This letter was written a month ago. He may already be dead." Ashok saw that the worker Devedas had yelled at earlier was returning with a wineskin and a basket of food. He snatched the skin from the red-faced and gasping inferior and took a long drink. The wine tasted almost as brackish as the water here. Then he tossed it over.

Devedas caught the skin, took a drink, and then spit it out with a grimace. "This is their good stuff?"

Ashok took a few rice balls out of the basket and then snapped at the worker, "I require a travelling pack, a few days' rations, and one of those silks to keep out bugs and snakes while you sleep. What are you waiting for? Move!" Ashok kicked the man in the leg for emphasis. He immediately dropped the basket and ran for his life. The inferiors were odd here, the casteless took up spears, the warriors didn't want to fight demons, and the workers were high-strung. Ashok hadn't even kicked him hard.

"If Mindarin is on his death bed, and he sent for you..." Devedas left that thought hanging.

"I'm sure it's for something else."

"There can be only one reason they'd call you back to the Capitol now."

Ashok shoved a rice ball into his mouth and began chewing as he gathered his belongings. If his mouth was full, he wouldn't have to answer. He knew Devedas had dreams of leading the Order. Ashok simply wanted to fulfill his responsibilities to the Law. Nothing more.

"I received no summons. They're going to promote you to his office rather than me." Devedas was silent for a long time, then he gave a bitter laugh. "Of course, a son of the finest of the great houses, who has a home to return to, and a sword that destines him to rule it, why not give him one more honor? What's a promotion to a man like that? But for a man who has sacrificed just as much in service to the Law, who has no house to return to, and no future except for servitude, who could use such a title to rebuild his family name... To a man to whom such an honor would mean everything, it is not granted."

Ashok choked down the too-dry rice, and regretted tossing aside the wine. "It's not a contest."

"Of course not, there can be no contest with Ashok the Fearless," Devedas raised his voice. "Because when you fight Ashok, all of his ancestors fight with him. I've done just as much as you have for the Order, only I've done it with the strength of my own arm, not that of the fifty generations who came before."

He didn't like when Devedas fell into one of his moods. "We all have a place in the Law. Accept yours, Devedas. There's comfort in that."

"That's easy for you to say."

"I don't know why I've been summoned, but if it's to take Mindarin's place, so be it. I don't want his authority. You know I never have. However, I'll do whatever I'm commanded and I'll ask for nothing in return."

"Your obnoxious inability to lie annoys me to no end." Devedas sighed as he stood up. "But it also makes it impossible to hate you."

Several warriors were hurrying their way, and one of them was carrying a large marching pack. It was still dark with sweat from the soldier it had been confiscated from. "I must go." He looked at his brother, and as was the custom in Vadal lands, gave a deep, respectful bow. Devedas returned the gesture. When he lifted his head, Ashok said, "Believe me, Devedas, if it were up to me, I'd much rather they picked you."

"I know. So who's in the grave, Ashok?"

"I buried a casteless."

"Did you kill him?"

"He killed himself through disobedience."

"What an odd thing to waste your time with." Devedas kicked at the freshly turned dirt. "Why would you do that?"

Ashok didn't actually know the answer. "Farewell, Devedas."

"Until we meet again, brother."

Chapter 5

Eighteen years ago

"You shouldn't be here."

"This is my place." Young Ashok crouched next to their tiny fire, trying to soak up enough warmth to get some feeling back into his hands. Three days of freezing cold and terrible terrain had taken its toll on his body.

Devedas was keeping watch at the mouth of the cave. They'd been warned that the wolves here were gigantic, big enough to latch onto a sleeping man's ankle and drag him out into the night before he could even scream for his companions to save him. Exhausted from the climb, the other acolytes had gone immediately to sleep. Devedas had volunteered to take the first watch. He nodded toward the snoring bodies, huddled together for warmth under their only blanket. "You're always so damned sure about everything. They've been in training for five years. I've been here for four. You've only been here for barely two. I'm impressed you've made it this far at all, but you're not ready."

"I won't let you down," Ashok assured the older acolyte. Opening and closing his hands, Ashok was pleased to see that only a few of his calluses had been torn off by the rocks and there was no sign of frostbite yet. That climb was one of the most difficult things he'd ever done. "Mindarin allowed me. If he thought I was going to slow you down, he would have forbidden me from coming."

Devedas snorted. "I think he was too surprised that the smallest kid in the program stepped out of line to try and tackle the Heart. I've never seen a man that fond of words struck mute before. We could die up here. Aren't you scared?"

"Probably." Ashok thought it over. It was hard to explain. He assessed danger and probability as well as anyone else, perhaps even better than most because he just couldn't work up any emotion about the subject, so he could say he *had* some measure of ability to experience fear. It just didn't *move* him like it did others. It was simply there, in the background, a suggested warning, nothing more. "Yes?"

"How old are you anyway, Ashok?"

"Twelve..." Ashok had to think about it for a moment. It was always cold and snowy in Devakula year-round. He wasn't permitted to have a calendar. Protector training was so tiring, unrelenting, and sleep was allowed at such odd, inconsistent hours that the days sort of bled together, so he wasn't actually sure what season it was. "I'll be twelve in the fall."

"Then you're the youngest to ever make the attempt. And it *is* fall."

"How can you tell?"

"If it was winter the snow would be over our heads instead of just up to our waists."

"Oh...I suppose I'm twelve then."

"Happy birthday."

"Thank you." There wasn't much room in the cave, but Ashok managed to get his sword out. It was an inferior design, made of regular boring steel, without any of the beauty or power of Angruvadal, but it was what he'd been issued, so he needed to make sure that it was properly maintained. The blade was clean, but Ashok wanted to make sure no moisture had been trapped in the sheath during the climb, which might cause rust. Sweat was saltwater, impure as the ocean, and he'd certainly sweated a lot during the day's journey up the mountainside. He removed a cloth and an oil vial from his pack and began carefully cleaning the sword. Ashok had never been good at conversation, but talking seemed to be the proper thing to do. "How old are you?"

"Sixteen, winter born." Devedas went back to staring into the dark. "You should turn back in the morning. There's no shame in not making it to the Heart for any of us, especially on the first try, and especially not for you. It wouldn't surprise me if some of them give up as well. I could see it in their eyes when we stopped for the night. If you're thinking about defeat, you've already lost. So you won't be going down alone. Turn back, Ashok. Our rations are half gone. It's only going to get colder, the air thinner, and you've heard the rumors, the seniors won't talk about it, but there's something far more dangerous than wolves living at the summit. Once we cross the glacier, we either reach the Heart, or the mountain claims us."

"You're the top acolyte in the program," Ashok said. Stronger, faster, tougher, and always confident, Devedas was easily the best among them. He was the one Ashok looked up to the most. "If anyone can make it, it's you."

"I'm not worried about me, stupid. I just don't want your sliding down a crevasse to your death to be on my conscience."

"Mindarin says that evil lives in the water. Snow might not be as impure, like saltwater, but it's still out to get us. That's why it makes itself slippery. Don't worry, Devedas. I won't be a burden, but if I start to slow you down, you may leave me behind to be devoured by wolves. I promise not to hold a grudge."

He chuckled. "Strangely enough, I believe you."

The two of them were silent for a long time. The only sounds in the cave were the crackle of burning twigs and the snoring of exhausted boys. Satisfied that his sword was clean, sharp, and ready, Ashok returned it to its sheath.

"You miss it, don't you?" Devedas asked. "The ancestor blade, I mean."

"Yes." It was difficult to explain what it was like, being away from something that had absorbed a portion of his life's spark. It gnawed at him, worse than hunger, or cold, or pain, a constant feeling of loss and weakness. "More than anything."

"That's why you're doing this now, isn't it? You think reaching the Heart will prove something. You can't go on living without that sword . . . I've seen it before. What happens to a bearer when they lose that bond, you'd rather die on this mountain than go another night without that sword by your side."

The older acolyte was correct. Most people were incapable

of understanding what it was like to lose a part of yourself, but proving himself worthy would earn it back. "You've seen it before because your father was a bearer like me."

"He was a great man and a hero. Our house was respected, feared even. And then one day our sword broke, shattered into a hundred pieces...Nobody knows what my father did to offend it."

Such a thing was always a possibility with the ancestor blades. No mortal man could fully understand their convoluted sense of honor, so when one chose to give up the ghosts...that was the end of it. Ashok had never heard Devedas speak freely about this subject before, so he listened intently.

"Just like *that,* it was all over. Allies abandoned us, friends betrayed us, and within a few seasons my house was defeated and consumed by another, without so much as a sternly worded letter from the Capitol in protest. Now we're just a poor province in some other family's lands. There was no inheritance for me, so I was obligated to the Order, because who wants a constant reminder of their family's shame around?"

"Every man has his place."

"Platitudes..." Devedas muttered as he stared off into the darkness. "It would have been mine. I know that sword would have picked me next."

"You can't know that. No one knows the will of the blade until they try and wield it."

"It chose my father and my grandfather before him. His father beat its bearer in a duel and proved his worthiness. They forged our house through the strength of their will." Devedas gave a bitter laugh. "My birthright. My destiny. My place...taken..."

"I am truly sorry for your loss," Ashok said, hoping that his sincerity came through.

Devedas studied him for a time, his expression inscrutable. "It doesn't matter now." He returned to his vigil. "I have this watch. Get some sleep. Tomorrow we have to climb to the top of the world."

Two of the acolytes had been too weak to continue and had turned back at the glacier, leaving only three to continue the test. There was no dishonor in quitting then. Part of being a Protector was recognizing your physical and mental limitations. They were assets to be spent in defense of the Law, not tossed away in futile gestures. Those who turned back would be able to try to attain senior rank again in the future, but for the three who remained, they had crossed the point of no return. They would reach the Heart or die trying. Another lesson of the Order was that once committed, you held nothing back.

The air was so thin it filled their lungs but provided no strength. Two more days of marching, climbing, tripping, and sliding across the bleak, white surface had left them incoherent with exhaustion. At one point the ice had broken beneath Ashok's feet, dropping him into a hole. Trapped and freezing, Ashok knew Devedas would have been justified in leaving him behind, but the older student had spent hours digging him out instead.

There were no more conversations during the night, as speaking took too much energy. They made their way across the mountains, following the landmarks the masters had spoken of. Sometimes on snowshoes, other times with picks and ropes, but it was always slow and difficult. No matter how tired he was, or how hard it was to keep his eyes open when they stopped, Ashok always made sure his sword was maintained. Mindarin had taught them that if they took care of their weapons, their weapons would take care of them.

A storm forced the acolytes to take cover for a full day, huddled in a shallow cave, miserable and shivering. On the final morning they ate the last of their dried meat and washed it down with melted snow. They'd resupply from the stores at the Heart or they'd starve. Acolytes often went days without food, but it was difficult to keep moving through terrain like this and stay warm on an empty stomach. Starvation was an excellent motivator to continue plodding on.

Noon of the final day was clear and bright, so bright in fact that they all had to wear leather strips over their eyes with small cuts to see through. Glare could sunburn the eyeball, leaving them blind and helpless. Despite the sun being visible, Ashok had never been this cold before. They were nearing the peak of the tallest mountain in the nation. He had never even imagined that this kind of cold could exist, but it was worth it, because from up here it was as if he could see the entire world.

Logically, Ashok knew it wasn't the whole world, not even but a small part of their continent of Lok, but it was still an incredible view.

"Magnificent." Devedas paused next to him and scanned the horizon. "It's almost enough to make you understand how the superstitious still believe in gods."

Ashok wanted to say something, but his mouth was so dry that he had to take a drink from his canteen before he could speak. The only reason the water hadn't completely frozen was because he kept it next to his body. He pointed toward the north. "Where the plains turn brown, that's the beginning of the great desert of House Zarger. I bet we can almost see the Capitol from here." Then he pointed toward the northeast, across the plains, to where another, smaller mountain range loomed. "Thao. And on the other side of those are the lands of Vadal, my house." He slowly turned in a circle, like the hand of a clock, still pointing, naming off great house territories as he went. "Sarnobat, Kharsawan, Akershan." He turned to the south where the mountains sloped down toward the distant sea. "Devakula."

"Home," Devedas agreed.

Ashok kept turning, he couldn't actually see those distant lands, but he liked to imagine that he could. "Makao." Then west. "Uttara, Harban." And a full circle back to the north. "Gujara, Vokkan."

"So you paid attention to Mindarin's geography lecture. I'd present you with an achievement ribbon but I didn't think to put any in my pack."

"Don't you understand, Devedas? All of those great houses? We're the ones who get to maintain the peace between them." Ashok gestured at the mighty expanse. Maybe the altitude was making him light-headed, but it was a lot to soak in. "All of this is our responsibility. Without the Law, there is no union, and without us, there would be no Law."

"You're a strange kid, Ashok," Devedas said as he started marching toward the summit.

Ashok took one last look at the world before resuming his journey. It was the strongest he'd felt in days.

Of the three who remained, Yugantar, five-year acolyte, was their oldest and most experienced student. He was the proud son of a chief judge in the Capitol, from a long and accomplished lineage, so it was rather shameful when he ran away and left Ashok and Devedas to die at the hands of the monsters at the summit.

"Get back here!" Devedas shouted, but Yugantar was already fifty yards away, clumsily sliding down the rocks, panicked and trying to escape. "Coward!"

When they'd first risen out of the snow all around them, Ashok had thought that they were only men, dressed in the pelts of some white-furred animal, only as they'd gotten closer he'd realized their visible skin was the color of blue river slush. At first his tired mind thought their bodies were painted, like a festival girl, but then he realized they had no faces. Their faces beneath their hoods were nothing more than a thin blue membrane stretched tight over a skull.

"Oceans!" Devedas swore.

Yugantar had been on point and seen them first. No wonder he'd run for his life.

The creatures hadn't made a sound, but they were spreading out, forming a circle around the two acolytes. Their mouths were sealed, their teeth visible through the stretched skin. *Do they eat? Or are they sustained on witchcraft?* They were armed with short spears and clumsy axes. Ashok counted six of them in total. Their appearance was unnatural. Thin as untouchables, they had no meat to them, but they didn't move like they were malnourished. They had no eyes, just round indentations in the sick fabric of their faces, but they seemed to have no problem seeing.

Strangely enough, Ashok still wasn't afraid, though he knew he probably should have been. This was the sort of thing stories were told about to scare children, or so Ashok had been told, because he really couldn't remember his own childhood. He raised his voice and shouted, "We're from the Protector Order on official business. It's illegal to block our way. Move aside."

Rather than answer, the things kept trudging through the snow toward them.

"They're abominations," Devedas hissed. "I don't think they obey the Law."

"Everything must obey or deal with the consequences. What are they?"

"I don't know. Witchcraft! You're the one that never forgets the lessons." Devedas drew his sword. The blade was southern, heavy and forward-curving, designed for chopping off limbs. He took one last look at their fleeing companion, probably debating if he should follow, but he turned back to the fight. "Damned idiot, Yug. There's nothing down that mountain but starvation. We get to the Heart or we die. Get ready."

Ashok drew his own sword. It felt clumsy in the thick fur mitten, but he was afraid to take it off because his skin would doubtlessly freeze to the handle and that would probably be worse.

They were on a rocky shelf, fifty feet wide, next to a wall of dark stone. Fallen snow was being blown about by the howling wind. As the blue-skinned monsters kept spreading out around them, Ashok realized that the leather strap protecting his eyes from the glare also took away much of his peripheral vision. They were in the shade of the rock so he tore the strap off. *Much better.*

The creatures were moving inward, crouched now, weapons clutched in their long blue fingers. Even with the wind, the snow here was still knee deep, so their movements were awkward and each step required them to lift their legs high to crunch back down through the hard snow. Maneuvering would be difficult. Outnumbered like this, if he and Devedas fell, they were as good as dead.

Devedas realized the same thing. "Get back to back."

Ashok moved around him, stomping down snow, trying to make a beaten area so he could have some footing.

"Try to look intimidating."

He wasn't sure how to do that. Ashok was tall for his age, but didn't feel particularly intimidating being outnumbered three to one by magical abominations. At his back, Ashok could feel Devedas shaking with nerves and anticipation. Personally, he still felt no fear. His only wish was that he had his real sword instead of this inferior thing. Angruvadal could sweep the creatures from the mountain with ease.

The monsters stopped. The acolytes were in the middle of a twenty-foot circle, hemmed in by the blue creatures' rough iron weapons. Ashok was surprised by how quiet the moment was.

Then they attacked.

The monsters didn't communicate in any discernible way, but they moved as one. The things lurched forward. He couldn't even call it a charge, more of a methodical approach through the deep snow, really. He'd been hoping they would clump up and get in each other's way like a proper mob, but they were coordinated, as a few moved to attack, while the others held back, waiting for an opportunity to strike.

A spear was thrust his way. Ashok turned it aside with the flat of his blade and then countered. The creature was bigger and had far more reach, so only the tip of his sword sunk into the thing's torso. It pulled back noiselessly. Another swung an ax at his head. Ashok parried it aside, then ran his sword down the handle, raising a cloud of splinters and then dropping one of the thing's fingers into the snow. That one also pulled away without a sound.

The rest of them kept coming.

One creature lifted its ax overhead, almost leisurely. Ashok lunged forward to drive his blade deep into the thing's guts. Straight and broad, his sword was designed for thrusting. A good puncture from a two-inch blade would take the fight out of any man, but the ax kept rising. Ashok turned the blade hard, ripped it out the side, and barely got out of the way as the ax was driven through the snow and into the rock below.

Snow was flying between the sharpened edges. The noise of steel striking iron reverberated off of the great stone wall. Devedas grunted as he was cut, but Ashok turned and ran that creature through the ribs before it could follow up. It put one hand on his shoulder and shoved him away. His sword came out, clean, with not a drop of blood to be seen.

The two of them were turning, meeting attack after attack. Devedas lowered his body and swung around to strike the monster closest to Ashok in the leg, while Ashok attacked over Devedas' shoulder and punctured a creature's neck.

The attacks stopped. His pulse was pounding in his ears. His breath was coming out in gouts of hot steam. There wasn't enough air. Ashok looked around, realized that all of the creatures had pulled back a few steps, as if collecting themselves. They weren't so much as shaking, and he couldn't tell if they were even breathing at all. Despite receiving several lethal blows, all six of them were still standing.

"They're not dying," Ashok stated.

"I can see that," Devedas snapped.

Devedas had lopped one of their hands off. The severed appendage was lying in the trampled snow at his feet, blue fingers still twitching, so he kicked it away in disgust. The monster who'd lost the hand went over, picked it up, and casually stuck it inside its furs for safekeeping. Perhaps it would reattach it later somehow. Ashok really didn't know that much about magical abominations.

"Run for the Heart. I'll hold them off," Devedas ordered.

Ashok didn't dignify that with a reply. He may have been young, but he'd done nothing but train his whole life. He was a son of the highest caste, and he'd be damned if he was going to run from witchcraft. Everything has a weakness. They just had to find it.

The creatures came at them again.

A spear was flung at him. He reacted and swatted it out of the air. A moment later another almost hit Devedas in the back but Ashok barely managed to knock it aside as well. Then the axes were falling, and they seemed ever faster this time. He moved between them, stabbing and slashing. A lucky move put him beneath a swing, and Ashok responded with a draw cut so deep into the monster's abdomen that it would have split any regular man nearly in two.

That monster calmly walked away, letting another take its place.

Ashok swung for a faceless skull, but it was mutely blocked by a raised ax. He stepped into it, and drove the tip through the space where the mouth would have been. He shoved until steel came out the back of its head and knocked its fur hood off. He shoved until the guard smacked into the stretchy membrane. It still tried to hit him, but he got his other hand up and grabbed onto the ax handle. *What does it take to kill you?*

Another monster stepped up to stab Ashok. Devedas intercepted it with a swing so hard that it left the spear splintered and useless. Then Devedas shoulder-checked the creature into the snow.

Everything had a weakness...Gravity was one of them. *Except for birds*, but luckily they weren't fighting birds.

"Breaking formation!" Ashok shouted. The two of them were hardly a formation, but that's what they'd been taught to say in training when moving apart. His opponent was bigger and heavier than he was, but Ashok had driven a sword through its face, and that gave him considerable leverage. He jerked the sword to the side, twisting its head around, and then he shoved. The two of them crashed through the crowd, sliding across the snow, toward the edge of the cliff. At the last second, Ashok yanked back hard, pulling his sword free.

The creature slipped on the ice and went to its knees, but didn't go over the edge. So Ashok kicked it in the chest and sent it rolling over the side. It disappeared in a cloud of ice crystals. He turned back just in time to catch the tip of a spear as it plunged through his thick coat. There was a flash of heat as the edge sliced through his skin. Rolling around the attack, Ashok hacked that creature in the neck. The soft flesh parted, but it still wouldn't let go of the spear. His boots began sliding across the packed snow as it shoved him toward the edge of the cliff.

Ashok snarled and hacked it in the neck again and again. The rubbery substance came apart beneath the well-honed blade until its head parted from the neck, and hung there, attached only by a flap of skin.

It still didn't die.

"Move right!" Devedas shouted.

Ashok didn't hesitate. He threw his body to the side, spear still twisted through his clothing, as Devedas crashed into the monster's back, sending it flying off the ledge and into space. The spear was yanked out, slicing a new cut across Ashok's body, just above the first.

The remaining monsters pulled away again, observing.

Ashok could feel the blood running down his stomach. Devedas was grimacing and there was blood running down his scalp from where he'd been struck. They were both panting. He was thankful for the chance to catch his breath, what little of it was available up here.

"Two down. Four to go," Ashok said. "Ideas?"

"Hack them to bits. Toss the bits over the side."

He'd been hoping for something better. "Good plan."

The monsters closed on them a third time. Either he was tiring faster than expected, or they'd grown much faster. The monsters seemed far more confident, and their weapon handling was vastly improved. There was nothing clumsy about them now. A minute of furious combat seemed to stretch on forever. Both sides fought with the savagery worthy of Senior Protectors. Ashok was only able to get in a single solid hit, slicing his blade through a few ribs before the things pulled back again. That one stood there, silently mocking him. Apparently they didn't have lungs either.

Devedas had done better than Ashok had, and had carved a massive chunk from one of the creature's legs. The monster was balancing itself with its spear, broken leg dangling in the snow, seemingly as calm as Ashok was. Then he looked over his shoulder to find that they'd been herded to the edge of the cliff.

"They're toying with us," Devedas gasped.

Sure enough, when they came for the fourth time, the creatures struck like lightning. Their strength was incredible. *Too
fast.* Devedas' legs were swept out from under him by a whirling
spear shaft. The monster smoothly recovered, raised the spear,
and launched it at Ashok. Devedas swung from the ground and
intercepted the killing blow, saving his life again.

Ashok stabbed at that monster, but a jolt of pain ran up his
arm as his sword was batted brutally aside by another. Ashok
fought with all the skill and savagery he could muster, until the
flat of an ax bruised his ribs and knocked the thin air from his
lungs. Something else hit him on the hip, cracking bone and
forcing him down. He swung for a monster's legs, but it leapt
effortlessly over the flashing blade. *Nothing is that fast.* Something clubbed him over the head, and by the time the lights quit
flashing behind his eyes, the monster he'd attacked had stepped
on his sword blade, pinning it to the ice.

It was curious. He'd always thought that at the moment of
death, he'd finally know what it was like to feel fear like everyone
else, but there was *nothing.* Ashok tried to draw his knife, but a
spear head was shoved through his hood and pressed against his
throat. *Strange.* He'd always thought that pushed to this point
he'd feel *something.*

"*Enough!*"

The cold iron departed, ripping away a bit of his skin with it.
The monsters pulled back again across the small battleground of
packed snow, leaving the two acolytes lying there, struggling to
breathe. Devedas got to his feet first. He grabbed Ashok by the
shoulder and roughly hauled him upright. One of his legs was
nothing but tingling, nonresponsive pain. Involuntary tears were
forming in his eyes and freezing there. He had to lean against
Devedas to keep from falling over. Neither of them could stand
on their own, but they both raised their swords.

The four remaining monsters silently parted to make way
for another figure. This one was also dressed in thick furs, and
Ashok's first thought was that the creature's chief had arrived to
finish them. Then the newcomer pushed back his hood, revealing dark human skin rather than a stretched blue skull. "Stand
down, acolytes. We start them tame for the challengers. Making
it to the fourth incarnation is impressive, but I don't believe you
would last more than a few seconds of their fifth."

Ashok recognized the speaker. He was tall and thin, but wiry strong, with graying hair and a weathered face. Ashok blinked his eyes and shook his head, but the man was still there. *Are my eyes broken?* He didn't think he'd been struck in the head, or maybe the lack of air was getting to him, because Ratul, Lord Protector of the Order, couldn't be here. Ratul had been at the base of the mountain to see them off.

"Master? Why... How?" Devedas stammered. "How did you—"

"Silence." Their swordmaster was known as Ratul Without Mercy, and he was more frightening than any witchcraft-fueled abominations. "You've kept me waiting longer than expected, but I must admit, that was an acceptable demonstration. I am not ashamed to have taught you."

Coming from Ratul, that was an incredible compliment, and Ashok was pleased to receive it.

His companion, however, was a bit more emotional in his response. "This was part of the test? We nearly died! What kind of brain-damaged fish-eater came up with this?" Devedas shouted as he wiped the blood from his face. Then he realized how unacceptable that emotional outburst was and lowered his head. "Forgive me, Lord Protector."

Ratul had a way of glaring with his narrow, heavy-lidded eyes that struck fear into all the acolytes capable of feeling such things. "You're lucky, Devedas. Long ago I cursed my instructor on this very spot for the very same reason. Offense has been given, but not taken. You have faced the guardians of the Heart. Don't worry about the two you tossed over the side. They'll climb back up shortly. If these had been men, you might have won. Enough questions for now." Ratul put his hood back up and began walking away. "Come with me. You have passed."

"What about Yugantar?" Devedas looked in the direction the other acolyte had fled.

"He didn't pass. The mountain can have him."

Chapter 6

Eighteen years ago

"If you'd not been here to guide us, we would've frozen to death before we found this entrance. The directions we were given were flawed for this last part. It would have led us to the wrong part of the summit."

"Correct, Ashok," Ratul said as he knocked the ice from the hidden doors. They were cut from the stone and camouflaged so well that they could have camped on them and never known. "The Heart is the most vital possession of the Order. Only those who pass the test may know the true location. It is possible that an acolyte may fail the test and flee the Order. They have already demonstrated their lack of character. They could talk. What then?"

The solution was obvious. "Execute them."

"Easier said than done in some cases, so it is better to deceive all the acolytes. Those who pass learn the truth. Should you ever speak of what you see beyond this point, your life is forfeit. If you are ever tortured for this information, it is better that you will yourself to die rather than give it up. If you ever tell of this place, you will be hunted down by the entire Order and destroyed, for the Heart is the source of our power."

Ratul did something with his hands, it seemed as if he were tracing invisible pictures on the stone, but whatever it was was hidden from view by his fur coat. The door should have been frozen solid, but it slid open with the grinding of stone against stone. Steep stairs led down into the mountain. Ratul started down and they followed. It was good to get out of the wind, but Ashok didn't like how there was no visible mechanism for opening the heavy door inside. Regulated magic was legal, but he had an instinctive personal distrust of the craft. Magic was made using the leftovers of broken ancestor blades and the remaining life spark of long-dead bearers.

"From this point forward, nothing you see can ever be spoken about with anyone who is not a Protector of senior rank or higher. You have already given me your oath. Whether it be a chief judge, the highest arbiter in the Capitol, the Thakoor of your house, or if the Forgotten himself descends from the heavens in a rain of fire and asks about this place, I don't give a damn, you will not speak with them about the Heart. Understood?"

"The Forgotten is imaginary, Lord Protector," Ashok pointed out.

"Damn, boy, you are a literal sort. Come on." Ratul started down the stairs.

The acolytes followed. Ashok was still having a hard time walking. His joint made a clicking noise in his pelvis with each step, and the pain was grating. The cuts on his chest burned, but the blood had dried to his undershirt enough to form a sort of giant cloth scab, so he was in no danger of bleeding to death. Devedas was keeping pressure on the laceration in his side, but the wound on his head was still slowly leaking through his hood. He was looking deathly pale and had vomited a few minutes before, but Ratul had denied their requests to stop long enough to tend their wounds.

Devedas slipped, stumbled down several steps, but caught himself on the wall before falling completely. Ashok grabbed him by the arm and helped him stand. Since one foot was numb, that almost caused both of them to go tumbling down the stairs. Some mighty Protectors they were.

He'd never been good at offering encouragement. "Keep going. It's not far now," Ashok said anyway.

"You don't know that," Devedas whispered.

"I can still hear you," Ratul said from below. "Your bodies are frail. Bones break, blood spills, and the Law is deprived of yet another valuable enforcer. That's what the Heart is for. When your own proves insufficient, it will beat on your behalf...But the boy is right, Devedas, it isn't much farther."

The magic door ground closed behind them, plunging them into complete darkness. Footsteps told him that Ratul was still descending. Devedas muttered something incomprehensible, and then the two of them limped along after their instructor.

The blindness was unnerving. The stairs continued. There seemed to be hundreds of them. Normally Ashok was so focused he would have counted, but now he was too tired to think. Something was making his nose itch. The mountain had been almost sterile. In comparison this placed smelled *old*. It was quiet except for the scrape of their boots against the stairs, their gloves along the walls, and Devedas' labored breathing. Ashok was taking a lot of Devedas' weight now as the older acolyte was having a hard time staying conscious. "Stay with me, brother," Ashok pleaded as Devedas' head wobbled around on his neck. If he went limp, they would fall. "I'm not strong enough to carry you."

Below them, Ratul began to whistle a tune. Then his footfalls changed. He'd left the stairs and reached a level surface. That gave Ashok hope. There was some rattling of metal on metal, and then the scrape of a firestarter. Thankfully, an orange light appeared. The glow spread as Ratul took the torch and touched it to a big fire pit. Whatever was in it was dry and immediately ignited. By the time he got Devedas to the bottom the chamber was filling with light and heat. His skin prickled. They'd been cold for so long that the warm air felt like being stabbed with thousands of needles.

"Bring him this way." Ratul ordered as he walked further inside and lit another fire pit. Ashok was having a hard time keeping up. "I was told there used to be lanterns here that never went out, but all magic breaks down eventually. The lights died generations ago, yet we make do. I sense a parable about society there."

Ashok stepped on an uneven part of the floor, and for whatever reason, that was enough. The strength went out from his injured leg. It crumpled beneath, and the two acolytes fell down. He hit the ground with a grunt. "Oh, what now?" Ratul muttered as he came back. He roughly rolled Devedas over and lowered an ear to his chest. "Hmmm...This one is worse off than I thought. He's bleeding to death and doesn't have enough sense to complain about it."

"He did complain, Lord Protector. However, you didn't listen."

"We're going to have to work on that unflinching honesty

of yours, Ashok." Ratul effortlessly hoisted Devedas up and put him over one shoulder. "Wait here. I must get him to the Heart immediately."

The master carried off the other acolyte, leaving Ashok alone.

He lay there on the hard floor for a time, flat on his back, letting his exhaustion seep from his body into the mountain. Ashok was incapable of fearing for himself, but it was interesting to discover that he could be worried about someone else's fate. He didn't want Devedas to die. Ashok had never had a friend before. Well, at least if you didn't count Angruvadal, but he wasn't sure if an ancient magical killing machine could actually be considered a friend.

The fire pits cast just enough light to see the high ceiling of the chamber. This place may have started out as a cave, but it had been worked and polished until the walls were smooth. However, there was large, rectangular section on the wall above him that was intricately carved and casting odd shadows. It took his eyes time to adjust enough to figure out what he was looking at.

It was a map.

Ashok had seen many maps. Mindarin used them during his lessons and had several posted in the training room. He'd seen maps of house borders, of the trade routes between them, even maps of all of Lok, where great rivers were lines and cities were nothing but specks. Only this wasn't like any map he'd seen before. He couldn't figure out what house's lands it was show-ing. Something was wrong with this one, he couldn't place his finger on it, but the map seemed totally unfamiliar. Legal borders changed over time, but coasts and mountain ranges didn't.

Then he picked out a few familiar shapes that would not have changed over time, like the Gujaran peninsula, and the western blob that was Uttara, the northern and westernmost parts of their nation respectively. "Impossible..." Ashok muttered as he forced himself to stand up. His leg burned and threatened to betray him again, but he needed to get closer. Ashok found another torch on the wall and lit it from the fire pit. He placed himself directly beneath the gigantic map and held up the flame.

This was a map of the *entire* world.

Their nation, the entire world of man, took up but one small corner. There were several other lands across the seas, some far larger than theirs, and hundreds of islands in between. As he moved the flickering torch back and forth, he realized there were thousands of carved dots casting tiny shadows. A quick check of the one continent he was familiar with revealed that the holes seemed to represent cities, with the bigger the shadow, the larger the place. Most seemed to correspond to the seats of the houses today, though there was no Capitol in the center, and there were a few dots where there was nothing today, but most matched... They had to be cities. When he went back to examining the rest of the map, he realized there were thousands of dots, spread across every landmass except for the ones at the very top and bottom. "Impossible," he said again.

Ashok couldn't say how long he stared at that map, memorizing every line, staring upward until the muscles in his neck began to ache and he got dizzy. It was easy to lose track of time when you found something so incomprehensible.

"It is rather impressive, isn't it?"

He hadn't heard the Lord Protector return. "Is Devedas—"

"That boy is too stubborn to die. As determined as he is to make up for his father's failures, it wouldn't surprise me if someday he was given my office."

Ashok turned back to the carving. "I don't understand this."

"Of course you wouldn't. This map comes from the time before the demons fell to the world."

It was forbidden to speak of the time before the Law in anything but the vaguest of terms. The acolytes only learned of it in passing, because it had been a dark and wicked time, so corrupt that it still influenced lawbreakers today. "The Age of Kings?"

"Before that, even. The houses were tribes back then. Fighting the demons is what forced us to name a king. It wasn't until long after we drove the demons into the sea that we discovered kings could be nearly as bad."

"We haven't been taught much about those days."

Surprisingly, Ratul didn't yell at him for concentrating on frivolous, useless things, and to the Lord Protector anything that wasn't fighting or preparing to fight seemed frivolous. Instead Ratul joined him beneath the map. "In ancient times, man had settled across the whole of the world. We were one of nine continents. There wasn't one nation like there is now, but hundreds of them, a multitude with different ways, different languages, traditions, different color skins, they even had different laws. They fought wars against each other, traded goods and thoughts, even animals. It was routine for man to travel across the sea in mighty ships."

"That's illegal, not to mention stupid," Ashok stated dismissively, even though he was talking to a superior.

"Not in those days. The oceans were just large bodies of water, nothing more, until there was a war that consumed the heavens, and the demons were defeated by the gods and cast down."

"Gods?" Ashok asked. Advocating the existence of such things was highly illegal.

"I speak metaphorically of course. Regardless of where they came from, there was a time before demons and a time after. They fell from the sky and began to destroy everything. Across the entire world, cities burned, and men fled before them. They nearly exterminated us. It wasn't until we used the black steel to drive them into the water that the oceans became hell. The demons have owned the sea ever since."

"Do you know where black steel comes from?" Despite spending years with three pounds of it riding on his hip, nobody had ever been able to explain it to him.

"There are only fantastical tales by those deluded enough to worship false gods," Ratul answered a little too quickly.

It was hard to imagine this ancient world of travelling foreigners and no supreme law to rule them all, until it had begun raining demons. Angruvadal had been forged in those days and it still remembered them. Ashok would have liked to see what that world had been like, but the memories locked in his sword were limited to battle after battle, and nothing beyond. Ashok could relive every fight of every bearer, but he'd never understand what any of them had been fighting for. "What do the fanatics say about the origins?"

Ratul gave Ashok that heavy-lidded glare, letting Ashok know there would be no good answer to that question. "The demons destroyed most of civilization, and what histories survived were questionable at best. They're locked away in the Capitol library now, under the careful eye of the Archivists' Order. The Age of Kings was based on lies, so the records that passed through their priests' corrupt hands were tainted until everything was twisted to serve their greed. Regardless of where black steel comes from, ever since our victory, man has controlled the land and demons have held the sea. We don't try to cross the water and they are not allowed to walk upon our land. This arrangement has held for fifty generations."

Scanning the dots on the other lands, Ashok tried to take it all in. Some of them cast much larger shadows than Vadal City, and the census said nearly a million people lived there... It was hard to imagine a city even bigger. "What happened to the people in all those other continents?"

"Who knows? Dead more than likely. The demons nearly ended us here. Perhaps other nations weren't so lucky. Did they discover magic like we did? Maybe in those other places the demons won and now those slimy things are the ones living on land."

"That would be trespassing. They should be punished."

Ratul actually appeared amused by that. "I admire your commitment, but sadly that's a bit beyond our jurisdiction to enforce, Ashok."

For now, Ashok thought to himself. He couldn't abide the idea of anything, demon or human, flouting the Law.

"Regardless, if any foreigners survived like we did, we'll never know. Crossing the sea is impossible, so for all practical matters, we're all that remain... You know this. Mindarin must have covered it in your lessons."

"Briefly." They didn't waste too much of the acolytes' precious training time on ancient history. Protectors were focused on enforcing the rules *now*, not dwelling in the past. How one got to the destination was not nearly as important as maintaining order once there.

"Myself, I'm a student of these things. I've read everything available about the ancients and sought out the best scholars in the Capitol to discuss our history." That was a surprise. Normally, Ratul only seemed interested in teaching them how to kill people more efficiently. It was hard to picture him actually *enjoying* something. "I've been fascinated by the subject my entire life. If I'd not been obligated to the Order, I might have made a fine Archivist, but enough of this. There is one final test for you." Ratul walked away.

Ashok hesitated. From the top of the mountain he'd been able to see into the lands of several great houses. At the time he'd not realized how truly small they really were. Taking one last longing look at the map, Ashok hurried and limped after his instructor.

More torches had been lit along a corridor. It led further into the mountain. "I'm curious, Ashok. Why did you attempt the test so early?"

He was required to give only honest answers to his superiors. "I don't think I can last another year without my sword."

Ratul grunted. "Thought so."

That didn't answer whether he'd get Angruvadal back yet or not, but it wasn't Ashok's place to question. He would prove himself or die trying.

They entered another, smaller chamber. The room was plain, but the shape of it gave the impression it had once been used for more. There were strangely shaped alcoves all around the interior, empty now, their original purpose a mystery. Ratul gestured toward an altar in the center of the room. "Behold, the Heart of the Mountain."

It was so black that it seemed to burn a hole in his vision. The hungry darkness seemed to absorb their torchlight. He had to turn his head a bit so that he could actually see it from the corner of his eye. The heart appeared to be a jagged, twisted mass of metal the size of a child. It was the biggest piece of black steel Ashok had ever seen, big enough to forge a dozen swords or thousands of valuable fragments. Some people had a sense for magic, and though Ashok had never been naturally gifted in that way, even he could feel the energy radiating from the Heart.

The metal device twitched. As he watched, it twitched again. It really was *beating*.

"This is the Order's greatest weapon, old as your precious Angruvadal, from the time when magic was common. We've kept it for over a thousand years. This is what makes Protectors more than men. When you touch it, you will take part of its power with you for the rest of your days. It will sting you and infect your blood. The influence of the Heart will be yours to call upon for the rest of your life. It can make you stronger, hardier, and hone your reactions. With sufficient concentration you can direct it to empower your senses, but it can only do so much at a time. You will heal faster and even survive wounds that would be fatal to a normal man, but it will not make you immortal. An injury sufficiently devastating will still kill you. It may stay death for a time, but nothing can postpone death forever. Well, nothing *legal* at least."

"I have already been touched by magic."

"Indeed. For one such as you, the defensive power of the Heart combined with the offensive skill bestowed by your ancestor blade, I can only imagine what the Order could accomplish with such a weapon at its disposal."

There was no better cause than justice, so Ashok didn't mind the idea of being a weapon in its behalf. "What if I'm unworthy?"

Ratul had a laugh like a dog's bark. "The Order decides who is worthy, and if you weren't, I'd have had the guardians toss you off that cliff. Magic can make you tougher, but it can't give you character. That's why our program is so harsh. Flawed acolytes must be weeded out. The Heart does not care about birth or honor. I imagine a casteless could take from it if one was clever enough to find his way in here. Only a bearer would think of such a question. Don't worry. It is not like Angruvadal. The Heart has no opinions of its own."

It was not his place to disagree, but in Ashok's experience, all black steel had ghosts inside of it. Some of them were just louder than others. He peered closer into the burning darkness. There was something *wrong* with the Heart. There was a weakness to it. "Lord Protector, you can see magic inside of things, can't you?"

"I have that gift, yes."

"How much magic is left within the Heart?"

Ratul didn't respond. Ashok looked over to see that the master was scowling. "Less than when I first saw it for myself, but enough."

When magic was worn too thin its container would fail. "What happens when the Heart shatters?"

"The Order will die," Ratul said simply.

Ashok moved away from the Heart. "Then I will not use up any for myself. Save the magic for someone better."

"I appreciate the sentiment, but that isn't how it works. No, Ashok, this is your final test. To become full-fledged Protector the Order requires this. I'm one of the few who can see magic, which means that when you touch the Heart, I will see you for what you truly are. This is necessary, for the good of the Order and for the sanctity of the Law."

"This is a command?"

"Yes."

Ashok nodded, stepped toward the Heart of black steel and placed his hands on it.

The world turned to blood.

✧　　✧　　✧

The promotion ceremony was over. Only two acolytes had attained senior status this season, not nearly enough to make up for attrition and their dwindling numbers, but one showed great promise, and far more importantly, the other possessed a sword that could supposedly defeat armies. Mindarin was excited at the prospects. However, Lord Protector Ratul seemed to be in a worse mood than usual.

The Hall of the Protectors was a vast stone fortress cut from the mountainside, far too large for their dwindling numbers. Mindarin joined his commander on the balcony overlooking the empty training ground. "I've been told that in times past, our numbers were so great that our formations took up this whole space when they presented themselves for inspection." Ratul snorted. "We used to be so respected that we received so many obligations that we had to turn some away. I can't even imagine. Now we can barely fill one corner with *children*. So this is what it feels like to preside over a dying order... But then I wonder if it truly has to be that way."

The acolytes were gone, allowed a few hours to celebrate some of their number successfully advancing or to mourn the one who hadn't made it back. It was their choice. Ratul went back to staring off into space, sucking on his teeth, mulling over something.

"What troubles you?" Mindarin asked.

"The truth..."

"That's an unusually cryptic pronouncement. You saw something strange at the Heart, didn't you?"

"Any other acolyte and I would have cut him down on the spot, but the Order *needs* that sword." Ratul sighed. "Dark times are coming, my friend."

Mindarin felt his hopes dashed. "Ashok then. Did you receive a prophecy?" Such a thing was rare, but not unheard of when dealing with the Heart. "Did it show you his future?"

Ratul spit over the edge and watched it fall. "Bah... I'm weary from the journey. That mountain seems taller the older I get. I don't want to talk about it now. It'll be dealt with in time. Good night, Mindarin." He left the rail and began to walk away.

"Did the Heart show you the future?" Mindarin called after him.

"No." Ratul didn't look back. "It showed me the past."

Chapter 7

As the sun rose across the desert, the spires of the Capitol's tallest towers were visible in the distance. It was the biggest city in Lok. There was no place farther from the sea, and thus purer, than the Capitol. Kept alive by endless caravans and mighty aqueducts, the city had grown out of this barren region to spite nature. It was the source of the Law, the home of the bureaucracy, and the depository of mankind's knowledge. It was in the middle of a desert, in the center of the continent, and though no rivers flowed here, all power did.

He had crossed jungles, mountains, plains, and desert, both low and high, over the last few weeks, riding from before dawn until after dusk, driving horses to exhaustion or death, and then using his office to confiscate more from the next town. Ashok had commandeered barges to cross rivers, climbed thousands of feet to cross mountain passes where the air was so thin that it made his head ache, and traveled hundreds of miles on the trade roads. He'd passed dozens of villages, a handful of cities, more caravans than he could count, and had dispatched one gang of bandits stupid enough to mistake him for a normal traveler in the dark. All of that brought him here, to the shadow of the Mount Metoro, to the greatest city in the world.

Protector Ashok Vadal, twenty-year senior, was not happy to be here.

"A wise man once told me that the place where they make law is the place where they're the least likely to obey it," Ashok muttered as he watched the spires. Of course, his only companion had no response but to snort and flick an ear. The horse was exhausted. That was too bad. It was his last mount, there were still miles to go, and now that the sun was up they needed to go faster. He thumped the animal with his heels. "My apologies, horse. I don't like this place either."

The duties of his office had taken him to nearly every city on the continent. Most of them were surrounded by the smelly farms and smoking industries of the workers, with scattered compounds belonging to the warrior caste between them, the slums for the casteless in the least desirable locations, and all of those quarters existed to serve the will of the much smaller governing caste who usually lived in some form of central castle or palace, separate and aloof. That's how society normally worked for the good and order of mankind.

The Capitol was different from every other city. There were still multitudes of workers who lived here to serve, and legions of warriors to defend it, but this was a city built from the ground up for the comfort of the greatest among men. There were disproportionate numbers of the ruling caste here. Within every caste were numerous subcastes, and levels within levels, until every man had a place. This was where the greatest among them gathered to conduct their houses' affairs. The lowliest bureaucrat still had rank and connections beyond an outsider's dreams. Every home was a palace, and each agency of the bureaucracy required a building that made those palaces look like a casteless shack.

The horse shifted nervously beneath him as it caught the scent of death on the desert wind. "Easy, horse. They have to hang the criminals somewhere." They certainly couldn't do it in town, where the governing caste would have to smell them rot.

To the north, separate from the city, high up the side of lonely Mount Metoro, was a familiar fortress. His dried-out eyes could barely make out the clouds of black dots dancing over the Inquisitor's Dome. *Vultures.* Hundreds of them. The executioners must have been busy lately, and recently too if the smell of decay was this strong, because bodies turned to jerky quickly under this sun.

The only good thing about his new orders was that he'd not been requested here by the Inquisition. When a Protector was summoned by the anonymous men in the masks and hoods, it was usually to deal with a lawbreaker using illegal magic, but once in a great while it was to be interrogated themselves. It was rare for a Protector to be questioned, but the Law declared that no one was above suspicion. Everyone answered to someone. Protectors answered to the Inquisition. Ashok would submit to their tortures if ordered, but he wouldn't enjoy it.

The Capitol was strange. It belonged to no house, but all houses heeded it. It produced nothing but words, but it was the richest city in the world. All houses had their own form of currency, but the Capitol issued banknotes, which could be traded and honored by all. The houses supplied the Capitol with resources and people, and in exchange the Capitol gave them Law.

Along the road, Ashok passed dozens of wagons flying the banners of many different houses. He thought about stopping one of the caravans to trade for a fresh horse, but by the time he dealt with all the needless pleasantries, announcements, and workers sucking up, he wouldn't be saving any time. Since he'd dressed in his full uniform for his presentation in the Capitol, he stuck out, and many of the drivers became obviously fearful when they saw a Protector approaching. Since it was legal for any enforcer of the Law to requisition whatever he needed to fulfill his orders, many poor merchants had been deprived of their goods along this very road after hauling them all the way across the continent.

Ashok knew there would be many sighs of relief as he passed them by unmolested. One eventually got used to being feared by nearly everyone he met.

The walls of the Capitol were too thin and constructed of sandstone. They existed primarily for decoration and would never survive a siege. The Capitol's real defenses were made of ink and paper. No matter how far it might drift from the letter of the Law, no house would ever make war on the Capitol, because there would be several other houses ready to curry political favor by turning on their neighbor. It was a careful balancing act, but it had kept the peace for hundreds of years.

The city never stopped growing. It had been a few years since his last visit, and he marveled at how many new structures there were, and how many old ones had been torn down and rebuilt. For the source of all order in the world, it was certainly chaotic.

The headquarters of the Order of Protectors were just inside the gate, between one of the vast bazaars and a workers' neighborhood. This position was strategic, separate from the decision makers, but close enough to still take orders. Compared to the rest of the government buildings, it was humble. Compared to the rest of the Order's holdings across the continent, it was ostentatious. Much like the walls, this building was also for show. The real—literal—heart of the Order was in the rugged mountains of Devakula, far to the south.

The bazaar was a packed mass of humanity, jostling about in the shade of hundreds of tents. The stalls came and went as merchants struck it rich or went broke. The arbiters and regulators didn't usually bother with this area unless someone important complained. Some fool was trying to sell elephants, and the poor beasts looked miserable in the heat. Their giant piles of dung covered half the road. The road that had been here the last time he'd visited was now blocked by someone selling chickens. A new path through had been created where there had been a spice merchant before. This lack of continuity offended Ashok.

"Protector business. Make a hole." Most people were quick enough to get out of his way. Though his horse did knock over a few workers, they were of low enough rank that nobody would notice. "You must have some warhorse in your blood," Ashok congratulated his mount.

The Order's compound was a prestigious posting for the warrior caste, so the soldiers guarding the entrance were always alert, and they had spotted his uniform above the crowd. "Who approaches?" one of them shouted.

"Ashok Vadal, twenty-year senior." The horse seemed very pleased to stop.

"You are expected, Protector," one of the guards said as he took the reins.

Ashok slid out of the saddle. "Take care of this animal. It's been tougher than expected." He patted the foaming beast on the neck, then walked through the inner courtyard.

Several acolytes were crudely sparring, which consisted of mercilessly beating each other with padded sticks. It was good to see that there were so many of them. Though they remained a small, elite organization, over the last decade their numbers had grown. As the Protectors had regained their status, the houses had obligated an increasing number of recruits, and since no one wanted to be outdone, they only sent their best. The acolyte running the drills saw him coming, and snapped at his younger charges to get out of the way. They quickly formed a line and bowed. Ashok didn't know any of them, so he gave but a small nod in greeting as he passed them by.

He could hear them whispering behind his back. *Black-hearted Ashok, the finest killer who has ever lived.* He didn't know them, but they knew of him.

The doors to the keep were open. In the high desert it was best to keep the air circulating. "Ashok!" the booming deep voice came from inside, followed a moment later by the broad-shouldered bulk of one of his brothers. "About damned time you showed up! Way to take your sweet time."

"Hello, Karno." Ashok outranked him, but they'd fought together, so he was used to Karno's plainspoken ways. He was from House Uttara, a land so poor that even their first caste were little better than farmers. Bad manners were to be expected from them. "Good to see you too."

The big Protector never seemed pleased, and he wasn't about to start now. "Forgive my abruptness. You can clean up later. The master's been waiting for you. Come on."

The compound was too quiet. He saw no other Seniors. Normally they only had a small garrison here, but he'd never seen so few experienced Protectors here. He went up the stairs, and the main chamber was just as dead. The only other living things were a couple of lazy dogs and a slave sweeping the floor. "Where is everyone?"

"Trouble down south. The Inquisition needed some muscle. Mindarin sent most of the Capitol garrison."

It had to be bad if they'd called up that many Protectors. "Makao again?"

"Not this time. Casteless uprising in House Akershan. Cultists of the Forgotten got to preaching the old religion. They even have themselves a false prophet. So some lunatic hearing voices got them all riled up and they murdered an arbiter. Can you believe it?" Karno snorted. "Bunch of idiots hiding in the mountains. Next thing you know they'll be crowning some fish-eater to be their king. The witch hunters are taking it serious though. They say the rebels have got their hands on some powerful magic. Fortress forged, I'd wager."

There were very few things more illegal than Fortress alchemy. They were the last open practitioners of the old ways in Lok, but their impenetrable island kept them from safe from the Law, and their smuggled abominations were a terrible source of corruption in the world. If it was truly that bad, then Akershan was where he would be going next. *Good.* Crushing uprisings was preferable to dealing with politics in the Capitol. At least the religious fanatics were honest. "I need to speak to the master."

"This way. I sent a slave to make sure he's awake." Karno lumbered down the hall. He was a head taller than Ashok, twice as big around, and shaggy as a bear in winter. He was one of the few men in the Order against whom Ashok actually had to work hard in order to win a sparring match. "I asked to be sent to smash this uprising, you know, but I got stuck here. The casteless back in my own house got uppity a few years back, murdered some of our warriors, and then Devedas slaughtered the lot of them, the lucky bastard."

"How is Mindarin?"

"Bad." He wasn't known as Blunt Karno just because he preferred to fight with a hammer. "Prepare yourself."

His father had died when he was very young. Ashok couldn't remember a thing about the man, couldn't even picture his face. Mindarin, on the other hand, had taught him everything he knew, made him everything that he was. The swordmaster was much more of a father than the one who'd passed on his blood. Everyone dies, but Ashok didn't have to like it.

They went up the stairs and stopped before a closed door. It was a sad comment that here privacy was worth more than the cooling breeze. Ashok reached for the handle but Karno stopped him. "Wait for the slave to come out. He can't even sit up in bed on his own or clean himself. Let the master retain what dignity he has left."

Ashok let go of the handle. "I was unaware."

"Most are. He was struck down months ago. The surgeons said it was a seizure of apoplexy. There was paralysis for a time, and only recently could he speak clearly again, but his body continues to deteriorate. The Heart of the Mountain is the only thing sustaining him."

"Is there no hope for him?"

"None. The rebels hiding in their mountain holes can pray to their false god for comfort, but for us, there's only the harsh truth that such a great man will be remembered. I'll leave you to your business." Karno stomped back toward the stairs, but paused before going down. "Whatever reason Mindarin called for you, whatever your assignment may be, I know you're the right choice. You are the best of us." He bowed.

He cared little for praise, but coming from one as honest as Karno, the words actually meant something. Ashok returned the bow. By the time he looked up, Karno was gone.

A few minutes passed. There was a single chair in the hall. The Order was supposed to be above petty house politics and devoted entirely to the rule of law. They kept an office here only as a demonstration of that fact, and they kept that office humble in an attempt to keep their power from going to their heads. The chairs weren't even padded. If they had guests then a slave would bring in a cushion. After weeks in the saddle, he wouldn't have minded that minor comfort. So Ashok remained standing. He was so tired that he probably could have slept standing up. He'd done it before.

The door opened and a slave came out. "The master will see you now," she said, keeping her eyes averted. Slaves were usually born of the worker or warrior castes, dishonored, demoted, and sold for some reason or another, but still needed to perform the necessary tasks that were above the filthy untouchable casteless, like tending to the needs of an honored hero suffering from disease.

"You may go," Ashok told her as he entered. The curtains were mostly closed. The room was far too warm. It took a moment for his eyes to adjust to the dim light. There was someone on the bed. He almost didn't recognize the skeletal figure propped up on a pile of pillows because he had lost so much weight. Mindarin was a shadow of himself.

"Lord Protector."

"Ashok." Mindarin opened his eyes. Despite his haggard appearance, at least they were as clear and focused as ever. "I knew you'd come, lad."

"I'm here to serve."

"As always... For that has been your life, to serve without question... Never to question..." His words were slurred and clumsy. It was an unjust fate for the one who had been their most eloquent defender. Mindarin had accomplished more with his words than with the sword, because in his case they had been equally sharp. To hear him now made Ashok's chest ache. "I knew that if I lived long enough for you to return, then this meeting was meant to be," the dying man wheezed. "Oh, how I wish I could be as pure in my devotion to the Law as you've been."

Ashok knelt next to the bed. "I am nothing more than what you made me."

"No. You were the creation of another. The Order merely gave you purpose. You are a sense of duty made flesh. You are the living avatar of the Law. You were a blank canvas and on it was writ devotion. You were the perfect student because you were designed to be. It is easy to be the ideal Protector when you have no choice in the matter." Mindarin gave a raspy laugh. "I suppose we are all slaves in some way."

That made no sense. Perhaps the master's mind wasn't as clear as he'd first thought. "I was obligated to serve by my house, but I took the oath willingly, and it is the best thing I've done."

Mindarin took a deep breath, as if preparing himself for a great labor. Ashok could tell that he was calling upon the strength of the Heart. When that borrowed energy was gone, the resulting strain would probably finish him off.

"Please rest. There's no need."

"I must." When Mindarin spoke again, his words were stronger, far more forceful. Here again this was the man Ashok had known. "When I was struck down and knew I was dying, I had to make a difficult decision. Summoning you here was one of the hardest things I've ever done. I realize cleaning the stain from my own conscience is no reason to condemn you, so now I offer you a choice, Ashok. On one hand, I can remain silent and you will continue to live your life. I offer you my place as master or you may return to your house with honor..."

It was as Devedas had predicted, the choice he'd been dreading, to retire in glory or continue to serve the Order. "I'll do whatever you ask of me."

"You speak too quickly. That isn't the choice...I'm offering your life, however you wish to live it, or the *truth*. Leave things alone, retain the lie, and do with the rest of your days whatever you desire, but the truth...the truth will *ruin* you. It will change everything."

Uncertainty was an unfamiliar feeling.

Mindarin reached out one shaking hand and laid it on Ashok's cheek. His skin was dry and thin as paper. "I have summoned you because I am selfish. I have failed the Law and failed you. My conscience isn't clean."

Ashok was no stranger to death, but right now he felt ill. "What would you have me do so you may die in peace?"

"Offering you this choice is enough. In that drawer is a message. It is the reason you are without fear. It is a secret known only to myself and master Ratul before me."

It had been years since he'd heard that name spoken aloud by another Protector. Just thinking of the former Lord Protector filled Ashok with disgust. "His secrets should remain hidden. Ratul worshiped the Forgotten while he pretended devotion to the Order. I'm ashamed he's the one I gave the oath to. He was a lawbreaker and a traitor."

"Yet he was also my dearest friend, and his beliefs saved your life. Before he fled to join the heretics, he told me what the Heart of Ramrowan revealed you to be."

"Ramrowan?" It was the first time Ashok heard the Heart of the Mountain given that unfamiliar name. "I know who I am. I know my place."

"Good. That is how it should be. If you wish to continue living, burn the letter and never think on this moment again."

Ashok was silent for a long time. "What manner of lie?"

"One that will cause no further harm, and I kept your secret for the same selfish reasons Ratul did. You have been our greatest instrument of justice. This Order is stronger than we have been in generations. We are respected, honored, even feared and it is a result of the legend you have created with that mighty sword. If you wish to know what Ratul saw in the Heart, read it, then do as you see fit."

Ashok stood up, went to the writing desk and opened the drawer. The only thing inside was a sealed letter.

"It's coded. If you wish, I will give you the cipher, but remember, sometimes lies are for our own protection. This is your choice. Do not make it lightly, Ashok."

Was this some sort of test? A trick? He reached for the letter, and then hesitated. "What does the Law say I should do?"

"For once in your life, do not make this about the Law!" Mindarin's words showed surprising strength.

"But the Law is everything." Ashok picked up the letter. His face was flushed, his hands trembling. He was growing angry and wasn't even sure why. "You know I was never one for your puzzles and word games. I'm not one of your riddles to be solved. I am a Protector."

"You are a killer."

"And the best one we've ever had!" Ashok snarled. "You tell me what to do and I do it. Point me toward the violators and I destroy them. Punishing the lawbreakers and striking terror in the hearts of those who even think of stepping over the line, *that* is my place. I follow orders. I keep *order*. I don't choose. There's no *choice*. If this is some sort of test of my worthiness—"

"Angruvadal decided that a long time ago, the question then became how many lies we were willing to tell to justify its decision." The borrowed vitality was beginning to leave Mindarin. His skin turned ashen, his voice lost its previous strength, and he seemed to melt back into the bed, once again, nothing but a shadow, skeletal as the guardians on the mountain. "It's remarkable what we can forget. We've forgotten our gods. Compared to that, what is one life? I don't have enough time left to keep the lies straight anymore, Ashok. With truth comes suffering. With ignorance comes freedom. Choose."

He quoted his lessons from memory. "There is no freedom. Every man has a place." Then he recalled the stubborn casteless who'd refused to give up his spear on the beach in Gujara. "Truth doesn't change the Law."

"Choose."

Ashok broke the seal.

Chapter 8

Twenty years ago

As the richest, most powerful house, Vadal was the last to be announced during the induction ceremony. Aunt Bidaya had prepared Ashok for this by explaining that it was all politics. *Vadal could afford to wait. It tells our rivals that we saved the best for last.*

Ashok found the Protectors' audience chamber to be surprisingly humble. Perhaps it was because he was used to the beauty of Vadal holdings that he connoted power with opulence. Except the Protectors were powerful and their audience chamber had less decoration than a Vadal horse stable. The simple room was crowded with representatives of every great house and their candidates for obligation. Everyone was dressed in furs or thick robes and their breath could be seen in the air. The windows were open. The ceremonial chamber wasn't heated. It wasn't as if a militant order with the blessing of the Inquisition couldn't afford to run the furnace. It was the Protectors' way of telling their guests that they didn't give a damn about anyone's comfort.

The representative from house Vokkan finished his long description of his charge's exploits, accomplishments, and championships.

The oldest was only thirteen years old, so he couldn't have done that much, but that was the game. The tales were surely exaggerated, but this part was all about trying to outdo the other houses. Whoever gave the most valuable obligations would be able to brag about it in the courts.

Ashok didn't understand these games that his aunt spoke about, but he understood honor, duty, and the Law. Each of those things demanded that he be here now.

The Protector in charge of the ceremony walked in front of the kneeling young men, inspecting them. Once satisfied, he made a mark on his scroll. "The Order thanks Great House Vokkan for their generous obligation of seven sons of the warrior caste and one son of the first caste." He sounded bored. "They will proceed to testing."

Despite the Order's power, the Protectors of the Law were few in number. A single master was presiding. His witnesses were a senior and a few other acolytes, barely older than the boys who were being obligated. While the presenters and their charges had decorated their winter clothing with ornaments, jewelry, and silks dyed the colors of their houses, the Protectors were dressed in drab cloaks, fit for workers. The master checked his list again as he moved to the end of the line. "Great House Vadal has brought... A *single* candidate? Your lady must not be aware of our failure rate."

The other presenters were curious. The dumb ones found that amusing. The smart ones realized that Vadal was up to something. The master stopped before the small Vadal contingent. He stood there for a while in the cold winter sun, taking his time. Ashok kept his back straight and his eyes fixed on a crack in the wall as the old man studied him. "Present your obligation."

The other presenters were arbiters and other courtly types. Ashok was the only one being introduced by a wizard. Kule was a small, quiet, odd-looking fellow. He stepped out of line and cleared his throat before speaking. "On behalf of Bidaya, Thakoor of Great House Vadal, as per our contract I obligate to the Order of Protectors the second son of deceased Jayesh of the first caste, who was once arbiter of Goda Province. Here is Ashok, aged ten years."

"A single candidate, and the youngest one here... This will end well," the Protector muttered. Everyone heard that, and there was a bit of laughter. Ashok kept his gaze fixed on a distant point and showed no emotion, just as he'd been taught. "What are his accomplishments?"

The other candidates had gotten long litanies of achievements. Ashok's was brief. "He is the chosen bearer of mighty Angruvadal." Kule finished his pronouncement and returned to his place in line.

The snickering died. Nervous whispers immediately rose among the other house's presenters. *Angruvadal?* Several of them broke protocol by turning their heads to try and catch a glimpse of the sword sheathed at the boy's side. All they would be able to see was that it appeared to be far too long for him to wield it worth a damn. They would be incorrect.

"What?" the old Protector glanced at the wizard, then at Ashok, then at his list, and back at the wizard. "House Vadal is obligating the bearer of its *ancestor blade?*"

"You are correct, Lord Protector." Kule bowed respectfully. "Which is why we believe just the one will be sufficient."

The other nervous young men who were being obligated to the Order kept their eyes forward. Ashok remained kneeling, motionless as the rest. He had been instructed not to move until told to move, nor to speak unless spoken to. He was *mostly* motionless, except for the shivering. That couldn't be controlled. The headquarters of the Protector Order, like most important things, was in the Capitol, but its training program was in the barren mountains of Devakula, so all of the boys from the warmer northern houses were having a difficult time. The annual ceremony was held during the winter, probably because any children who died along the hard journey through the passes saved the Protectors the effort of having to weed out the weak later.

The Protector's mood changed from bored to angry very quickly. He'd probably had some small speech prepared, but it had been forgotten once he'd learned someone had brought something so deadly into his castle. "The ceremony is concluded. The presenters will be escorted out. The obligated will be shown to their quarters. Except for the Vadal delegation. You stay here."

The other houses complied, the boys looking nervous or happy to have made it this far, while their political masters seemed frustrated or curious by this new development. The senior ushered everyone else out, and soon it was only the master, the wizard, and Ashok who remained in the giant, freezing room.

"What is Vadal playing at, wizard?"

Kule smiled, showing his oddly pointed teeth. "There is no game here, Lord Protector, merely a demonstration of our house's extreme devotion to the Law. All of the details are in the contract which was presented to your representatives in the Capitol. It has already been approved by the judges. All that remains is for you to accept the obligation of this child as acceptable. All that we have asked in return is that should Ashok perish, the sword be returned to its rightful house so that it may choose a new bearer."

"Stand up!" the Protector shouted.

Ashok leapt to his feet. The Protector circled him, eyeing the sword sheathed on his belt. The handle and guard were dark and unremarkable.

"Draw the sword."

He did as he was told. Three feet of black steel was freed from the leather. Angruvadal wanted to know who it was supposed to cut. *No one yet. Be still.* When the sword came out, his shivering ceased. He held it out with one hand, horizontal to the floor, careful not to take up any sort of fighting stance so that Angruvadal would not get the wrong idea.

Angruvadal was shaped like a typical sword of House Vadal. Most likely, they were based on it. Unlike most swords in Lok, Angruvadal was straight, not curved in any way. It was double-edged, sharp enough on either side to effortlessly lop off a man's arm. The grip was long enough for two-hand use. Though the pommel, grip, and guard didn't give off the same eye-searing glow as the blade itself, they weren't separate pieces, but seemed to have grown organically from the whole. For something so valuable, there was absolutely no ornamentation to it at all—not that there was any way to decorate Angruvadal, since it was made out of a material that couldn't even be scratched.

Most people were afraid to come too close to the blade because they'd heard the stories, but not the Protector. He loomed over Ashok and demanded, "Hold it up toward the lantern so I can see." Ashok did so, and they both watched it devour the flickering light.

"It is truly one of the most dangerous things in the entire world," Kule warned.

"It burns the eye to look directly at it," the Protector whispered as he stared into the blade. "It is said that a warrior with one of these can break an army by himself."

"History has repeatedly demonstrated that to be true." Kule had hunkered back down into his coat to hide from the chill, nearly disappearing until only his tiny black eyes poked out over the fur. "It can slay demons as if they are normal flesh and bone. Lawbreakers will tremble before its wrath. Imagine what the Order could do with such a tool. And now it is yours to direct . . . for the good of the Law, of course."

The Protector realized that he'd been drawn in until his breath was steaming on the sword. He was so close that Ashok could remove the top half of his head with the flick of a wrist. A man could lose himself staring into that abyss. He stepped back. "Sheath it. Now."

Angruvadal felt disappointment at being put away.

The other Protectors had returned from shooing out the presenters. They were watching as well, seemingly just as fascinated as their master. "Is it true?" the senior asked.

"It's the real thing, and it didn't take his life for daring to pull it, so we can assume this is no fraud," the master said.

"Imagine what we could accomplish with a bearer in our ranks," the senior said.

"Answer my questions carefully, boy. Answer them as if your life depends on it, because it truly does."

"Yes, Lord Protector," Ashok said.

"Your house has given you to us. Do you willingly give your life over to the Order?"

He hadn't asked that to the others, except the others didn't possess an ancient device capable of destroying them all. "Yes, Lord Protector."

"You will follow your instructions without question?"

"I will."

"You will do exactly as I say. I am Ratul, twenty-five-year master. This is Mindarin, eighteen-year senior. If I am indisposed or dead you will answer to him. Now, keep your sword sheathed and remove it from your person." Ashok unbuckled his sword belt. The Protector stuck out his hand. "Give it to me."

"Master!" one of the acolytes warned. "It will destroy you."

"According to tradition, only if I should try to wield it." The old Protector took hold of the belt strap. The sword hung there, leather creaking, as he held it at arm's length. Ashok could tell the sword wasn't offended. Ratul addressed the sword with far more respect than he had given any of the representatives of the great houses. "We mean no disrespect, Angruvadal. First the Law must be upheld." Then he passed the sword to the senior Mindarin, who took it without hesitation, though he was careful not to touch the sword itself.

Kule looked on as if this was all mildly amusing.

The master roughly put his hands on both sides of Ashok's face. The boy flinched, but the Protector dragged him over and forced Ashok's eyes open with his thumbs. He stared *through* Ashok's eyes and there was a terrible pain inside his head. Ashok didn't flinch. "I thought so." The Protector let go, and the pain subsided. "There is magic in this boy."

"Some," Kule agreed.

"What have you done to him, wizard?"

"As a child, Ashok suffered a terrible accident. A fire in the middle of the night and his family perished. He alone survived, but was found in the ruins of their home, with heart, mind, and body broken. Since he was of the first caste, our Thakoor had me put him back together. Good thing, too, since he was later chosen by the sword. No illegal magic was used in the healing, I can assure you. My notes about his treatment are available to Inquisition auditors if you would like them examined."

"I do not trust you."

Kule may have shrugged. It was difficult to tell beneath the thick coat. "Then you must ask yourself, Lord Protector, does your Order want access to the sword or not?"

The master folded his arms, seemingly deep in thought, staring at Ashok. Not having his sword at his side was unnerving, so Ashok found the crack in the wall and fixed his attention on that again.

"The mere presence of such a device within the Order will deter lawbreakers," Mindarin said, still carefully holding the sword as if it were a serpent that might bite him. "I believe it to be worth the risk. I will accept responsibility for this one."

Ratul nodded slowly. "Very well...If Ashok cannot be controlled you're the one that has to try and kill him. Note, I said *try*. You've not seen what a bearer can do." He turned back to Kule. "Wizard, your house's obligation has been accepted. Get out."

Kule bowed again, then turned and shuffled out the door without another word. Even though Ashok had lived in the wizard's household while he'd been healing from the accident, there wasn't so much as a farewell. Ashok kept staring at the crack while the Protectors clustered around the hanging sword.

"Do those Vadal fools have any idea the risk they are taking? Are their heads crammed so far up their own asses that they think being the talk of the Capitol is worth losing their house?" Ratul mused.

"Maybe a great house is really that devoted to upholding the Law?"

They all laughed.

It was almost as if he had been forgotten entirely. Ashok was temporarily thankful, but that moment passed and Ratul returned his attention to him. "Ashok. You are now an acolyte in the Order of Protectors. Your training begins immediately. Devedas will escort you to the barracks. That will be all."

One of the acolytes stepped forward. "This way." Though he was not that much older than Ashok, he already carried himself like a Protector, and to Ashok's inexperienced eye appeared to be nearly as dangerous as the others.

The other newly obligated had all been armed. Ashok looked to Mindarin, and then to his sword, hanging there, creaking against the leather. "May I have my sword back now?"

"No," Ratul answered.

"Why?"

Ratul frowned, then nodded at one of the older acolytes. That one stepped forward and struck Ashok in the face. The force snapped his head back on his neck and sent him crashing hard into the floor.

Blood came rolling out of his nose and he could taste it on his lip. Ashok could feel Angruvadal's desire to help. *No...* He had made a mistake. Ratul's actions had been correct. Ashok held no animosity. The sword was content.

"Questioning an order? Already you're off to a fine start."

"Lord Protector, if I may..." Devedas interjected. "This one isn't like the others. That sword is more than a weapon to him. Part of his fire is inside it forever. To a bearer, losing his blade is worse than one of us losing an arm."

Ashok wiped the blood from his lip, got up, and stood at attention. Devedas was correct. He couldn't even remember a time before the sword.

"Hmmm... You would know of such things. What did your father do after he was deprived of his ancestor blade?"

"He slowly went mad until he flung himself into the sea to be devoured by demons, Lord Protector," Devedas answered.

"Seems reasonable... So, Ashok, I'll grant an answer to your question as to why you cannot have your sword. Our program does not test fifty generations of a house. It does not test the strength of your ancestors. It tests you and you alone. You will survive or perish on your own merits, not by the memories within your sword. You will have no advantage over your brothers. If you fail and live, it will be returned to you. If you fail and die, it will be returned to your house along with your corpse. If you go insane, the nearest ocean is two hundred miles that direction, but since we're on the side of a mountain there are plenty of places to leap to your death if you are so inclined. You certainly wouldn't be the first acolyte to do so."

Ashok continued staring at the wall. Ratul correctly took that as assent.

"Know this, Ashok, there is no room in the Order for weakness, so I will not give you a crutch. To do so would only make you weaker than you could be. The Law is only as strong as those who enforce it. If you last long enough to prove that you are worthy on your own to be one of us, then I will return your sword. Until then it will remain in our vault. Don't worry. None of us are fool enough to try to use it, and if anyone unworthy attempts to steal it, we both know what the sword will do to them. You are dismissed."

The barracks were as frigid as the audience chamber. There were no beds, just woven mats on the floor. Devedas directed Ashok toward one corner. "You will be issued a uniform and basic supplies. Get some rest. Tomorrow is going to be the hardest day of your life. Then it will get worse."

"Thank you for explaining my hesitation to Master Ratul."

"It was the truth, nothing more. That's our job. When you've gained the respect of your seniors you'll be allowed to speak freely as well. Until then, it's best if you keep your mouth shut."

"Your father was a bearer?"

"Perhaps I did not emphasize, mouth *shut*," Devedas said. "At this rate I'll be amazed if you last a week."

Ashok bowed. Annoyed, the older student just shook his head and left the barracks.

The sleeping mat was very thin. He could feel the cold of the floor seeping through it already. It was going to be miserable to sleep on. Kule had warned him that the Protectors thrived on discomfort, but knowing something and experiencing it were two separate things. With the sword, he could do anything. Without it, he was only human. His devotion to the Law would have to carry him through.

Ashok realized the barracks were too quiet. The other newly obligated acolytes were all staring at him. He studied their faces. Already they knew he wasn't like them. He would never be like them. No matter how hard they trained, or how much courage they had in their hearts, or strength in their arms, they would never be his equal. So be it. The Law said that every man had a place. His house had declared his place to be here.

He stared back at the others. They were doing their best to hide their doubts and fears, but Ashok didn't need to hide what he did not possess. They didn't know what they were yet. He knew exactly what he was.

"Rest, brothers. Tomorrow we demonstrate our conviction to the Law."

He lay back on his uncomfortable mat, knowing that he would show Master Ratul that he was worthy, and get his sword—and the rest of himself—back. While the others tossed and turned, longing for home or having nightmares, Ashok had no trouble sleeping at all.

Chapter 9

Protector of the Law, Ashok Vadal, twenty-year senior, rode through the lands of the great house that shared his name, dwelling on what he'd lost, what had been taken, and the legal questions pertaining to the proper way to end his life.

A light rain fell, more of a mist really. Ashok didn't mind the rain. Water that came out of the sky was water's purest form. It hadn't had a chance to become corrupted yet. It wasn't until it collected that it turned malicious. The night was dark and chilled. It gave him an excuse to keep his hood up and his distinctive insignia covered. It was best if word of his arrival didn't spread. He was still riding the same poor, tired horse that had taken him into the Capitol, and from there all the way across the northeastern portion of the continent to Vadal. He'd only worn out one horse this time. There was no reason to try hard to reach this particular destination. Time was no longer of the essence, and the long weeks had given him time to think.

All that time hadn't dulled his anger in the slightest.

Damn Mindarin. Damn Ratul. Damn them both along with their lies. Mindarin had put a curse on his head. Ashok had been offered a choice, to be a liar like them, but that was nothing but an illusion. The master must have known there was no way

Ashok could continue living once given this knowledge. Ratul had broken the Law by allowing him to live to begin with, and ever since then the Order had perpetuated fraud in exchange for power. For the first time in his life Ashok was angry that the religious fanatics were deluded and there was no eternal soul and no eternal punishment, because they were dead, but that wasn't enough. They still needed to suffer for the mockery they'd made of the Law... The Law was *everything*.

Protectors routinely sacrificed their lives so that the houses could have stability. Though he could understand the strategic reasons for why the masters had kept up the lie, he could never forgive them. And thus he would never forgive himself. Ignorance of the Law was no defense for violating it.

A cluster of lanterns told him there was a checkpoint ahead. Anyone crossing house borders was required to stop and present their travelling papers. A few wagons were waiting to have their cargos inspected and papers stamped. This was a busy trade road, so the checkpoint was practically a fort, but with the rain there wasn't much of a line tonight. Protectors were of the highest caste, so all he needed to do was display his token of office and ride through, but since he was trying not to draw attention to himself, Ashok got into line. As usual, his horse was glad for the chance to stop for a bit.

"Almost there, Horse," Ashok told the animal as he dismounted. When you spent months on the road with the same beast, you had to call it something, and he had never been one for titles, so Horse would do. Horse didn't care. It just stuck its face into a trough of collected rainwater and drank.

The wagon ahead of him was nothing but a cage on wheels filled with a cargo of untouchables. It was hard to tell how many, because they were packed together. The cage didn't have much of a roof, more of a canvas sunshade really, so the casteless had clumped together to try to stay warm in the rain, until they got to wherever their betters thought they belonged. Their clothing was nothing but rags. The adults wouldn't make eye contact, but the children were staring at him, hungry and miserable. They looked tired, wet, abused, and completely used to it.

The casteless knew their place.

A merchant of the worker caste was standing next to his wagon, awaiting his inspection. He had an umbrella, a respectable coat, and shoes that probably kept his feet dry. He was clean, groomed, and even a little bit fat. He was even allowed a sword for protection. Ashok had never paid much attention to the workers' ranks, as he was above them all so their relative differences were meaningless, but from the fine attire this one probably fell somewhere in the middle, above the laborers and farmers, but below a skilled craftsmen or a banker. Another worker was driving the wagon, he was below the merchant, but far, far above the casteless.

The workers knew their place.

Warriors of House Vadal were manning the checkpoint. They were fit, strong, and proud. They wore armor, not so different in design from Ashok's own, but not nearly as expensive or well-constructed. Their weapons were cared for, and unlike the merchant's sword, they didn't require a permit to possess one. The soldiers seemed bored. This bureaucratic necessity was beneath them, but their duty required them to be here, biding their time until the next fight, when their house would spend their lives as readily as the workers spent money.

The warriors knew their place.

Through the door of the checkpoint, he could see that a low-ranking arbiter was sitting on a padded stool behind a large table. A brazier next to him provided warmth and enough light to make sure the travelling papers weren't forgeries. He collected the tariffs, stamped the papers, and wrote in his ledger. The bureaucracy was required to lead and organize, and it was what made sure the rest of the castes worked as designed. Only the lowest of the governing caste would be assigned to such a duty, especially during the slow hours of the night, but even then this man could command all of the others and they would obey without question.

The first caste knew their place.

All men had their place within the Law...except for him.

What am I?

Ashok was an anomaly, and that made him an abomination as much as any creature of witchcraft or demon that slithered from the sea.

The arbiter declared the merchant's papers to be in order. The warriors opened the gate, and the casteless rolled on to their destiny. When it was Ashok's turn to present himself to the arbiter, he simply opened his cloak and displayed his insignia. The arbiter immediately began babbling about how the allegations of bribery against him were nothing more than slander and to please have mercy. Since it was against the Law for a Protector to investigate his own house, this man's possible crimes were not Ashok's problem, but a few stern words assured him that this particular arbiter would make no mention of his passing through. He was able to return to his journey, with Great House Vadal being unaware that the bearer of its mighty ancestor blade had returned.

Ashok knew he needed to be destroyed, for there was no place for a man without a place, but that was where the legal conundrum arose. There were certain obligations for a bearer. The blade's continued use was far more important than the fate of a single bearer. His existence was a crime, but so would be his execution. A dishonorable death might cause the incredibly valuable sword to shatter. Suicide was a coward's death and would offend Angruvadal. Much thought had gone into his problem and what solution would best satisfy these competing requirements during the long journey, but this would have to be a question for the judges. He didn't care if he lived or died as long as justice was served.

Regardless of his fate, there was one last thing to be done before giving up his office and submitting himself to judgment.

The ones who created this fraud had to die.

Justice demanded it.

Chapter 10

Among the warrior caste, Jagdish was of low rank, young age, and minor status. His position on the Personal Guard of Great House Vadal had been earned due to his exemplary courage in battle, and the fact that his disregard for tradition and disrespect for stupid commanders had gotten him thrown out of his last unit. Jagdish thought of himself as a brilliant strategist who'd found himself working for careless fools, so he'd been happy to take the promotion. If he'd known the Personal Guard mostly stood around looking pretty while the first caste threw lavish parties, he'd have avoided the promotion and stayed patrolling the border. Continual skirmishing against other houses was always exciting. Watching the firsters drink themselves into a stupor was boring. Listening to high-ranking warriors—who were only of such status because their fathers had been great men—brag about their imaginary accomplishments was offensive. Rich workers pranced about in their silks and gold ornaments, as if their wealth made them equal to the first and second castes. These vapid, useless people annoyed him to no end.

"I wish they'd called off this affair," Jagdish whispered to Derang.

The other warrior kept his expression neutral. They'd been

ordered not to display any emotion. It made a better show for the honored guests. "A little rain is no reason to cancel a party, Jagdish."

He'd been thinking of the recently arrived news about the border raid by House Sarnobat. Fifty men captured and a town pillaged demanded an immediate, exceedingly violent response, preferably with an entire legion of troops to put those uppity Sarnobat bastards in their place. Of course, Bidaya Vadal had spent more on decorations for this ball than she had equipping that particular garrison, so Jagdish doubted the thought had even crossed her mind.

The dress uniform was uncomfortable and wouldn't so much as slow a sword unless he got lucky and it hit one of the multitude of medals pinned to his chest. And thinking of swords was another annoyance, since he wasn't even allowed to wear his in the main hall. They were limited to knives, because it was a fad in the Capitol that wearing a sword at a party was an insult to the safety provided by the hosts, so the great houses had—as usual—copied Capitol fashions. That ridiculous custom had been carried to the illogical end of even limiting the men who were supposedly providing the host's safety. If this was a proper warrior's celebration, you wouldn't be able to walk ten feet without tripping over a real weapon. Jagdish longed to take off the frilly uniform, throw it in a fire, and then return to the other warriors to take a sword in hand to smite his enemies for glory, as he'd been born to do.

Derang tried to hide a yawn and failed. Luckily none of their superiors noticed.

The main hall of the palace was a huge room and it was filled with people. Vadal was the lushest, richest house, so no expense had been spared to demonstrate that fact. The ceiling and walls had been decorated with so many flowers that it made Jagdish's nose itch. Musicians played. Women sang. A multitude were dancing in their colorful outfits, the young and beautiful trying to impress each other, and though he doubted any of those high-status young warriors knew a damned thing about fighting, Jagdish had to admit that they were all very good dancers. *So that's what the privileged practiced while the rest of us learned to swing a sword . . .* This was the sort of event where suitable mates were found and marriages arranged between the highest of each caste. Jagdish didn't care. He was of no importance, so he'd be assigned a wife eventually. Hopefully she wouldn't be too ugly.

Between each song, more arrivals were announced. They must have picked the house herald based upon whoever was the loudest person in the city. The man had a voice that could be heard over a battlefield, and as guests arrived, he would bellow out their names, offices, and status so that the entire hall could hear. The celebration had drawn guests of the highest status, and they'd even been joined by representatives of several other houses. Those ambassadors were probably the reason Bidaya had put out enough food to feed a village for a year. Vadal never tired of rubbing their wealth in other houses' faces.

Derang looked like he might yawn again, so Jagdish stepped on his foot to warn him. The elderly leader of House Vadal had finally made her appearance, and she'd had guards flogged for far smaller offenses. The tune ended. The dancers came to a stop.

"Thakoor of Great House Vadal, widow of bearer Bhadramunda, mother of Chief Judge Harta, and lady of this house," shouted the herald with the loudest voice in all of Lok. *"Bidaya Vadal has graced us with her presence."*

Bidaya was standing on the balcony. She appeared haughty as ever, dressed in the richest silks of Harban, jewels from Kharsawan, and feathers from colorful Gujaran jungle birds. The giant warrior, Sankhamur, a beast of a man and Bidaya's personal champion, stood behind her. She didn't have a voice like the herald, but when you were that important, everyone made sure to listen closely. "Welcome to my hall." Bidaya possessed a patient and patronizing smile. "Dance, drink, and feast. Enjoy the hospitality of Great House Vadal, for this season we have been truly blessed for our obedience to the Law."

Bidaya was a terrifying old woman, and she'd ruled this place with an iron fist ever since her husband had died over two decades ago, through multiple house wars and the deadliest of politics. The guests obediently lined up to greet her, acting like she was their favorite grandmother. Bidaya began walking down the stairs, with Sankhamur shadowing her and cataloging every potential threat in the room. The giant's eyes lingered on Jagdish for a moment but Jagdish took no offense, as he was probably the second best fighter in the room, and a good bodyguard truly trusted no one, especially not his fellow warriors. Jagdish was jealous. The wickedly curved blades Sankhamur was carrying certainly stretched the Capitol's polite definition of the word *knife*.

The musicians began playing again, and those too young or too unworthy to greet the Thakoor returned to their merriment. Jagdish went back to watching for trouble. At worst, he'd probably have to remove anyone who became too drunk or smoked too much poppy and began molesting the slaves in public. If they were of higher station—which was likely—the most he could do was ask them politely to take it somewhere private. More important people were arriving. Derang seemed too nervous now to yawn.

There was some commotion at the entrance of the hall, a few raised voices suddenly silenced. Jagdish walked to the side so that he could see better. A tall, broad-shouldered man in a rough travelling cloak was showing something to some very chastised-looking guards. The guards bowed deep, and then fearfully moved aside. The dark, wet hood was very out of place among the bright, stylish guests. Panicked, one of the house servants ran to the herald and whispered in his ear. The herald looked like he might go into shock.

A female singer was in the middle of a verse, and the musicians hadn't even gotten the signal to stop, so the drums were still pounding when the herald made his rushed announcement.

"After twenty years away, Bearer of mighty Angruvadal, Protector of the Law Ashok Vadal has returned!"

It couldn't be. The music came to a crashing stop midverse. The dancers froze. There were many audible gasps. Every head turned to see. Ashok was a legendary figure in this house. Very few of them had ever met the man who bore their sword. "My ass, that's the bearer. There's no way," Derang whispered.

The tall man untied his cloak and let it fall on the floor in a wet heap, revealing that he wasn't dressed for a fancy party. In muddy boots, and plain, damp clothing, he looked like a regular traveler, nothing more. When he turned, a sheathed sword was visible at his side. Jagdish couldn't tell if that was *the* sword. You'd think that you'd feel *something*.

The newcomer wore the token of the Protector Order on a chain around his neck. That insignia was like a warning sign proclaiming this man could kill whoever he felt like, whenever and however he desired. His skin was darkened by the sun except for where it consisted of lines of white scar tissue. He scanned the room, seemingly taking everything in at once, and there was nothing polite in that gaze. It was as if he was passing judgment on them all. His eyes passed over Jagdish, and the warrior felt an involuntary shudder. Those eyes were cold, hard as the veteran warriors who'd seen so much that they were past feeling. This was a man completely devoid of mercy.

Bidaya broke the uncomfortable silence. "Can it be? Has our noble Lord Protector returned home after all these years? Now we have even more reason to celebrate."

The newcomer began striding across the hall with purpose. The guests nervously moved aside, crowding toward the edges as if a tiger had just entered a pen full of sheep. The tales said Ashok Vadal had killed a thousand men. Seeing this one here, Jagdish could almost believe it. "Is that really him?" Jagdish whispered.

"I don't know. Hardly anyone ever met the bearer before they sent him off."

When the crowd parted enough that Bidaya could see him clearly, she called out, "Ashok, it has been so long. Is it really you?"

The newcomer stopped in the middle of the room. He slowly turned, taking it all in. "I have returned."

"You've grown up," Bidaya exclaimed. She was trying too hard to sound overjoyed. Jagdish could have sworn that he heard an element of fear in her words. "At last you've come back to us, and you've brought our precious Angruvadal home! Has your obligation ended? Is our house's time of suffering finally over?"

"No." Ashok turned back to glare at the Thakoor. "The suffering of this house is only just beginning."

It hardly seemed possible, but the room got even quieter. The uncomfortable silence dragged on for several seconds as Bidaya's forced smile slowly died. "What brings you back to your people, nephew? Are you on Protector business?"

"Tonight, I don't represent the Order." Ashok seemed to mull that over for a moment, before reaching up and lifting the chain over his head. He held the token in his hands, staring at it for a long time, as if trying to make a difficult decision. Horned and fanged, that predatory visage symbolized the Law. The Inquisitors hid their faces behind it, but Protectors wore it over their heart. Then Ashok dropped the amulet on the stone. It made an audible *clang* that made some of the guests jump. He looked up, dark eyes narrowed dangerously. "I have come on a personal matter."

Jagdish looked down at the discarded symbol, and then back up at the grim, determined man who'd put such a high-status thing aside, and the experienced warrior felt a sick, sinking feeling in his stomach.

"Of course, nephew. There's no need to trouble our guests with family business. Let us retire and discuss it."

"No. Because this is a legal matter there must be witnesses. Your guests will do. I require restitution."

The Thakoor tilted her head to the side. "I am afraid I—"

"*Restitution.*" Ashok kept his voice down, low and dangerous. Like the rest of the crowd, Jagdish found himself leaning forward to hear his words. "The Law is clear that when one is deprived of his property, he may seek a suitable compensation from the offender."

"The bearer must be exhausted from his long journey." One of Bidaya's senior arbiters stepped forward. "Allow us to prepare a room so that he may rest for—"

"Silence," Ashok snarled. He didn't so much as raise his voice, but nearly every occupant of the hall took a nervous step away from him. Jagdish realized that Ashok's hands had curled into fists and the man was trembling with anger. "I require restitution."

The giant Sankhamur sensed the danger as well, and moved forward, placing himself between his charge and Ashok. Bidaya held up one hand and Sankhamur paused. "Well, nephew, whatever is it that you require restitution for?"

"A casteless."

Bidaya forced herself to laugh. It was a hollow sound. "A casteless? Oh my. All this drama over a casteless? I thought it was something important!" She kept laughing. The sycophants and fools joined in. Even the privileged warriors who didn't understand the terrible danger in their midst chuckled nervously. "Whatever is the matter? Did one of my guests run over one of yours with their carriage tonight?" The laughter in the room grew as they made the mistake of thinking Bidaya had just ended the tension, but Jagdish saw more rage building behind Ashok's eyes. "Whoever ran down a casteless, please pay our Lord Protector for his dead so that we all may return to our merriment!"

"Restitution requires equal value. I demand a life for a life."

The laughter tapered off. There was no joke here. Someone was about to die, and most of them were beginning to realize

it. The guests exchanged nervous glances as they tried to figure out what Ashok was getting at. Jagdish slowly moved one hand to the dagger in his sash.

Bidaya's expression turned hard. All the pretenses are gone, and now they could all see the iron fist of House Vadal. "A life? Will any do, or do you seek one in particular?"

"Your life, aunt."

There were cries of outrage. Sankhamur drew his blades. Ashok and Bidaya were staring at each other with icy hate.

"That is enough, Ashok. I know why you're here. Speak no more, or wound this house forever," she warned.

"What is the meaning of this?" demanded a senior judge from the Capitol. "You may be a Protector, but that doesn't allow you to insult your Thakoor! What could possibly be so valuable about this casteless you speak of?"

Bidaya shook her head, almost as if she was pleading for Ashok's silence.

But Ashok would not grant her that mercy. "The casteless was my mother."

Chapter 11

Twenty-five years ago

It was hard work to mop up so much blood. Luckily there had been so many opportunities to practice lately that he'd become very good at it. He may have only been a child of the non-people, and a small, sickly one at that, but you didn't need to be strong to clean up blood, only committed. When he was done, the stone floors were so clean you couldn't even tell that a man had just been gutted there like a pig. He had been doing such a good job at scrubbing up the blood that the overseer had not had him beaten even once over the last few weeks.

After the whole men had stormed out in frustration, and the other casteless had carried the dead warrior's body outside for cremation, the boy found himself alone in the main chamber of great house Vadal, on his hands and knees, pushing a red puddle.

Only he wasn't really alone. The sword was there, watching him.

Wringing out his rag over the bucket, he saw that the water running over his hands was still very pink. There was much work to do.

When the Thakoor of House Vadal had died, they had placed his terrible magic sword in the main chamber. Casteless did not usually live as long as whole men, but there were a few among them old enough to remember the last time this had happened. They warned the other casteless what to expect. Until the ancestor blade was satisfied, the whole men of the warrior caste would be tense and quick to anger. Do your jobs, stay out of sight. The warrior caste loved to spill blood, but they considered it beneath them to mop it off the floors. That was *unclean.* Even the lowest of the workers thought they were too good to play with corpses and blood and guts. That was work for the casteless, so some of them would be sent into the main chamber. If they were chosen, look only at the ground, do not speak unless spoken to. If they were lucky, they would not be killed by frustrated warriors. If the Forgotten had mercy on them, the sword would pick someone sooner rather than later and life could return to normal.

It had not taken long for the sword to begin killing whole men. That last Thakoor's ashes were still warm when the first of the warrior caste tried to take up the sword. A few minutes later the overseer had arrived in the casteless quarter looking for help to remove the body parts.

"Why take the boy?" his mother asked.

The overseer frowned. "Why not?"

"He's weak. He'll just be in the house slaves' way."

The overseer was casteless as well, but even amongst the non-people, there was order, and questioning his commands could lead to a beating or worse. The overseer seemed like a huge, muscled beast to the small child, especially when he roughly grabbed the boy by the wrist. "I got strong men for lifting bodies. He's got small fingers to get into the cracks. I don't want no stained mortar and I don't want the main chamber stinking of death. Got it?"

His mother had lowered her head in submission. The casteless did as they were told. They worked and they died at the pleasure of their betters. That's how it always had been and how it always would be. Such was the way of the non-people.

The overseer had given him a rag and a bucket. They were his most prized possessions.

✧   ✧   ✧

The first time he had entered the main chamber, he had tried to heed the elder's warning, but he had been too tempted, and had lifted his head to see. The inside of the great house was truly as amazing as the house slaves proclaimed it to be. The floors were flat stone, not dirt. The walls did not have holes in them, and in fact, they were covered in carvings and paintings of animals and birds, mountains and trees, and heroic scenes of warriors defeating demons. There was food everywhere. This one room was big enough to hold ten casteless barracks. It was more than he could comprehend. But it wasn't the vastness of the great house that intimidated him, it was the sword.

There was no ceremony to it. The sword was just lying there on the floor where the last warrior had flung it after severing his own legs. Though there was blood on the walls and the floor and in every crook and crevice and joint, there wasn't a drop on the sword or anywhere close to it. In time, he would learn that this was normal for the ancestor blade, as it did not want to stain itself with unworthy life, which was good, because the boy was scared to get close to the sword.

He'd overheard the warrior caste speak of the dead Thakoor's sword. It was said whoever carried it could defeat entire armies by himself. Only this kind of sword could easily kill a demon from the distant and terrifying ocean. Even the mightiest heroes were scared of the ancestor blade. The boy took their fear and made it his own. He was casteless. The Law declared that his kind were not even allowed to touch a weapon. His experience with swords consisted of seeing them in the hands of warriors when it was time to intimidate or execute.

This sword was not like those. This one was...beautiful. It hurt his eyes, but he couldn't help but look anyway. Realizing that he'd been staring, he'd quickly averted his eyes. There were still warriors present. If a whole man saw a casteless looking at the sacred ancestor blade of House Vadal, he'd surely be killed. In this room, his life was worth absolutely nothing.

Only the warrior caste did not see him. The casteless were typically beneath notice. They were simply there to do the things whole men should not have to. They wrapped the body parts in old blankets and carried them down the stairs to the furnace. He was so small that it was a real struggle to carry just the man's leg, and this one had been cut off at the knee.

Then he'd been put to work pushing thick blood around with a rag and carrying buckets of water up and down the stairs until the main chamber was spotless. The overseer had inspected it carefully. If any blood got into a gap and began to rot, he'd have to smoke the smell out with hot coals, and the smoke might upset the great house family. The pale stones took the most scrubbing to keep from staining. It was hard, but it was better than the typical unclean duties of tending swine, cleaning sewers, or burning corpses.

The first few weeks were very busy, as members of the warrior caste from across all of the lands of house Vadal tried to take up the sword. There was so much blood to clean up that the child found himself working in the main chamber more often than not. The overseer allowed him to stay hidden in there during the day, so he didn't have to walk back and forth to the casteless quarter to fetch laborers.

The boy was able to watch many of the warriors' attempts to wield the sword. Few ended in crippling injury or death, but all ended with blood.

There was a shadowed alcove in one corner of the main chamber, well hidden behind a few hanging tapestries. The boy squatted there, waiting, his precious rag clean and his bucket filled to the brim with soapy water. He liked his alcove. It was cool out of the sun, there were no biting insects, and best of all, the whole men could not see him, but he could see them. The overseer had dumped a few buckets of wash water over the boy first, so his betters wouldn't detect the pig, ash, and dung smell of the casteless.

It was the first time he'd observed whole men. The Law declared that they were separate and better, but outside their armor shells the warriors didn't seem so different from the non-people. They were strong and proud until the sword opened them up, then they screamed and bled the same color as a casteless. Above the warriors were the members of the great house. They didn't look so different than his family, only they were far better fed, wearing real clothing, and carrying themselves without constant fear. But the Law said they were superior, so that was the way of things.

The house slaves began preparing the chamber by lighting lanterns. That meant that it was time for another attempt. Men in uniform, their station far beyond his understanding, arrived to serve as witnesses. The sword ended up in a different place every time, depending on where the last user had dropped it after it cut him, but the witnesses always stood as far from it as possible, as if it might become angry and cut them as well. They boy knew that was foolish. The sword only judged those who tried to wield it. He was only a casteless blood scrubber, and he already understood the sword better than the whole men in the fancy robes.

Someone stopped directly in front of his alcove so he could no longer see the proceedings through the gap in the tapestries. He stood up to try and see past them, but his view was being blocked by two people. He didn't dare move the fabric or risk moving enough to slosh any water from his bucket.

"Who is it this time?" one of them asked.

"A pair of havildars from the coast," a woman answered.

The young man chuckled. "Has our house grown that desperate?"

"What do you know of desperate? Sixty of our best soldiers have tried and failed. Ten of our own caste have been carried from this hall cut or missing limbs." The woman sounded very angry, so the boy squished as far back into the corner as possible. Though he understood everything she said, her words were different than casteless speech, clear and not nearly so rough. These two were of the first caste. The angry woman continued. "We've been without our ancestor blade for nearly a month. The other houses are circling like vultures, and there are open discussions in the Capitol about our shame. If the sword does not choose soon, it will be seen as a sign of weakness."

"My apologies, mother...But a mere havildar? That's a nothing rank. Normally it would choose our greatest. For it to pick someone so low would be unseemly."

"They are both young, but accomplished enough. Regardless, we are far beyond courtly matters now. The warrior caste is troubled. There are whispers that perhaps Angruvadal will not deem anyone worthy to wield it. If no one is chosen, then its magic will die. Other houses' ancestor blades have died before, usually from treachery or dishonor, but whatever the reason, those great houses have perished soon after their swords. Perhaps you should try to take Angruvadal up yourself, firstborn."

"I'm not the soldier father was."

"Of course you're not, Harta. And we'd hate for it to mark up that pretty face of yours. Now be silent. The warriors are here."

He couldn't see, but he could still hear. He'd already watched the sword maim dozens of others, and he figured that this wouldn't be any different. The men in the robes announced the warriors by name, and their father's name, and their father's father. The boy still found that most curious. Casteless were not allowed to have a family name. Next the announcer listed their offices and exploits. That part normally took far longer than the test itself, only these introductions were shorter than normal. It sounded as if these warriors hadn't dueled much or attended very many battles. Now the boy really wanted to see if the sword would treat them any differently from the proud ones it had already flayed.

"My lady, you do us all a great honor by attending this event. I will take up Angruvadal and serve with distinction, as your husband did before."

"Proceed, Havildar," the angry woman in front of the tapestries commanded.

A hushed silence fell over the main chamber. There were footsteps as the first man approached the sword. He must have been very brave, because there was no hesitation, just the scraping of metal on stone as the sword was lifted. The boy could feel the tension. All of the observers were holding their breath. *Could this be the one?*

Then the screaming began.

Nope.

The screaming abruptly stopped. The sword must have really disapproved of this warrior, because it had not taken long to make its decision. From the noise and the gasps of the crowd, it had been a particularly violent death. The woman of the first caste swore beneath her breath, but the boy was close enough that he was surprised to learn that even the highest of the high used the same profanity as the lowest of the low.

"Next," she snapped.

This warrior sounded much younger and not nearly so cocky. "I will do my best, my lady."

Luckily the man in front of the alcove had stepped to the side so the boy could peek out again. The first warrior had stabbed himself through the chest and it looked like he'd done a messy job yanking it back out through his guts. This one was going to be at least a five-bucket job. Sadly, he was bleeding out right on top of the palest stone in the entire floor. The boy would be scrubbing until his hands were raw tonight.

The second warrior was standing by the sword, looking flushed and timid. As usual, the dying man had flung the sword clear across the main chamber. Maybe that was why the witnesses tried to stand so far away, so as to not be sliced by accident as a disemboweled warrior flailed about. Despite just ripping a man in half, the gleaming black sword was clean. Wearing an expression like he was about to pet a cobra, he knelt down and extended one hand, but hesitated.

"Do it," the lady of the house ordered.

He did. The warrior slowly lifted the sword from the floor. He grimaced when the handle bit into his hand. The boy didn't know why the sword did that, maybe it wanted to taste them first? He stood up straight, held the sword pointed at nothing, and waited for its decision. This one had an honest face, so the boy hoped that the sword wouldn't be too hard on him.

Several seconds passed. The crowd was growing hopeful. They began to whisper excitedly, but the boy could already tell this wasn't right. The man was concentrating so hard that he was red-faced and sweating. Veins were standing out in his forehead and neck. This warrior was the strongest one yet, and he was most certainly a good man, but he wasn't the *right* man.

Then it was as if the warrior's limbs moved on their own. The muscles in his arm twitched and contracted. The dark blade flashed and he gasped as it parted his flesh. The sword clattered back to the stone at his feet. He stepped back, one hand pressed to the long weeping cut on his other arm.

It wasn't even deep enough to sever any tendons. It had only cut him enough to teach him a lesson. The sword must have really liked this particular warrior.

"Forgive me," the young man said through gritted teeth. "I was found wanting."

"What did you see?" the woman demanded.

"So much..." It was as if he didn't know how to put it into words. "It was as if the eyes of every warrior who has carried this blade before were upon me. There's a thousand years of courage stored within, waiting for... something." The warrior stumbled, then fell over on his backside. The men in uniform went to him to staunch the bleeding. "I'm sorry, my lady. I'm becoming a bit faint."

"Get out," she snapped. "All of you, be gone from my house. Come back when you have someone worth a damn."

The boy was glad the sword hadn't chosen yet, because when it finally did he'd have to give up his comfy job of blood scrubber.

It would be dawn soon. He'd spent the entire night cleaning the pale stones. He'd scrubbed until his fingers had grown soft and his calluses had begun peeling off. He had to be careful not to add his own blood to the mess, so he'd torn scraps from the bottom of his shirt and wrapped his fingers so he could continue.

Up and down the stairs, he'd carried that bucket so many times. Down red, up clean, over and over, until he was satisfied that the main chamber was perfect. The house slaves told him that this big room was normally only used for parties, where members of the first caste and the highest-ranking warriors and richest workers would gather to dance and eat more meat than the entire casteless quarter would consume in a season. He suspected they were teasing him.

The boy had not seen the other casteless since they'd taken the warrior's body to the furnace. There were guards patrolling inside the great house, but they didn't pay any attention to him. He'd be inspected by the overseer when he was dismissed to make sure he hadn't stolen anything. It was just the boy and the sword in the main chamber, so there was no one to punish him for speaking. He had been alone with the sword so many times over the last few weeks that it had become his only friend.

"Why did you spare the last warrior?" the boy asked the sword as he inspected the seams for any errant spatter. Of course, the sword did not answer. The only time it made any sound was when it was whistling through the air or hacking through bone. "Why do you only hurt some but kill others? I think it is because you like them better. The whole men think they know you, but I don't think they do."

The sword lay there, as long as he was tall, and made out of some dark metal that he'd never seen before. The boy walked around it carefully. "You don't have ears so you probably can't hear me, but mother says I talk just to hear myself anyway. You don't have a mouth to talk, but you still let everybody know what you think!"

It was hard to find tiny specks of blood by lantern light alone, and a few times he found himself picking at something that was actually a brown spot on the rock itself. Even though he'd practically memorized every single stone set in the floor, he scrubbed at them just in case. "I probably shouldn't talk to you because I'm not a real person, but you're not a person either. I don't know what the Law says about that."

Then he noticed a fat drop of blood that he'd somehow missed, but only because it was *beneath* the sword.

The boy was suddenly very afraid. That had never happened before.

"I mop around you every night, but I can't mop under you," the boy said. "I could slosh some water on you...." The tools the older casteless were issued sometimes rusted. Could this sword rust? If the whole men would have him severely beaten for missing a drop of blood, they'd surely murder him for making their magic sword rust.

Very carefully, he reached for the drop with his rag-wrapped fingertips. He didn't know what the parts of the sword were called, but the part that protected the fingers was resting on the floor and lifted up the part the warriors tried to handle. If he was careful, he could sneak under that without touching anything.

He bumped it with one shaking knuckle. "I mean no disrespect." The sword didn't answer, but since it didn't remove his fingers, it didn't seem to mind. He wiped away the drop with a fingertip, but there was still a stain there on the stone. If he let it sit it would become a permanent blemish on House Vadal and he'd be beaten to death for it.

There had to be a way to move the sword without offending it... They'd put it here somehow after the Thakoor had died, after all, but he was not a trained warrior. He was a child of the non-people. He didn't know any other way. "Forgive me, sword, but I have to fulfill my duty."

The boy looked at the filthy rags wrapped around his hands. That would not do. It would be wrong to touch the sword with something dirty, so he unwound them until it was just raw, clean skin. Then he took a deep breath, reached out, and took hold of the handle.

It was far lighter than it looked.

The sword bit into his palm.

The guards found him some time later, lying on the floor, barely conscious, and raised the alarm.

Weak, confused, it was like waking up from a bad nightmare, and when the boy realized he was still holding onto the sword he began to panic. "I'm sorry!" Hot tears began to stream down his cheeks. "Please don't kill me."

But the intimidating guards seemed more terrified by this development than he was. Most of them seemed too stunned to react and stood there clutching nervously at their swords. One ran for help. Another even dropped to his knees, bowing to the boy as if he was of the highest caste.

"I was only trying to clean the blood," the boy cried. "Take it back!" But his fingers would not unclench from the hilt. He tried to pry them off with his other hand, but they wouldn't budge. He managed to get to his feet. The tip of the sword was dragging along the floor and slicing *through* the stone. "I'm sorry!" He lifted the sword so it would do no more harm. "I'll fix that. I promise."

The boy turned in a circle, and found that he was surrounded by warriors. Each one took a fearful step back as the blade pointed at him. Even in the hands of a child, there was no mistaking how incredibly lethal the sword was.

"Why have I been awakened?" It was the woman, the angry one all of the warriors deferred to, the one who was in charge, the one who was going to have him whipped to death in the dungeons for his insolence. Then she was staring right through the boy at the sword he was waving about and her expression changed from icy rage to shock.

"The blood scrubber picked up the ancestor blade," one of the guards explained.

"As if Angruvadal would choose a casteless!" She began to laugh, only it was a bitter, mirthless sound. "Give it a moment and he'll slice his own throat."

"He's been holding it for several minutes, my lady. It doesn't appear to be turning on him."

"Well...oceans."

"This is impossible," one of the guards stammered. "Only the best warrior may take up the sword. This has never happened before!"

"As far as anyone knows, it isn't happening now." The woman appeared to be deep in thought. She frowned at the boy. "Do not speak a word about this to anyone. Summon my advisors."

"Are you comfortable, child?" the woman asked him.

The boy nodded. The lady of the great house didn't seem so angry with him now.

"Good. Drink up."

They'd given him some cushions to sit on and a cup of wine. He was still scared, but something in the drink had made him very sleepy. The sword had finally allowed his fingers to release it, so it was resting at his side. Though he wished they would, no one had tried to take the sword from him yet.

"I'm sorry I took it." He was having a hard time speaking. It was like his tongue was too big for his mouth. "You can have your sword back."

"I'm afraid it doesn't work that way, child. An ancestor blade cannot simply be given or taken."

A few other members of the first caste had joined them and then they'd gone to a smaller, more private room. It was covered in silks softer than anything he'd ever felt before and the air was filled with perfumes that made his face itch. The woman in charge was named Bidaya, because that's what the other important whole men called her, except for the youngest one who kept calling her "mother." The young man was pacing back and forth nervously while the others sat. The boy was very sleepy, but he could tell that the young man was very upset, even more so than the others, or maybe he wasn't as good at hiding it yet.

"You should have had the guards execute the little fish-eater on the spot!"

"That would have been foolish, Harta," one of the old men in robes stated. He had white hair and a bushy beard. "Your mother was wise to proceed cautiously. What's done is done. Angruvadal chose this casteless for some unknowable reason. He is the bearer now, and one does not simply *execute* a bearer."

"Speaking of which..." The young man stopped his pacing long enough to look the boy over. "Are we in danger? What's to stop it from slaughtering us all?"

"Besides the fact that he's probably only five or six years old and the sword is bigger than he is?" Bidaya snorted. "Calm yourself. The boy is no danger. His drink is laced with a bit of the sleeping poppy. I'm surprised he's still awake at all."

"You should have just poisoned it and saved us all the trouble," Harta complained.

"That would be unwise," the old man said. "The sword has spoken. If we went against its wishes, Angruvadal might construe that as an act of treachery. To murder the bearer of an ancestor blade is a terrible dishonor against a house. Traditionally, the only way to remove a bearer is through a proper duel, and he is far too young to legally enter into a duel."

"Damn it, Chavans, the judges don't have to know," Harta shouted.

"I'm not worried about what the judges think. I'm worried about what the *sword* thinks. Why do you think there are so few of them left? There were once hundreds of black steel weapons and now there are only a score, if that many. If the blade feels its house is no longer worthy of protection, then it will perish. The surest way to prove we are unworthy is by murdering its bearer."

"A duel isn't murder under the Law...Neither is falling asleep in the bath, and this stinky little creature could certainly use a bath."

"No one has ever accused an ancestor blade of having nuance, Harta. If we murder the bearer, no matter how clean we keep our hands, the sword might shatter."

"So what?" Harta waved his hand dismissively. "Killing the brat is worth the risk. Even if it breaks, it isn't like father used that sword in decades. There hasn't been a demon washed up on our shores in my lifetime. Vadal is the strongest of the great houses. We don't need to rely on some superstitious artifact when we're this well positioned in the capitol."

"It isn't just the blade itself, but what the blade symbolizes," Chavans argued. "Losing our house's sword will make us appear weak, and our allies in the courts will turn on us."

"I'd rather not have an ancestor blade at all than bear the scorn of having it carried about by casteless scum!" Harta kicked a pillow for emphasis.

"On that point, heir, we are in agreement," Chavans said. "However we proceed, no one can ever know of this shame."

The sleeping poppy was making it hard for the boy to keep

his eyes open and there was a pleasant humming in his ears. While Chavans and Harta continued their debate, Bidaya was absently studying the boy. He'd seen that expression before on the face of a butcher about to take apart a hog, only he found that he was too tired to care.

Harta had gone back to pacing. "Worst case scenario: we kill the casteless, the sword shatters, and then we give the shards to Kule's wizards to play with. I know they're constantly raiding the treasury to buy black steel fragments and demon parts enough as it is."

"If you believe that's the worst that can happen, then you lack the imagination necessary to someday rule this house," Chavans replied. "If this scandal were ever brought to light, it would ruin us. We would become the laughingstock of the council. Our warriors would revolt before they would follow a non-person into battle. The Capitol would send the Protectors to execute us all."

"Enough, both of you," Bidaya said. Chavans and Harta closed their mouths. She looked over her shoulder at the last person in the room. This man had not spoken this entire time. He was so quiet and unassuming that the boy had nearly forgotten he was there. "The boy must go, but we can't jeopardize the sword. What do you think, Kule?"

The boy shivered. It was a name that was spoken of only with fear and superstition among the casteless of House Vadal. From the stories, he'd expected a fire-breathing giant dressed in demon hide, raven feathers, and baby skulls, but Kule just seemed like a small, quiet, soft-spoken type. If he'd been casteless he would have been too frail to work and would have been sent to the pleasure houses to be abused for the whole men's amusement. But everything was different when you could work magic.

"Kule?"

The terrifying wizard was cleaning beneath his fingernails with a talon that had been cut off a bird of prey. "Send him to the Protectors," he answered absently.

"What?" That seemed to alarm Harta. "Are you mad? What would that bunch of fanatics want with it? How does that solve—"

Bidaya held up her hand and the heir immediately fell silent. "Continue."

"The answer to our conundrum lies with history. It has been a very long time since a great house has volunteered the service of the bearer of their ancestor blade to the Protectors of the Law. The last time that happened, impoverished Akershan's obligation died after a few years, but they gained the Capitol's gratitude for a generation. For mighty Vadal to give such a gift would be seen by the judges as an incredible act of devotion. Our foes will believe that we are so confident in our defenses that we do not even require the blade's presence. Angruvadal exists to serve, and there is no honor greater than to dedicate a life to protecting the Law. Everyone wins."

Except me, the boy thought to himself. All he knew about Protectors were that the non-people were taught from birth to never break the Law, because then the Protectors would come for them.

"The life of a Protector is one of hardship and service, but it is not usually a long life..." Chavans mused.

"That is correct, Arbiter. Their lives tend to be glorious and brief. Their average member doesn't survive their obligation. Our only terms would be that when he is inevitably killed fulfilling his duty, the ancestor blade must be swiftly returned to its rightful house so that it may choose its next bearer. Then we can put this unfortunate incident behind us."

"The Order is brutal. With any luck he'll die in training." Chavans smiled. "Yes. This course is honorable and brief."

"Foolishness," Harta declared. "The Law is clear on the separation of castes. What happens when the most ruthless of all its enforcers discover that we not only violated the Law, but insulted them in the process by sending them this...this...farm animal?"

The wizard smiled. Perhaps it was the poppy, but the boy thought Kule's teeth were too sharp. "I will make sure the boy tells them only what we wish him to."

"Your potions may be able to cloud the mind, but they can't pass a casteless off as a whole man." Forgetting his earlier fear, Harta strode over to the boy. It probably helped that by now he was barely able to keep his eyes open or his heavy head from drifting toward the cushions. Harta roughly put his hand on top of the boy's head and rubbed it around through his hair as if searching for something. "Everyone knows casteless have horns."

"That's only a myth," Chavans snapped. "Did you not pay any attention in your studies? They are mentally defective savages, but they're still physically human."

Embarrassed, Harta backed away, wiping his hand on his robe because he'd touched something filthy. "They're still coarse and stupid. This charade will fool no one."

"Protectors are not known for their polite company, firstborn, but rather for their viciousness, a quality which casteless have in abundance," Kule explained patiently. "The Order will be so pleased at having access to an ancestor blade that they will over-look his limited intellect. Vadal encompasses a vast territory. I have no doubt we can find some backwoods, inbred village for him to hail from."

"My scribes keep the Vadal genealogy," Chavans said. "It can be arranged."

Kule, satisfied that his nails were clean, stuck the talon back inside his sleeve. "I assure you, grant me a bit of time and no one will ever suspect this little thing was not born a whole man."

"Very well, wizard, you had best not disappoint... Giving our best to the Order... Only Vadal cares enough about the Law to make such a sacrifice," Harta muttered. "Yes, I could sell that in the Capitol. Let those Vokkan monkey-humpers try to suck up to the chief judges over our trade disputes after that."

"What of the boy, Kule?" Bidaya asked.

"What of him, my lady?"

"Can you truly make him believe he is one of us? Can you truly make something forget what it really is?"

The wizard was confident. "It will take a great deal of effort and expense, but my art can obscure its memories and construct new ones in their place. I will give it a new foundation built upon a total devotion to the Law. Upon that foundation I will build a most obedient servant."

Bidaya seemed intrigued. "While you're at it, can you remove his fear?"

"It will take some doing, my lady. Emotions are stamped upon us. Cutting off one may damage the others. May I ask why?"

"I want my family's sword back as soon as possible."

"Ah, yes, of course. That is wise. The bold die first. I will erase his sense of fear. As for erasing the evidence of the rest of his existence, that is up to you."

"Very well, we will proceed with the wizard's plan. Chavans, how many others know of this?"

"Six guards, mere nayaks, so no one of rank sufficient to cause a scandal if they die. I saw to it that they were all confined to the palace and allowed no visitors."

"Excellent. Come up with a crime and execute them for it. Murder all the house slaves and their overseer as well."

The boy protested. The house slaves had been kind and fed him, but his cries meant nothing to the first caste.

Bidaya turned back to the boy. "Do you have a family?"

He didn't want to answer, but the sleeping poppy made it so the words just fell out. "I have a mother."

"You don't know who your father is? Of course not. Since the sword chose you, I'm assuming you're my dead husband's bastard. And all this time I thought he had better taste than to slum about with a fish-eater whore...Chavans, before you kill the overseer, have him take you to the casteless quarter, find the boy's mother, and kill her. In fact, let us err on the side of caution. Find whatever slum he called home and burn it to the ground. Kill everyone he's ever known. Make it certain."

"It will be done," the old man assured her.

"Please don't, my lady," the boy begged. "I can keep a secret."

"This is for the best, child. Go to sleep now. Tomorrow will be a new day."

Chapter 12

Ashok remembered the hands of a child, covered in blood... Now they were the hands of a man, hardened, and trembling with barely controlled rage. The spell was broken. It was all coming back. This was it, the very place where the fraud had begun.

Lies. Slander. The crowd whispered about his allegations. *Outrageous.* They looked to their Thakoor, but Bidaya seemed incapable of responding. Ashok knew that the truth had momentarily robbed Bidaya of her serpent's tongue. She should have known this day would come.

Her silence was damning. The whispers began to change. *Could it be? What does it mean? Born of an untouchable makes him untouchable. A casteless bears our sword?*

"What was her name?" Ashok whispered.

Bidaya mumbled something incomprehensible.

This time he bellowed with all his might, *"What was her name?"* The mob flinched away.

"Why would I remember?" Bidaya shouted, her face flushed red. "I don't remember the name of some wretched casteless whore any more that I remember the name of the pigs we butchered for dinner. They're equally inconsequential. You were nothing. She was nothing. You were a whim of the sword. I *made you*, petulant child."

"You broke the Law," someone in the crowd charged.

"I saved this house!" Bidaya screamed back. Then she realized she'd said too much and tried to compose herself, but it was too late. Face had been lost. Word would spread. "I deny these charges. The Protector has lost his mind. He's a foul liar. You wish to make this a legal matter, Ashok, then so be it. You wish a life for a life, then as the Law allows, I demand a duel. Who among you has the courage to defend the honor of this house? Who will fight on my behalf?"

Several young men of the warrior caste immediately stepped forward. Their volunteering forced some of the hesitant soldiers to action so they wouldn't lose face. They began to assemble in front of Bidaya. Most were too naïve to realize what they were facing. Some knew. They were aware of what an ancestor blade could do, threshing men as if it were a scythe and they were wheat, but they would willingly die for their master because that was what warriors do.

"I will have my restitution," Ashok warned. If she expected bloodshed to turn him aside, she was sorely mistaken. His anger would only be quenched when Bidaya was dead at his feet. "I don't want to kill these men, but I will."

Most of them were young, dressed in brilliant uniforms, and wearing commendations earned as a result of their station rather than their own skill, yet there were a few among the perfumed peacocks that carried themselves like experienced combatants. One of them wearing the uniform of the Personal Guard raised his voice. "If you wish us to commit suicide on your behalf, my lady, we shall gladly do so, but there is no such thing as a duel when an ancestor blade is involved. Only slaughter."

Bidaya wore an evil smirk. Let the world say that the Protector had gone mad, slaughtering warriors of his own house, men who'd broken no law, who had no chance against an invincible black steel weapon . . . Bidaya would surely die, but not before she'd preserved her name. Ashok was so furious that he thought about cutting them all down regardless, but he would give her *nothing*.

"You are wise, warrior." Ashok drew his sword. The group before him flinched. They could feel that it was eager to kill. *Not today.* Ashok lifted Angruvadal high, then slammed its point deep into the floor. The black steel penetrated the stone like it was soft wood. He let go and stepped away, leaving the sword there, upright and vibrating from the impact.

Now it was fair.

He walked over to his opponents, stopping when they were only a few paces apart. Half of them had already drawn their dress knives and were jittery with nerves. "Who will contend with me?" Ashok suspected it would be the fearsome bodyguard next to Bidaya. That one looked eager enough.

But Bidaya put her hand on the giant to keep him in place, then looked over her prospective duelists. There were a dozen to choose from. Ashok could tell what she was thinking. Without the sword, a warrior had a chance to defeat him. If he died in combat, Angruvadal would be satisfied. She could still salvage this situation. Bidaya had already proven herself so dishonorable that her next words shouldn't have come as a surprise. "All of them."

"My lady?" asked the same veteran as before, unsure at the command.

This was an execution. She meant for the lies to die with him. "You heard me, Jagdish, *all* of you."

Those with integrity hesitated, torn by such a command. The rest rushed forward, eager to curry their Thakoor's favor.

A young warrior lunged, driving his dagger at Ashok's face, but the Protector knocked his arm away. Another gave a wild swing at his midsection, but Ashok darted back. Then he had to move again to avoid another blade, and another. But even without Angruvadal in his hand, he retained much of its wisdom, and had trained in the fighting arts of the Protector Order where Ratul had allowed him no crutch. Ashok flowed like water between his foes. He swatted aside an arm, then slammed his elbow into that warrior's chest, knocking him down. Another stabbed at him recklessly, but Ashok caught him by the wrist and twisted, throwing him off balance, and used his momentum to snap bones. The warrior cried out in pain as Ashok spun him about and flung him into his allies.

They were coming from every direction. A cut was directed at his back, but Ashok was too fast. He stepped into it, caught the arm, locked up on the elbow, and ground that joint into fragments. Then he dragged the arm back up and put the warrior precariously beyond his center of gravity. The others were still attacking, so he twisted the arm harder, steered the warrior between his body and danger, and dragged his meat shield toward the center of the dance floor.

Many guests were fleeing, but others remained to watch the spectacle. Ashok observed his opponents. The inexperienced were getting in each other's way, tripping each other up. The careful were flanking, looking for their moment. Ashok twisted the arm harder and the boy screamed. The reactions of his opponents told a story. Those who cringed were vulnerable. Intimidation made them afraid. Fear made them clumsy. That took care of most of them. Only one of them had a face as expressionless as Ashok's. He made eye contact with that veteran, then he ripped the captive warrior's knife from suddenly nerveless fingers and plunged it into its owner's throat. He dropped the gurgling, choking warrior to drown in his own blood.

Ashok held up the bloody weapon as if to say, *now I have a knife.*

That was sufficient to strike fear into a few more of them.

To their credit, most didn't hesitate. The warriors came at him in a rush. The veteran tagged him in the side, but not deep enough to strike his vitals. The ceremonial blades were short, but they were kept razor sharp. He met them, clashing, striking, then moving aside, but always slicing. Ashok was calm. There was only action, reaction, and blood pressure.

An arm wasn't withdrawn fast enough, so Ashok split it open from wrist to elbow. Realizing the Protector was too fast to trade blow for blow, a warrior tried to tackle him, but Ashok drove the dagger into that one's thigh. When he ripped it out a bright spray of femoral blood drenched the floor. He caught another arm and leveraged it around, stabbing that warrior repeatedly in the chest before dropping him into the puddle.

There was a burning sensation as a steel edge parted the muscles of his back. Ashok dove between them, rolling across the stone, palm, forearm, shoulder, and then springing instantly back to his feet facing his attackers. He split a kidney in half, then stepped on the back of a knee to force the warrior down to have his throat slashed. Kicking that one between the shoulder blades caused the body to fall forward and trip up an advancing ally. That distraction gave Ashok the time he needed to put three fast puncture wounds into that attacker's torso.

That was over half of them dead, severely injured, or crippled and moaning on the floor.

The remaining warriors came at him, trying to entangle him.

If he became immobile, he would die. They fought across the hall. Feinting, striking, constantly moving. Ashok was cut again on the chest. He was kicked in the leg. While blocking a knife thrust a fist caught him in the eye. He opened that warrior's stomach. Rolling round another, he opened that one's armpit, but lost the unfamiliar knife when the blade stuck in a rib and the slick handle slid from his grasp.

Ashok backed into a table. It was a failure of awareness. Luxurious food fell off the table and plates and glasses shattered. A wounded man sacrificed himself by throwing his body against Ashok. The sudden impact caused the table to collapse. As the rest closed on them, Ashok rolled through the food and blood and broken glass, spied a large two-tined meat fork and picked it up. The warrior grabbed him by the leg to keep him in place, but Ashok stabbed the fork through his hand and pinned his palm to the floor.

Now there were only three. Ashok scrambled for maneuvering room as one of them broke a table leg over his shoulder. It had far more reach than their little dress knives. He spied a lost dagger and scooped it up as the improvised club slammed into his calf. Grimacing, Ashok turned, dodged the descending club, and hit that warrior in the chest. Ashok pushed forward, stabbing repeatedly, piercing between the ribs, until he tripped over his pinned comrade and fell flat on his back.

Two remain.

A collision with the experienced veteran knocked him aside, both of their arms flying back and forth, free hand attempting to keep the other's blade away from the guts, but a feint and a quick twist of the wrist put a deep cut through the muscles of Ashok's abdomen. This one was extremely skilled, but Ashok had touched the Heart, and the one Bidaya called Jagdish was only a man. They clashed again. Skin opened. Steel hit bone. Both parted with cuts. The winner dripped, the loser gushed, and the veteran had to stumble away, reaching for the deep laceration that had suddenly appeared in his bicep. Ashok used the distraction to lash out with a boot hard enough to snap bone. Jagdish fell as his broken leg collapsed beneath him.

Ignoring his many wounds, Ashok started toward his false aunt. Blood was running down his back, leaking down his legs, and leaving a trail of bloody footprints in his wake. He should have collapsed, but it turned out that the Heart of the Mountain still beat even on behalf of a casteless fraud. The floor was littered with the dead and crippled. Injured warriors were trying to keep pressure on their wounds. A few of the fops were crying. They'd not expected this sort of dance tonight. All this blood in this place seemed *so* very familiar. The remaining guests were watching in shocked disbelief. Bidaya wore a mixture of disgust and fascination on her face.

The giant bodyguard was patiently waiting his turn.

One.

"Kill him, Sankhamur."

Though thick with muscle, there was nothing slow about this one. The giant came down the last few steps and leapt onto the dance floor, a thick blade in each hand. He was as big as Blunt Karno and with the reach to match.

They began circling each other. Sankhamur used the two-blade stance of a westerner, one knife out to create distance and the other down low at his side. That would be the one he'd kill with. For such a big man his footwork was smooth, and he closed swiftly, lead blade flicking back and forth. Ashok stayed ahead of it, and sure enough, once committed, the other blade swept up to eviscerate him. Endless training had prepared him though, and Ashok's unconscious reaction enabled him to move aside in time and counterattack.

With one of his knives lost and sliding across the bloody floor, the giant walked away with a deep cut on the back of his hand. Sankhamur paused to admire his injury, then looked at Ashok and nodded in appreciation. Now this was a proper duel.

Ashok lunged forward, blade flashing. Then he retreated as Sankhamur countered. Fast as the eye could follow, they went back and forth. Short, brutal flicks of the wrist, aimed at veins and arteries. Blood flew, from new cuts or old, Ashok couldn't even tell, but even he was beginning to weaken. Sankhamur fought like a sea demon and his fists were like iron. A vicious blow to the body lifted Ashok's feet from the ground. A rib broke. But he came back down swinging the knife.

Sankhamur intercepted it, edge against edge, and the fine steel nicked and locked together. They turned, and the giant should have hurled him down, but with the Heart of the Mountain, they were equals in strength. Ashok was closer to the ground, however, and he was able to use the leverage to push Sankhamur back. The two of them wheeled about, striking each other, throwing elbows and knees that landed with bone-jarring force, both wanting to free their blades, but also not wanting to let the other escape. Ashok couldn't twist this one's joints. The bodyguard was too strong and Ashok's free hand was too slick and wet. Sankhamur hit the steps and tripped back, Ashok still on him. Some of the foolish guests didn't get out of the way in time and they were smashed between Sankhamur's bulk and the wall. Both he and Sankhamur ignored the screaming.

They were so close Ashok could smell his breath, wine and cheese. Somehow Sankhamur's free hand had gotten hold of Ashok's knife hand, and Ashok's free hand had hold of the wrist that ended with Sankhamur's blade. The giant smashed Ashok's nose with his forehead, and Ashok slammed a knee into the bodyguard's groin, but neither would let go. Sankhamur's feet slid out from under him and Ashok threw his weight down on the man.

And then the giant's grip slipped.

That heartbeat-long mistake was all it took. Hand free, Ashok plunged the small knife into the top of his chest, just over the collar bone. Sankhamur roared in his ear and thrashed about. The wounded hand landed on Ashok's face and shoved, twisting his neck so hard that it felt as if it would break. Veins standing out in his forehead, the giant tried to force Ashok back, free his blade, anything, but Ashok wouldn't budge. He got an angle and began stabbing, the little blade darting in and out, perforating the bodyguard's chest.

Losing too much blood, Sankhamur slowly sank down the wall, fingers twisted into claws and tearing into Ashok's face, but his slide exposed his throat, and Ashok adjusted and stabbed him just beneath the ear.

Eyes wide, the two combatants stared at each other for a time. Competence turned to confusion as the blood drained from Sankhamur's brain, but still he struggled. The truth of the moment was enough to make Ashok forget his rage. This was a waste of a great warrior. But justice was not yet fulfilled, so Ashok twisted the knife and sent Sankhamur to the endless nothing.

Panting, Ashok stood up. He was dizzy. The sick feeling in his stomach and the cold in his limbs told him that even the Heart had reached its limits. It was stop now or perish. The worker trapped beneath Sankhamur's body was crying for help. Other than that, the room was deafening in its silence. He limped away from the wall, turning to gaze at the shocked onlookers who were staring at him in wide-eyed disbelief.

Bidaya...

The woman he'd always believed to be his aunt had crossed the hall and was standing next to mighty Angruvadal. "Your selfishness has ruined everything."

"What was her name?" Ashok asked again as blood dripped from his split lips.

But Bidaya was past listening. As her fraud had unraveled, so had her life, and all that remained for her was to rage. "This sword made this house, and now it's destroyed it. It never should have chosen you!" She leered at the crowd, a caricature of the wise leader they'd thought they'd had. "What does it say about the men of this house, when none of you were worthy? You useless, preening warriors were so awful that it would rather choose an untouchable. This is your fault, too!" She kicked one of the corpses.

"What was my name?" Ashok whispered.

"My own son lacked the spine to even try. My warriors were too useless. Your failure gave us this casteless abomination! This is no Protector!" Bidaya screamed as she went to the sword. "I'm the one that protects us all. I should have done it myself!" She wrapped her tiny hands around the handle and pulled it free.

"My lady! No!" shouted one of the arbiters.

Defiant, she held up Angruvadal for all to see. "See! I should have done this to begin with! My house, my sword! I'm the one who made Vadal great! I'm the one who has kept you safe and made you all rich! I'm the one who—"

The sword found her *unworthy.*

Bidaya's expression contorted in horror and revulsion as the muscles of her arm moved against her will. She tried to fight it, but the sword was very unforgiving. Black steel flashed as Bidaya struck herself in the side of the head. The blade sliced so quickly and cleanly through the front of her skull that it was as if it wasn't even there. Angruvadal spun from her fingers, struck the floor, and slid, coming to a rest at Ashok's feet.

Faceless, Bidaya stood there a moment, until her brains slid out and the Thakoor of Great House Vadal collapsed in a heap.

Ashok bent over and picked up his sword.

It didn't shatter at his touch.

The main hall was covered in blood and corpses. The guests were too stunned to speak. Some had begun to cry, whether for their dead Thakoor or the bleak future of their house, he didn't know. More warriors had arrived, and they were lining the balcony, bows ready and arrows nocked, but they saw the black steel blade in his hand and hesitated.

The Law required a bearer to defend himself. He would have no choice. Enough decent men had already died to expose this corruption. Ashok found the highest-ranking of the archers and gave a small shake of his head. *That would not be wise.* The commander agreed. The bows were lowered.

Ashok picked out a guest wearing the silver insignia of a judge. "You..."

The judge swallowed hard. "Me?"

"Yes, you. I wish to turn myself in as a violator. The Law has been broken. I'm guilty of murder, treason, fraud, and I'm certain you'll think of many more crimes to add to the list. I am a casteless by birth but have been illegally bearing weapons and pretending to be a whole man. My responsibility..." Ashok held up the sword and the judge pulled away fearfully, "will not allow me to commit suicide. I require legal counsel and punishment. Where may I be imprisoned until judgment is pronounced?"

"Urm..." That had been an unexpected question. "There's Cold Stream Prison just south of the warrior district, outside the city gates."

He gave a small bow. "Thank you. Please tend to these wounded. None of them deserves to die."

Ashok took one last look around the main hall of Great House Vadal. This is where the only life he'd ever known had begun, and this is where it had ended. Then he turned and limped from the room without looking back.

The symbol of the Protector Order remained, abandoned in a puddle of blood.

Chapter 13

Several weeks passed before anyone came to see him.

There were a few sets of footsteps in the hall, heavy and armored. They stopped on the other side of the door. "This is his cell, Lord Protector."

It was about time. They wouldn't have sent a Protector for anything other than dispensing judgment. Ashok was eager to meet his fate. There was nothing to do in prison but stare at the walls. He'd never been one for meditation, and he didn't particularly understand the concept of self-pity, so he couldn't even sink into a proper depression like so many other prisoners did.

"I must warn you, he's still got the sword."

The guards hadn't even attempted to take Angruvadal from him. Word of Bidaya's final party had reached the prison before he had. He'd respectfully asked to be directed to wherever he needed to wait for his judgment. The Protector in the hall must not have cared that Ashok was armed, because the heavy door creaked open a bit. They didn't even bother to lock the cell, since there wasn't anything they could do to stop Ashok from leaving if he decided to. It was an unusual situation for everyone involved.

For most of the prisoners the guards would simply storm in, barking orders, and administer beatings to anyone who didn't get on his knees quick enough to suit them, but with Ashok it was different. There was a polite, almost timid knock on the partially open door. "Prisoner, you have a visitor." And then the poor warrior got out of the way so the Protector could enter.

"Leave us."

Devedas.

His old friend stood in the open doorway, Ashok sat cross-legged next to the far wall. One was in splendid armor, the other in blood-stained rags. A beam of sunlight from the single small window cut a dividing line between them.

Devedas looked as if he'd been stabbed in the gut. "Is it true?"

Ashok nodded slowly.

Blinking rapidly, Devedas looked away. "It can't be. It has to be a mistake."

"It isn't. I was born an untouchable." Ashok stood up to meet his fate. It wasn't fair. Devedas already had more blood on his hands than any one man should ever have to bear. He shouldn't have to execute his best friend as well. "I knew they'd send someone, but I hoped it wouldn't be you."

"Nobody sent me. I'm here on my own."

"You've not come to pronounce judgment?"

"I had to know."

Ashok spread his hands apologetically. "I'm sorry, brother."

"Don't call me that!" Devedas suddenly roared. He took a step forward, fists clenched. "How dare you call me 'brother'?" Spittle flew from his mouth as he shouted. "Damn you, Ashok! After all we've been through... After everything we did for the Order, for the Law? How *dare* you?"

"I only recently learned the truth. I never intended to deceive anyone."

Devedas was shaking. Protectors were taught to avoid showing emotion, but tears rolled down his cheeks. "You worthless whoreson, fish-eater bastard. You were the best of us. I *believed* in you. We all did."

"You were mistaken, as was I."

"Who knew the truth then?"

"Mindarin, Ratul, Bidaya... Dead. Harta knew as well. All that remain are the wizard Kule and Arbiter Chavans." Ashok didn't know where they were, or if they were even still alive. "They are beyond my reach."

"Not mine," Devedas vowed. "I'll see to it they pay."

"Thank you."

"I don't want your thanks," Devedas snarled. "I want you to have never existed. I want your name stricken from the records. I want all references to your deeds scrubbed from the world. You've mocked the Law and brought shame to our entire Order."

"For that I will pay," Ashok agreed.

"And I'll volunteer to be the one to swing the executioner's blade when the time comes!" Devedas shouted.

There was an unfamiliar pain inside Ashok's chest. For a moment he felt so weak that he thought that the Heart of the Mountain had abandoned him. "Very well."

Devedas lowered his voice. "What happens to Angruvadal?"

"I don't know."

"All this time... You've thought you were better than me. I was deprived of my family's ancestor blade because of the sins of my father, but you... You're not even a real person. How did it pick *you*?"

That was a question Ashok had asked himself many times, even before he'd known the truth. They stared at each other. *I am casteless. Should I avert my eyes?* But that didn't feel right either.

"I could prove which one of us is worthy once and for all." Devedas placed his hand on his sword. His feet shifted into a dueling stance. He seemed furious enough to try it.

"Don't..."

"You unfeeling thing. Black-Hearted Ashok, with no more conscience than some wizard's automaton. I should cut you down and end this now."

It was tempting to just lift his chin and expose his throat. All it would take was a moment's hesitation, and his scandalous existence would be purged from the world. No one would know that he'd accepted a dishonorable death... Except he'd know, and so would the sword. "I may not be a whole man but I still honor the Law. My judgment hasn't been pronounced. This isn't an execution, it's a duel. If you draw your sword, as a bearer I'm obligated to give my best."

"Offense has been taken," Devedas stated the prerequisite terms for a legal duel.

"Offense has been given." There was no denying that fact. "But remember what happened last time we fought," Ashok warned. "Angruvadal found you wanting once."

"I was only a child then."

"So was I..."

The scar on Devedas' face was a constant reminder of what happened when jealousy overrode common sense. They'd come down from the mountain, brothers, until celebratory drink and poisonous envy had made Devedas think that he could claim another family's sword for his own. Ashok's love had overridden Angruvadal's desire to kill that day, but he knew it wouldn't be enough now.

There was a subtle shift. Anger had been replaced by a focused intensity. Devedas was ready to draw and strike. Angruvadal hung from Ashok's waist, and it was screaming at him to end this threat.

"Haven't I caused enough evil already?" Ashok asked softly. "Don't make me do this too."

The long silence was painful.

Devedas slowly moved his hand away from his sword.

The decision had been made, and the Protector backed toward the open door. "If I ever see you again, Ashok, I'll kill you. You have my word."

"Goodbye, Devedas."

The cell door closed. His brother was gone.

They called him unfeeling, remorseless, a black-hearted killer the likes of which the world had seldom known, but that wasn't entirely true. The wizard Kule may have shattered his mind, stolen fragments and filled the gaping holes with lies, creating a parody of a rational, feeling, law-abiding man, but it would have been better if Kule had taken it all. Instead, he'd left behind emotions that Ashok could barely articulate, and would never fully grasp. Ashok sank to the floor and wept.

Months after bringing justice to Great House Vadal, something woke Ashok in the middle of the night. He was lying on the pile of straw that served as his bed. At first he thought it must be the rats again, but the cell itself was dark and quiet. The noise was outside. A small bit of moonlight came through the iron bars of the small window until a shadow blocked it.

Someone had climbed up the stones to his window. From the sound, they were unarmored and barefoot, so it wasn't one of the prison guards. No one else should have been on the grounds at night.

"Who has come to stare at the freak now?" Ashok snapped.

"You are indeed most curious. I've never seen a prisoner with a sword before."

"What do you want?"

"I've come to speak with you, Protector."

"I no longer hold that office."

"On the contrary, you are a protector in the truest sense. It is in your nature. You've just been protecting the wrong thing." The stranger's manner of speech was odd. He was a westerner, probably from Uttara or Harban, but there was something else there as well, a sort of roughness to his pronunciation. He spoke well enough, but certainly wasn't of meaningful status.

"Who are you?"

"I am Keta, the Keeper of Names," the stranger answered.

That was an odd title. "Of what house?"

"I have no house."

"No house?" It was possible he was obligated to an order that Ashok was unfamiliar with, the Capitol certainly had enough bureaucracies that it was impossible to keep track of them all. "Of what caste?"

"Free men have no caste."

Free? This Keta was insane. The prison had a section for raving lunatics. One of them must have gotten loose. "No one is allowed in the square after dark. The guards will punish you when they find you."

"No worries. I'm very good at not being found. Warning me like that though makes me curious. Do you still seek to enforce the Law?"

Old habits die hard. "That is no longer my place."

"What is your place?" Keta asked.

Good question. There had been no word yet about what was to be done with him. "For now, my place is here, awaiting judgment."

"Aren't we all? Only you are thinking of the fallible judgment of man, and not the all-seeing judgment of the gods."

"There's no such thing as gods." Ashok wasn't in the mood to listen to the ramblings of a crazy person. "You're treading dangerous ground, Keeper. Talk like that is grounds for execution."

"As you'd know, having personally executed so very many! What a terrible burden that must be. Do all of those deaths trouble you? Don't be so hard on yourself, Protector. Everyone has faith in something. You simply put your faith in the Law instead of the gods. But now your wise judges don't have a clue what to do with you. You've caused quite the predicament."

The lunatic had a gift for understatement. The Capitol would want him executed and Vadal wouldn't want to risk the destruction of their sword. Eventually the judges would come to a consensus, and until then he would remain a voluntary prisoner. Ashok rolled over on his straw pile. "I'm going back to sleep."

"But I've come all this way. Wouldn't you like me to answer your questions?"

"What questions?" Ashok asked, annoyed.

"The ones that Bidaya couldn't answer that night. You asked for names, and I'm the one that knows them all. The casteless of these lands prefer to give simple descriptive names. Your mother was called Addis, named after a type of flower because she was such a beautiful baby. Bidaya had her suffocated. You didn't ask, but if you are curious, your father was called Smoke, named because his father was a cremator of bodies. He was sold to another house and died of sickness during the journey, only a year after you were born."

Ashok leapt to his feet. "How do you know of this?" he demanded.

The man was hanging from the bars. All that was visible of him were eyes and the whites of his teeth. "As I said, I'm the Keeper of Names. It's my duty to know. Your parents named you after the season of your birth, because the day you were born was when the first leaves died and turned to gold. So to answer your question, your casteless name was Fall." Keta let go of the bars and dropped into the shadows.

By the time Ashok reached the bars, the strange man was already gone. The prison grounds were completely devoid of life. To disappear like that the Keeper of Names had either been a wizard or the remainder of a dream.

Fall . . .

Shaking his head, Ashok returned to his bed of straw to continue his self-imposed exile.

Chapter 14

Grand Inquisitor Omand lived for the game.

The Chamber of Argument was often filled with heated rhetoric, but it had been particularly bad lately. The recent casteless uprisings were a matter of contention, and now the houses suffering from them had someone else to blame. Debates had turned into fist fights, offense had been freely given, and several duels had been fought. The usual ceremonial guard had proven insufficient to keep order, and had been replaced with a few masked Inquisitors armed with truncheons and very little patience. That had gotten the politicians quieted down.

Mostly.

"Enough of your slander! These charges are filthy lies, nothing but calumny and defamation," Chief Judge Harta Vadal shouted from the speaker's podium. "This report was written either by a liar or a fool."

"Outrageous!" Another judge rose from the stands and bellowed his response. *Why do they bother to set out a podium for the opposition speaker when they usually just yelled from the audience?* Omand recognized the offended as one of the minor officials from Akershan. "How dare you insult my arbiter?"

"If your arbiter didn't wish to be insulted, then perhaps he shouldn't have delivered such an incoherent screed to the committee!"

"We wouldn't even need this special committee if your mother hadn't turned some casteless pig dog into a warlord!" Several other judges roared with laughter.

"Order!" The presiding judge banged his staff against the floor. The laughter tapered off, but Omand counted the remaining smiles. Those would be Vadal's foes. Then he counted the frowns or looks of righteous indignation. The allies. The ones keeping their faces impassive or expressionless were the undecided that needed to be convinced one way or the other. "The Chief Judge has not finished his rebuttal. The staff has not recognized the judge from Akershan. Now be silent!" The staff struck the floor again for emphasis.

The official from Akershan sat down and the great game resumed. That round had clearly gone to the offended. Omand loved to keep score.

Chief Judge Harta's jaw was clenched, and he lowered his head and pretended to study his notes as his political foes in the gallery continued snickering. Omand observed that Harta's normally calm demeanor was slipping. He was an eloquent speaker, but he had a temper. Quick anger gave some men power, but it made others stupid. Omand decided that Harta fell into the latter category. The murder of Bidaya had put him off his game. Harta was sweating like a man about to go beneath the torturer's knives. Omand was an expert on such things.

"This is an internal house matter which does not concern the Capitol. There is no need to involve the bureaucracy. We all grieve the loss of my mother. Mark my words, the traitor, Ashok, will be punished for his crimes."

"By dying of old age?" someone in the back bellowed.

The presiding staff hit the floor again before anyone had a chance to laugh.

Harta scowled at the gallery, but he seemed unable to locate the speaker. The normally eloquent judge looked mad enough to declare offense and demand a duel, but only a fool did that before figuring out who his opponent's champion would be. Omand had missed the speaker's identity as well, but his men were providing security and he had spies everywhere, so they would give him a full report about every passed note and whispered conversation later. Very few things happened within the Capitol without Omand's knowledge.

"Continue," ordered the presiding judge.

"The demands for the traitor's immediate execution have been noted. Believe me, my fellows, no man wishes for the traitor's blood more than I. My own dear mother perished because of his evil. My heart cries for vengeance." Having always had a good sense of the dramatic, he paused to look around the room before continuing. If he'd not been so high-born, he would have made a fine actor. "Yet, I would charge that these demands are nothing more than thinly veiled schemes designed to endanger mighty Angruvadal, and thus the safety of my house."

Some of the undecided were nodding. It seemed that Harta was hitting his stride. He was appealing to the other houses' desire to protect their own ancestor blades. *Good recovery,* Omand thought. Very few played the game as well as Harta.

"Vokkan is perched like buzzards to our west." There were several angry shouts from that section. "Sarnobat are slavering wolves to the southeast." More outraged cries, but the staff didn't fall. Omand was curious what favors Harta had plied the presiding judge with to let Harta get away with such inflammatory speech. "They say they demand justice, but it isn't justice they seek, it is advantage. They would risk Angruvadal to weaken their neighbor..." Harta stared directly at the biggest group of undecided judges. "And they would do the same to you."

The Vokkan and Sarnobat delegations began loudly booing. Now the staff came down along with the demands for silence. A scuffle broke out in one aisle, but before it could get out of hand one of Omand's inquisitors bashed an arbiter with a club and dragged him from the room by the beard. That shut them up.

"Order!"

Omand was sitting in the roped-off section reserved for important guests who had no vote, but who were of high enough status to attend various committee meetings if they wished. The only other occupant today was the newly promoted Lord Protector. It was always hard to guess a Protector's age, since to a courtly man they all looked like leather that had been left out in the sun too long, but he was still a handsome sort, provided you didn't mind scars. He had a reputation for being intriguing and mysterious to the courtly ladies, but Omand had no need to guess about anything, because he knew everything there was to know about this man. He was the firstborn of a house that no longer existed, the son of a disgraced bearer, and the Inquisition spies said that he had been a close friend of the fallen Protector. Omand was curious to see how easily he would be provoked, so he leaned over and whispered. "Your Order has been strangely silent on this controversy. What is your opinion on the matter?"

"We form no opinions. An opinion will be issued to us." The reports said that this newly promoted Lord Protector could be rather charming when he wanted, so the fact he was only coldly polite to Omand told him how he felt about the Inquisition. "Then we will fulfill our duty."

"Of course you will. You are Devedas?" He extended his hand in the southern tradition of greeting that he'd been told the Lord Protector favored. "It is a pleasure to finally meet you in person. We've corresponded by letter before, about that... peculiar situation your Order faced a few years ago."

"The Order appreciated your discretion." Devedas didn't shake his hand.

"I am—"

"I know who you are, Inquisitor. The mask fools no one."

"They aren't necessarily meant to be disguises, Protector."

"I'm familiar with the concept of intimidation, only we don't hide our faces." Devedas pretended to watch the bickering politicians. "Why are you here? Shouldn't you be off burning witches, or is the committee filled with traitors?"

You would be surprised. But Omand only chuckled, as if that was a good-natured jibe between peers. "It pained me to turn down your request to investigate Chief Judge Harta. His word outweighs that of an untouchable, even one accomplished enough to pretend to be a whole man for twenty years, and Harta says that he had no knowledge of his mother's fraud. However, I assure you, the Inquisition will keep an eye on him."

Devedas glowered in silence.

Omand asked a question that he already knew the answer to. "So did you know the fallen... this Black-Hearted Ashok?"

"Yes." Devedas didn't elaborate further. Who could blame him? There was nothing but shame in declaring that you'd once been friends with the most infamous criminal in the world. Omand knew that the Lord Protector had recently travelled all the way to Vadal to speak to the traitor in his prison cell, and though he wished he knew what had been said there, he couldn't know *all* the secrets.

Omand waved one hand toward the intricate carvings and colorful murals that decorated the vast and beautiful Chamber of Argument. No expense had been spared to decorate such an important place. "So what do you think of the Capitol so far?"

"It's hot," Devedas muttered.

A beautiful young woman had approached one of the speaker's podiums during the commotion. The colorful scarves told everyone that she was from House Zarger. Despite her age she wore the insignia of a high-status arbiter, so most of the judges would probably think she'd either married well, or slept with the right Thakoor. Omand knew that this one actually impressed some very powerful people with her keen intellect and earned her appointment through cunning. The desert house hadn't taken a stand one way or the other yet, so most of the gallery was actually paying attention. The staff gave her the floor, and when she presented, she had the melodic voice of a songbird. "I believe we all agree the fallen Protector deserves the dishonorable death of a criminal, but his sword, and by extension, House Vadal, do *not* deserve to be punished. The loss of an ancestor blade weakens us all, and leaves all of us more vulnerable to the demons."

There were shouts of agreement from Vadal's allies. "What is your name, reasonable Arbiter?" Harta asked with a smile.

"Artya Zati dar Zarger, Order of Census and Taxation. *However,* the casteless *uprisings* are being spurred on by rumors about this Ashok. The casteless take courage from his murderous rampage. They speak of an untouchable armed with the most powerful magic, who has slaughtered whole men and who still lives to spite us. As long as he lives, Ashok inspires them to more rebellion and increased violence." As she continued, Harta's smile slowly died. "The fallen Protector has become a rallying cry for the criminal underclass."

"The report is exaggerated."

"I do not speak about the Akershan report. This unrest is spreading. I've seen it in my house's lands with my own eyes."

There was an uncomfortable rumble throughout the entire room. Everyone had occasional problems with their non-people, but it was uncouth to admit it in a public forum. The Akershan delegation had several villages sacked and officials murdered by

Fortress magic before they'd swallowed their pride enough to request witch hunters from the Inquisition. It had taken a false prophet stirring up a full-on rebellion for them to accept the shame of needing the Capitol's help to control their non-people. Freely admitting to unrest in Zarger was a curious development. Everyone was paying attention now.

"The non-people are increasing in boldness and depravity. Their degenerate nature is idle, but quick to riot, and now all of them are whispering about the Lawbreaker in Vadal. Your inability to detect this fraud has endangered us all."

Harta was in a difficult position. He could attack Atrya as a liar, but he needed Zarger's votes and couldn't risk giving offense. Omand enjoyed watching him squirm. He suspected that Harta had known about Bidaya's plot to conceal the blade's choosing a casteless boy all along, and given an excuse he'd love to torture a confession out of the pretentious little fop, but even Omand had to tread carefully about charging Chief Judges with crimes. He noticed that Lord Protector Devedas was also studying the Chief Judge with barely concealed disgust. *Interesting...* Before Harta could formulate a response the murmuring had died down and Atrya resumed speaking.

"Our houses suffer because of the sickness in Vadal, but we are all infected. Do not blame Great House Vadal or their honorable leadership for being victimized by this casteless scheme. No one doubts Ashok must be dealt with. When a cancerous rot is found a surgeon doesn't leave it alone and allow it to spread, but rather the disease is excised immediately for the good of the entire body. No one doubts Ashok must pay, and for now he is quarantined, but this underlying sickness must be destroyed. Let us allow the surgeon to do it in the manner that is least likely to kill the patient. Ashok is a *symptom*. He is not the disease. We would treat this symptom, but the body remains sick...The real disease is the *casteless*."

She's good. And the Grand Inquisitor wasn't easily impressed. His allies had chosen wisely.

"That is not the current topic," the presiding judge warned.

"On the contrary, it was a casteless who stole an honor he did not deserve and brought shame to one of the Capitol's oldest and most prestigious orders. If the Protectors of our Law can be so easily deceived, are we not all vulnerable?"

Omand glanced over at Devedas to see his reaction to the slander of his order. The Protector was leaning forward on his seat, knuckles pressed to his mouth, bitter, angry, yet apprehensive at the same time. The Protectors were politically vulnerable right now, and Devedas knew it.

And that is why the Inquisition wears masks.

"Let us be honest with ourselves. Black-Hearted Ashok, no matter how deadly the magic he bears, is but one man, and he has already turned himself in to the authorities. The real danger is the non-people he has inspired. If there were no non-people to riot and disturb the peace, then he would be nothing more than another common criminal, and none of us would care what Vadal decided to do with him. The casteless are an infestation, a plague. They consume our resources and give nothing in return. They're barely more than wild animals, savage and uncontrollable. I say we have tolerated them long enough."

Harta seemed glad for this diversion. "Indeed, they're foul creatures, but the Law determines the castes. There have always been untouchables, and we're required to allow them to live."

"That was before one of them stole a sacred ancestor blade!" exclaimed a regulator from Harban. Omand smiled behind his mask. That man might have been high status, but he'd been bought and paid for as surely as any slave. Omand had commanded him to agitate on this topic and his timing was impeccable. "Artya speaks with wisdom."

"What would you have us do?" shouted another judge from the opposite end of the gallery. "There are millions of them!"

"Millions of mouths to feed!" responded Omand's plant. "Kill the locusts and be done with it."

"Drive them all into the sea like we did with the demons," said a woman sitting off to Omand's side. "Let's see if they float."

"Why not?" Artya asked. "No good comes from the casteless. We're already allowed some measure of population control and Thakoors can execute them as necessary to maintain order, but why not dispose of them once and for all?"

Omand carefully studied the council. No one was fool enough to speak up for the lives of the untouchables, but they were still valuable assets, especially in the houses that required vast amounts of manual labor. The Vokkan and Sarnobat delegations seemed angry that the subject had been changed away from harming their powerful neighbor. The rest knew this would go nowhere. The topic of exterminating the untouchables came up every so often, but that was a lot of work.

"The casteless are property, are they not? If they are property, then why are we not allowed to do with them as we please? The Law wouldn't require us to keep a pet dog that had turned rabid. Another false prophet has arisen in the south, and his meddling has disrupted the flow of trade. We are all aware of the Law as it stands, but times have changed. We are a nation of industry now, and the casteless are no longer necessary. The lowest of the workers can take on their vital duties."

There were a few token representatives of the second and third castes seated in the very back of the Chamber of Argument. Omand carefully studied the workers' faces. These were wealthy among their kind, but they were ants here. They didn't look happy at the idea of their people handling sewage, carcasses, and other unpleasant things, but it wasn't like these particular quality individuals were in any danger of getting their own hands dirty. They'd simply create a new division for their undesirables and obligate them to the work.

Of far more interest to Omand, however, were the faces of the warrior caste's representatives, and they had sent no fools. Those assigned to observe the Chamber of Argument were usually experienced commanders, crippled in battle and no longer able to fight, but still sharp and not easily riled. They hadn't grown up playing the game, but they were good at thinking fast and keeping their emotions in check. Exterminating the casteless would be their caste's responsibility, and it would be a huge undertaking. Omand needed their support, but the warriors just sat there, straight-backed, focused and stern. *Hard to tell...*

"I officially propose destroying all of the untouchables," Artya said, advocating the death of millions about as dispassionately as discussing the weather. Several others shouted their agreement, making the proposal official.

"A proposal has been put forward." The presiding judge hit his staff on the floor. "You raise interesting questions, Arbiter Artya, but there are thousands of pages of regulations pertaining to the mandatory continuation of the casteless bloodlines and the dispensation of property. The committee has not done sufficient research on this point of law to discuss it at this time. We must understand why these regulations exist and if they are open to interpretation or amendment." The scribes and legal experts sitting in the rows behind the presiding judge began to whisper among themselves. *Oh, how they do love a good legal question.* "I hereby obligate the Order of Archivists to research this topic and prepare a report."

Omand found it satisfying that the judge picked the Archivists and not the Historian Order, but he had made preparations either way. That report would say exactly what he wanted it to say.

"If it is acceptable to both the offender and the offended, the committee will reconvene on this topic in sixty days."

Considering the bloated, ponderous nature of the bureaucracy, Omand would be surprised if they finished their report by then, but Harta and the representative from Akershan were both eager to agree. It bought Vadal more time to figure out how to deal with their shameful prisoner, and Akershan would be delighted to have their rebellion put down once and for all. Once word trickled down through the castes that the Capitol was thinking about cracking down on all the untouchables because of the actions of their violent few, the non-people would silence their own troublemakers as they always did.

"Idiots," Devedas muttered to himself.

"What's that, Lord Protector?"

"Nothing."

Omand smiled beneath his mask. Surely Devedas was marveling about how soft-palmed bureaucrats could so flippantly discuss slaughter on this scale, when most of them had never even killed their own dinner. *Welcome to the Capitol, Lord Protector.*

The meeting was adjourned so all the important people could return to swindling, bribing, coercing, seducing, and blackmailing each other. The Capitol rarely changed. There were minor shifts in the balance of power, and houses came and went, but for hundreds of years things had stayed basically the same. They all knew Artya's proposal would go nowhere, because extreme changes to the Law damaged their comfortable entropy, and annihilating millions, even if they were wretched non-people, was rather extreme. The wind and sand would erode the city walls away before this august body committed to anything so drastic.

Unless of course, they had no choice.

Omand was extremely pleased. The game had gone well for him today.

Chapter 15

After the public farce was over, the real business was conducted. There was a small Census and Taxation office across the street from the Chamber of Argument, except this compound had secretly been claimed by the Inquisition. Omand had made certain that none of his twenty important guests had been followed. Though only a few of them were fellow Inquisitors, all of his guests wore masks or veils to protect their identity. Their insignia and tokens of office were hidden. Omand was the only person who knew who everyone really was, and he was the only one whom they all knew by his real name. He wasn't particularly worried about any of them betraying him, because who would they betray him to? They all knew he had ears everywhere.

The Capitol was a web of plots and secrets, and Omand was the spider at the center.

One of his men brought in their final arrival. She was wearing a veil and introduced with a code name, but only an imbecile wouldn't recognize the young arbiter from Zarger who had caused such a stir earlier. "Excellent work." Omand congratulated the newest member of his conspiracy. "You had them eating from the palm of your hand like adorable baby birds."

Artya gave him a very respectful bow. "It was my pleasure,

but my Thakoor wasn't expecting me to make any proposals. We were to remain neutral for now. I'll be severely reprimanded, possibly even demoted."

"Don't worry, a year from now when we're rounding up all the untouchables you'll be hailed as a visionary."

"I'm sure he will wait to see what the scribes' research finds before he announces my punishment." Artya sighed.

The arbiters would debate, the scribes would pore over the scrolls, and a new report would be presented on the casteless problem. Omand already knew what those reports should have said because unlike most, he remembered their history. Legally speaking, the casteless were a necessary evil, kept around because of the vague threat of an even greater evil. To the dispassionate Law, it was all a matter of value, so to get what he wanted, Omand simply needed to rebalance the scales.

"I wouldn't worry too much," he assured her. Artya was rather attractive, and she struck him as intelligent, articulate, and conniving, all useful traits. If she had the stomach for hurting people, she would probably do rather well as an Inquisitor. "If the punishment is too severe for you to remain with your house, then I'm certain an important assignment could open within the Inquisition. Your Thakoor owes me an obligation or two."

"I am humbled by your generosity, Grand Inquisitor." She even managed to sound sincere as she said it, so she was also an excellent liar. It didn't matter if she had an aversion to torturing confessions out of witches or not, when someone of his status offered an assignment, it was accepted.

The other conspirators were already seated on cushions around a low table. The slaves who brought their refreshments were deaf, and if he had even the briefest suspicion that any of them was paying too much attention he'd have them strangled and buried in the garden. It was amusing to him that most of his guests didn't know how to eat or drink while wearing a mask. Silk was best if you were planning on eating. Decorative porcelain or metal masks were saved for formal occasions, or when one needed to make a statement. The trick was to keep it tight across the bridge of the nose and loose over the mouth and chin, then stick with finger foods in public. *Amateurs.*

One nice thing about taking over a census office was all of the maps and population tallies were already here. Most of the non-people had been located, numbered, and registered for their convenience, because all houses had to pay annual property taxes, and casteless were just a fleshy form of property, similar to—but sometimes less valuable than—livestock. For years Omand had been gently suggesting that the casteless were a terrible threat to society, so he'd been steering the many competing bureaucracies of the Capitol into doing all his preparatory work for him. Maps were spread across the table, and he was glad to see that the few members of the warrior caste who had joined his secret cabal were already making plans about how to conduct their war of extermination.

"Greetings, my friends," Omand told his fellow conspirators. "Today we welcome a sister to our ranks." There was some polite clapping as Artya took her seat. "Excellent. Thank you."

Omand surveyed the room. These were the people who were going to help him achieve his goals. Staging a coup and overthrowing the government was simply not a one-man job. They were all here for different reasons, politicians, warriors, wealthy bankers, even wizards, but the important thing was that they were all useful and connected. "Today I bring fantastic news and a wonderful opportunity before you. After today's reading of the offense, you are all aware of the situation in the north, but you may not yet comprehend the dire situation in the south." He nodded at one of the masked men to proceed.

This conspirator was from the affected house. "The rebellion is far worse than what has been reported before the committee. This prophet has inspired many to join their cause, and as a result he's built a small army of religious fanatics who've been waging war against House Akershan. They've destroyed multiple settlements, disrupted trade routes, and sabotaged many of the iron mines. There's no doubt that this is the costliest rebellion any house has experienced in generations."

Most of the cabal took some sick pleasure at that news. They may have been united in their desire for power, but everyone retained some bias in favor of the house he'd been born into, so it was natural to delight in the suffering of another. It was poor Akershan that was burning instead of their ancestral holdings, so that was a cause for rejoicing.

Though they were all in disguise, it was easy to pick out the warrior caste among them from their sheer physical presence. The courtly types looked frail in comparison. One of his warriors spoke, "To be fair to our southern brethren, from examining the tactics of the rebels, I believe that some members of the higher castes have joined with them and are providing training and logistical support. This is no mere casteless mob."

"Impossible," said another.

"They're certainly not fighting like fish-eaters," said his southern spy. His real name was Faril, and it was his family holdings that were being torched. "Their leadership is hiding in the mountains and we've not been able to root them out. Someone has been supplying them with illegal magic, and there've even been indications that they've been in contact with Fortress."

A warrior swore. "If only we could get an army across the sea without being torn apart by demons we'd destroy those lunatics once and for all."

Omand watched their reactions carefully. Fortress had earned its name by being unassailable. The island was tantalizingly close to the mainland. The strip of ocean separating them was so narrow in a few places that in the coldest years a brave man could walk across the shifting ice floes. Over the centuries different houses had tried to send armies across, but any activity on the ice inevitably attracted swarms of demons. Small groups had made it to the island, only to perish against the great stone walls as the fanatics rained fire and thunder down on them.

As much as it galled the bureaucracy to have anyone not bend their knee to the Law, after many fruitless sieges and thousands of dead warriors, most of the first caste liked to pretend that the island of fanatics didn't exist at all.

"It has been years since an army has tried to cross the channel," Artya said.

"The fanatics cross somehow," Faril spat.

"Doubtful," said a northern judge. "That's nothing but rumors southern houses use to excuse their inability to keep their untouchables in line. More likely it's their lax standards of discipline stirring up trouble, than witches from Fortress."

Omand put an end to that myth before his meeting degenerated into prideful house bickering. "It is extremely rare, but such crossings have been documented before." No one, not even the best minds of the Inquisition, had been able to figure out how they snuck across even during warm years. Theories ranged from magical flying devices to secret tunnels beneath the ocean floor.

"Recently, some of our soldiers have been killed by Fortress forged weapons, so either they're smuggling things across, or worse, someone has taught the rebels how to recreate their alchemy here." Faril paused to let that sink in. Now *that* was serious. No house wanted that madness spreading to their lands. The warrior caste was especially terrified of weapons which could make the lowest among them equals in battle to someone who'd spent his whole life training. "The rebels refuse to fight unless they have overwhelming numbers, and when they don't they simply flee and blend back into the casteless slums to hide. Normally the rebellious would be given up by the other non-people with a few bribes or threats, but this prophet keeps the masses silent, through fear or adoration, we don't know. Purging entire casteless quarters has only caused more to join his army."

"Protectors have been slaughtering the rebels stupid enough to stand and fight, but they can't find this prophet either," supplied another conspirator. As the warriors were easy to spot, so were the courtiers of the first caste, with their smooth inflection, fine clothing, and skin that never saw direct sunlight because there was always a slave there holding an umbrella. He addressed Omand directly, "Even the witch hunters you've dispatched haven't been able to catch him."

"That's because I've ordered them to look in the wrong place," Omand explained patiently. That announcement caused quite a stir. "Calm down. I've had Inquisition spies hidden among the prophet's followers for quite some time." There seemed to be some confusion at that, and the southern members were aghast. Of course, with their home lands being ravaged by savages, an emotional response had been expected, but that was just part of the game. It was good to occasionally remind the other conspirators that he knew more than they did. "I've spared their prophet's life because a competent foe is actually a good thing for us right now. If our plans are to succeed we'd need a villain eventually, and all these years I'd thought we'd have to manufacture one for the houses to unite against when the time came..." Omand raised his hands theatrically toward the heavens and spoke like the actors did when portraying a religious fanatic in a play, "*but the gods will provide!*"

"But what about my property?" Faril demanded. "My family is—"

"Your sacrifice has been noted. After we've consolidated power, you will be rewarded." And just because a little bribery now was more certain than the promise of great bribes later, Omand added, "In the meantime, I will see to it that you are compensated for your material losses."

"So you think this is the crisis we've been waiting for?" Atrya asked.

"It is a fine start, but sadly, no. We need something *better*. Every few generations some delusional casteless who can manage to string a few coherent sentences together gets them all riled up with talk of the Forgotten and tales of make-believe. A false prophet is hardly a unique threat. In time this rebellion would be crushed like all that have come before, and things will return to the way they've always been. The houses will go back to squabbling, never-ending competition over scraps, while the Capitol bloviates and guides with a lenient hand, and we will remain a nation in name only."

Faril spoke, "We all know such stagnation stands in the way of progress. For society to improve, the Capitol must assume greater central control." *With us in charge,* but that went without saying. "But if a mass casteless rebellion isn't enough to force the houses to give up their autonomy, what is?"

"Something truly *epic,* a threat so vile that even the most independent Thakoor will beg for the Capitol's help." Omand was rather proud of his idea. It was rare that such a wonderful intersection of opportunity and good fortune arose. It would be a crime not to take advantage of it. "That my friends, is where our fallen Protector and his legendary sword come into play."

"He's so devoted to the Law that he's voluntarily rotting in a Vadal prison," said a courtier. "We all heard the offended's asinine complaint today, but what does Black-Hearted Ashok have to do with an uprising in the south?"

"Nothing...Yet."

Chapter 16

Rada was happiest at times like this. The Presiding Judge had sent out a detailed information request. Such an assignment would send her into the oldest, dustiest, quietest parts of the legal archive for literally weeks on end. She could read and research, moving from one book or scroll to another, coming out only to sleep and eat—when she occasionally remembered to—and then back to the archives. She'd read all day, and then make notes all night by lantern light until the eye strain made her head throb, and then she'd do it again the next day. Once all of the possible legal questions were exhausted, only then would she write her report.

It was wonderful.

This particular report was about the ramifications of the proposed destruction of the casteless. Having lived her entire life in the glorious Capitol and being obligated to the prestigious central library most of that time, Archivist Rada had never actually met a casteless, so it was difficult to comprehend the idea of killing all of them. She'd seen the filthy non-people mucking out the storm drains on her way to the library a few times, but for the most part the casteless who lived in the greatest city in the world remained invisible. She'd pulled the latest reports from Census and Taxation for the judges, so she was aware of how many of them there actually were, but understanding numbers on a ledger was different than picturing them as living things. It was a good thing Rada was an academic, because she only had to report on what was actually written in the Law, and didn't have to delve into the difficult things like interpreting or enforcing those laws.

This was a rather confusing issue, and one that the legal library had not worked on for quite some time. There had been many regulations pertaining to the casteless passed over the last few hundred years, and those laws were based upon prior laws. So she'd pulled those, and found that they were based on even earlier laws, and those were reworked versions of even older laws. In fact, it turned out there had been a group of people regulated to be untouchables since the Age of Law had begun over eight hundred years ago. This was all rather exciting to Rada, because ancient history was a controlled topic, and could only be reviewed under certain circumstances with approval from the Order of Historians, and they were a tiny, secretive bunch. The only order more tightly controlled than the Historians was probably the Astronomers.

This case was giving her an excuse to read all sorts of interesting things!

"Here are the works you requested, Archivist." One of her assistants entered the room, grunting beneath the weight of a stack of old books. *Thoom.* He dropped the books on the library table in front of her, which raised a great cloud of dust.

Rada took off her now dust-speckled reading glasses and wiped them on her sleeve. Glass of this quality was expensive, even by her family's standards. Satisfied the precious lenses were clean, she put them back on, glanced over the stack and took in all the titles at once. "There are only nineteen here...Where's Ingragdra's *First Volume of Historical Proceedings?* Where's Melati's *Testimony of the Prior Age?*"

"I'm really sorry, but I couldn't pull those." The assistant was a little scared of her. "The Lord Archivist declared there's no reason for us to look at the early histories on this subject."

"What? That's asinine. My assigned topic clearly relates!"

"General access to information about the prior age is prohibited. You'll have to take it up with the superiors."

Rada sighed. She'd hoped to do this without trading favors. "Tell me something I don't know."

"The books you're requesting are in a section I'm not allowed into. My apologies, my lady, but you'll need written permission to enter."

She thought about yelling at her assistant, but that wouldn't accomplish anything. It wasn't like some low-status librarian was going to fight with the Lord Archivist. *That's my job.* She needed to talk to him about this fascinating but troubling assignment anyway. Her investigation had found a few irregularities, and librarians *hated* irregularities. Since she only needed her glasses to read, she put them back in their case. It was better not to risk such expensive things on a hike through the library. "Fine. I'll get permission. You stay here and . . . dust . . . or something."

It took Rada twenty minutes to get to the Lord Archivist's office. She walked fast, but the Central Library was just that big, and it wasn't laid out in a very convenient fashion. In a nation based upon laws, they all had to be collected somewhere, and after hundreds of years of additions to make room for all of the new regulations, decrees, and studies, the library was probably the biggest building in the world. Despite the library's vast size, she only passed a handful of people on her journey. Because information was valuable, access to it had to be strictly controlled for everyone's safety. Her Order was kept small, and approved visitors were rare.

Once she got to the Lord Archivist's office, she didn't wait for the secretary to announce her, but rather just barged right in. The secretary was used to that and didn't even try to slow Rada down. The head of her Order was sitting at his desk, smoking a pipe, reading a letter, and seeming rather annoyed. "What is it now?" He looked up. "Oh. Hello, Rada. What brings you up from your warren to the sunlight of the top floor, my dear?"

"I've come to yell at you."

"Ah, excellent. I should have my underlings thwart you more often, as that's the only time you care enough to visit your poor, lonely old father." He put his pipe down and placed his hands on top of his desk, as if preparing himself for important news. "So what has provoked your outrage this time, daughter? Ink that is slightly too blue? Lantern oil that creates too much smoke?"

"Your cheap oil may have shaved fewer notes from your precious budget, but it caused a premature yellowing of valuable papers, and the Law mandates *black* ink for inventory forms," Rada stated.

Her father grinned. "And such fanatical attention to detail is why you will someday be the one sitting in this chair, listening to junior librarians complain about paper cuts. Your mother and I are very proud of your accomplishments, Rada. If you bothered to dine with your family occasionally you'd probably hear that once in a while. Come outside for once, child. We miss you. The library has been here for five hundred years. It will probably still be here tomorrow."

Outside meant people, and Rada didn't like people. Books were much easier to deal with. "This is serious."

"And so is finding you a husband. I tell other families that I have another daughter of marriageable age and they don't believe me, because no one outside of the library ever sees you. It is said that spotting Radamantha Nems dar Harban is like witnessing a mythical creature, like a unicorn or a whale."

"The legends say that whales were fat." She really didn't want to talk to her family, but she was willing to make sacrifices for her duty. "*Fine.* I'll come to dinner."

"Excellent. We'll see you tonight."

"I'm very busy, I was thinking perhaps tomorrow—"

"Tonight, it is. So what can I do for you, Senior Archivist?"

"My section has been assigned an important duty by a special committee of judges and I require access to the restricted collection to continue my research."

"Hmmm..." Her father scratched at his beard. There were crumbs in it. "Those books are controlled for important reasons. The Age of Kings was a time of madness."

"I'll file an official request if I have to. It's very important."

"The foundations of the Law were laid during a very turbulent era. Sadly, when you get that far back into the writings, even those from the early part of this age, reason and science were intermingled with religious fervor, and we all know no good can come of works polluted with lies."

"What good are books that no one is ever allowed to read?"

"Talk like that can cause trouble. The Inquisition burned anything they thought was too dangerous long ago. We were lucky they allowed any questionable writings from that time to survive at all, so it is best not to even remind them that part of the library exists. But you do raise a wonderful philosophical question. Let's save it for dinner. In the meantime it would still be best if you limited your research to more contemporary writings."

Rada appreciated his concern, but it was her nature to continue pushing. "That's the problem. The newer records are incomplete."

"Incomplete?" Those were fighting words to the Lord Archivist. "Impossible."

"Some of the items on the catalog are missing."

"More than likely they're just shelved in the wrong place."

That was insulting. That had to be the sort of thing that the warrior caste got into duels over. "Nothing in my section is *ever* shelved in the wrong place. I've checked and rechecked. They're gone. Minutes of debates, prior studies on this topic, disappeared. And I'm afraid a few books..." she leaned forward conspiratorially, "have been *defaced*."

"Saltwater!" It was rare to hear profanity out of her father, but books were her family's life. "What kind of vile scum would harm a book?"

"Several pages were torn out of each one. I can't say when this happened. It's been decades since these were last inventoried, but each time the pages that were taken were related to the same topic. The only reason I found them at all was because of this assignment."

Her father was obviously concerned. Damaging library books was a serious crime, punishable by death. "And what is this research topic of yours?"

"I'm to find if there are any potential legal ramifications for eradicating all the casteless non-people."

It was odd. Unlike most in their Order, her father was of such high status that he actually had windows, so he had the darkest skin of any librarian Rada knew. During the summer he could almost pass for a worker. She'd never seen him turn pale before. Father looked as if he was going to be ill, and for a moment, the hands on his desk were actually being used to steady himself rather than for show.

"Are you all right?"

"I'm fine, Rada," he lied. He was clearly not. "I didn't know you were working on that project. I thought that was assigned to Senior Archivist Gurman?"

"Gurman's an imbecile. He's a political obligation because his family donated enough money to add a wing to the library. I'm not entirely convinced he's even literate. I traded assignments with him. He's lazy, so it was easy to convince him to swap."

Her father took several deep breaths to compose himself. "You shouldn't have done that."

"I thought you'd be proud. While Gurman's section is research-ing legislation pertaining to irrigation and soil erosion for some minor house court, my section is helping the presiding judge. It's obvious which one is the more important job."

"And on some subjects, doing a thorough job results in punishment rather than a reward," he muttered. Agitated, he drummed his fingers against a desk. "This isn't good, Rada, not good at all. There are plenty of scribes working on this issue. It will be enough without delving into ancient history. For your report just use what you already have. Pay no mind to the rest. It is of no concern."

"I can't—"

"No concern!" he shouted.

Rada flinched. Her father hadn't raised his voice to her since she'd been a child. "Why are you yelling at me?"

"I'm sorry. Just...Finish your report. I'll take care of not-ing the damage on the inventory. Stay away from the restricted collection. If the committee cares so much, they can ask the Historians."

"But *my* report would be incomplete. There seems to be something dating back to the founding of the Law concerning the casteless that's missing. As it stands, the Law mandates their continued existence, but why it requires this is confusing. I'm supposed to provide a historical context. I can't turn in a flawed report to the judges. It'll bring dishonor to the library."

"That's on my head, not yours. I'll sign off on it."

"That would be dishonest!" Leaving out information was the same as lying. She'd learned to be a scholar from her father, and academic honesty always trumped all other concerns, so this was a very troubling conversation. "Do you know what was on those missing pages?"

"Of course not. It was probably vandalism, nothing more..."

"It seems too much of a coincidence for it not to be sabotage."

"You know what? On second thought, forget the report. You're done." Her father was extremely agitated. Normally he was a very calm and rational man. "This was Gurman's assignment, not yours, and you were wrong to take it. I'm giving it back to him."

"Father!"

"That's final. Go do your report on watering plants or whatever it is. I'll hear no further argument."

"Fine!" She stood up and stormed away, planning on giving his office door a good slamming. *And then she noticed something on the wall...*

"Come back here!" Her father turned to his writing desk, and rummaged about for supplies, until he found a scrap of paper. Using a fine glass pen he scribbled a quick note. Rada became nervous. She'd never been officially reprimanded before. Her record was spotless. He passed it over but she couldn't even read it without her glasses. "Give this reprimand to Gurman for shirking his duty, and count yourself lucky that you're not getting one yourself. If everyone in the government did whatever they felt like instead of what they were told, the Capitol would descend into madness."

"I'm sorry, Father."

The Lord Archivist got up and went around his desk to her, trying to act like he wasn't upset, but she'd never seen him so flushed and nervous before. "Now back to work, silly girl. I'll tell your mother to expect you for dinner."

She accepted his awkward hug, then hurried out of the office, hoping that he wouldn't notice she'd stolen a spare ring of keys from its peg on the wall.

Rada missed the family dinner that evening because she was too busy sneaking into the library's restricted collection.

She'd thought about putting the keys back and doing as her father had instructed, but she was curious to see what all the fuss was about. All her life her father had lectured about the importance of their order putting integrity above all other concerns. Archivists took no side. The Capitol depended on their honesty and thoroughness. Good law couldn't be built upon a foundation of bad information. So what was it about this casteless problem that could cause her father to ignore such a fundamental philosophy?

Rada working late wasn't remarkable to anyone, especially as she often lost track of time, fell asleep between the stacks, and was found there in the morning. So she'd waited until all of the other librarians and archivists had left for the evening before going down to the lowest level. Just in case anyone else was working, she kept her lantern hood down so that it would only illuminate the steps right in front of her. As a Senior Archivist, she could go *almost* anywhere she wanted in the library, but it was better to avoid questions.

Hardly anyone ever descended into this section. This was part of the original building that had been added onto for hundreds of years. It was solid, but ugly, and lacked any of the fancy ornamentation now common to government buildings. She'd been told that they had once stored statues from the prior ages down here, but the Inquisition had taken them all away back when her grandfather had been nothing but a junior archivist. The only statue that was left had been too heavy to move easily, so the Inquisitors had smashed it with hammers until it was unrecognizable. But if Rada squinted just right, she could imagine the shape of the smiling fat man grandfather had spoken of.

There was a desk for a watchman, but there was no one posted there at night. The warrior caste had obligated a single old cripple to the library to serve as a guard during the day, but on the rare occasions that Rada had walked through this section, he'd been taking a nap. She put her glasses on long enough to read the visitor log at the guard post. No wonder the old soldier with one arm was usually asleep. It had been months since the last librarian had been let into the restricted section, and five years since the last outsider had signed in. *Lord Protector Ratul...* *Never heard of him.*

Rada paused at the entrance. Going past this point meant she would be breaking a rule. She didn't think of herself as a rule breaker. If she was caught nosing around in here, she might even be questioned by the Inquisition, and frankly, those masked bullies terrified her. Rada almost turned back before she decided that she was being stupid. Nobody would know, and damn it, she was curious. She had to try a half a dozen keys from the ring before finding the one that opened the heavy lock.

Once inside the restricted collection, she fully opened her lantern. There were shelves filled with books, so it looked pretty much like the rest of the place, only dustier. She was a bit surprised how small the room was. After years of not being allowed inside, she'd built it up in her head that the restricted collection would be far more impressive. Like most forbidden things she'd sampled over the years, reality was a bit of a letdown. She locked the door so her search wouldn't be interrupted.

It was believed that books had been common long ago, but when the demons had arrived, they'd ruined most of them. During the Age of Kings they'd started binding books again, but many of those had been lost when that age had descended into evil. Most of the works from the tumultuous time between the ages were scrolls or unbound stacks of paper. It wasn't until reason returned and the Age of Law began that proper books had as well. Now her Order even had marvelous pressing machines that allowed them to make multiple copies of a page at a time. If Rada had her way, the world would be flooded with books and everyone would know how to read—but that was just her being silly, and she knew it.

There were shelves filled with wooden boxes and piles of paper, and unlike most of the regularly accessed parts of the library, it had been quite some time since this place had been properly inventoried and organized. This could take a while.

One nice thing about the Capitol was that the air was very dry in the desert, and since this part of the library was deep underground, the temperature never fluctuated. It was the perfect environment for preserving paper. Rada put on her soft gloves. Many of these works dated back to the first centuries of the Age of Law, and some from even before that, back when mad kings reigned, or even before, when demons rained from the sky and lived on the land, so these works would be *very* delicate. They would need to be handled with the utmost caution. She pulled her scarf over her mouth, because even moist breath could damage an old book. Then she put on her glasses so she could actually see.

Rada began her search.

It was easy for a voracious reader to lose track of time when given access to new books. But then her lantern ran out of oil.

"Saltwater."

Rada had been sitting on a stool, reading Melati's *Testimony of the Prior Age* when she'd been plunged into total darkness.

No need to panic. She'd spent her entire life inside the library, so ending up in the dark in a windowless room wasn't particularly remarkable for her. The worst part was that she'd been interrupted. The book was fascinating, and the casteless question was far more complicated than she'd ever imagined, certainly more complicated that the modern judges suspected, and in fact, it was astounding that so much had been forgotten about this particular topic over the centuries. She held the delicate page between her gloved finger tips so as to not lose her place.

Then Rada realized that there was no way that she could have run out of oil already. Sure, Melati's words were difficult to decipher because their language had evolved so much, and it was hard to sort out the truths from the myths, but she'd only skimmed about a hundred pages, so she'd not been down here that long. Why had her lantern gone out?

Blind, she slowly reached toward where she'd hung the lantern on the wall with her free hand. She was hesitant, waiting for her fingers to bump hot glass, but instead they hit something soft. *Cloth?* It was hard to tell through the gloves, but that hadn't been there before. Then as she lifted her hand, she touched a *face.*

Surprised, Rada screamed and nearly fell off the stool, but a hand clamped onto her throat and choked off the sound. The ancient book was torn from her grasp. The fingers around her neck were like iron. She was lifted off of the floor by the neck. As she thrashed about, the man didn't seem to care as he carried her effortlessly across the room and slammed her hard against one of the shelves. Several books fell on the floor, and she inadvertently kicked the priceless artifacts as she thrashed about, but he didn't let go of her neck. Desperate, Rada remembered her ceremonial knife and pulled it from her sash, but her assailant swatted it out of her hand with bone-jarring force, and then he squeezed her neck, just *a bit* more.

She couldn't breathe.

"Quiet, Archivist, or I'll snap your neck," the man said. He pulled her over, so close that she could feel his hot breath on her ear. Terrified, she began to black out. "I know anatomy like you know books. You'd be amazed how little pressure it takes to snap a neck, especially a scrawny one like yours. Scream again and I'll kill you."

The grip relaxed just a bit, and Rada gasped for breath. "Please don't hurt me."

"If and how much you will be hurt is entirely dependent upon the honesty of the answers you provide." His voice was neither old nor young, but it was frighteningly calm. "Do you understand?"

"Yes." She couldn't understand how someone had gotten in. There was only one door, it was locked, and she would've heard it open. *A wizard?*

"I have magic," he said, almost as if he'd read her mind. "So if you lie, I'll know. What have you read so far tonight?"

"Ancient history, nothing more."

"A history of the untouchables, yes?"

"Yes."

"The War in Heaven? The Sons of Ramrowan? The fall of the kings and their priesthood?"

"Yes," Rada wheezed.

"Too bad. You should have listened when your father warned you not to come here...Yes, child, the walls have ears."

The walls have ears? That was a common saying about the Inquisition. Rada hadn't thought she could be any more afraid, but she'd been wrong. "You're an Inquisitor?"

"I don't know." His voice was a menacing growl. "Are you a witch?"

"No! I was only trying to research an assignment from the judges!" Hot tears had leapt from her eyes and were streaming down her face. "Please..."

The shadow gave her throat a bit more of a squeeze, fingertips on her artery, and it was enough to make her almost pass out. "I'm familiar with your task. That's why I'm here, to ensure the integrity of your investigation. Now it's too late and you know things you aren't supposed to know, which makes me wonder if you can keep a secret. Can you keep a secret, Rada?"

Rada tried to nod, but couldn't move her chin up and down with his iron hard fist there. "I won't tell."

"Good answer. My inclination is to kill you, but I have friends who hold a great deal of respect for the Lord Archivist, and they wouldn't want the embarrassment of a daughter of the first caste hanging from the Inquisitor's Dome. So due to that respect, you will be given one chance. *One.* You will never speak of this. You will finish your report, but there'd better not be any mention of these old histories. There's no need to confuse the judges with superstition or the ravings of religious fools. Use what you have been allowed, nothing more. We'll see what you write long before the judges will, and if my friends don't like it, I'll come back. Do you doubt me, Radamantha?"

"No." She flinched as he stroked her face with his other hand.

"Good job," he said as he removed her glasses. There was a crunch as he ground them to bits in his fist. "We'll be watching."

He let go of her throat and Rada sank down to the floor. The room slowly filled with light. Her lantern was glowing again.

Ancient books and little bits of sparkling glass littered the floor. She was alone and her throat was bruised and aching. The book she'd been reading was missing. The door was still closed and locked.

What have I done?

Chapter 17

‹‹‹‹‹‹‹‹‹‹‹‹‹‹‹‹‹‹‹‹

Grand Inquisitor Omand was stuffed. Say what you would about his not-so-gracious host, but among his household servants was one of the best chefs in the Capitol. "Thank you for the wonderful dinner, Durmad, but I'm afraid I really must be going. I've got a long journey ahead of me tomorrow."

The Lord Archivist was terrified but trying not to show it. Having the leader of the Inquisition show up unannounced at your estate for dinner tended to have that effect on people. "Where are you going?"

"I have business in the north. Vadal lands." Omand waved his hand dismissively. "As you know, an order's work is never done."

His host sat on the cushions, staring at the nervously picked-at plate of food in front of him. The food was excellent, so Omand was sad it was going to waste. It would be rude to ask to finish Durmad's plate, and besides, Omand was getting a little soft around the waist as he reached middle age. The lady of the house had already made some excuses and fled at the earliest opportunity. Even the servants were scared to come into the room to clean their plates.

"Well, it has been a pleasure to see you again, Omand..." the Lord Archivist said, hopeful that the Inquisitor was actually leaving now.

"Always. My only regret is that your eldest daughter was unable to join us."

The Lord Archivist looked up and swallowed hard. "My daughter?"

"Yes, Radamantha, I believe, is her name. I've been told she's quite the lovely girl, takes after her mother. You truly have a beautiful family, Durmad. Don't worry. I'm sure she's just working late and she'll be home soon."

"She'll be home soon?"

"Yes, that is what I said, isn't it?"

The Lord Archivist, wide-eyed, nodded. Omand noted that there were crumbs in Durmad's beard.

"Important work, preparing all those reports for the judges. I look forward to reading her findings on the casteless question. It will be good to have such an important topic presented by someone so respected for her thoroughness. See to it she finishes them in a timely manner. Take care of that girl of yours, Durmad, for I foresee a bright future ahead of her." Omand stood up, adjusted his mask, and then gave his host a polite bow. "I'll see myself out."

Omand took his time strolling down the hall, admiring the artwork and the excellent wood carvings. The Lord Archivist stayed planted there, staring and sweating until Omand was out the door. Omand had no doubt that the instant he was out of sight the old man would send a runner to the library to make sure his precious daughter was still in one piece.

I love my job.

His driver, Inquisitor Taraba, was waiting outside the estate, standing next to the carriage, holding the door open for his superior. "How was your evening, sir?"

"Excellent. Finest spiced duck I've had in years, steamed in some sort of chewy leaf I'm not familiar with. Absolutely delightful. Find out who their chef is and steal him," Omand ordered as he climbed into the carriage. Taraba closed the door behind him, and sure enough, waiting within the shadows was Sikasso.

He was sprawled across the carriage's opposite seat as if taking a nap. Sikasso wasn't a member of the Inquisition. Quite the contrary, he was a leader of an organization that wasn't supposed to exist anymore, but if it did, would surely be an enemy of the Inquisition. The assassin was an average-sized, unassuming man, somewhere between the age of twenty and forty, with a completely forgettable face. Tonight he was dressed like a junior librarian, tomorrow he'd appear to be something else. Neither of them spoke until Taraba had whipped the horses and the carriage was rolling through the Capitol.

"It is done," the magically enhanced killer said, revealing that he'd not been napping after all. "The girl at the library won't be a problem."

"Not a problem dead, or not a problem compliant?" He had, after all, insinuated she was still alive to the girl's father, and he'd hate to have gotten it wrong. Omand had a reputation to keep up.

"Alive as requested. I'm not one of your masked thugs, out there carelessly breaking knees and thumbs. My people are artists. Besides, intimidating the firsters is easy. Most of them are so insulated from violence that even the suggestion of it makes them fold. She'd probably never been threatened before in her whole life. I'd have your men keep an eye on her, but I don't think she'll talk to anyone. All that easy living makes firsters soft."

"I've found that to be true myself." Over the years Omand had tortured confessions out of members of every social stratum, from the lowest casteless scum to chief judges. Everyone cracked eventually, but the ones who were the least used to sweating and bleeding usually cracked first. "A fantastic evening all around, then. Better her respected name on the report than some drunken fool who the judges will mock." Omand reached into his robe and pulled out Sikasso's payment. He tossed over the pouch. "Are you ready for our journey to Vadal?"

"I look forward to it," the assassin said as he opened the pouch and studied the contents. If his Inquisitors had a smile as unnerving as Sikasso's, then there would be no need for them to wear masks. Satisfied that the black steel fragment was of the agreed-upon weight, the pouch vanished from Sikasso's hands. "When the Protector's sword shatters, then we get the pieces."

"If . . ."

"When," Sikasso stated. "The road you're sending him down can only end in dishonor, and we'll be there when it does. The fragments are mine."

"That is fair." An entire ancestor blade worth of magical black steel shards was worth a fortune, but so were the services of Sikasso's organization. "You know my expected timeline."

"I think your schedule is optimistic at best. I've killed more than my fair share of Protectors over the years, but I've always wanted to fight a bearer."

Omand chuckled. "If everything goes according to my plan, you won't need to."

"You assume he'll still do as he's told. No man is that devoted to the Law, Inquisitor."

"On the contrary, Wizard, from what I've learned of this Ashok, you might be surprised."

Chapter 18

"Where's your cane?" Pakpa asked.

"I threw it in the river," Jagdish answered. He'd be damned if he presented himself to his new assignment looking like a cripple. Besides, his leg only really hurt in the mornings, or when it was too cold, or too hot, or when he walked, or put too much weight on it. He spread his arms so she could see his new uniform. "How do I look?" he asked his new bride.

"Like the finest warrior in all of Vadal," she lied, or perhaps she was so still so happy to have been assigned a higher-status husband that she actually believed that. To Jagdish, when he looked in the mirror all he saw was a warrior so pathetic that he'd managed to lose a duel even when his opponent had been unfairly outnumbered, and who'd had a Thakoor die under his watch as a result. It had taken months for his arm and leg to heal enough to return to duty, but by then, the story had spread, and no fighting paltan wanted him.

"The finest warrior? I doubt that."

"You will make an excellent risaldar."

Pakpa meant well, but she'd grown up in the worker caste. She couldn't grasp the nuances of rank and assignment within the warrior caste hierarchy. To her, being married off to a miserable failure of a soldier was still a huge step up in life. She didn't understand that his new promotion was really intended as an insult. Only the worst places received names related to water, and he was being sent to Cold Stream.

Jagdish kissed his wife. "I must go. I can't be late."

He limped from their small home, through the streets of the city, south toward his new assignment, guarding the very bastard who had ruined his life.

The fallen Protector's appearance had changed. He'd not shaved or cut his hair since the slaughter. His beard was long and unkempt, his hair wild and filthy, and now he truly looked like the casteless dog that he was. Like the other prisoners, he was dressed in gray rags.

The only noticeable difference was that sword.

"What does he do?"

"Nothing much, Risaldar Jagdish," the prison guard told him. "We let them out into the yard for most of the afternoon, but he keeps to himself. I think the other prisoners are scared of him. He exercises, sword forms mostly, then runs several laps around the yard, but that's it. When their time is up, we ask him to return to his cell, and he does. Then he just sits there and stares off into nothing."

Jagdish stood at the tower railing, looking down into the yard and the prisoners who'd segregated themselves into groups. Most of them were here because of crimes not severe enough to warrant execution, but a judge had found them to have temperaments unfit for a period of slavery. His new charges were mostly thieves, debtors, and deserters. The roster said he had a few murderers and rapists from the warrior caste, who would serve their time and then be returned to duty, where murder and rape weren't necessarily crimes as long as they remembered to only do it to their approved enemies and not their own people. He also had some workers guilty of that level of crime who'd not been executed, which told him they came from families with enough money to bribe a judge. Then there were the hostages, warriors taken from other houses in border raids, held here until their families paid a ransom or they were traded for Vadal men being held in other lands.

But none of those mundane prisoners interested Jagdish right now. "Has the prisoner caused any problems?" He had five hundred charges, but there was only one who could be *the prisoner*.

"None, sir. He's unfailingly polite. In fact, Nayak Suchart was surprised by one of the more violent prisoners, who started choking him with a length of chain. Before any of us could get there, Ashok appeared and beheaded the attacker. Cut his head right off like it was nothing. Then he just walked back to his cell. Saved Suchart's life, more than likely."

"Yes. I'm sure they call him the Black Heart because it overflows with mercy."

"I wouldn't say that, Risaldar. It wasn't mercy so much as annoyance. He told the prisoners that were watching that he wouldn't abide anybody breaking the Law in his presence... Scared them, that's for sure. Assaults have been down and we've not had a single riot since he's been here. We used to have fights between the different hostage gangs all the time, but now they're all scared of getting on his bad side. Most of the prisoners seem happy, you know, having a bit of entertainment."

"The Law didn't condemn them here to be *happy*, Nayak," Jagdish said, not that he particularly cared about the nuances of the Law. He just wanted to fulfill this dead-end detail until a proper war started, because then his value as a border scout would far outweigh his reputation as a lousy personal guard. "What do you mean, entertainment?"

"The duels, sir...Wait...You've not been told about the duels?"

"I'm a soldier. Nobody ever tells me anything. What duels?"

"Chief Judge Harta's orders. Anyone who wishes to try and take the magic sword is allowed to duel the prisoner for it. We're required to let them fight. They show up all the time. Not just warriors, but Harta even said to allow workers. Maybe he thinks somebody will get lucky or the sword will find somebody it likes better? Hell, he's even let men from *other* houses have a shot. Said if an outsider won, they'd be given a Vadal obligation and promoted to the first caste!"

That reeked of desperation...But a promotion to the highest status was a rare thing indeed. Jagdish watched the prisoner, who had found a lip of rock on the perimeter wall and was doing chin-ups with his fingertips. "How many has he beaten?"

"I don't know, but probably every fool crazy enough to try and earn himself a better place in the entire region. So far? He's been here six months, so forty-five, maybe fifty. I'd have to check the guest log at the gatehouse. I'm surprised you haven't heard."

"I've been preoccupied lately."

"We've even had a problem with spectators bribing guards to come inside so they can watch. That's what got our last risaldar transferred. The judges must've not liked that one of us thought of a way to take bribes for something before they could…" He trailed off when Jagdish didn't laugh.

"That nonsense ends. This is a prison, not a circus."

"Well, it's been like we've had our own personal arena and the prison has a champion gladiator. This must be how the first caste live in the Capitol," the guard said with a wistful tone.

"How many of these challengers has the prisoner killed?"

"Not more than ten or twelve, I think. It looks like he tries to let them live. Most, he soundly beats, then he gives them a lecture about how to fight better before sending them on their way. Them who piss him off, though, they go into the furnace in *parts*. The Black Heart doesn't strike me as the patient sort, but he's got a particular sort of honor to him."

The fact that one of his guards seemed so impressed by the prisoner annoyed Jagdish to no end. Only the lowest of his caste were given this assignment. There was never any chance for glory, but plenty of opportunity for failure. If they fulfilled their duty, none of their betters would ever notice, but if one of their prisoners escaped or killed a guard, there would be plenty of shame. The prison guards didn't get to do the things a warrior was born to do, so it was no surprise they would be impressed by a fighter of the Black Heart's skill.

"I want to speak to him."

"You sure that's a good idea, sir? I mean, I heard you were there that night…"

"Tomorrow, after exercise, send the rest back to their cells, but have the prisoner stay in the yard. I will meet him alone."

That night Jagdish lay in bed beside Pakpa, thinking about what he was going to do the next day. Most would say it was foolish, but as a proud warrior, he couldn't let such an opportunity pass. Low-born, without any connections, the only other way he could rise in status was to become a war hero. A duel made perfect sense, except for that whole dying part.

He couldn't sleep. Not because of nerves, but rather because Pakpa snored. Her wheezing sounded like the giant machines at the workers' foundry on the other side of the military district's wall.

How can someone so beautiful snore like an elephant?

Not that Jagdish minded that Pakpa snored and constantly rolled around in her sleep, gentle as an ox, shaking their small, flimsy bed, and occasionally scratching him with her toenails, because her positive traits far outweighed those few negatives. As a warrior of low birth, he'd expected his arranged marriage to be to an ugly, stupid woman, but he'd gotten lucky. The workers had traded one of their loveliest daughters to his caste for additional security on a trade route, and Jagdish had been single and recuperating from his wounds, and thus available in time to sign the arbiter's treaty, so it had all worked out.

Even his arranged marriage had been meant as an insult, marrying him off to a baker's daughter, instead of a proper strong woman of the warrior caste who'd provide him with superior sons. His children would be looked down upon as half-caste. Only he liked coming home to Pakpa's warm smile and kind words, and he had no doubt she'd provide him with many wonderful children. Jagdish had actually come to love his wife, and she seemed fond enough of him.

So he didn't want to die tomorrow.

He must have sighed, because Pakpa snorted herself awake and rolled over. "Huh? What's wrong?"

"I can't sleep."

"How come?" She sounded confused. "Was I snoring? My sisters always accused me of snoring."

All he could see in the dark was her lovely general outline, but he had no problem picturing her beautiful face. "No. Your sisters lied because they're jealous. You sleep like a songbird, delicately perched in a tree." He thought about telling her what he was going to attempt—to better both of their lives—but he didn't want to make her worry. "Go back to sleep."

Pakpa rolled back over. "I love you." She was snoring again within a few seconds.

Jagdish resumed staring at the ceiling beams, pondering dueling and death.

✧   ✧   ✧

The next morning Jagdish watched the man he feared the most easily defeat one of the best warriors in the world.

Their guest was announced at the gate house as swordmaster Nadan Somsak dar Thao, from their mountainous southern neighbor, who had won high status through countless victories, until he'd become the Thakoor of a vassal family. His skin was covered in tattoos designed to strike fear in his enemies and he had a herald to read off a list of all the warriors he'd bested. He'd hired musicians to play drums and was even accompanied by an arbiter who announced that his travel papers had been approved by Chief Judge Harta himself, so Nadan Somsak had showed up with an entourage, legal standing, a great deal of fanfare, and a chip on his shoulder.

He walked to the center of the prison yard, spread his ink-covered arms wide, and shouted, "Bring me the fallen Protector so that I may defeat him! I have come to claim Angruvadal as my own! I will destroy the criminal and the whole world will sing praises to my name."

"He's a cocky one," said one of the guards. "I've got ten notes says the Black Heart beats him in under two minutes."

"You're on, but only because he'll slow down to give that tattooed mountain thug some pointers."

All of the prison staff who could temporarily escape their duties had climbed the walls and towers to watch the duel. Jagdish noted that they were all making bets, but not a single one was betting on the challenger, but rather on how long he'd last or whether his life would be spared or not. The prisoner might have been the vilest form of criminal, but he was *their* criminal.

Havildar Wat was his second-in-command, and he joined Jagdish on the wall. "They've gone to fetch the prisoner." He reached beneath one of the lamellar plates of his armor and pulled out a watch on a chain. "With your permission, sir, I'll keep time. That way none of the men get into fights over who loses the bet."

A timepiece small enough to fit in a pocket was rare and expensive. "How did you afford that, Wat?"

The young warrior grinned. "My winnings from betting on these duels, Risaldar. You see, there are marks for every minute of the day. It's supposed to be very accurate."

Jagdish had to squint, and even then he had a hard time seeing anything that small. "Remarkable."

The drummer was beating a steady cadence. The man from Thao was still shouting below them. "Bring me the traitor Ashok, so that I may cut his throat and spill his casteless blood! The whore-spawned abomination must pay for the curse he's brought upon this weak people!"

"What's his problem?" Wat asked.

"The Somsak were a small house, renowned for their skill, supposedly some of the best mountain fighters in the world," Jagdish explained. "Then a winter plague came through a few generations back and wiped out most of their army. Thao moved quick and invaded while they were weak. I suppose all those farmers were tired of being raided and decided to finish it once and for all. They say the Somsak bearer singlehandedly held a mountain pass while fighting five hundred Thao warriors, but his ancestor blade shattered on the very last one's shield. They've been a vassal house ever since."

"That's quite the story, sir."

"I've no idea if it's true or not, but the Somsak think it is."

"Still no reason to make an ass of himself."

While the challenger continued his rant, the guards opened a gate at the far end of the yard and Black-Hearted Ashok entered. There were no drums, heralds, or fanfare. He seemed far calmer than the night Jagdish had first seen him.

Nadan Somsak turned and saw Ashok coming. "I smell the ocean! It must be a casteless." He hawked and spit in the dirt. The drummer quit playing and hurried out of the way. "Come here, so I can crack open your skull and wipe my ass with your brains. Look at you. You're nothing. I can't believe this is the casteless scum who made the Protectors into a bunch of dupes and fools."

Ashok tilted his head to the side. Since he didn't bother to raise his voice, it was difficult to hear what he was saying from up on the wall. "My life is of no value. I have no status, so you are allowed to insult me freely, but it is illegal to slander an approved order, so please refrain from maligning the Protectors."

"The Protectors are a bunch of stuck-up idiots, all swagger, no heart, no balls, and wouldn't be worth saltwater if they didn't have the Capitol to prop them up. All the Protectors could be casteless as far as I know. You're just the only one dumb enough to admit it. It wouldn't surprise me if the lot of them had been sired by demons and squeezed out of whores. I piss on the Protectors."

The warrior from Thao had succeeded in provoking the

prisoner's anger, and Black-Hearted Ashok's emotionless mask slipped just a bit, giving Jagdish a glimpse of the man he'd fought that night in the main hall of Great House Vadal.

"Hey, Wat, I'll bet you two hundred notes against that little timepiece of yours that from the time the prisoner draws his sword to winning, you can't count to ten."

The young warrior was happy to take advantage of his naïve commander. "You're on, Risaldar."

Jagdish checked his new pocket watch. He could feel the gears turning inside through the thin metal body, almost like holding a mouse in his hand and feeling the vibration of its tiny, rapid heart. All one had to do was turn a knob several times a day, winding the springs inside, and a needle turned with the time, pointing at all the little dashes on the side that represented the minutes of the day. Though it was easier to just look in the sky and see where the sun was to know what time it was, this was truly a marvel of mechanical science. He'd heard that in the Capitol there were clocks now with *two* needles, so accurate they had one pointing at the hour *and* another for the minute.

His guards were watching from the walls. They'd seen the limp and the giant scar on Jagdish's arm. They'd heard the versions of the story that had filtered down from the Bidaya's party guests, and now they were curious to see if their new commander was crazy enough to fight the Black Heart *again*...

I wonder what times they are betting on?

Jagdish was alone in the yard. There was a dark spot in the dirt in front of him where Nadan Somsak had bled that very morning. Surprisingly, the Black Heart hadn't killed the foul brute. He'd simply drawn and struck him once, fast as lightning, right through the cheek. Nadan Somsak was returning to his mountains without a tongue. Jagdish wondered if Nadan had a wife. Would she be happier that he could no longer speak? Would Pakpa still love him if he came home missing any body parts? If Ashok cut off his ears, then at least he would be able to get some sleep.

Jagdish smiled.

The gate opened and the fallen Protector entered. He pulled back his matted hair, looked around, and seemed a bit surprised to see someone wearing a guard's uniform waiting for him, because the prison guards had seen enough of his duels to know better.

As Ashok approached, Jagdish put the marvelous little clock back inside his armor.

"I am Risaldar Jagdish, new commander of the Cold Stream Prison garrison."

Ashok bowed. Jagdish hadn't thought through the etiquette. The prisoner was technically a casteless, which meant he deserved no respect, but he was also a bearer, which meant he deserved great respect. The prisoner must have realized why Jagdish was standing there so awkwardly, because he said, "I'm a legal anomaly, but I'm not worthy of your respect. I was born an untouchable and I'm a criminal."

Jagdish gave him a small bow anyway.

Ashok seemed confused. "There's no need to be respectful to me."

"Well, I honestly hadn't thought of it that way." Jagdish shrugged. "You beat a dozen warriors in a knife fight. If that's not worthy of respect, then I don't know what is."

"A curious way of looking at things. Fighting is what I do. You wouldn't praise an ox for pulling a plow. How may I be of service, Risaldar?"

Jagdish mouth was suddenly very dry. "I wish to duel."

Ashok tilted his head to the side, curious. "I'm only a casteless, and you're a warrior, but may I speak freely?"

It was an odd request, as Jagdish was having a very hard time thinking of the most terrifying combatant in the world as an *inferior.* "You may."

"Why?"

"I wish to prove myself to Angruvadal and earn my family's place in the first caste."

"You have a family? Children?"

"A wife."

"She'll miss you if you die?"

"Yes."

"Then walk away, Risaldar," Ashok warned. "There's nothing to be gained by dying here. I remember you. You were there the night of my crime and you were the best among them."

"No. I was second to Sankhamur."

"In experience, perhaps, but in integrity, you alone questioned Bidaya's dishonorable commands, and you alone had the wisdom to not try to fight against an ancestor blade. How many of you died?"

"Eventually, six of us succumbed to our injuries."

"My apologies for your brothers, but it would have been all of you, and perhaps some of the bystanders, if you hadn't shaken me from my anger and reminded me of what was right. Then, despite your misgivings, you still followed your Thakoor's command. Obeying such a command is one of the most difficult things for a warrior to do."

Jagdish hoped that his men couldn't hear him from the walls. "I was shamed by that defeat."

"You fought well. There was no shame there."

"If I wasn't good enough, then I should have died. I've been mocked by my betters ever since. They say that if I had been stronger, then our Thakoor would still be alive and our house wouldn't be vulnerable. Enemies harass our borders because of our weakness, which means my brothers are out there fighting and dying, and I'm not even allowed to help. This assignment is my punishment. They want me to have to look every day at the face of the man who ruined me."

"I may have broken your leg, but it's obvious I didn't break your spirit. The Law says a warrior's life belongs to his superiors, but your superiors are willing to spend your life stupidly. Anyone who mocks you is a fool, and would have done no better in your place. The next one who tells you that, tell him to come and see me."

Jagdish actually laughed. "That'll go over well."

"If they're so very brave, then I'm easy enough to find."

"True, but it is simpler to insult my courage than it is to test their own. My purpose in life is to fight, serve my house, and prove myself in combat. I can't do that if I'm wasting away the rest of my days babysitting hostages and criminals. I don't see much choice but to fight you. Who knows? Maybe I'll get lucky."

"And maybe I'll be unlucky and kill another good warrior who deserves better. I'm tired of killing. If you wish to take Angruvadal, then I'm required to wield it, and when Angruvadal is drawn, mercy cannot be promised. I'm legally obligated to do my best against everyone who tests me, and I know you're good enough that I'll actually have to try."

"Thank you." For an unstoppable killing machine, Black-Hearted Ashok seemed to be a very reasonable man.

Ashok appeared to mull something over for a moment. "So we can agree. You don't want to die, and I don't want to kill you. I have an idea, Risaldar. You're good, but you're not good enough to beat me today. I mean no offense."

"If I was offended, I'd suppose we'd just have to duel about it."

"True." Ashok said thoughtfully, as if Jagdish had brought up some brilliant legal point. "But here is my proposition. I've nothing better to do, and I'm obligated to remain here until judgment is pronounced. While I await execution, I can teach you. Eventually you could be good enough to beat me, and then we can have a proper duel."

Of the many possible outcomes of Jagdish's challenge, he'd not expected that. But if he could learn even a fraction of Ashok's skills, surely he could redeem himself among his caste. "Hmmm... Interesting. I'm listening."

"I have no status. You're the commander of this prison. There's no reason you can't order me to spar against you with practice swords. I'd have no choice but to obey. Let the city know that Risaldar Jagdish has so little fear that he trains against a monster. Let's see if any of those high-status warriors have the spine to do that."

"What kind of madman is brave enough to spar against such a fearsome killer? I like it. Let those soft-palmed fops lord it over me in their estates, because in their hearts they'll know that Jagdish is braver than they are. Ha! I like this plan." Jagdish turned and shouted at the guards along the wall, who were nervously waiting to see if their commander was going to get butchered or not. "You! Go to the armory and bring back two wooden swords."

There were a lot of confused looks shared, but one of the nayaks ran off to fetch some practice weapons as directed. He doubted any of the men would win the betting pool today.

"I must caution you, Risaldar. I am trained in the ways of the Protector Order, and our methods are unforgiving at best. It isn't uncommon for our acolytes to die during training."

"I'm no mere student, Prisoner. I'm a four-year veteran who has seen a house war and more border skirmishes than you have fingers."

Ashok smiled as if Jagdish had just told a very amusing anecdote. "Of course, Risaldar. I'm sure this will prove enlightening."

"Very well. We will meet here every day..." Jagdish pulled out the pocket watch. He opened the lid and pointed at the slowly moving needle. "At *this* time."

Ashok glanced down at the watch. "What does that mean?"

There were a lot of little marks. "I don't rightly know."

Chapter 19

The presiding judge slammed his staff against the floor. The sudden noise brought the meeting to order. The judges, arbiters, regulators, courtiers, scribes and other various functionaries all took their seats in their sections that were carefully sorted by house, status, and rank.

Bang! "Several months ago this committee asked for a report to be generated pertaining to the proposed eradication of the casteless. The report is prepared and the meeting will come to order." The staff came down again. *Bang!* Considering they'd been using the Chamber of Argument for hundreds of years, Senior Archivist Rada wondered how many times they'd had to replace the floor with all that staff-banging. She'd have to look it up. "Honorable judges, representatives of the great houses, your scribes have been provided with a copy of the Order of Archivists' report. Are there any questions pertaining to the report?"

Rada was in the scholar's section far behind the presiding judge. She could see most of the chamber from here, and she glanced about fearfully, waiting to see who would condemn her first for submitting an incomplete and academically dubious report to this august body. Surely someone would realize how shoddy it was. There were Inquisitors standing in the aisles to keep order. Once a judge pointed out her errors, one of those Inquisitors would drag her away for execution. Sure, she could say that it was some nameless Inquisitor who'd forced her to leave out pertinent information, but who would believe her?

Several minutes passed as the judges flipped through their provided summaries. Rada was sweating and she couldn't stop one leg from vibrating nervously, but nobody stood up to accuse her of fraud or treachery.

Since there was no shouting or cries for Rada to be dragged through the streets and lashed to the Inquisitor's Dome to sunburn, wither, and die, the presiding judge was able to speak freely. "As you can see, there appear to be no real legal mandates pertaining to this topic. There is some confusion as to the origins of the idea that the untouchables were somehow protected and a few oral traditions, but nothing in the actual statutes can be found. The last time a full report was done on this subject was two generations ago, and the only references found in that report pertain to customs, not laws. The idea that some number of casteless must always exist appears to be a tradition formed by the great houses hundreds of years ago."

"Our ancestors didn't have to put up with so damned many of them. They breed like rabbits!" someone shouted from the judge's gallery. Many laughed. Rada had flinched at the noise, certain that it would have been someone from the unpopular and neglected Historian's Order calling attention to her lies, but it had only been a stupid joke. Besides, there weren't that many Historians, and none of them were here.

"Indeed," the presiding judge said. "Let us honor the wisdom of our ancestors, and be respectful of their traditions as we debate. However, since there are no legally binding covenants the committee is free to vote as they see fit. Before we begin, does anyone have any amendments they'd like to make before this report is entered into the permanent records of the Capitol?"

She could stand up now and speak. There was a mistake. A page had been left off the summary. There was some pertinent history that really mattered to the discussion. Saying there was an error would bring dishonor to her family, since her father had signed off on this report himself, but being blamed for a mistake was more honorable than committing fraud. She didn't know what her father knew about the Inquisitor's threats, but after he'd put her back on the assignment he'd made her swear that she would only use the contemporary records. Even he—the respected head of an order—was afraid. She could say something, anything. *This is my last chance to tell the truth.*

But Rada didn't get to find out if she was that brave or not, because one of the Inquisitors patrolling the aisles had stopped directly next to her seat. She looked up, and he was staring right through her, his eyes nothing but black holes in his metal mask. Sharp teeth in a leering, hungry mouth, it was the face of the Law. He had a polished club in one hand, and was resting it in his other palm, fingers tapping an absent beat against the wood.

We'll be watching.

Rada put her head down and kept it there. She never should have stolen this assignment from that drunken imbecile Gurman.

"Since there are no comments, the report will be entered into the official records and used as the basis for all future discussions on this topic. The debate will now commence. The staff recognizes Arbiter Artya Zati dar Zarger."

When Rada looked up, the Inquisitor had continued down the aisle and a beautiful woman had gone to the podium. She had such a lovely voice that it was almost like she was reading a poem, rather than estimates of how much it would cost to round up and slaughter millions of untouchables.

Though Rada had never met a casteless and had been brought up thinking that they weren't people at all, now that she knew where they came from, Rada discovered that the discussion was making her nauseous. She certainly didn't buy into any religious nonsense about forgotten gods and their prophecies, but now that she knew the untouchables' history, she knew the term non-people to be inaccurate. They were a filthy, degenerate, and evil lot, but still people, and now these judges were arguing their fate without all the facts.

From watching them, she doubted any of the judges would really care, even if they knew the truth behind the Law, since their only philosophy seemed to be one of selfishness. But that didn't make Rada feel any better. *I'm a dishonorable coward and a failure of a librarian.*

The debate was heated and seemed to go on forever. Rada didn't like being around people to begin with, so listening to them bloviate, lie, and call each other names was particularly difficult to deal with, but she forced herself to stay. She had to see what she'd caused. The scribes around her were enjoying this and rooting for different factions as if this was some sort of contest.

The judges spent hours yelling at each other. Some houses didn't seem to mind their casteless so much, because their labors earned money for their Thakoors. Others hated them, but even they had to admit that destroying them would be expensive and time-consuming. Nobody would admit to liking the untouchables, but other than a few who railed against the *casteless menace*, it didn't seem like the proposal would go anywhere.

Rada breathed a sigh of relief. Maybe she'd be able to return to her library soon, without having helped eradicate a quarter of the world's population.

A judge from Akershan had reached the podium. The staff recognized him and gave him the floor. Rada wasn't sure what he was talking about at first, as she didn't really keep up on current events, but he was complaining about a huge rebellion in his lands. The news must have been dire, because it even got the annoying scribes to shut up and pay attention.

"The false prophet's army has burned the vital town of Hamilwa. Three Protectors were in the area. *Three* . . . Yet somehow he was able to sneak right past them to flee back into the mountains unharmed."

"Such a failure is unacceptable!" shouted someone in the crowd.

"I'm not so sure it was a failure at all . . ." said the judge from Akershan. "It is said that the only way you can escape the Protectors' wrath is if they aren't *that* inclined toward catching you to begin with."

A shudder went through the crowd of *oohs* and *ahhs*, and many whispered *how dare he?* Rada didn't understand people very well, but even she understood that a dire insult had just been given.

"What are you insinuating?" There was only a single individual sitting in the section set aside for honored guests and visiting dignitaries, and that man stood up, folded his arms, and glared at the speaker. She didn't know who he was, but Rada was fairly certain he was even more out of place here than she was. He looked more like a younger version of the crippled, battered representatives of the warrior caste than any of the governing caste here, but he was sitting in an important section, indicating a very high status, at least equivalent to her father's station.

The audience seemed shocked to hear this one speak up. "Don't dance around. Give your accusation or shut your idiot mouth."

The presiding judge banged his staff on the floor. "Please, Lord Protector Devedas. Representatives of orders must not speak in the chamber unless questioned."

"My apologies, your honor. I assumed I was being questioned when this honorless dog insinuated that some of my men are traitors. If that was his intent, my answer is no, and my inclination is to give him the back of my hand," the Protector said.

The audience roared and the presiding judge did his best to punch a hole in the floor with this staff. "Order! Order!"

She had to admit the Protector was a rather handsome man, lean and muscular, with broad shoulders and narrow waist, and a strong, square jaw. Rada didn't like people, but she could still appreciate natural beauty as well as any woman. However, unlike the pretty first-caste men she'd associated with, this one looked like he could murder the entire chamber and sleep well at night.

But the Akershan judge wasn't deterred. "Is the idea of a traitor amongst the Protectors so outlandish? How quickly we forget what brought us to this debate to begin with! We must examine the possibility that your men allowed the criminals to escape. Everyone knows the Protector Order was already infiltrated by one in league with the rebels."

"Who is this *everyone* who knows so much? Ashok had no connection to your rebels."

"How would you know, Lord Protector? He went undetected among you for twenty years. A reasonable man would ask if there are more like him. Perhaps the Black Heart was able to corrupt other Protectors with his lies? There were rumors only a few years ago of one of your predecessors who fell into religious madness... Whatever happened to him? I believe his name was Ratul."

Rada looked back to see the reaction. The Lord Protector seemed angry enough to strangle the judge on the spot. He'd already walked out of his section, into the aisle, and was heading toward the podium. The judge grew frightened and fled. An Inquisitor intercepted the Protector and put out one hand to stop him.

"If you want to keep that hand, remove it from me *now*."

The Inquisitor slowly backed away.

"Lord Protector!" the presiding judge shouted. "I implore you to calm yourself. Your place is to enforce the Law, not to threaten its authors. I'm certain he's very sorry for this inadvertent insult, and will issue an apology to your Order. Isn't that correct?"

The Akershan judge had fled back to the far corner of his section, surely hoping to put as many of his friends' bodies between himself and the Protector's wounded pride as possible. "Yes, your honor. I didn't intend to give any offense. That's the truth!"

"Truth?" Devedas spat. Then he looked around the Chamber of Argument. Most would not meet his gaze. "I don't think the residents of this honored chamber would recognize truth if it was crammed down their throats."

"Lord Protector! That is enough!"

"No, it isn't. The judges sit here in the shade, fat and comfortable, as you casually propose a slaughter beyond imagining. I've traveled Lok from one end to the other, seen every great house, and I can assure you, though the casteless are individually weak, they are *many*, and when the warriors do as they're told, *all* of the untouchables will rise up. Unlike most of you, I've seen bloodshed, and far too much to take such delight in it. All of you, pronouncing judgment about things you barely understand, spending lives like they're banknotes, and questioning the integrity of those who've sacrificed more than you can imagine..." Devedas picked out one particular chief judge wearing Vadal colors to glare at. "Even while *criminals* lurk among you like rats—"

"Protector!" the presiding judge snapped. "You are dismissed."

Devedas gave a very stiff bow toward the presiding judge, then he turned and strode from the room. The Inquisitors at the door rushed to get out of his way.

The instant he was gone the Chamber of Argument lived up to its name, descending into shouting and general mayhem.

"How dare you insult the Protectors?"

"He protests too much! Investigate the Order for treachery!"

"If the rebels can corrupt even our finest, then surely all the casteless *must* be destroyed!"

One of the men sitting next to Rada was giggling, then he leaned over and whispered to another scribe. "That southerner sounds like a grunting ape compared to Mindarin the Eloquent. I bet the Order is regretting promoting Devedas to the Capitol now!"

"That fool has no idea how to behave in polite society," his friend agreed. Apparently the polite thing to do was lie and insinuate horrible things with impunity, all while never expecting any repercussions. "With a traitor in their midst, the last thing the Protectors need is more shame. Their support will vanish."

This place was *unclean*. It really made Rada want to return to the quiet of her library.

The arguments calmed down and the regular debate resumed, but Rada had heard enough, so she slipped out. Inquisitors watched her the whole way, or at least she felt like they did. She didn't think anything was going to be decided about the casteless right now, but worse, she'd helped lay a flawed foundation. She had no idea what horrible decisions might be made in the future because of her cowardice.

There was only one thing Rada came away from the Chamber of Argument certain of. There was no way that angry Protector who'd boldly stated the obvious truth could be in league with the Inquisitor who'd forced her to lie.

Chapter 20

Rada stood in front of the mirror and examined the complicated dress. It was constructed of the finest silks and dotted with ornaments. She frowned. "I look like a whore."

"I thought that was your plan."

"I don't have to like it."

"You're such a prude. This is the height of fashion now," her little sister told her. "You'd know that if you ever left the library. No wonder you haven't been assigned a husband yet. No other families can even tell you're a girl beneath those librarian's robes you always wear."

"My arms are bare."

"We live in the desert. It's hot."

"You can see my *knees*." Rada awkwardly bent over to try and pull the silks lower.

That caused her sister to cluck disapprovingly, then reach over to untie one of the knots on Rada's neck, further loosening a shirt which was already strategically loose in some places and tight in others. "You've got to give the boys a bit of a peek when you bend over."

Though they were the same size, Rada had never borrowed any of Daksha's clothing before. This outfit bore no insignia for house or family, the rank was indeterminate but still suggested a great deal of wealth, and was designed for anonymity at the secret parties thrown by the bored young people of their caste. "Father allows you out of the estate dressed like this?"

"Father pays about as much attention to the outside world as you do. I could paint myself purple and ride an elephant through the streets naked and I doubt our parents would notice." Daksha was far more typical of a first-caste daughter than Rada was, since she was primarily interested in marrying well. "You're not nearly as pretty as I am, but you're passable. So tell me, Rada, who is this man you wish to impress?"

She didn't want to impress anyone. She wanted to prevent the systematic execution of millions of untouchables, stop a terrible breach of one of their oldest laws, and free herself from the guilt of fraud, but she needed to do it in a manner that would avoid the Inquisition's notice. She didn't know if they really were following her, but ever since her experience in the restricted collection, she'd been noticing more masks wherever she went. "I can't tell you."

"Fine. Make me guess. I'm glad you like real boys and not just the imaginary ones in books. I was worried about you. Passing up marriage all these years to obligate yourself to a library always struck me as foolish. I figured you'd spend the rest of your life alone, reading books, until you shrivel into an old childless crone, and die between those shelves, and no one would ever notice until some junior librarian tripped over your mummified corpse."

That didn't sound so bad.

"It's good to see you come outside and live life. I know our family status comes from father's position, but you can't live your life through someone else's words. You need to do things that someone will want to write about!"

Daksha shouldn't insult books. This particular idea had come from a book. The central library held all manner of books, including foolish romances designed to titillate empty-headed girls like her sister, but it was one of many the catalog had suggested under *clandestine meetings*. She almost avoided it as trash, but the basic idea—disguising herself as a pleasure woman—seemed sound. Though Rada's goal was far different than the woman in the romance, she also needed to meet with a certain man while avoiding detection.

Rada covered her mouth and nose with the colorful scarf and

tied it tight against her neck. Her sister had changed her hair and put paint around her eyes. In the mirror a stranger stared back at her.

"Is he handsome?"

"Yes," Rada answered automatically, then cursed herself. "No."

Daksha laughed at her. "Well, he must be of lower status since you're wearing a disguise. Forbidden love is exciting. Except father is so desperate to marry you off at this point that he'd accept lower status... Wait... Is he lower *caste?*" She began to giggle because the idea was so scandalous. "Is he a worker? A merchant, I'll bet. But no, you've never cared about having nice things. I bet you've fallen for a warrior! Trust me, they may have muscles, and they're fun to play with for a bit, but they're all stupid, and you certainly can't bring one home to meet Father! I can understand though, warrior boys are passionate— Wait... You know about... well... you know how everything *works*, right?"

"Daksha, stop!" Rada exclaimed, embarrassed. "Of course I do." She'd read several texts on the study of biology, so she was practically an expert. This was an important mission, so there wasn't time for foolishness, but Rada twirled in front of the mirror a few times, and had to admit that she was a little impressed that she made a convincing woman of ill repute.

"Not my best work, but you'll do."

Daksha had been sneaking out for years and had never been caught by anyone other than Rada, and that was only because they used to share a room. "So what's next?"

"The trick is to crawl beneath the back fence without getting your dress dirty. Come on."

When Rada had discreetly inquired about Lord Protector Devedas to some of her gossipy junior librarians, it turned out he had already developed quite a reputation around the Capitol. Most Protectors chose to live a rather ascetic lifestyle, but it was said Devedas loved the *companionship* of women. As long as the Protectors were obligated to their Order, marriage was forbidden, but spending time with designated pleasure women was legal. However, the junior librarians whispered that because of his legendary *prowess*, Devedas had no shortage of willing companions seeking him out, including many thrill-seeking—often already married—ladies of the first caste.

She had never cared for social things, as society was just a complicated collection of individually annoying people, and she didn't like most people to begin with, but as far as Rada understood it, consorting with the lower castes was a bit of a game to many women of her highborn status. There was a certain sport to seeking out handsome warriors. Unapproved relations between castes could result in severe punishment for the lower and public embarrassment for the higher. They might have all been sworn to uphold the Law, but technically speaking a dashing young warrior was committing no crime if he was unaware of his companion's marriage status, and the Law was all about technicalities. Hence, the fashion of bored first-caste ladies disguising themselves as lowborn pleasure women, a situation which she'd been assured added to the excitement.

It made Rada question how many of her peers had secretly been sired by warriors... Most of the tall, athletic, dumb ones probably.

The plan was simple. She would pretend to be such a woman, thus avoiding the eyes of the Inquisition, and once she had the Lord Protector alone, she would tell him of the forced fraud. She would simply gloss over the part where she had disobeyed orders and broken into the restricted collection, and she would leave out the part where her father had knowingly signed off on an incomplete report as well. Then he'd do whatever unpleasant things it was Protectors did to lawbreakers.

Confident that she hadn't been spotted leaving her family's estate, Rada made her way across the Capitol. There wasn't a single Inquisitor spotted along the way, not that she would have known if one had been watching her because all they had to do to blend in was take off their frightening masks. Other than the fact that she didn't normally attract the attention of leering men, she'd passed through the workers' neighborhoods and into the markets without incident. A woman of her status wouldn't normally enter the grand market after sunset. That's what servants were for. Crowds made her uncomfortable and her mother had often warned her that there were rampaging gangs of rapists and murderers frequenting the lower districts after dark, but it *seemed* safe enough.

Now all she needed to do was present herself to the Lord Protector. He would immediately be overcome with desire, and once he swept her into his compound, she could reveal the truth. Part of her was tempted to hold off on the truth-revealing part, but that was the same part of her that had secretly enjoyed the romance novel.

Her simple plan fell apart as soon as she arrived at the Protectors' compound and discovered it was walled and had guards posted at the gates, and of course those gates were closed. Rada cursed her foolishness. What had she been expecting? An entrance marked *pleasure women deliveries?* The romance she'd read was of no help. That man had been expecting their secret meeting, and if she started making bird whistles to draw his attention it would just cause the local merchants to look at her funny. She had to find another way in. While she thought through her predicament, Rada pretended to shop at one of the many stalls in front of the Protectors' compound. One in particular was selling glass pens—a fantastic invention beloved by all librarians—which was when Rada made the enlightening discovery that the merchants' prices went *down* when their potential customer was attractive and showing off some skin.

There was a commotion and the crowd began parting. "Protector coming through, miss, best to get out of his way," the pen merchant warned her. "Some don't take kindly to being delayed." She did as cautioned, temporarily getting her hopes up, until she saw that this wasn't the Protector she was looking for. This one was a huge, ugly man, carrying a great big hammer over one silver-armored shoulder. Despite being big enough to shove anyone out of his way, he seemed remarkably polite in letting the lower-caste shoppers pass. The guards saw the Protector coming and opened the gate for him.

This was her chance. It was like the crowd opened up for the Protector and then reformed in his wake, so she walked into that uncomfortable mass of annoying humanity and followed him all the way to the entrance. Over the last few yards the crowd thinned down to nothing, and then she was standing there before a couple of warriors and a really scary-looking man with a hammer designed for bashing people's brains out.

Somehow the Protector heard her over the noise, or maybe even smelled all that ridiculous perfume her sister had slathered her in, and he turned around to study her. He may have looked like an ox, but surprisingly he had quick, intelligent eyes that wouldn't be so out of place on a librarian. He had a very deep voice. "Can I help you?"

"I'm here to see Lord Protector Devedas," Rada proclaimed.

"Do you have an appointment?"

She hadn't expected that. Rada had no idea what to say. Did pleasure women make appointments? "Yes?"

The Protector glanced at the guards, one of whom shook his head in the negative. He turned back to her. "I'm sorry. What's your name?"

She damned near blurted out her real name, but choked it off just in time. Rada hadn't thought of needing a fake name. Obviously all those married first-caste ladies carrying on their scandalous secret affairs with the Lord Protector had fake names. "Daksha." It was the first thing that popped into her head.

"I am Protector of the Law, fifteen-year senior, Karno Uttara." He planted himself squarely in her path, like a massive, unyielding steel wall. "It's a pleasure to make your acquaintance. What is your business with Lord Protector Devedas?"

"A personal matter." Rada realized that by lying to this man, he was legally justified in taking that hammer from his shoulder and whacking her with it, and that hammer was nearly as big as she was. All that would be left of her would be a red smear across the market. The merchants would have to discount their stained goods. So telling the truth was very tempting, but she couldn't risk speaking freely yet. *The walls have ears.* "A very, very *personal* matter."

Karno didn't seem convinced, neither did the two warriors behind him, who traded grins as they leaned on their spears. This wasn't going well. *What would Daksha do?* She was a natural flirt, and Rada had observed her use her skills to manipulate men into doing whatever she wanted, so Rada tried to channel her sister and gave the Protector what she thought of as a saucy look and a wink.

"Is there something wrong with your eye, miss?" he asked, expressionless.

"What? No. I'm fine . . . You see, I'm a pleasure woman, come to . . . you know . . . for the Lord Protector."

Karno nodded slowly. "Of course. May I see your obligation documents and arbiter's stamp?"

Uh-oh. Rada didn't even know they had such a thing, but everything else was regulated, so why not that as well? She'd begun sweating. "I left my papers in my other dress."

"Of course. I'll take you to him. Follow me." Karno turned and walked through the gate.

Rada breathed a sigh of relief and followed. The guards got out of her way and closed the gate behind them. Inside the compound was a courtyard, but rather than manicured grass like would be found in a typical first-caste estate, this was nothing but packed dirt and gravel, and several young Protectors were currently practicing their swordplay across it. "Thank you, Protector Karno. I am—" and the next thing she knew she was falling. Rada landed hard on the ground.

Karno was standing over her. Somehow he'd swept her legs out from under her and dropped her right into the dirt. Rada hadn't even seen him move. She'd never thought something ox-sized could be that fast. "If you're a pleasure woman, I'm the presiding judge." Karno bent over and ran his rough hands through her clothing. For a moment she thought he was going to assault her, but he'd only been searching her, and removed her knife and the pouch that held her replacement glasses. While he inspected the items, he lowered his hammer and let it rest on her sternum. Even with most of the weight still being taken by his arm, it felt like it could crush her flat.

"Ooof!"

"Expensive knife, pretty but hardly optimized for killing." He sniffed the blade. "Not poisoned. If you're an assassin, you're remarkably bad at it. Who are you really? And don't waste my time lying. My arm is getting tired." He let a little more of the hammer's weight rest on her.

She hurried and pulled down her scarf, revealing her whole face, not that it mattered since he didn't strike her as a library regular. "Senior Archivist Radamantha Nems dar Harban of the Central Library." Getting hit with a hammer was certainly not how the romance story had turned out. "I really do need to speak to Devedas. It's a matter of life and death."

"That should be obvious." The young Protectors had witnessed Karno toss her down had run over and formed a circle around them. Though they were only armed with practice swords, they all looked more than capable of beating her to death with them. "Fetch the Lord Protector," Karno ordered one of them. That boy took off at a sprint.

Karno looked into the pouch, saw the expensive spectacles

inside, removed them and let the pouch fall. There was something else very valuable in that pouch, but Rada managed not to audibly gasp when it struck the dirt. Karno held the glasses up to his eyes.

"Be careful with those. I need them to see!"

"I know what they are." Karno frowned as the world doubtlessly turned blurry for him. Then he looked down at her. "Soft. The ink-stained fingertips of a scribe, the skin of someone who never sees the light of day, and a mark on the bridge of your nose where you usually wear these things, more likely an archivist than an assassin, and certainly more firster than some low-status worker unlucky enough to be born too pretty. I believe you're telling the truth this time." Then he lifted the hammer off of her. Surprisingly, he extended one hand to help her up. She took his hand. It was hard enough to crush every delicate bone in her hand, but somehow remarkably gentle. He hoisted her right to her feet. "I don't normally shove down government officials, but occasionally our Order receives unwanted guests, witches, blasphemous creations, demonic hybrids, that sort of thing. You have my sincere apologies, my lady."

Daksha's expensive dress was torn. She'd never hear the end of it. "I can't imagine any of Devedas' many other secret female guests are greeted in such a terrible manner."

Curious, Karno tilted his head to the side. "What secret female guests?"

"His affairs!"

"What affairs?"

And that's what Rada got for listening to the gossip of junior librarians.

Now *this* was just embarrassing.

"In a way, I'm flattered that you'd believe such rumors about me, but I'm not in the habit of doing things that could cause my Order to be blackmailed, especially in this hive of stinging insects. I swear all these fools do is try to blackmail each other. It's like the favored sport in the Capitol." Lord Protector Devedas sat across the table from Rada in the small study. Servants had brought in refreshments and then left the two alone so they could speak privately. "No offense intended if there are any politicians you're overly fond of."

The list of people Rada actually liked was a very short one. "No offense has been given." It felt odd to give such a formal answer.

"Other than that, and the part where you tried to lie to Blunt Karno, a man who can sense lies like a soaring eagle can spot rabbits, your plan showed initiative. Well done, Senior Archivist Radamantha."

"Thank you." He was only humoring her, but she'd take the compliment. Even though she'd seen him outraged in the Chamber of Argument, and he'd been furious enough to duel then and perfectly polite now, Rada couldn't help but be intimidated by this man. There was just something about him that told her this was the most dangerous individual she'd ever met, and that included the Inquisition wizard who'd threatened her. That danger made him a lot more interesting than the scribes she normally associated with. "Please, call me Rada."

"Wine?" He poured her a glass. Up close, he was older than she'd expected, probably ten years her senior. Devedas had a kind smile, but it was offset by the massive scar that crossed his face. He caught her looking and touched the white line with his fingers. "This? I received it in a duel. Needless to say, I lost."

"I didn't mean to stare."

"It is kind of hard to miss. This is my little reminder that one shouldn't try to take something that isn't his, but that was a long time ago."

There was no way this man could have ever stolen anything. "I'm sure you've won many duels since," Rada said, and then realized how stupid that sounded.

"A few, but as a swordsman gets older he understands there are some fights he's not meant to win... Now, your identity is safe and your visit is only known to people who I trust. Not even the strongest wizards can spy within these walls. You can speak freely here."

Earlier it had been easy to think about lying to the Protectors about her own crimes, but with those piercing eyes looking through her, such an omission had suddenly become very difficult. "I recently provided a report to the judges concerning the legal history of the untouchables."

"I was there that day." His expression suggested he'd enjoyed it as much as she had.

"That's when I saw you and knew you'd help," she exclaimed, and wished that she hadn't, because that sounded childish. "I mean, you were actually *honest*."

"That isn't necessarily a positive trait in the Capitol. I brought shame to my Order and discovered I lack the temperament for court. Other Protectors will be handling those duties on my behalf from now on." Devedas shook his head, as if the whole thing was rather amusing. "What can I help you with?"

Rada's mouth was suddenly very dry. She drank more of the wine without even tasting it. "The report... There was a problem." For someone as devoted to the ideals of the library as Rada was, this was like admitting to the foulest deed possible. Feeding babies to demons would have been better. "The report was inaccurate."

Devedas blinked slowly. "And?"

"On *purpose*. It wasn't my fault. I was forced to leave things off. But only because I was threatened! They'd kill me if I didn't."

"Oh." He sensed her hesitation. "Listen, you might have broken the Law, but I'm not going to judge you now. The Law allows leniency for crimes committed under duress. The important thing is that you're trying to correct your mistake. You're safe. I won't allow anyone to hurt you."

It was so easy to believe him that Rada told of the events in the archives.

Devedas listened intently the entire time, and his expression darkened when she spoke of the Inquisitor. When she was done he seemed to weigh his words very carefully. "That is troubling. I'll do my best to find this man, but you have no evidence this wizard was actually from another order, let alone one as important as the Inquisition, and you can't take a criminal at his word."

She certainly hoped he was right about that, but the sabotage worried her. "But what of the conspiracy? The missing pages?"

"The Order of Inquisition is powerful, and frankly, currently better favored in this city than either of our orders. You can't expect me to accuse the Inquisition of wrongdoing on just your word."

That stung. "Then I didn't need to dress up and make a fool of myself to come here."

"I'm not disparaging you. It was wise to be discreet. Besides, I think you look lovely," Devedas said, obviously trying to put her at ease, and just for a moment his smile was so damned charming that Rada could see how rumors got started. "This isn't the first time the threat of violence has been used to sway the making of law. What is it they forced you to leave out?"

"It was some ancient history about the beginning of the castes. References to the origins of the untouchables were struck from all of our newer records." The whole thing sounded insane to put it into words. Her father had often told her that good information was the foundation of good law, but someone was trying to sabotage that foundation. She found the whole thing incredibly offensive.

"I think those advocating for their slaughter are fools. I can reassure you that I honestly don't think anything will change."

"I hope you're right."

It was surprising how Devedas could go from charming to somber so quickly. "I don't hope. I fight. I think about logistics. There are whole regions of Lok where the majority of the residents are casteless. Some houses depend on their labor to feed themselves. Our nation would rip itself apart. Most of the judges aren't foolish enough to do something like that, but if they are..." Devedas shrugged.

"We can't allow them to hurt the untouchables."

"That isn't our decision to make. The council will decide, laws will be written, and then we'll follow them."

"You don't understand, Lord Protector. The Law only exists *because* of the casteless!"

Devedas laughed. "The most perfect system of governance in the history of the world exists because of the casteless?"

"I have proof." Rada took out her glasses case and reached beneath the padding for the folded scrap of paper she'd hidden there. She regretted not wearing gloves, and as delicately as possible extracted the damaged treasure. "This was the page I was reading when I was attacked." She wanted to be clear that she would never willingly damage a library book. "I accidentally tore it out when that man grabbed me." She placed it on the table and steered it toward Devedas. He stared at it. "Oh, I'm sorry. Can you read?"

"All Protectors are literate..."

"I meant no offense, just that most warriors..."

"Actually, I was born into the first caste. When I'm not traveling the countryside cracking skulls like a barbarian, I *enjoy* books."

He read the scrap. Rada bit her lip, hoping he would believe her. She didn't have her glasses on, but she'd memorized what it said.

The Lord Protector finished and was quiet for a very long time. "How old is this?"

"The original is from the dawn of the Age of Law. This was a copy transcribed hundreds of years after."

"You believe this to be accurate?"

"Of course. That's one of the duties of my Order. To preserve the words of older documents we often make new ones. Now we use the press, but this is how it was done for generations. We pride ourselves on our accuracy. I'd have more evidence, but this is exactly the sort of thing that's been stolen. I've been afraid to return to the restricted collection to search for more." She'd seen that her father had posted more guards around the library, so hopefully the saboteurs had been scared off, but she suspected their work was already done.

Devedas was deep in thought. He finished off his wine and set the cup down far too hard. "The idea of a conspiracy offends me. I will personally oversee this investigation."

"If they find out I told you—"

"Protectors of the Law aren't known for our discretion. We're usually more *direct* in our investigations, but you have my word that I will do my best." Devedas reached out and placed one rough hand on top of hers. Rada was surprised that she was suddenly feeling very flushed. Even with the scar the Lord Protector was perhaps the most handsome man she'd ever seen. He let go of her hand and stood up. "You'll be safe. I'll have my men escort you back to your estate."

Rada surprised herself by exclaiming. "Wait!"

Devedas paused. "What?"

She didn't want to leave yet. "My disguise, the rumors," Rada blurted. She had no idea what she was doing, maybe Daksha was right, and it was time to have some experiences worth writing about. For once she was doing something extremely important, she actually felt pretty, and that made her bold. And on the spot Rada decided that, damn it, she was going to seduce this Protector. "Maybe it would be safer if I returned to my estate in the *morning* instead?"

"I see." Devedas smiled.

It turned out that some rumors were true.

Chapter 21

Thwack!

"Excellent," Ashok told Jagdish. "You almost hit me. Good work."

The risaldar stumbled away, one hand pressed to his bruised ribs. He caught himself on the prison wall and held himself there, trying to catch his breath. If they'd been using real blades, Jagdish would be dead, and they both knew it. "That was good?" he gasped.

"Well . . . Better." Ashok respected Jagdish. Ratul had taught them there were two types who could become great swordsmen, tigers and hounds. Tigers were naturally gifted, fast, graceful, and everything came easily to them, but tigers were proud, so were resistant to learning. Hounds were not born lucky, but they simply would not quit, and they just kept grunting along until the job was done. Jagdish was a hound. It was too bad Vadal hadn't obligated him, because he would've made a good Protector. Jagdish's skills had improved greatly over the last few months they'd been training together, and if he'd done this well during their knife fight Ashok might have gotten injured.

Jagdish pushed himself off the wall, lifted his shirt, and grimaced at the spreading bruise. "Damn! That hurts."

"My swordmaster told me it has to hurt, or you can't learn." Ratul may have lost his mind and descended into the madness of religious fervor, but he had been an excellent teacher before that—among the best there had ever been. "A balance must be struck between severe injury—which makes you unable to train further—and the tag-and-slap games those who play at combat mistake for training. So, as my master used to ask, is it squirting blood or is a bone sticking out?"

"No."

"Then we can continue."

"If it wasn't for this bum leg, I could take you," Jagdish lied. They both knew his leg was completely healed at this point, and besides, Ashok routinely defeated everyone, so it wasn't like Jagdish needed an excuse. "At this rate, by the time I'm ready to retire and you're about to die of old age, I'll be ready to duel you."

"Keep winding your little clock, but I don't think time will save you. The judges may move like snails, but they're not that slow." It had been fall when he'd faced Bidaya, and winter was just starting. He'd been imprisoned here for over a year now. Even by Capitol standards, he must have given the judges something interesting to argue about. "Justice isn't swift, but it is, by definition, correct. My corpse will be decorating the Inquisitor's Dome long before either of us can grow old."

Jagdish picked his wooden sword out of the dirt. "Then I'd better work harder."

"A wise answer."

"How in the ocean's name are you this good? I've trained my whole life."

Ashok shrugged. Fighting had always come easily to him. "Strike your opponent while avoiding their strikes. Hit them before they hit you. If they put something in your way, move it, then hit them. They're easier to hit if you knock them down first. There is no showmanship, no flash, only hitting and not being hit. Don't make it complicated."

"Yes, yes, I got the fundamental philosophy the first hundred times you said it, but I was the best in my class, from the house with the greatest warrior tradition in Lok, and this is ridiculous. All of the legends about Protectors are true!"

"Warriors train to fight other warriors. Protectors fight everything." That was only part of it, but he'd made a solemn vow to never speak of the Heart of the Mountain. The truth of it was, ever since touching the Heart, the movements of regular fighters seemed sluggish in comparison. It wasn't fair, but anyone who got into fair fights could expect to lose half the time.

"It's like you know what I'm going to do before I do it, every single time!"

"I don't have to have Angruvadal in my hand to feel its influence. Every fight it has ever experienced, I've experienced. It makes you predictable."

"Then perhaps I should be unpredictable!" Jagdish must have picked up a handful of dirt when he'd retrieved his sword, because he threw it at Ashok's eyes.

With Angruvadal helping, he could pick out every grain of sand suspended in the air. Borrowed lifetimes of experience enabled him to respond without thought. Ashok simply closed his eyes and felt the stinging bits bounce off his skin as he swayed to the side. He felt the wooden sword pass through the ragged remains of his shirt as he calculated all the angles and the most efficient way to respond to Jagdish's lunge. Time returned to normal and Ashok was already turning, bringing his own blunt practice blade up, and he struck Jagdish in the armpit with a push-cut that was hard enough to break skin and toss the young warrior on his back.

Jagdish landed hard and swearing. The guards watching along the wall had a good laugh at their commander's misfortune. He was enough of a man to let them watch, and they'd gained respect for their leader seeing him try to beat the unbeatable, without fail, every single day. So the laughter was all in good fun. Soldiers fought harder when they knew their leader had guts. "Are you all right down there, sir?"

"Get back to work!" Jagdish shouted at them.

"Come on, Risaldar! You think in a thousand years nobody ever thought to throw sand in a bearer's eyes?" Ashok tapped two fingers to the side of his head. "I've got the memories of someone who fought a duel where both combatants stood on the back of an elephant in here!"

Jagdish groaned as he sat up. There was a dark spot of blood showing through the side of his shirt. "I'll have Wat fetch us some elephants for tomorrow then. That'll give the men a good show."

Ashok extended one hand to help him up. It was an unconscious movement, something an equal would do for a friend. Ashok realized too late that he'd just broken the Law, but the warrior didn't seem to notice and he took Ashok's hand anyway. Jagdish might have hesitated to accept the help before, but when you fight against a man every single day, it became easy to forget the caste of their birth. Ashok hauled him to his feet.

Jagdish leaned his practice sword against the stone wall. "I'm done."

"Calling it a day already?"

"I don't think I have a choice." He pointed at the highest guard tower, where one of the men was waving a flag. Red was for potential danger, green was for regular business, and blue was for high-status visitors. This flag was blue. "They must be flying heraldry. Someone important is coming to visit. Damn it, I wasn't told of any inspections."

"Perhaps it's a judge, finally come to condemn me," Ashok said hopefully.

"Don't say that," Jagdish said as he picked up a towel and wipe the sweat from his face. "I'd miss our practice sessions."

"Don't worry, Risaldar. After they execute me, you could still try to become Angruvadal's bearer."

Jagdish paused. The idea of becoming a house's bearer wasn't something any honorable warrior took lightly. "Do you truly believe I'm worthy?" he asked earnestly.

Ashok thought that over. It was a curious thing for an honest whole man to ask a vile criminal about worthiness. "I only know of one man who may be more deserving, but it is Angruvadal's decision to make, and no one can truly understand how black steel thinks. However, I'll put in a word with my sword and ask it to not mangle you too badly if it finds you unworthy."

Jagdish paused, thoughtful. "Does that work?"

"I don't know. There's only one way to find out, but I won't be around to see if it cuts your hands off or not."

"Maybe I won't miss these practice sessions that much after all..." Jagdish muttered as he limped toward his office. "Wat! Return the prisoner to his cell."

Ashok enjoyed the bright winter sun on his face until he was put back in his hole.

They were coming for him.

The footsteps were getting closer. Some of them weren't wearing guard's boots, or prisoner's bare feet or coarse sandals, but fine soft shoes. The prestigious visitors were approaching his cell. Ashok's pulse quickened.

It was strange to be so excited for his own death, but the wizard Kule had burned away all that he had been before and replaced it with devotion. He'd proven that he was an imperfect servant of the Law, but the Law was still his foundation, his purpose, and now it required him to perish. As long as he lived, he would remain an aberration, an element of chaos in an otherwise orderly system. So Ashok would go to his death, not just willingly, but eagerly.

They stopped outside. "This is him." *Jagdish.* "Do you wish an escort?"

"We require privacy." Ashok didn't recognize this voice. "Go home, Risaldar. You're bleeding on your uniform."

"If you would allow it, your honor, I would like to stay and hear the prisoner's fate."

"Clean yourself up, you disgrace. You may return tomorrow."

Footsteps retreated as Jagdish was cast out of his own prison. *That was disrespectful.* But then Ashok corrected himself. He had been away from society for a year, and too much familiarity with the lesser classes had made him soft. A judge could do almost whatever he wanted to his inferiors, and they'd best accept those decisions. Ashok got on his knees, ready to accept his.

The door opened. Three men were standing in the hall, and in the instant before he put his forehead to the floor, he saw that one was wearing the blue-gray and bronze of a Great House Vadal judge, another was wearing the white robes of an Arbiter Superior, but most importantly, the one in the center was dressed all in black and wearing the ornate golden mask of the Grand Inquisitor himself, one of the most powerful people in the Capitol.

Ashok kept his face down. They wouldn't have sent such important men if the time of his judgment wasn't at hand. His heart rejoiced.

"Rise, Ashok."

He lifted his head. The three men had entered and spread out. There were lesser Inquisitors in the hall. The arbiter seemed very nervous about the hems of his fine robes touching the straw.

The Grand Inquisitor stopped directly before him. It was hard to tell in the uniform, but he seemed to be an average-sized man, gone a bit plump, and the only parts of his body that were visible were his small dark eyes and the crow's feet around them. "You are aware of who I am?"

"Grand Inquisitor Omand Vokkan."

"Correct. I wish to make this official so that there can be absolutely no question as to the validity of your sentence." He reached into his sash and pulled out a piece of gold jewelry, shaped like a raven. "You recognize the symbol of my office?" Ashok nodded, so Omand handed him some folded papers. "Here are my documents."

Ashok had no reason to doubt him, but Omand must have been as much a stickler for the letter of the Law as Ashok was, so he carefully inspected the papers. They had been signed and stamped by several extremely high-status officials. *The criminal Ashok the Black Heart is remanded into Inquisition custody to be dealt with according to the Grand Inquisitor's wishes.*

"Do you concur?" Omand asked the Vadal judge.

"He's all yours." This was the one who had insulted Risaldar Jagdish. The haughty judge spit on the straw. "Good riddance."

Omand looked to the arbiter.

"This transfer of custody is witnessed and approved."

"Thank you, honorable gentlemen. Now I need to speak with the prisoner alone."

The two of them walked out. A lower-ranked Inquisitor entered, placed a stool behind Omand, then left, shutting the door behind him.

"Inquisition business." Omand sat down and made himself comfortable. "This shouldn't take long."

And then Omand remained there, perfectly still, silently studying him for several long minutes. It was difficult to tell what a man was thinking when you could only see his eyes. Such silent judgment probably unnerved most prisoners, but it meant nothing to a man incapable of fear. So Ashok studied him back. What he found behind those eyes was intense, cold, and somehow broken. Ashok knew it well, because he'd seen something similar every time he had ever looked into a mirror. It took hard men to maintain the sanctity of the Law.

"I will truthfully answer any questions you have to the best of my ability," Ashok stated. "If you wish to confirm the accuracy of my answers, I will not resist any tortures you wish to apply. You have my word that Angruvadal will remain sheathed in your presence."

"It is my understanding that you were an unwilling victim in this fraud."

"I had no knowledge of my true origins until last year. When I found out, I took action."

"You never suspected the truth, or doubted the false past which was created for you?"

"I did not, but ignorance is no defense. I was born a casteless and took honors which were illegal for me to take, so I must be punished."

"You won't ask for mercy?"

"Of course not." Mercy was a strange concept that Ashok had always struggled with. Mercy was merely the weak trying to rob judgment. "I'm guilty."

"So the Law truly is your essence... Kule wasn't lying about you."

Kule? Ashok tilted his head. "You know of the wizard's treachery?"

"Yes. He has been interrogated and punished."

Had Devedas brought them to justice? His former brother would never forgive him, but Ashok had known that Devedas would do the right thing. "How?"

"That is not your concern."

"Harta? Chavans?" Ashok had no problem going into the eternal nothing, but he would die easier knowing that they'd gone first.

"I'm aware of Bidaya's conspirators, and they will all be dealt with in time." Omand waved one hand dismissively. Harta was an extremely important man, so doubtless the Inquisition had to tread carefully, but nonetheless, Ashok was glad justice would be satisfied. "They're not why I'm here. One other question, an unofficial curiosity really... If you are such a devotee of the Law, why kill a member of the First to avenge a casteless? Was it so personal because she was your mother?"

"Regardless of my personal beliefs, Bidaya had committed crime."

"Oh, so you weren't avenging your mother, you were avenging the Law? If only I'd known your motivations were so pure all along, I wouldn't have had to come all this way."

Ashok paused for a long time, mulling over the Grand Inquisitor's sarcastic response. He had sworn to tell the truth, so he was obligated to continue, no matter how uncomfortable those truths were. "I've had time to think about it since. Bidaya didn't just take my mother from me, she made it so that she never existed at all.

Gone. As if they never were. I know that I shouldn't care, but that *offended* me. Anger clouded my judgment that night. It still clouds my judgment now. There's no excuse for the evil I've done."

"It is good that you recognize the magnitude of your crimes."

Even now, after all this time rotting away in a prison with little else to do but try to remember, he only had tiny glimpses of his real past before the sword—a white smile on a tanned face, eyes bright and proud of her boy, a gentle hand picking bits of grass from his hair as they huddled together for warmth in one corner of a crowded shack—and for all he knew those were fabrications of his imagination. "Forgive my words, Inquisitor, for they sound harsh, but to the ocean with Bidaya. I know that the casteless are little more than animals, but she was *my mother.*"

"You learned the truth in the Capitol. Having just made the same journey myself I know how long it takes." Omand rubbed his lower back, as if he was so terribly road-weary from what had probably been a ride in a carriage filled with cushions. "This was no heat-of-the-moment crime of outrage. You had weeks to calm yourself, to seek legal counsel from the judges or to speak with your Order, but instead you committed an act of public, premeditated butchery, supposedly for the Law, but really for someone you can't even remember."

"I would do it again," Ashok said.

Omand nodded thoughtfully. "I've come to give you your new orders."

That was a strange choice of word. Orders implied some necessary action on his part. There was only one order that seemed likely to be given, and his sword would disapprove. "Am I to kill myself, then?"

"That seemed to be the logical choice, but the Vadal delegation wouldn't hear of it. They didn't care what was done with you, as long as you died by a hand other than your own, preferably in combat, but they grudgingly accept execution. They're willing to take *some* risk to get their sword back, but they refused to simply throw it away. It took some debate before they agreed to turn you over to me. So no, Ashok, you will not kill yourself, though when you hear your orders, you may wish to."

He couldn't imagine what else it could be, unless they wanted him to walk from here to the Capitol, naked and barefoot, probably starving and dueling every desperate fool along the way, all so the whole world could mock him before he presented himself at the Inquisitor's Dome to be strung up and sunburned to death. But if a penance walk was what justice required, then he'd gladly do it. "I will serve."

"Have you been to the lands of Great House Akershan?"

"Yes. The Order has sent me before."

"Good. I'm sending you again."

Akershan was the far to the south. It was a cold, desolate place, with tall, rocky shores overlooking an icy sea infested with demons. Yet just beyond the ice coast was Fortress, the impenetrable island of criminal fanatics and their deadly magic. *Ah, a suicide mission.* This was a much better death than he'd hoped for.

Ashok's expression must have changed, because Omand hesitated. The condemned should not *smile.* "Yes?"

"Since I'm to die, it is wise to let me take some lawbreakers with me. I will gladly attack Fortress."

"You would, wouldn't you!" For the leader of such a nefarious, secretive order, Omand laughed like a regular man. Ashok had expected something with more cruelty in it. He didn't understand why the Grand Inquisitor thought that was so funny, but then Ashok pictured Angruvadal, lost on the floating ice or sinking to the bottom of the sea where demons lived.

"It would be best if I left my sword here. Once I'm dead, it can choose a new bearer. That is the most honorable solution."

The Inquisitor wiped his eyes. Tears were just another form of saltwater. "I must say, Ashok, you're everything they made you out to be and more. Breaching Fortress is a task that entire legions have failed at, but you would surely try. From your reputation, you'd probably even discover a whale that miraculously hadn't gone extinct and train it to carry you across the sea!" The way Omand's mirth disappeared so quickly suggested it had never existed at all. "I'm afraid your assignment is far more mundane than that. A prophet has risen among the casteless in Akershan and started a rebellion."

He had heard something about that from Blunt Karno. It was surprising that over a year later this would still be a problem. "Do you wish for me to find and kill their prophet?"

"Finding and killing seems to be your solution for everything, isn't it?"

Ashok shrugged.

Omand leaned forward on his chair and lowered his voice conspiratorially. "Yes, you will travel to Akershan and find him."

"Very well."

"Only you're not to kill him. You will *protect* him."

Ashok blinked. "I don't understand."

"Since it was your title for twenty years, I'd have assumed a greater familiarity with the concept. Your orders are to find the casteless prophet, pledge your services to him, join his rebels, and do as he commands. He is to be your new master." Omand paused to let that sink in.

It was the Inquisitors who skulked about in the shadows, pretending to be things that they weren't. Inquisitors often lied about who they were to infiltrate cults and criminal conspiracies. They were skilled in deceit and trickery. "I'm no Inquisitor."

"I'm not speaking of going undercover, Ashok." Omand's voice had turned low and dangerous. "Oh no, you're far too noble for that. You're many things, but you're not a liar. There's no hiding your identity. You'll present yourself to this prophet as yourself, Ashok the Black Heart, the casteless murderer, the fallen Protector, in all your infamy, and you will swear allegiance to his cause and his false gods, and you will follow his orders as if they had all the might of the Capitol and spoke with the voice of the presiding judge himself. You will serve for the rest of your days. That is your punishment."

Mind reeling, Ashok couldn't respond, couldn't speak, could barely think. It was as if the prison cell was spinning around him.

Omand pulled out another piece of paper and handed it over. "Read this."

It was as Omand said. The written orders were clear. Ashok was to join the casteless rebels. Ten members of the committee had signed off, and it was stamped by the presiding judge.

Their word was law.

"Why?"

"The *why* never mattered to you before. Do you question the validity of these orders, prisoner?"

"No."

"Good. But the dumbstruck look on your face amuses me, so I will tell you *why*. Every man has a place. You're a casteless criminal, so your place will be with the casteless criminals. This is your obligation. This is your sentence. The rest of your pathetic life will serve as an example to any who dreams of transgressing. If you were a normal man, I would take away your life, but your life is the Law, so I'm taking that instead."

Ashok couldn't breathe. This was worse than death. This was banishment, and not just banishment from a house, but banishment from all of society. This was the most dishonorable punishment imaginable, not just dying as a lawbreaker, but living as one. In a daze, he tried to unbuckle his sword belt, but his fingers had become too clumsy.

"What do you think you're doing?"

"Leaving my sword here. Angruvadal can't be dishonored like this."

"The sword goes with you."

"No. It can't." Ashok looked up, confused and hurt. The sword was more important than the bearer. Bearers lived and died, but the sword symbolized the strength of a house. "It'll surely be destroyed."

"The Law has spoken. You're still the bearer."

"But Great House Vadal—"

"Never should have let your foulness pollute the world. Now they will pay for their transgressions," Omand hissed.

There had been no Vadal signatures on the second document. Judgment had been given to more than just Ashok today.

"Listen carefully now. For you to fail in keeping these instructions is to disgrace the sanctity of the Law even more than you already have. These are your final orders. You will take Angruvadal and you will leave tonight, in secret. You will sneak out like a thief. You will speak to no one. You will let no guards see you. All will believe you to be a coward and an oathbreaker. You will leave Vadal as quickly as possible and not look back. You will travel to Akershan without delay. Allow no one to stop or detain you. You're forbidden from ever speaking of this meeting. You are bound from ever talking about these orders or the names upon them. As far as the world knows, you are nothing but a casteless criminal with a magic sword. Thus says the Law."

"Thus . . . thus says . . . the Law."

"Do I have your oath?"

Ashok couldn't form the words.

"Give me your oath!"

"I swear to follow these orders," he whispered.

Omand reached out and snatched the papers from Ashok's fingers. "I told you that you'd rather kill yourself." He stood up, walked away, and thumped his fist against the door. An Inquisitor on the other side opened it for him.

Ashok felt as if he'd taken a severe blow to the head. It was taking all of his concentration to stay on his knees and not fall over. He thought about taking Angruvadal out and plunging it into his guts. It would have hurt far less.

This was a betrayal of *everything*.

Omand paused in the doorway. "I must admit, of all the many terrible things I've done in my career, this is the harshest punishment I have ever dispensed. Farewell, Ashok."

Chapter 22

〰〰〰

Jagdish drank his beer and thought about his latest shame. Both were bitter.

The warriors' hall was loud. The air was filled with pipe smoke. Drinks were flowing freely. News had spread quickly. Representatives from the Capitol had gone to Cold Stream to deliver judgment to the Disgrace of Vadal. By the time Jagdish had gotten here, wanting only to drink his anger away, all the other warriors were already talking about it, so he'd listened in annoyed silence.

"It was the masks that came for him. That means he's going to roast on the Inquisitor's Dome."

"Naw. Beheading."

"But no ax! They'll use a wood saw. Slow and squirting and kicking. I heard that's how they do it in Vokkan, and the Grand Inquisitors from House Vokkan."

"You're a moron. Harta won't allow that. Not *honorable* enough. With our luck they'll send a whole paltan to fight the Black Heart, make it a nice and proper bearer's death they can write songs about...The arbiters will probably sell tickets."

"They wouldn't do that...Would they?"

"Oceans, Nayak, they'd gladly spend fifty of us to wrap this mess up. In a generation there'll be a play about it in the Capitol.

The tragic final scene will be the actors playing us getting cut to pieces so the bearer can have a right honorable enough death." That warrior was fairly drunk by this point. "I bet the actor playing Harta will deliver a fine speech, knee deep in the paint supposed to be our blood."

"What do you think, Jagdish?"

Of course, they wouldn't leave him alone about it. Oh no, he'd been there that terrible night. Jagdish had actually fought the Black Heart, then he'd bravely kept him imprisoned, and Jagdish was the only man who had the balls to command that monster to spar against him. Or at least, that's what many of the Vadal warriors were saying. The ones who thought Jagdish a fool were smart enough to only say it behind his back.

Jagdish took his time looking at the many warriors sitting around the long table, and the others who were standing around the edges, all eagerly awaiting his opinion. He'd drawn a crowd. The hall had even quieted down a bit to hear what he had to say. Jagdish poured the last of the beer down his throat. The cheap watery swill wasn't nearly strong enough tonight. "All I know for sure is that's the last of my month's beer allotment."

"You can have one of my ration, Risaldar!" exclaimed one of the youngest, who signaled a slave to bring another pitcher.

Maybe being the resident expert wasn't *all bad.* That was like the...eighth? Tenth? He couldn't remember, but the soldiers kept them coming, so he wasn't complaining. The pitcher was set in front of him, and Jagdish refilled his mug. "I was sent away before I heard. The sentence will probably be announced tomorrow." The younger warriors seemed let down, the veterans were used to never being told anything, but all soldiers liked to guess about how their leadership was going to screw them next. "It could be execution or it could be another duel. I just don't know."

"Bidaya threw a bunch of us at him before, and what a mess that turned out!" shouted one of the drunks. Then he realized nobody was laughing, and he was catching a few angry glares from his friends. "No disrespect, Risaldar."

Jagdish just kept drinking, pretending to have not heard. He'd weathered far worse insults from far more important people.

"So if it's to be a fight, Jagdish, you know him better than anyone, how many of us will they have to toss at that maniac so he can die happy enough for the sword not to break?"

"If the judges rule that way..." Jagdish mulled it over. "Hmmm...Tough question. Honor would demand a sporting duel, and that's hard when there's an ancestor blade involved. Depending on the ground and what we're allowed to bring, pole arms, maybe bows, it'll square up quick, even with him using Angruvadal, our armor, numbers, and reach go a long ways. Give us space to maneuver, we'd do better. A close engagement where Ashok could get his back against something solid and only fight a few of us at a time...Tricky."

"Come on, Jagdish. We all figure if that's how the judges decide, you're probably the man leading the charge."

He hadn't thought of that, but he was certainly expendable enough. "To make it sure? Assuming I'm given fully equipped veterans, of the best Vadal has to offer, I'd ask for a paltan."

A few mouths fell open. Jagdish knew Ashok's capabilities far better than they did, and he'd just suggested *fifty* experienced men to give them a fair fight.

"We might have a chance if I'm allowed archers." Jagdish took another drink. "Winning would still be questionable. To minimize casualties I'd want two full paltans at once."

"A hundred men against one?" A risaldar from another legion had walked up to their table. "I do believe this man has had too much to drink!"

Jagdish looked down at his mug. *Sadly, not even close.* "You don't know what you're dealing with. Anyone who underestimates the Black Heart is a fool. You might think the stories are exaggerated, but legends exist for a reason. They say he's only a man..." Jagdish chuckled and shook his head. "Even without the sword in his hand, he's something else."

"He's evil," agreed one of the drunks.

"He might fight like a sea demon, but I can't call him evil. But he's not good either. Ashok simply is." Jagdish had been thinking about this for quite some time, so the words seemed to fall out. "He's like a weapon disguised as a man. We don't say a blade is good or evil, do we? What it gets used for depends on who is wielding it. Our house loved him until we lost control and the blade cut us instead. I've seen him spare lives when he didn't have to and I've seen him try to better warriors who'd just tried to defeat him. Evil? Not really...No doubt unfeeling, merciless even, but at the same time Ashok is everything our caste should aspire to be, fearless, unflinching, with a personal code of honor stronger than the Law itself."

Everyone was staring at him.

Damn. Maybe he had drunk too much.

The newcomer had taken offense. They may have been of the same rank, but Jagdish had just stepped over a line. "Are my ears broken, or is a fellow officer of Great House Vadal paying respects to a casteless murderer?"

"Shut your mouth, fish breath!" One of Jagdish's more inebriated listeners stood up so fast it knocked over his chair. "Or tomorrow you'll be shitting out your teeth." He shoved the newcomer. The other risaldar pushed him back, knocking the drunken soldier to the floor. Several other warriors around the room leapt to their feet. Their caste was always looking for a good fight.

"Enough," Jagdish snapped. He'd been dishonored enough for one day. The last thing he needed was for these fools to go about wrecking the warriors' hall on his behalf. Brawls and even knife fights were common here, but his reputation had suffered enough already. "Our guest is correct to be offended. I misspoke. The Black Heart is a foul creature, and I look forward to whatever his sentence is, as any of our caste should. To say otherwise would be foolish. No offense was intended."

One might question the sanity of the man who trained daily against a killer, but it was still stupid to test his skills. The other risaldar sized him up, decided he would probably lose, and gave Jagdish a small bow. "No offense has been taken."

Duel avoided, Jagdish finished off the beer, then shoved the mug across the table. He'd have loved to cut the smug off the other warrior's face, but there was only one man Jagdish wanted to fight right now. "I'm going home. I've got either an execution or a battle to prepare for tomorrow." Many of these men had served with him before, and a few were his subordinates from the prison's day watch. They might have had questions for him about his opinion of the prisoner, but they knew to get out of his way.

The area outside the hall was much quieter and the air cooler. Jagdish paused beneath the red lanterns to catch his breath. Across the street a group of soldiers were smoking and lounging in front of a brothel. One of their junior nayaks had passed out drunk in the gutter. Everywhere else in the city, their caste had to be on their best behavior, but in this district, dignity was quickly forgotten. At least, before abandoning him to visit the pleasure women, the young soldier's companions had rolled him onto his side so he wouldn't drown in his own vomit.

Tomorrow Ashok would probably be dead or beyond his reach, and Jagdish would be deprived of his chance for glory. Other warriors of far higher status would try to take up the sword, and surely Angruvadal would choose one of them long before a low-status nobody like Jagdish had his chance. That wasn't justice. None of them had fought Ashok. None of them had the courage to strive against him every day... Only Jagdish did... But then again, that training made it impossible for him to maintain any illusion of being able to defeat Ashok himself. He felt cheated, but logically he knew the only thing he was really being cheated of was the opportunity to get slaughtered in a lopsided duel. Angry, and not exactly sure why, Jagdish walked down the road until he reached the main street through the warrior's district.

If he turned north, the road would take him back to his house and his loving wife. If he turned south, the road would take him through the city gates, and beyond that was Cold Stream Prison.

Jagdish took out his pocket watch. The hand said it was after midnight. The arbiter had commanded him to stay away from the prison until tomorrow.

By the letter of the law, it was tomorrow.

Chapter 23

Vadal City stretched before Omand, hundreds of lights and tens of thousands of lives, all beneath him, literally and figuratively. As an honored high-status guest, the Grand Inquisitor had asked for one entire tower of the great house as his temporary residence. He'd told them that he preferred to be above the odor of the city, and thus required the highest possible altitude. Normally these rooms were reserved for the Thakoor's immediate family, but the local authorities had been quick to grant his request. Unlike most men of his status, Omand didn't care about personal comfort. A humble inn would have done just as well, but he'd been curious to see if they'd oblige his extreme request. It was good to occasionally test various great house families to make sure they were sufficiently frightened of his office.

The Vadal castle was ancient, constructed in the days when man could still cross the seas, though most of it had been torn down by demons then rebuilt during the Age of Kings. There were still spots on the walls where the original carvings had been defaced to remove the likenesses of the old forbidden gods, though Omand could trace the dusty outlines with his fingertips and guess at what they'd shown. Most people were unaware that there had been a multitude of different religions to choose from before the Age of Kings, and from the shape of the scars in the stone he could tell that the tribe who had gone on to become the Vadal had been one of the strange ones who'd worshipped the god with an elephant's head and the blue lady with four arms. Omand chuckled at their foolishness and moved on.

The Vadal tower wasn't nearly as magnificent as anything in the Capitol, but it would suffice. The important thing was that the roof made for an excellent place to hold a clandestine meeting.

Omand looked up when he heard the beating of huge wings. A giant obsidian vulture materialized from the darkness overhead and landed smoothly on top of the tower. Still in motion, twisting and smoking, feathers melted into steel, and talons turned into boots. Within a few steps the bird was gone and a man in shining armor stood before him. Omand was impressed. His own magic was stronger, but Sikasso was extremely gifted. The assassin bowed to the Grand Inquisitor. "Good evening, my lord."

"I like the uniform. A very nice touch."

He spread his arms, proudly displaying the lamellar armor of the Protector Order. "A rare and expensive collector's item, but an elaborate plot requires a meticulous dedication to detail." Sikasso lifted his eyes. They were still glowing from the aftereffect of the transformation. "Ashok has escaped the prison."

Of course he had. "That man is as reliable as the sunset."

"If you'd realized he was truly as devoted to the Law as everyone made him out to be, you wouldn't have needed to bring me along."

"Perhaps," Omand mused. "But every man, even Ashok, has a limit to his devotion. If there was any imperfection in Kule's work, and even a scrap of conscience remains, then you will prove most vital."

"The walls didn't even slow him. As you predicted, no alarms were raised. He's running south, staying off the roads, and sticking to the fields. The route he's taking, the only place to cross the river is at Sutpo Bridge. He's making excellent time and should be there by dawn."

"That's splendid news." This wasn't familiar territory, but Omand had memorized the locations and strengths of every garrison, Vadal and its neighbors both. Sutpo was strong, but not too strong. He couldn't have asked for a better location. "Are you prepared for what's next?"

Sikasso feigned insult. "As one artist to another, you wound me, Inquisitor. Are you ready for my men to proceed?"

"The local judge is floating face down in the river. The Arbiter Superior will be found in his stateroom sometime tomorrow missing his head. I have a hunch that orders from the Capitol saying Ashok is to be executed will be found in his desk, but as for his head?" Omand spread his hands apologetically. "I'm not sure where that wound up . . . So yes, I do believe there is no turning back now."

The assassin nodded. "Just don't forget our deal." Then Sikasso took several fast steps and leapt over the side of the tower.

Don't forget our deal? Omand chuckled. He was staging a coup. There had been so many bargains struck, with so many nefarious groups and dark forces that it was becoming a challenge to keep track of them all. He walked to the edge and looked down. A black shadow flew over the castle wall before disappearing into the darkness.

The Grand Inquisitor leaned on the parapet and studied the city. Because of the smoke and steam rising from the workers' district, he couldn't make out the Cold Stream prison's watch-fires from here. There was no way he could see his plans unfold, and that saddened him a bit. Omand had been waiting a long time for this. Deciding the air was too chill, he returned to the stairs, content in the knowledge that by morning the actions of his pawns would shake Great House Vadal to its foundations, and as news spread it would strike fear into all of the houses. In time everything would be destabilized, and it would take a firm hand and strong leadership to restore order.

It was a tragedy. A great revolution had just begun and Omand was the only one who knew about it.

Chapter 24

Jagdish tripped on a loose stone, stumbled, and almost fell over.

Maybe trying to sneak in a duel to the death with Ashok before he could be executed wasn't the best idea, considering how many beers he'd had tonight, but damn it, Jagdish was a warrior, and he wasn't going to sit around and let some high-status ponce steal Angruvadal from him. So Jagdish put his hands on his knees and hung his head until the dizziness passed. Vomiting seemed like a good idea, but a bad waste of alcohol, so he resumed his journey, until a few minutes later his guts disagreed with him and he had to pause to throw up in the grass.

Jagdish wiped his beard on his uniform sleeve. He felt lighter. *Now* he was ready to duel.

The walls of his duty station loomed before him. Commanding the Cold Stream garrison had been intended as a punishment, but it wasn't really that bad an assignment. There were some damned good men under his command, and Jagdish had to admit that his daily sparring sessions had made him a much better fighter than when he'd started here.

There was supposed to be a bonfire along this section of road after dark, so that the guards in the watch tower could spot anyone approaching the gates, but nobody had lit the wood piled in the

Both moons were bright tonight, and there was quite a bit of light to see by, so maybe the night watch had simply gotten lazy. Jagdish looked up at the tower, but nobody had spotted him and begun waving a signal flag. He scowled. *Somebody's getting reprimanded for this.*

There were two entrances on the north wall, a big gate for wagons, and a man door next to it. There should have been a guard near each, but he didn't see anyone. Jagdish could be lenient at times, so he didn't mind them having a chair. He'd even allowed a small shack to be built so they could have shade in the sun or protection from the rain, but there was no one in the shack either.

There were vines growing up the stone walls, and Jagdish leaned against them while he caught his breath. They were soft and cool, and it was very tempting to go to sleep, but he only wanted to catch his breath before he started yelling at someone. He was really wishing that he'd not drunk so much earlier, but then again, Ashok had told him that he needed to be unpredictable, and showing up to a duel to the death drunk off his ass? Even Ashok wouldn't predict that!

Sufficiently composed, Jagdish banged on the man door with his fist. "This is your risaldar! Get out here, Nayak, and open this damned door! Let me in so I can claim my magic sword!" Even though the wood was extremely thick, he could hear commotion on the other side. *Good.* That meant that not all of his men were sleeping or screwing around while their commander was gone. Then he noticed something shiny lying in the grass. He went over and kicked at it with his boot. There was a solid *clunk.* Curious, Jagdish bent over and discovered that it was the blade of a halberd. The shaft was stuck into the bushes. It was one of the arms issued to his gate guards. Swearing, he pulled the pole arm free. "Somebody is getting ripped for this stunt. This is dereliction of duty!"

There was a loud metallic clang as a gate bar was removed. Jagdish turned back to discover that it was the larger door being opened, for some reason. That was odd. Now he could hear voices, lots of them, and more coming. The heavy wood parted and torchlight crept through the gap. Jagdish shielded his eyes, and it took his befuddled mind a moment to realize that the figures on the other side weren't wearing the blue-gray and bronze of Vadal warriors, but were dressed in sack cloth and rags.

Prisoners.

"Oceans." Jagdish took up the halberd in both hands. "Guards! *Guards!* They're escaping!"

The massive door flew open behind the weight of dozens of bodies, and suddenly Jagdish was standing alone in front of a mob.

He'd never sobered up quite so fast in his life.

"Return to your cells!" Jagdish ordered in vain, because they were already surging toward him. The issue halberd had a small ax blade for chopping, and a long spike for thrusting, and Jagdish aimed that spike at the first prisoner in line. "Stop!"

But it was like they hadn't even heard him. A terrible cry went up, part desperation, part terror, and part exhilaration at being free. Only the first prisoners in line had seen him, and unluckily for them the ones behind shoved them forward, right into the path of Jagdish's blade.

He hadn't even thought about it. The reaction was automatic as he stabbed a prisoner in the chest. The hardened steel was designed to punch through armor, and it went through the thin man almost as if he wasn't there. Skin split as easily as paper until the ax blade ground against ribs and stopped him flat. The prisoner screamed in agony as the mob kept shoving him forward. Jagdish's boots slid across the gravel as all that energy was pushed down the haft. Then he was surrounded by bodies. Sweat gleamed in the firelight. He could smell the fear. *This is madness.*

Yanking the spike free, Jagdish stumbled back as the dying prisoner fell and was trampled by the bare feet of the fleeing mob. Jagdish swept the wide blade back and forth, biting into arms and legs. "Return to your cells!" But the prisoners just kept pushing past him, some already limping and bleeding from earlier altercations, and Jagdish kept on swinging. More tried to run right over him, while others realized there was some sort of resistance ahead, and went crashing off to the sides through the bushes. Jagdish realized that the prisoners were terrified, but not of him. Pushing past a desperate warrior with a razor sharp pole arm was preferable to whatever they were running from.

There were too many of them. Someone hurled a torch at his face, and Jagdish was barely able to move aside, even though it singed his mustache and left his vision flashing and orange. A thin prisoner wearing nothing but a loincloth screamed and leapt at him. Jagdish smashed him in the face with the butt of the halberd, dropping him to the ground. Another thrust a stolen guard's sword at him, but Jagdish desperately parried it away, and then sliced through that prisoner's stomach. That one seemed almost surprised as he lurched off to die. His freedom hadn't lasted very long at all.

"Return to your cells!" Jagdish bellowed, but they were having none of it. Then most of the mob was past him, sprinting down the road or scattering into the fields. His initial reaction was to run after them, because when something ran, a wolf's reaction was to chase it, but Jagdish wasn't just a warrior, he was a commander. *My men!* What had happened to his men?

The prisoner he'd struck in the face was crawling into the grass. A swift kick to the ribs flipped him over, then Jagdish pushed the spike against his throat. "What's happening here? Talk or die!"

Blood spilled from the prisoner's broken nose and painted his teeth. "The Fallen went to killing the guards, then all of us too!"

"What?" Jagdish pushed the spike in enough to break the skin. "Don't lie to me!"

"It's true! I swear. Some other Protectors came, demanding to see him. The guards opened the gate, but they started cutting your boys to bits, then went cell to cell, hacking everyone down, and we're next if you don't let me go. Please, please..."

Such fear couldn't be faked. Jagdish stepped back. This was madness. There was no way Ashok would do such a thing. The prisoner scrambled to his feet, clutching at his bloody throat, and ran into the darkness. The torch that had been thrown at him was still lying in the road, burning. Other prisoners were scattered around him, moaning or dead. He couldn't even remember hitting that many of them, and then he looked down and realized he was covered in blood. "My men..." Jagdish started toward the gate in a daze.

More prisoners were running across the inner yard, but they were efficiently cut down by a figure who materialized behind them before they could reach the open gate. At first Jagdish thought it was one of his guards, but then the figure stepped out of the shadows, intricate armor gleaming with silver inlays, and the golden symbol of the Protector Order on his chest.

"What's going on here?" Jagdish demanded.

The Protector started toward him. His hood was up, and in

the shadows beneath all Jagdish could see was the stubbled edge of a strong jaw and eyes that seemed somehow too reflective. It wasn't Ashok, but it was one of his former brothers, and thus nearly as intimidating.

The Protector didn't answer.

"I am Risaldar Jagdish, commander of this garrison. You will answer me. What law have we broken?"

The man kept walking, sword held down at his side. He tilted his head, acting as if he'd not heard, or he was confused, and instinct screamed at Jagdish that the Protector was trying to close the distance so he could strike. As he got closer to the torch, Jagdish could see that the Protector's gauntlets and boots were soaked and dripping with blood.

"To the sea with you then." Jagdish took up the halberd in both hands and shifted into a fighting stance. He aimed the spike at the Protector's chest. "Come and try me."

White teeth reflected the moons. The Protector was smiling. Now they understood each other.

They circled around the torch, sizing each other up. Jagdish had a few feet of reach advantage, but if the Protector could slip inside the arc of the longer weapon, then he would be at the mercy of the swordsman. The Protector's vitals were shielded by some of the best-crafted armor in the world. Jagdish was wearing a cotton uniform with his own vomit on it. He had been taken by surprise after a long night of drinking, and interrupted a Protector who was already warmed up by a killing spree.

I should have gone home to Pakpa.

The Protector lifted his sword, almost as if he were showing it off. There was a gentle curve to the blade, a slashing style that the horsemen of Zarger preferred, nothing like the broad, straight swords of the northern houses. Then he reached out with the sword, tapping at the end of the Jagdish's halberd, almost as if this was a game. Jagdish tried to knock the steel away, but his move was clumsy, and the Protector turned the halberd and stepped back, seeming to enjoy himself.

"You've arrived too late." Like his sword, his accent was from the high deserts, but Protectors hailed from every house. "Pathetic drunk."

"Only on special occasions," Jagdish muttered. What the hell had he been thinking? Here he was, being intimidated by a Protector, when he'd come here fully prepared to be struck down by one in a desperate attempt to win honor. Jagdish's grip tightened on the wood. *To hell with him.* "What have you done to my men?"

But the Protector didn't answer. Instead he lunged forward, catching the blade of the halberd with his sword and trying to shove it aside. Rather than step back as the Protector must have expected, Jagdish kicked the torch. It flew forward and bounced off armor, sparks flying, and as the Protector twisted away, Jagdish followed, stabbing with the halberd. The spike glanced off the lamellar shoulder plate, but Jagdish kept on him, stabbing, lifting and cutting, forcing the Protector back. The halberd came back, flecked with silver paint, but no blood.

Jagdish was enraged. "This is my prison! These are my men!" The Protector countered, lunging forward, striking at the halberd shaft, trying to force it down, but the warrior was having none of it. When his attacker made it past the spike, Jagdish turned and slammed both arms forward, crashing the length of wood into the armored chest. The Protector went flailing back, tripped over one of the dying prisoners, to crash against the stone wall.

There was a burning sensation on his shoulder. Jagdish glanced down to see that his uniform was hanging open. He'd been cut. *Didn't even see that one coming.* He roared, lifted the pole arm, and went after the Protector. Jagdish hacked through vines and ivy, and sent a shower of dust from the wall beneath, but the Protector had already scrambled aside.

The Protector counterattacked, blade flashing through the air. Jagdish tried to block, but he'd put himself too close to the wall, and the haft scraped against stone, slowing it *just* a bit. He felt the cut as a terrible fire burned down his ribs. Grimacing, he moved away from the wall, striking with both ends of the long weapon, trying to make distance, but the Protector followed, constantly swinging, his blade a blur of motion. Splinters flew from the halberd shaft, but better splinters of wood than bone, and Jagdish sacrificed his weapon to save his life.

The halberd went flying across the road.

The Protector's eye instinctively followed the bouncing pole arm, just for a heartbeat, but that was enough for Jagdish to launch a kick into his opponent's leg. Nothing broke, but it pushed him back long enough for Jagdish to draw his own sword.

They were back where they started. Only now Jagdish was bleeding and his foe was not. Slick, hot blood was running down his belly, but not fast enough to drop him yet.

The Protector's hood had fallen back, revealing a hard, square face. "You're better than expected."

"You're worse," Jagdish said honestly. Ashok was far faster than this one. With all his clumsy mistakes, if he'd been fighting the Black Heart he would've been dead five times over by now. It seemed that not all Protectors were created equal.

They met in the road, sword blades flying. Jagdish's issue weapon was a traditional Vadal broadsword. It was heavier than his opponent's weapon, thus a bit slower, but it was also longer, and the extra mass was sufficient to knock the lighter blade aside. The Protector kept slashing at him, but even with the fog in his head, Jagdish's muscles remembered what to do. Months of training with the finest killer in Lok had prepared him. He caught the edge with his flat, and then again, always moving, interrupting his opponents lightning quick swings with fast strikes of his own. The Protector seemed to grow frustrated. Unlike Ashok, this one actually seemed capable of getting tired.

Jagdish pressed the attack, cutting and thrusting. His arm burned, but he kept it high, no delay, never settling into a pattern, and never, ever letting up, even for an instant. The Protector over-extended. Jagdish used his sword to push the blade further astray, and then slugged the Protector in the face hard with his left fist. A jolt ran down Jagdish's arm, but that square jaw gave and the Protector took a few halting steps back, stunned and hurting.

He might have finished him then, if it wasn't for the interruption. "Enough games. We've got work to do." Jagdish spun around to see who else was speaking. There was another Protector coming out of the prison, wiping his bloody sword on a torn scrap of Vadal gray. This one was an average-sized man, neither old nor young, but obviously in command.

The Protector he'd been fighting put one hand to his face, and shoved his broken jaw back into place with a sick *crack*. Jagdish flinched. No matter how tough a man was, that should have put him down. The Protector moved his jaw side to side, and then opened and closed his mouth a few times. Satisfied it was in the socket, he spoke as if no injury had occurred at all. "Let me finish this, Sikasso. It isn't often we find a real challenge."

"You call this a challenge, Lome? He smells like a brewery."

"He's more skilled than he looks."

"Make it quick." Sikasso tossed the bloody rag that had been a guard's tunic on the ground and sheathed his sword. "I've got a message to deliver. Use your magic and finish this mope."

"That'd be cheating," Lome said, eyeing Jagdish suspiciously. "A good fight makes life worth living."

"It's getting paid that makes life worth living." Sikasso began walking across the grass. "I don't care what you do, but if you don't catch up in time, you're not getting your cut. I'm off."

"You're not going anywhere!" Jagdish bellowed at him. He'd have his revenge on these Protector dogs, and he was angry enough to fight their entire order at once to see it happen.

But then Sikasso seemed to... *melt*. Silver dripped into black. Jagdish blinked, uncomprehending, as the Protector spread his widening arms and leapt into the sky. It was almost as if a hole formed in the world. There was a color, but not one that his mind could comprehend or record. Where Sikasso had been was an absence of sight, and then *something* came out the other side. He thought he saw feathers, but then he had to look away because the searing darkness burned his eyes. There was a beating of wings and a slap of air, and then Sikasso was gone.

"Witchcraft!" Jagdish roared as the abomination soared into the night. "You're no Protectors of the Law!"

His opponent laughed. "Your Law is for the weak, and you're not worth losing my share." Jagdish turned back to see that Lome had lifted something small from a chain on his belt and he was clutching it in his hand. More of the eye-stinging magic was emanating from that fist. Lome began whispering something that made Jagdish's ears ring.

Jagdish charged.

Things had changed. This time he didn't even stand a chance. Lome parried every attack effortlessly. A grin appeared on the murderer's face, and it began to widen as he chased Jagdish back. It took everything he had just to survive. Lome seemed gleeful. Flats met, the curved sword slid down steel, and Jagdish nearly lost his fingers. The false Protector moved like the wind.

He's toying with me.

Lome hit him incredibly hard in the side. It would have been a killing blow, but he'd used the spine of his blade just out of spite. Lome did it again. It was like being beaten with a steel rod. Now *this* was like fighting Ashok. He batted Jagdish's sword away, then kicked him in the torso hard enough to lift him off his feet and fling him down the road.

Jagdish hit the ground hard, rolling, stomach heaving, simultaneously gasping for breath and retching his guts up. He could feel the shape of the footprint embedded on his chest. Jagdish tried to stand, but Lome was on him, and a fist clipped the side of his face, driving him back into the road. Stars spun behind Jagdish's eyes.

"That was for breaking my jaw." Lome kicked him in the side to roll him over. He stepped on Jagdish's sword, pinning it. "That really hurt!" The false Protector stood over him. The chain hooked to his belt was dangling, and at the end of it was something small and impossibly dark, swinging back and forth. When he tried to focus on it, the object stung his eyes.

No wonder I lost, fighting a damned wizard. Jagdish tried to curse him, but all that came out was a wheeze.

"I've enjoyed this." Lome lifted his sword to deliver a decapitating blow. "But I've got places to be," he said just before his head opened like a red flower and Jagdish was hit by a shower of blood and teeth.

Armor clanking, Lome flopped to his knees. There was an angry roar from behind him, a flash of movement, a terrible *thud* from another impact, and then Lome collapsed in a heap. A huge man appeared, standing over the wizard, holding the giant iron beam the guards used to bar the gate. It normally took two guards to lift the thing, but now it was being held by a single person, and there was blood and hair stuck to that massive bar. He lifted the beam in both hands, thick muscles straining, and brought it down on the wizard's head again. Red and white chunks flew in every direction.

Seemingly satisfied that Lome's skull had been thoroughly smashed, the big man spit on the nearly headless corpse, then tossed the iron beam into the road. *Clang.* He wiped his bloody hands on his clothing, and Jagdish realized his clothing was nothing more than a wool blanket with a hole cut out of it for his large head to poke through.

A prisoner had just saved his life.

"Looked like you could use a hand, Risaldar...What's this then? I knew I smelled magic..." The big man knelt down, took up the chain and tore it from Lome's belt. "Demon bone! That'll be worth a few notes!" Then he picked up the Zarger blade. It looked like a toy in his hands. For a moment Jagdish thought the prisoner might use it to finish him off, but instead he used the sword to cut a strip from the dead man's cloak, which he roughly shoved against the gash on Jagdish's chest. "Lay still. You're hurt and there's no rush. Far as I can tell your friends are all dead. You have my word I'd no hand in that. It was this fool and the other one." He stood up. Jagdish recognized him as one of the worker-caste prisoners, but right then couldn't remember his crime or even his name. "No offense to your fine hospitality, but I intend to escape now. Just hold onto that rag tight as you can and make sure you keep pressure on that wound."

Jagdish was still recovering from getting the wind knocked out of him. He couldn't have stopped the prisoner even if he'd felt like it, but he needed to understand what had happened here. He managed to croak, "Ashok?"

"The Black Heart? He weren't involved."

"How do you know?" Jagdish gasped.

The big man grinned. "Because some of us lived!" and then he ran away.

The warrior Jagdish lay bleeding in the road before Cold Stream Prison, surrounded by bodies, as the torch slowly flickered and went out.

Chapter 25

Ashok sprinted through the night, leaping over fences and ditches, crossing open fields as quickly as possible to stay out of the moonlight. He'd not worn shoes the entire time he'd been in prison—he'd given his fine boots to one of the guards—so the soles of his feet were a callused mass, but they'd still taken a beating tonight, and were bleeding from many small cuts. His arms and face were scratched from crashing through brush trying to stay out of sight. The only living things that had spotted him had been farm animals that he'd startled awake or birds he'd flushed from the trees. His lungs ached and his muscles burned, but rather than slow down, he'd called upon the Heart of the Mountain and pushed on, far past human endurance. He set a brutal pace that the most athletic warrior could have only kept up for a short burst, and Ashok kept it up for *hours*.

The exertion made it easier not to think about his orders.

Akershan was on the far end of the continent. He'd die if he kept this up. Such a journey could take months this time of year and required planning. This area was all farms and pastures, but as he went south he'd enter the hills and then the mountains, and as the altitude climbed the temperature would drop. By the time he reached Thao lands, the snows would be deep. He would need food, clothing, supplies, and preferably horses. Ashok had no idea how he'd get such things now, because his entire life when he'd needed something he'd just requisition it from his inferiors. He'd been of the first caste and a senior member of a prestigious order, so that had been his right.

But now he had nothing, no symbol of office, no rank, and no place. How did the casteless find food and shelter? He'd never cared enough about them to pay attention. Workers traded with money, but Ashok possessed no banknotes. Omand had declared he was to be a criminal, and criminals just took things. He was passing small villages and isolated farms, and there was nothing the workers there could do to stop him if he stole their property, but the idea sickened him, and Ashok kept running instead.

He stayed off the main road, but kept parallel to it as much as possible. This might have been his homeland, but it was unfamiliar territory. The moons had helped keep him pointed in the right direction whenever the terrain forced him away from the road for most of the night, but the bright Canda had sunk behind the distant mountains and tiny Upagraha had faded away as it always did. A thin fog had rolled in. The sun would be up soon, and the farmers had already risen for their long day's toil. There were occasional travelers on the road, mostly on foot, but some on horses or mules. Ashok could have easily taken one of them, but orders or not, he didn't think of himself as a highwayman.

Crashing through a small stream soothed his feet, but it was only temporary, because the wicked water simply softened his flesh so the ground afterwards hurt even more. He paused long enough to slake his thirst, but didn't drink his fill. That would only slow him down. Then it was back to running.

That narrow, shallow bit of water made him think, though. He'd have to cross the Martaban River soon. It was too wide to leap across and too deep to wade. It was fresh water, not nearly as evil as the violent saltwater of the sea, and they were so far inland that it was doubtful a demon would stray this far from Hell, but that wasn't the problem.

Like all people raised in the highest caste, Ashok didn't know how to swim. Whole men only used water to drink and bathe, otherwise it was better left to their inferiors. The impure and sullied worked around the source of all evil. Submersing yourself completely was madness, and only a fool would *swim*.

So he'd need to cross at one of the few bridges or find a ferry. He couldn't follow the Capitol's orders if he drowned, and the idea of leaving Angruvadal on the bottom of a river was absurd and offensive.

Suddenly his foot plunged into a gopher hole, and his momentum caused him to crash into the dirt. Being tired and distracted had made him clumsy. He wouldn't be able to obey his orders if he tripped in the dark and snapped his neck either, and it was truly darkest before dawn, so Ashok lay there, face down in the damp grass, breathing hard, trying to collect himself.

What am I going to do?

Kule had taken away his fear, but Ashok felt a weak sickness inside his chest. *Dread* . . . Close enough. It did no good to be mad at the Capitol. It was their place to give punishments, and this punishment was truly a masterpiece. Not only would Ashok suffer in the most terrible way possible for the rest of his life, but everyone in the land would see his example, serving out the rest of his days in the service of a false god.

Resigned to his fate, Ashok rose from the dirt. He'd wrenched his ankle hard, and it was throbbing and swelling as he set out. The tendons protested, but he ignored the pain, and continued on, but a bit slower now.

By the time the eastern horizon was beginning to turn orange, Ashok reached the river. He heard it long before he saw it, a deep energetic sound. The ground around the river was marshy and covered in tall reeds. He moved across the dry bits of land until he stood at the bank. Here the river was wide, cold, swift-moving death. He tossed a stick in the water and watched as it was swept away instantly. Ashok could fight anything that walked on land or crawled out of the sea and have a good chance of winning, but he knew he'd perish if he tried to make it across that.

Even then, it was tempting.

It would be simple. He could drive Angruvadal into the ground to wait for its next bearer, then step over the edge and let the water have him. He knew from watching the Inquisitors torture witches that drowning was painful, but a relatively quick way to die. Eventually his bloated, soggy corpse would be carried out to Hell for the demons to devour. That would be decisive and final, nothing like the harsh, lingering punishment the Capitol had dreamed up for him.

Ashok put one hand on his sword. *I can't dishonor you like that.* He stepped away from the bank.

In the distance there was a dark shape in front of the rising sun. It was taller than the fog and the lines were too straight to be part of nature. *A tower.* Probably a checkpoint, and if there was a checkpoint, that meant there was a bridge. Ashok set out toward it, carefully picking his way through the tall reeds. No one could be allowed to stop him, and he had no travelling papers. So sneaking across was preferable to fighting. He'd ruined enough lives already.

Creeping forward through the mud and weeds until he was close enough to get a clear view of the checkpoint, Ashok could see that the squat tower was made of red bricks. The silhouette of a single archer was visible on top. Next to the tower was a small wooden barracks, and from the size there couldn't be more than a handful of warriors stationed here. No stable or feed, so they didn't even have horses to pursue him if he was seen. The final building was the arbiter's office. Smoke was rising from the chimney. Other than the single archer, he saw no other guards. Hopefully most of them were still asleep.

Behind the buildings was the bridge and he could see why they'd built it here. The ground was higher and the river narrower, so the wooden bridge was shorter and tall enough for the local barges to move beneath it freely. A large raft covered in barrels and crates was moving toward the bridge. There were figures on both sides, pushing their way against the current with long poles. Ashok didn't know if those who moved cargo on the rivers were casteless, or if there were any workers low enough to have an obligation so awful.

On the opposite shore was a small village consisting of a trading post and a handful of buildings. As much as the idea of stealing disgusted him, he would have to find food there. Even with the Heart to sustain him, all of his running had left him famished.

Ashok assessed the options. It was tempting to just run across, but the last thing he wanted to do was cause these warriors to give chase. Since the bridge was constructed of crossed wooden beams, he could probably climb across the bottom, staying out of the archer's view, but he couldn't see the underside from his current position. The archer was looking in the opposite direction, so Ashok moved out of the reeds and made his way through the tall grass toward the bridge.

A dog began barking. The sudden noise shattered the quiet morning. Ashok froze. The archer turned toward the sound, which was coming from behind the arbiter's building. The barking stopped abruptly, turned into a whine, and then that was cut off as well, as if someone had grabbed the dog by the snout and squeezed its mouth shut.

Sinking as low as he could into the grass, Ashok called upon the Heart of the Mountain, but this time to heighten his senses rather than his stamina. Immediately his exhaustion magnified, and he was nothing but a skin sack of aching muscles stitched together with pain, but sounds and scents seemed to grow stronger. He could hear the rolling of water over the rocks below, the chirp and clicks of insects, even the muted thumps of the barge poles as they punctured the unseen muck.

A horse snorted.

That distant sound had come from a copse of trees a quarter mile behind the tower. When he focused in on that area, he made out other noises, the creaking of leather—saddles and gloves twisting on spear shafts—and the ping and rattle of armor.

Warriors were waiting for him.

It made no sense. How could they know? There was no way a messenger could have gotten here ahead of him. His initial thought was to circle back, and ambush the ambushers, but these were Vadal men, fulfilling their obligation, and Ashok was the lawbreaker.

Enough killing.

There had to be another way across the river. He would find a hole to hide in until nightfall and then try again. Ashok had made it back to the edge of the reeds when he heard a new noise echoing from the direction he'd come from, horses and hounds, and lots of them. The vibrations and sounds were distant but they were heading this way. If they were coming from the prison, they'd have his scent. There would be no hiding from those dogs, and he'd have no choice but to fight. Even drastically outnumbered, he would more than likely win, but in doing so, lose.

Ashok looked toward the bridge. It was now or never. Calling upon the Heart was instinctive, and as the distant sounds faded so did his physical weakness. Quivering muscles became strong again. A quick glance confirmed that the archer was looking away, so Ashok bolted for the bridge, moving as fast as he could.

The dog began barking again.

The road here was made of tiny, sharp stones, and the gravel crunched beneath his bare feet. The archer heard the noise, turned, and began shouting. Immediately, the door of the arbiter's building flew open and far too many soldiers poured out, bows already strung and arrows nocked, eager for a fight.

How had they known?

Still sprinting, Ashok grabbed hold of Angruvadal and pulled the terrible sword from its sheath. Immediately it suggested a hundred ways for him to annihilate every potential threat.

But Ashok kept running.

The archer in the tower let fly first. Instinct told him when and how to turn, and the shaft of the arrow exploded into splinters as Angruvadal struck it from the sky. He dodged left and right as several other bowstrings thrummed. The soles of his feet struck wood as arrows embedded themselves in the bridge. Something tugged inside his mind, and Ashok knew to always listen to the sword's warnings. He threw himself to the side, behind the first of the bridge supports, as an arrow flew through the space where his head had been. *Thump. Thump.* He could feel the impacts as more arrows struck the wood at his back.

He stepped out, took in the releasing strings, the flashes of red fletching, and a picture of the future formed in his mind. Ignoring the ones that would miss him anyway, he turned Angruvadal in his hand, an extension of his destructive will, and he intercepted the speeding arrows. Several shafts split into kindling in a series of black flashes, and Ashok remained standing, unharmed.

That so unnerved a couple of the warriors that they stopped shooting, but most of them were already drawing more arrows from their quivers. Behind the arbiter's building, someone blew a horn to alert the horsemen. Ashok turned and ran.

The great bridge was a hundred yards long. He was halfway across it in a few heartbeats, but had to stop so suddenly that it put splinters into his feet when he saw that there were warriors on the other side as well. They'd been concealed in the village until the horn had sounded, and now they were spilling out of the workers' huts, archers and halberdiers both. Ashok looked back toward the tower. The waiting cavalry had come thundering out of the distant trees. He was surrounded.

The barking war dog had escaped its handler and was running

after him. It was a large brown beast, a hundred pounds of angry muscle and sharp teeth. Such an animal could easily take down a normal man and rend the life from him. Ashok waited patiently for the war dog to catch up, and then he snap-kicked it in the mouth. It yelped as it flipped over the railing to tumble into the river far below.

He turned back toward the village. The halberdiers had formed two ranks, shoulder to shoulder, and begun their advance. The archers were behind them, waiting for the order to engage.

"Let me pass," Ashok shouted.

A risaldar was standing behind the line. "Surrender or die!"

One of the archers either slipped or mistook his officer's response as a command to release. Angry, Ashok watched the lone arrow come speeding in, then reached up and caught it. He snapped it in his fist, then let both pieces drop to clatter against the boards. That put a stutter in the halberdier's march. "Do you know who I am?"

"You're the Black Heart, but no criminal is a match for the Sutpo garrison," the officer proclaimed. His men let up a nervous cheer. That only made it worse. Ashok didn't want to kill anyone, especially warriors that had such courage and commitment to duty. "Surrender or perish, lawbreaker."

Angruvadal painted another picture in his head, showing how prior bearers had survived situations similar to this. A plan was presented, and he saw himself charging, moving between the halberds, and cutting a swath of blood through the village, leaving a pile of dead warriors behind him.

No.

With Ashok stubbornly refusing to kill innocent men, Angruvadal had no other answer to give him.

"I cannot surrender."

The arrows fell like rain.

In a flash of black steel, Ashok dodged and struck more shafts from the air. When he tried to keep moving, he realized that his foot was pinned to the bridge. An arrow had gotten through his defenses, and the shaft had gone cleanly through the top of his foot and embedded itself deep in the wood. He tugged, but that only caused a flash of pain so sharp that it nearly staggered him. While they prepared the next volley, Ashok bent down, took hold of the arrow, snapped the end off, and then carefully lifted his foot. The wooden shaft disappeared through a red hole that quickly filled with blood. At least they were using narrow armor-piercing tips instead of broad heads.

Wincing, he set his bloody foot down, and then limped to the edge of the bridge and looked down at the swift-moving river. The big cargo barge was directly below him, but it was a *long* drop.

Hooves hit one side of the bridge while armored boots hit the other. The fierce whistle rose again as the morning filled once more with flying death, but by the time the arrows landed, Ashok was already falling.

He hit the barge hard, smashed through an empty crate, and collided with the logs beneath hard enough to shake the entire craft. Ropes snapped and water sprayed over him. Bones had cracked, but none had snapped off to poke through his skin, so he could continue.

When Ashok stood up, the small crew was staring stupidly at the man who'd fallen out of the sky. The two with the poles were obviously casteless, but they must have been eating well, since they were fit and appeared strong from their labor. The third and final one was a worker. He was a tiny man, probably a licensed overseer since he was openly carrying a short sword. But when that cheap little iron pig sticker was drawn free and fearfully pointed in Ashok's direction, Angruvadal instantly slapped it from his hands, and there was a splash as the cheap sword landed in the river.

The warriors were swarming the bridge above. There wasn't much time.

"Can you swim?" Ashok demanded. The two casteless nodded yes. Of course fish-eaters knew how to do something so undignified, but the frightened worker just squeaked a sound that sounded like *no*. The edge of the barge was only twenty feet from the nearest bank, and he wasn't very big for a whole man. "Very well," Ashok said as he sheathed Angruvadal, grabbed hold of the struggling worker by the belt and the collar, spun him hard, and flung him across the distance. He almost made it—probably would have if not for all that flailing—but from the size of the splash and the clack of rocks beneath, the worker had landed in the shallows. He came up thrashing and gasping, scrambling to get out of the water.

One casteless took the hint and had already dived into the river by the time Ashok turned back, but the other one was pointing at him. "It's you! You're the one the Keepers have been preaching about! You've truly come to free us!"

Ashok snatched the pole from his hands, and then kicked the babbling casteless over the side. He disappeared with a splash.

The barge swayed beneath his feet. It was a *very* uncomfortable feeling. As soon as the casteless had stopped pushing against it, the current was already carrying the barge back the way it had come, but not nearly fast enough.

Thunk.

Above, archers were sticking their bows over the side. Ashok jammed the pole down and felt it stick in the mire, then he pushed with all his might, sending the barge spinning away from the bridge. He didn't have to have Angruvadal in his hand to feel its warning, and he ducked behind a stack of barrels as more arrows came streaking in. He kept one hand on the pole as it dragged through the water, because if he lost that, he'd have no way to steer. All he could do was hope that no missiles struck his exposed arm. His cover blocked most of the arrows, but a lucky head slipped through a crack to stab him in the hip.

Within seconds the barge was bristling with arrows. It was a large, slow target. Ashok peeked over the wood, through the new forest of shafts, and saw that some warrior had gotten the bright idea of lighting fire arrows. A torch was swinging back and forth, setting fire to oil-soaked rags. They must have been prepared to ignite the bridge rather than let him pass. Good for them.

The cavalry was wheeling their horses around and galloping back so they could follow him along the shore. This cumbersome raft would have to land somewhere, and they would be waiting for him.

Ashok grabbed hold of the arrow stuck in his hip, but the tip was embedded in his pelvis and didn't want to come free. Prying now might crack the bone, and that would slow him down too much to outrun a horse, so he left it there. He got out from behind cover, dragged the pole up, and then jammed it down again, pushing the raft further from the bridge. Normally two men did this, but he was working with the current rather than against it, and Ashok was far stronger than any two casteless put together. More arrows flew past him, but he focused on getting out of their range, rather than trying to block or dodge them.

Flaming arrows began to fall on the barge. That was the kind of quick thinking initiative Ashok had always liked to see the warrior caste's officers exercise against criminals. In normal circumstances he'd order a commendation for such cleverness, but it wasn't so pleasant being on the receiving end. The bulbous fire arrows weren't as accurate, and had shorter range, so some landed in the river in bursts of steam, but the barge was an easy target, so many more were sticking in the wood. Thankfully, the barge was so damp that the fires weren't catching.

A fire arrow struck the lashed-down pile of barrels. He'd been concentrating so hard on the physical struggle that he'd neglected to pay sufficient attention to his surroundings. A thick liquid was dripping from where the barrels had been struck. A strong smell hit his nostrils.

Words had been roughly stenciled on the barrels. *Lantern oil.*

Already leaking from the earlier hits, the barrels burst into flames. Ashok drew Angruvadal, and in one movement he sliced through the thick ropes lashing the barrels down. He had to get them off before—

A barrel burst. There was a roar and a flash as the oil ignited.

The concussion nearly knocked him over the side.

Ashok found himself face down, one arm in the river, and he flinched and jerked his hand out. He sprang up to discover that his ragged shirt had caught fire. He shrugged out of it and hurled it away, only to find that his long, matted hair had caught fire as well. He smacked it out as he assessed the damage. Nearly the entire barge was burning. He'd lost the pole and it was floating away. Smoke was obscuring the bridge. He couldn't steer and was at the mercy of the current. The sound of impacts told him that the warriors were still firing arrows. A puddle of flaming lantern oil was eating its way toward him. Ropes were snapping as the logs making up the barge's backbone spread apart. He didn't know if he'd be immolated first, or if the barge would sink before the fire got him.

He was going to have to enter the water.

Ashok sheathed his sword. *Forgive me, Angruvadal, but I must submerse you in evil.*

At the edge of the barge, he paused, the evil water just beneath his feet. He knew what he had to do, but part of him didn't want to comply. The idea of vanishing beneath the surface was repellant.

Maybe I can feel fear after all.

And then an arrow struck Ashok square in the back.

The river rushed up to meet him.

Chapter 26

"Ashok has escaped then. So how many warriors did he kill along the way?"

"None, Inquisitor."

Omand took the pipe from his mouth. "None?" He'd been expecting reports of great slaughter. In fact, he required slaughter, not discretion. If he'd wanted discretion he certainly wouldn't have picked Black-Hearted Ashok to be his villain. "Really? Not one?"

"I suppose he kicked a dog, but that was about it. They had him surrounded, cut off on both sides of Sutpo Bridge, but rather than fight his way through, he leapt into the water," Sikasso reported.

"He *swam?*"

"It appears that way," the wizard answered. He didn't sound nearly as incredulous as Omand, but since the magical assassins of the Lost House routinely engaged in all matter of blasphemous behavior, swimming probably wasn't that remarkable to them.

"Our fallen Protector is full of surprises. The only time I like surprises are parties thrown in my honor, or wrapped gifts. Does this strike you as a gift, Sikasso?"

"It does not, Grand Inquisitor."

They had the top of the tower to themselves. His men had secured the floors around his guest quarters and swept them for spies, magic, and secret passages. Everyone not part of the Inquisition had been sent away, granting Omand some measure of privacy. However, at the base of the tower, the number of Vadal warriors posted as guards had recently doubled, suggesting his hosts had found the body of the murdered arbiter. His hosts most certainly knew about the rampage through the prison, but they'd not mentioned it to him yet. They were playing it carefully. When they could no longer hide the news, there would be lots of bowing and apologizing, and the Inquisition would be showered with obligations and concessions to make up for it. Omand was looking forward to that part. As soon as he was officially notified of the escape, he had a very special favor to ask of House Vadal.

"We've not found his body or his sword, but my men are searching the river bottom now."

"An easy enough task when you can transform into a fish, I suppose."

Sikasso tilted his head to the side. "You speak as if you've never used the black steel yourself, but I can smell it on you, Grand Inquisitor. You're a far greater wizard than you let on."

Omand waved one hand dismissively. "I am nothing." He'd not been the most successful witch hunter in the history of the Order as a result of cunning alone, but he liked keeping his true capabilities secret. It was good to keep his opponents guessing.

"Of course." Not even Sikasso was bold enough to push that topic. "My apologies for prying."

"This is most curious." Omand returned the pipe to the stand. Vadal tobacco was truly the finest there was, far better than the bug-infested garbage that he'd grown up with, and he would have enjoyed finishing it, but he had work to do, letters to write, and hosts to manipulate. He didn't bother to put his ceremonial mask back on. Sikasso had seen his true face many times already. "So, when you say he's escaped, you mean Ashok is truly missing, as opposed to one of your men being so eager to lay his greedy hands on an ancestor blade that he saw his opportunity and murdered Ashok during the fight?"

"That is the risk you take when you hire us, but no." Sikasso was still wearing his stolen Protector armor. It was so spattered with dried blood and caked with mud that the silver no longer gleamed. The wizard was civilized enough to remain standing, and not soil the fine silk pillows with his filth. "You have my word. My men are scouring the countryside and watching every possible path. We will find him."

"And then you will *watch* him. I know it pains you so, but he's still more valuable alive than dead for now." Omand could see the greed in Sikasso's eyes. He was a collector of magic, and Ashok was walking around with a treasure trove of it. Despite all his talent, all that power and cunning, Sikasso was just as easily manipulated as any other man. As long as Omand could supply him with what he wanted, he would remain a dog on a leash. "Don't worry, Sikasso. You'll have that sword in time. This is Ashok we're talking about. If he's alive, just follow the inevitable trail of corpses. If he's dead, then you'll find the sword somewhere. If the warriors do manage to kill him, make sure his body and the witnesses disappear, and I'll simply pay you to create chaos in his name from then on."

"That would be far simpler."

"I'm the Grand Inquisitor. I didn't earn the title by being *simple*."

"Your plans are beyond my meager imagination, my lord."

"On the contrary, I believe you have a far better grasp of politics than you let on." That dig was payback for the assumptions about Omand's magical abilities. The assassin's house had managed to survive undetected in a lawless no man's land for generations, so Sikasso was extremely astute. "I assume that when Ashok failed to provide a convincing enough display of savage casteless rebellion, you did it for him?"

"We killed most of the warriors there and put the village to the torch. I had the local arbiter's head stuck on the tallest pole. One of my men wrote *the casteless will rise* in his blood across the bridge."

"A nice touch."

"The survivors don't know what hit them, but they believe it was the Black Heart and a few Protectors. Soon everyone will tremble at the mention of Ashok. Dead or alive, his legend will grow."

"See? You get it. You would make a fine Judge."

Sikasso smiled. "My job is more honorable."

"True." Simply killing people was far easier than manipulating people into killing each other for you. Omand was excellent at *both*. "Tomorrow I begin my journey back to the Capitol.

Casteless rebellion and renegade Protectors? I imagine someone of strong moral character will need to keep order during this time of turmoil."

"We'll continue our search. I'll contact you when I have news." Sikasso gave the Grand Inquisitor a small bow, walked to the tower's open window, stepped through, and dropped silently from sight. Omand had to admit that no matter how many times he worked with the twisted men of the Lost House, that manner of exit always remained unnerving. Omand did in fact have incredibly powerful magic, but shape shifting had never been among his many skills. He liked his body—aging and flabby as it was—to stay in one piece.

There was a polite knock on the door. Omand put his mask back on.

A moment later Inquisitor Taraba entered. "Good evening, sir." He took note of the open window and the billowing curtains. "You've received word from the assassin?"

"I did. Things are proceeding well." He could tell his subordinate had something else to say. "You may speak freely. I can tell that he's gone."

"I just spoke with one of our spies among the Vadal. Did the assassin tell you that one of his men died at the prison? His head was stomped into paste so there's no danger of him being identified, but he was also disguised as a Protector."

"Our dear friend neglected to mention that." Omand chuckled. That had to sting. There weren't very many members of Sikasso's Lost House. Losing even one would be frustrating.

"I don't trust the assassin."

"That's perceptive of you, Taraba. I fully expect Sikasso to betray us at some point. That's the nature of such men."

"Then why—"

He held up one hand to stop his subordinate. The Grand Inquisitor wasn't in the habit of explaining his actions to anyone, but Taraba was a young, extremely capable—and most importantly—*loyal* Inquisitor. Though he lacked the imagination to ever rise to Omand's position, Taraba was valuable, and deserving of mentoring. "Sikasso's kind are addicted to the accumulation of magic. I've employed them to shadow a man carrying around some of the strongest and rarest magic in all of Lok. Normally such an item would be considered off limits because they couldn't afford to anger a great house or an order and still survive, but Ashok is dishonored and disowned. There's no one to avenge him. I've planted the idea that even if Ashok dies, our mutually beneficial arrangement may continue. Being an intelligent man, he will think it through to the logical conclusion. This is a rare opportunity for Sikasso. Eventually greed will overcome sense, he'll murder Ashok and take his sword. It would surprise me if he wasn't plotting such a move already."

"Why use them then?"

"Because the services of the assassin's house are very *expensive*. They require payment in black steel or demon parts. I'm only paying them to follow, observe, and facilitate. It would be far costlier to hire them to assassinate a bearer, and this way when they do inevitably dispatch Ashok, their greed will force them to hide it from me. They will lie to my face and I will gladly continue to pay them for it."

Taraba was far smarter than he looked. He grasped the implications right away. "They'll keep committing atrocities to blame on the Black Heart. You don't care who causes them, as long as the great houses fear a casteless rebellion."

"Correct. Their unreliability makes them reliable. Plus, it saves us the expense of having to dispose of the extremely dangerous Ashok ourselves once he's outlived his usefulness. The Inquisition has a budget to keep."

"That's brilliant, sir."

"I do my best," Omand said with false humility. Tomorrow was the beginning of another long journey, and he needed his rest. "Take this letter with you. As soon as our hosts see fit to inform us about the horrible embarrassment of losing the prisoner, have their wizards will this to their fellows in the Capitol."

Taraba took the letter. "Speaking of costly, instantly sending a message such a distance will use up whole fragments worth of magic."

"Time is of the essence, lad. Our Order must know that there are other Protectors in league with the rebels! All of the Protectors are now suspect and action must be taken. House Vadal will be so ashamed they'll be glad to do this favor for the Inquisition, and what's a bit of black steel compared to that? Tomorrow will be busy, so I believe I'll retire for the evening. Leave me." His subordinate immediately turned away, but on second thought, there were so many exciting things happening that Omand found himself in a festive mood. "Taraba, wait . . . Have our hosts send up a pleasure slave for my amusement."

"Yes, sir."

"And make sure the girl is someone . . . that won't be missed."

The young Inquisitor swallowed hard. It was one thing to torture people as part of your obligation, but another to do it for amusement on your own time. The Grand Inquisitor knew he had a reputation for having *peculiar* appetites. "Of course, sir." Taraba bowed, then fled the tower.

Omand rose from the cushions, walked over, and closed the window. The night was chilly.

Chapter 27

The Capitol's grand bazaar was very quiet in the hours before dawn. It was about the only time the place was relatively calm, but even then, there were still hundreds of workers getting their booths ready and stocking merchandise for the busy day to come. Rada was very familiar with the bazaar at this hour, because over the last few months this was the time that she'd normally sneaked away from her secret rendezvous with Devedas to go back to her family estate.

It was that familiarity that told her something was wrong. The merchants had stopped working. They were all looking back the direction she'd come from, and there was nervous whispering. She overheard the word *Inquisition* repeatedly. Frightened, Rada hid among the people who were arriving to work and tried to blend in while she eavesdropped. A large group of Inquisitors had been seen on their way to the Protectors' compound.

The judges often proclaimed that only the guilty feared the Inquisition, but everyone knew that was a lie. Rada was innocent. In fact, she knew that she was the victim, but she was still terrified of the Inquisition. The Law gave them the power to sweep up anyone they suspected of treason or dealing in the forbidden arts, and many of those who were taken were never seen again, and if they were, it was only as desiccated corpses decorating the top of the Order's foul dome.

Logically, she knew she should have run, but Devedas had been investigating a supposed Inquisitor on her behalf. Was it possible that he'd angered them? Was her lover in danger? She had to know. So the librarian made her way back toward the Protectors' compound, doing her best to blend in with the merchants. The workers were afraid of the Inquisition too, but they were morbidly curious when the Inquisitor's attention was on someone else.

It was rare to see more than a few masked Inquisitors at a time. Judging by the number of lanterns, there had to be hundreds of them. It was like an army was marching through the bazaar. She'd never have guessed there were so many in the Capitol. Rada knew there were only a handful of Protectors present. During her many recent visits to their compound, the most she'd ever seen at a time was ten, and most of those were barely more than children. They were a relatively tiny order, spread thin over all of the continent. Why send an army of Inquisitors if they weren't intending to arrest the Lord Protector?

This is all my fault.

The Inquisitors had stopped in front of the compound's wall. The gates had opened and a lone figure was waiting there to greet them. Rada's heart skipped a beat when she saw that it was Devedas. He was wearing nothing but a sleeping robe tied around his waist. A small group of Inquisitors broke off, their black armor made them look like gliding shadows, and they approached Devedas. She tried to get as close as possible so she could hear what they had to say, but luckily, the lead Inquisitor shouted his accusation so loudly the whole block could hear.

"There has been treachery in the north! I bear a message for Lord Protector Devedas."

For once the market had fallen silent enough to listen.

"You found him." Somehow Devedas managed to sound bored, like an army beating down his door before dawn was of no particular note. "Speak."

"By order of the Council, the whereabouts of all Protectors must be accounted for. The Protectors within the Capitol are to remain confined to their compound unless authorized. If requested, Protectors must submit to interrogation at the Inquisitor's Dome."

Devedas didn't so much as raise his voice. "What is the meaning of this?"

The lead Inquisitor must have practiced beforehand, because he delivered his message with gusto. They must have wanted the whole city to know. "The traitor Black-Hearted Ashok has escaped, killing members of the governing caste and hundreds of others across House Vadal."

"Escaped? Why would he bother? The traitor only wants to die."

"He was aided in his escape by Protectors of the Law."

The crowd in the bazaar gasped.

"Lies."

"It was confirmed by a multitude of reliable witnesses."

"Then they are mistaken," Devedas snapped.

"The Council has declared that until the Protectors of the Law have been freed of this treacherous corruption, the entire Order is suspect. Until those loyal to Ashok have been purged, the Protectors are—"

Devedas began walking away.

"Where are you going?" the Inquisitor demanded.

"To get dressed so I can go argue this foolishness with the judges."

"Was I not clear? You're not allowed to leave your compound!"

Devedas stuck his head around the wall and surveyed the many lanterns. "What did you bring? Two hundred men? I have twenty senior Protectors here." Rada knew that was a huge exaggeration, but the way the Inquisitor took a few steps back, he didn't know that. "We'd be finished with you in time for breakfast. If you plan on keeping us here, you'd best come back with real force."

"You would flout the Law? You threaten to turn your blades against servants of the Capitol, like unto the Black Heart!"

"You made your speech, and I'm sure by sunup the entire Capitol will be talking, but now you're beginning to annoy me. Go tell your masters that I'll demonstrate exactly how much love this Order retains for the traitor by delivering his head to the council myself." Then Devedas snapped an order and his men closed the compound's doors in the Inquisitor's face.

Chapter 28

Dreams of drowning tormented him until the ache in his chest brought him back to consciousness. Ashok lay there, taking stock of the pains in his body. There were healing puncture wounds in his back, side, and foot. Everything hurt, but his lungs were especially sore. He remembered being swept along, out of control, breaking the surface to gasp for air before being dragged back down. He'd been disoriented, flailing, crashing against rocks and tangled in clinging underwater vines, as his air had run out, his lungs had burned, and evil water had flooded in to destroy him.

And at that last instant, he had known fear.

"Why are you laughing?"

He'd not realized he had been. "Because they didn't take everything from me after all." Wherever he was, the light was poor. Small bits of sunlight came through cracks above and there was a single candle burning next to him. It smelled like *river*. He was flat on his back, on a thin blanket, on a plank floor. He'd used the Heart too much, and it felt like his skull was split in two, but Ashok turned his head far enough to see who'd spoken. There was a woman kneeling next to him. She had the candle, but was wearing a scarf and a hood so he couldn't make out any of her features. "Where am I?"

"Hiding."

Not a very specific answer. It took a moment to collect his thoughts. From the odd, stomach-churning sensation of rocking, he figured that he was on another barge. Angruvadal was still sheathed at his side. That was good. Even as loyal as he was to his sword, he would have had a very difficult time going back into the water after it. "Hiding where?"

"This compartment is used for smuggling contraband past checkpoints. It may offend you to know this, Protector, but no one likes to pay taxes."

"I'm not a Protector anymore. How did I get out of the river?"

"The Keeper was given a vision where to find you and we fished you out of the river."

"But I drowned. How am I alive?"

"The kiss of life...I shared my breath with you."

That made no sense. "Witchcraft?"

Now it was the woman's turn to laugh. "If I had magic that strong would I be on a barge piloted by untouchables? You're looking a bit jumpy there. I've got to remember your kind likes to execute first and ask questions later. It's nothing like witchcraft. It's just an old trick. When someone drowns, push out the water in their chest, then force your air into their mouth to fill their lungs while they can't. Sometimes they live, sometimes they don't."

Ashok had never heard of such a thing, but he didn't normally associate with brazen criminal women.

"A useful trick to know when you've spent as much of your life around water and morons as I have. Try not to move. Your wounds began to heal as soon as I pulled the arrows out, just like the Keeper said they would, but there was a poison on one of those that struck you. It was like nothing I've seen before, and I've seen some nasty ones. I forced you to drink some soothing tea, but even then, I'm amazed you're alive. You've been unconscious for several days. I expect you will remain weak for a few more." She got up and left him.

Ashok must have fallen back to sleep, because the next time he opened his eyes the sun was higher in the sky and there was a bit more light sneaking through the cracks. Outside, men were singing, a rough, rhythmic, working song. He was in a wooden room with an extremely low ceiling. His headache had subsided. A thin man was sitting cross-legged on the floor next to Ashok's blanket. He was probably close to Ashok's age, but losing his hair. He was wearing simple clothing, cleaner and in better repair than what most casteless would possess, but without any of the insignia a worker would normally wear to indicate his station. He didn't carry himself like a warrior either, head up, shoulders squared, but more like someone who simply didn't *care* how he presented himself at all. The man had a bucket at his feet and a ladle, which he pushed toward Ashok's lips. He was so thirsty that he drank without question.

It was wonderful. Water was eager to murder them all, but man couldn't live without it. It was a very spiteful arrangement.

"Hello, my friend. It appears that you are feeling better. It turns out that Protectors are as difficult to kill as the legends make them out to be. Pierced, burned, poisoned, and drowned, yet still among the living. I knew you were the one I've been waiting for."

The voice sounded familiar. He'd not gotten a very good look at him that night, but Keta had been a memorable lunatic. "You came to see me in prison. . . . You called yourself the Keeper of Names."

"That is correct. I am Freeman Keta."

"A free man?" Ashok snorted. "There's no such thing."

"Of course you would believe that. Your only freedom has been to serve in an approved manner, which if you think about it, is entirely contrary to the very concept."

"I remember all that nonsense about not belonging to any house or caste."

"I'm impressed that you can remember anything at all. That poison was strong enough to drop an elephant."

The warrior caste didn't use poison. The Law declared that to be a cowardly assassin's weapon, which meant Ashok hadn't been the only lawbreaker on that bridge. It had to be something rare and extremely potent to have this much of an effect on his body. Those who touched the Heart of the Mountain were immune to most poisons, and if he were ever exposed to this particular mixture again, the Heart would be ready to counteract it and there would be no effect at all.

One song completed, the casteless began a new song outside. He found the song strangely familiar.

"May I ask you a question, Fall?"

"That isn't my name."

"That's how it was recorded in the book."

"What book?"

"The most important book of all books. The book that tells us who we really are, but I'll call you whatever you wish, even if that name is a lie." Keta dipped his head in apology. "So, *Ashok*, why did you try to escape at the bridge rather than fight? There weren't that many warriors between you and freedom. From the stories I've heard, they wouldn't have been able to stop a bearer. Why not cut a path through them? Why risk your life instead? Why put yourself in the water?"

That wasn't a question. That was many questions, and the answers were so complicated that Ashok wasn't sure about them himself. "I didn't want to kill them."

"You kill everyone. Why not these?"

"I don't know."

"You chose the unknown rather than the familiar. I believe you will be doing that quite a bit in the near future. I believe before you discovered the truth, you would've killed them all without a second thought. You've been lied to for so long that now you see the whole world is crooked, but the Forgotten knows that you'll learn to see things as they really are. I don't know your mind, but you going beneath the water is a sign. Did you know that among the beliefs of the old tribe, before the kings, some believed in a thing called baptism? It represented rebirth. A man would be submerged beneath water, and when he came out of the water, it represented a rebirth, a new beginning. This is your new beginning!"

"I'm on a barge of fools," Ashok muttered to himself.

"What caused you to leave the prison? The last time we spoke, you seemed content enough."

Duty. But Omand had ordered him not to speak of it. "My reasons are my own."

Keta grinned. "We both know that's a lie! You *own* nothing. Even your most prized possession owns you, not the other way around. You've never determined a thing for yourself. Blind obedience has carried you through life like this river carried your body to me. You go where the current takes you, *Ashok*."

He was still dizzy and nauseous, but Ashok sat up. Keta seemed surprised that he was able to do that already, and he was even more surprised when Ashok grabbed Keta's collar, twisted it tight, and dragged him over to whisper, "Listen carefully, Keeper. I've no patience for lectures. Who are you and what do you want?"

"Of course you're impatient!" Despite being on the edge of strangulation, the Keeper didn't cower. He was made of sterner stuff than his appearance suggested. "I should have known the Forgotten would pick a man of action. I understand. Believe it or not, I was a lot like you once."

Ashok sincerely doubted that. "The Forgotten? So you're one of those fanatics."

"I serve the Forgotten. That's what a Keeper is. It's an office in the priesthood, left over from the Age of Kings. You'd think an expert on murdering the religious would already be aware of such things."

"I never needed to know the particulars." Their kind disgusted him. Devotees to the old ways were enemies of all that was good. He drove his knuckles into Keta's neck. It wouldn't take much effort to crush his throat. "You're all the same to me."

The Keeper grimaced as his face turned red. "It has been proclaimed that you must meet the prophet. I'm the only one who can take you there," he gasped.

"How do you know I seek him?" Ashok demanded.

"You already are?" That seemed to surprise the Keeper more than the threat of strangulation. "We've been expecting you."

"Explain."

"You may have a mission from man, but I have a mission from the gods. Ultimately they take us to the same destination. I'm supposed to convince you of the truth. I've been called to be your guide."

"I need no guide. I travel alone."

"Your teacher, then!"

"There's nothing you have to say that I want to learn. If I have been reborn, it is as a man with even less patience for foolishness than before." Ashok squeezed harder.

"Your Order has been searching for years and failing. You can't meet the prophet until the Keepers arrange it. A test... You must..." Keta was about to pass out. *I have to proclaim you worthy first!*"

"I see." It was tempting to snap the fanatic's neck and get off this blasphemous barge, but Ashok let go of Keta, who scrambled back, gasping. "I will pass your tests. You will take me to this prophet."

Keta rubbed his bruised throat. "I won't if you're attacking the Forgotten's loyal servants."

"Very well. I will respect your office for the duration of our journey. You will take me to him." Ashok found the next few words so extremely distasteful that they were difficult to speak. "I will become his servant as well."

"What?" That statement was so surprising that it registered even through the indignity of being choked with his own shirt. "I've not . . . But . . . You're already—"

"You are not so eloquent that you've swayed me into worshiping your false gods, Keeper. I have my reasons. Do we have an agreement or not?"

Keta seemed thoughtful, if a bit intimidated. However he'd expected his god to deliver the miracle of the cooperative Protector, this certainly wasn't it. "We have an agreement."

Chapter 29

The others were up top, in the dying sunlight, poling their huge cargo barge along against the swift current. It was tedious work, and Keta was impressed by the seemingly endless stamina of the casteless who lived upon the rivers. The men worked in tandem, singing a song with a rhythm that told each one when to push so that no distance was ever lost to the relentless water.

Thera was sitting on a crate, sharpening one of her many knives. She hid the blade inside a sleeve when she heard Keta climb up the ladder. Those who dared to carry arms in defiance of the Law became very proficient at concealing them. "How goes it, Keeper?" She must have noticed the spreading bruise on his throat. "Not well, I take it."

Keta sat next to her. He was troubled and trying not to show it. "Some of us are more set in our ways than others."

"We've got ourselves a whole man who has spent his entire damnable life eliminating folks like they're vermin, and he's supposed to be the meanest man ever turned out by an order of right hard bastards. He can't be the one. This is stupid."

Since Keta had assumed his office in the priesthood, he wasn't used to having people supposedly on his side scoff so openly, but he didn't mind. Doubt kept him from getting a big head.

"The Voice made it sound like he is. I don't know what put him on it, but Ashok was already on the right path. He was already seeking the prophet."

"Why? How?" Thera obviously didn't like that at all. "What does that mean? To kill?"

"No, to *serve*." She had an incredulous look on her face. "I know. I thought the same thing. This has to be true. I have faith."

"And I have knives, so if he's not the one we're looking for, and you decide this is some Inquisition plot to get close to us, say the word. I'll wait until he's sleeping and cut his throat. A magic sword can't do much for him while he's asleep, and he won't be so indestructible with a gash from ear to ear."

Thera may have slit more than her fair share of throats, but he doubted killing Ashok would be that easy, even coming at him while he was asleep, and the rebellion couldn't afford to lose her. "We might not understand the wisdom of the gods, but this is all part of the Forgotten's plan. I'm sure Ashok is the one."

"Good. I didn't stick my lips on some bastard firster's food hole for no reason. You better know what you're doing."

"I might not, but the gods always know what they're doing."

"Keep saying that, Keeper, and you might start believing it yourself."

She was trying to goad him into another religious argument, but Keta let it pass. On their long journey north they'd had many philosophical debates, most of which had been brief, heated, and usually left him feeling annoyed, angry, or depressed. It was remarkable that Thera, who had personally been through so much, could believe in so little.

Thera cleared her throat and spit over the side. "My faith in the Forgotten isn't as strong as yours, but I'm sure it'll last until the rebellion runs out of notes to pay me."

Her admitting to such base motivations just made Keta sad. "I know my interpretation of the vision is correct, Thera. Just do as we planned. We're supposed to be here."

"We'll see." She rose and put her hood up. "In the meantime, if our Protector decides to start dispensing judgment, you're on your own, and I'm swimming for shore. He might be able to fight, but he can't swim to save his life." Then she walked away.

"He's stubborn enough he might put rocks in his pockets and walk across the bottom to pursue you!" he shouted after her, but she just gave him a profane gesture and continued walking. He sighed, then watched the passing river and the setting sun while listening to the laborers sing their rhythmic pace.

Keta had been preparing for this moment for years, yet he was still plagued with doubt. The Forgotten had long ago taught what must be done, and now it was Keta's duty to prepare the way for the gods' triumphant return. He'd known this would be difficult. His new charge was a product of the callous governing caste. Ashok's cruel, distrusting nature shouldn't have come as a surprise to him.

The two of them came from extremely different backgrounds, but they shared the same teacher.

Sometimes I really wonder why you picked me for this, Ratul . . .

Chapter 30

Four years ago

"The demons must be emerging from the sea again," the overseer said as he entered the storehouse.

Alarmed, Keta the butcher sprinted to the entrance, meat cleaver in hand. He looked toward the distant shore, but saw no monsters. The ocean was its normal blue, not blood red like the last time. "Are they coming?" he gasped. It had been nearly twenty years since their last incursion into the lands of House Uttara. "How do you know? Have you seen them?"

Yet the overseer wasn't panicking like most men would if they'd seen such horrors. "Calm yourself, butcher." The large man scowled as he moved one hand to the whip at his side. Like all overseers, he was a hard man, but unlike most appointed to his station, not a totally unkind one. Such disrespectful questions could earn a beating. They were both casteless, but even amongst the lowest of the low, there was order.

Keta bowed his head. "Forgive me. I was little the last time the demons came. They slaughtered everyone." Realizing that he was still clutching the sharpened cleaver, Keta quickly dropped it onto a nearby table. The Law said his kind were not allowed weapons, only tools necessary to perform their work. "Fear made me speak out of turn."

The overseer let go of the whip. "I've seen the ocean beasts myself. Only a fool would be unafraid. There have been no raids, yet." Remarkably, he even took the time to answer the young man's questions. "This morning I was told that one of the Protectors of the Law is on his way here."

Keta's mouth was suddenly very dry.

"A Protector is coming all the way from the capitol." The overseer scratched his head. "That's a long journey and this house isn't so big to warrant such a visit. I bet demons have been seen along these shores again. What else could attract a Protector's attention?"

An uprising...but Keta didn't speak. The Protectors kept order between houses and the castes in their place. He could only pray to the Forgotten that it was demons from the Haunted Sea and not another purge that brought such a perfect killer into their midst...*What a horrible thing to wish for.*

"Regardless of the reason for the visit, the master wants his holdings in top shape for a visitor of such high status." The overseer glanced around Keta's storehouse. Cured meats hung from chains. Barrels of salted fish were neatly stacked in the corners. The storehouse was already extremely neat and organized, as Keta had learned a long time ago that the best way to avoid trouble was never to *cause* any. "I can't imagine a warrior who can kill demons with his bare hands inventorying meat, but clean everything just in case."

"As you command, it will be done."

"And one other thing..." the overseer leaned in conspiratorially. "I heard the master giving instructions. If it is demons and we're raided, the warriors are to protect the master's household first, then the town, then the livestock next, and once the cows and pigs are safe, only then see to the casteless quarter." The overseer's disgust was obvious. "It's nice to know that years of loyal service has made it so that our master values the chickens more than he values the lives of my children."

Was this a test of his obedience? "That is how they are valued according to the Law."

"I don't think demons honor the Law..." The overseer's eyes darted toward the discarded meat cleaver. "I'd keep that handy if I were you."

"That is just a tool necessary to fulfill the responsibilities assigned to me." Keta said automatically. "I would never—"

"Of course..." The overseer nodded, pretending he had not noticed the way Keta had held it earlier. "It's just a tool. I forget myself. That's not a wise thing to do with a Protector coming. I will spread the word. Get back to work."

He waited until the master's man had left the storehouse before returning the meat cleaver to its place on his apron. The overseer was correct. The master and the Law were correct. A sharpened piece of steel was just a tool. The spears, knives, and clubs Keta had been secretly stockpiling beneath the barrels of fish were also just tools.

His *mind* was the weapon.

"I think the overseer might join with us when the time comes," Keta whispered to his fellow conspirators.

"He strikes me as the master's man," Baldev said. "I wouldn't trust him."

"I don't know. He seemed truthful. I think he's had enough of the Law. Same as us."

"The overseer's words are worth saltwater." Govind's teeth were visible in the dark when he grinned. "Besides, he's given me the whip one too many times for no good reason. He's getting his throat cut, same as the rest of the master's pets, when the time comes."

There was a constant low level of noise in the bunkhouse, as was bound to happen when you packed over two dozen casteless men, women, and children into one shack, so they weren't too worried about being overheard. There were many other bunkhouses just like this one on master's lands, and each one had its own conspirators as well.

"When the time comes? We keep talking about that like it's the return of the Forgotten." Baldev was casual about his blasphemy. "If this Protector is on his way because of us, the time needs to be now. We need to strike soon."

The dirt floor was covered in straw. Everyone slept on top of their personal belongings to keep them from getting stolen during the night. Keta rolled over on his meat cutter's apron to stare at his friend. "Are you mad? We're not ready. There aren't enough of us."

"The master's house only has a hundred warriors. We've got twice that now."

"Have you been out in the sun too long, Govind?" Keta was actually surprised the fisherman could count that high. "Your duty is to mend the nets. That's all you do. Sleep, eat, shit, screw, and mend nets, and then complain about mending nets to us before you repeat it all the next day. Your whole life you've worked on nets. How good are you at mending nets?"

"I'm really good at mending nets."

"So if I grabbed any two men here, and sent them to the beach tomorrow, they together would be able to handle nets as good as you by yourself?"

"Of course not. It takes time."

"Exactly, stupid. The warrior caste's only duty is to fight and train to fight. That's all they do. That's all they care about. You hear them on the other side of that fence, hitting each other with wooden swords from dawn to dusk. They're as good at their duty as you are at yours. No, we wait, until we have enough to overwhelm the house all at once. And then when we win, and we win fast and clean, all of the casteless in this province will rise up and kill their warriors too."

Baldev was the strongest, but he knew Keta was the smart one. "And there's so many of us that even the other houses won't be able to do a thing."

"This province is the ass end of the land. We've got cursed ocean on three sides. The other houses are too busy fighting each other to send an army to deal with us, and by the time they do, we'll have formed our own army. A real casteless army, only then, we won't be casteless anymore. We'll be whole men, like them, and even the Law will have to recognize us."

"Just because you're the only one of us who can read makes you think you're so smart," Govind snarled. "You steal one of the master's books about strategy and you think you're such an expert. You're a dreamer."

The book had merely given him new ideas. Govind had no notion of just how much of a dreamer Keta really was. They were focused on freeing themselves, but Keta wanted to free *all* of the casteless in every province. He wanted to see the great houses in flames. Even though they weren't allowed to speak of the old ways or practice any of their traditions, Keta knew in his heart that the Forgotten was real, and though they had abandoned their god, their god would never abandon them.

"We keep doing what we're doing. Find more like us, willing to fight and smart enough to keep their mouths shut. When the day comes, we'll know. Soon, my friends, it'll be very soon."

Govind grunted. "Fine . . . We'll wait then. And while we wait this Protector will show up, breathing fire, kill us all, eat our souls, and we'll be so much better off . . . I'm going to sleep."

Keta lay on his back, stared at the logs of the ceiling, and tried to ignore the screaming of hungry babies.

Baldev waited a minute before whispering again. "What are we going to do about the Protector, Keta?"

"Nobody will talk. Our plan is safe."

"And if it's not?"

They'd all heard stories about what the Protectors of the Law were capable of. "The Protectors are only men, Baldev. They're only men."

"You are wrong."

Keta woke up with a start. He sat up in the straw, and his first instinct was to move his hands about to make sure no one had stolen his belongings or the meager amount of food he had stashed. It took him a moment to regain enough sense to understand that it was very late, and the bunkhouse was too quiet. The snoring, grunting, and farting of the packed-in bodies seemed muted, like his ears were plugged. But he'd heard a voice . . . Keta looked around, and flinched as he realized somebody was sitting in the straw behind him, only a few feet away.

"The Protectors are more than men now. It is best to think of them as a one-man army, or perhaps a one-man inquisition. They are warrior monks of the highest caste, whose bodies and minds have been broken by hardship and reformed by magic, and if one of them is trying to kill you, then you will more than likely die."

Keta slowly put one hand on the handle of his cleaver. Squinting, he tried to make out the visitor's features in the dark. The stranger was very old, probably forty years at least, thin even by casteless standards, and dressed in fabric made of the coarse woven fibers common to one of their station. "Who're you?"

"Someone who has been listening to your plotting and been

rather amused by it. Our people were thrown down forty generations ago. Do you really think in all those years you are the first who has thought he could destroy the Law?"

"Quiet!" Keta hissed. The old man wasn't even whispering. He scanned the room, but everyone appeared to be asleep. "Are you trying to get us killed?"

"You are doing a fine job of that without any help from me. Besides, none of them can hear us. We may speak freely."

Keta snorted. "What? Are you supposed to be a wizard or something?"

"Yes, Keta the butcher, something like that. I am Ratul, the Keeper of Names, and I have come to help you shake the foundations of the world."

Keta did not speak of the strange visitor to anyone, especially his fellow conspirators. They would have either thought he was mad, or that it was some sort of elaborate ploy to expose them, but a Keeper of Names? They were a tale that casteless mothers would tell their children to give them enough hope to sleep at night. Even talking of the Forgotten's clergy was a violation of the Law. Only a babbling madman would claim to be one. Yet Keta had to know the truth.

The next night he waited for everyone assigned to his shack to fall asleep before sneaking out the back window. His sandals didn't make much noise on the grass. There were so few warriors here that he wasn't worried about being seen, but even if he was he'd never been caught violating curfew before, and more than likely could plead his way out of it by saying that he was going to visit one of the women assigned to a different shack. He'd probably only get a beating to show for it at worst. As much as the higher castes would never admit it, Keta suspected he was too valuable at his duties to start chopping his limbs off for such a minor infraction. He did the work of a butcher and a storekeeper, and it would take far too long to teach another casteless to read the inventory ledgers.

The tide was high. The surf was crashing against the black rocks. Ratul was waiting for him there.

The madman did not turn to look as Keta approached. "Did you know that in the days before the sky opened and the demons fell from the heavens, that man actually moved across the waters in great vessels?"

"That's foolishness." The ocean was pure evil. There were only two things to be found in the ocean, death and fish. And fish were only good to feed to the casteless, as whole men would never touch something tainted by unclean saltwater. "Why would anyone do such a thing?"

"Because we are not alone, or maybe we are now, but we were not then. There are other lands, as big or bigger than this one, and isles, so many isles, thousands of them in between."

Keta knew that there were islands. On a clear day some could even be seen on the horizon. He remembered a time many years ago when some of the casteless decided to try to make it to one. A false prophet had a vision, saying they could go live in a place beyond the Law's reach, and be whole men there. He said the Forgotten would protect them during their journey. Many fools had gone with him on their pathetic cobbled-together boat, while the rest had watched, curious, along the shore. Of course, the demons had come from the deep and consumed them, and the master of the house had laughed and laughed at the foolishness of his non-people.

"There used to be trade, of ideas, things, animals, and crops. Men explored and settled and made new lives and bore children who'd do the same. Now that the demons own the sea, I wonder if those other lands have become as dark and isolated as this one, or if they still live at all? Here, Ramrowan pushed the demons back into the sea. Maybe the Forgotten didn't send other lands such a hero."

He had heard so many conflicting myths and stories, but this was new. "Ramrowan?"

"They've done such a fine job stomping out our history here." Ratul looked at Keta for the first time. "When our God defeated the demons in the War in Heaven, they fell here and began a great slaughter. Mortals could not slice the hide of a demon so God sent one of his generals to the world to protect us. It was Ramrowan who united all the houses and pushed the demons back into the sea. Thus Ramrowan became the First King. We built a great temple at the spot where he fell to the world, and a city sprung up around it. It is still the Capitol today."

"The Law says that there are no gods and no kings," Keta said suspiciously. "There is no temple in the Capitol and there is certainly no king over the houses."

"The Law did not exist then. In those days there were prophets who taught God's will. After Ramrowan died the prophets said that the demons would return again, and only the blood of Ramrowan would be able to smite them. If this blood line died out, we would all perish with it. The sons of Ramrowan were to defend us and their bloodline could never die, or we would be defenseless before the demons. They each took a hundred wives and had many more sons who each took many more wives. Their lives were sacred, and far more important than lesser men, so the first of the castes was born."

"There have always been castes!" Keta insisted. "I read it in a book!"

"Heh . . . You can read? I knew that I chose well. No, butcher, the Sons of Ramrowan were the first caste, and as time went on other castes were created to serve their whims. First were the workers, then the warriors, then the merchants and most of the others that we still have today, all of them created to see that every desire of the Sons was granted. All wealth was theirs to take. Any woman they desired was granted as another wife, because what are the wishes or property of any one house compared to our eternal security from the demons? The priests enforced the will of the ruling caste. They began to replace their god's teachings with the desires of the Sons of Ramrowan. As the numbers of the first caste grew, so did their greed and pride."

"We will rise up and kill them all," Keta spat. "They are still horrible today!"

"Yes . . ." Ratul turned back to the waves. "Yes, they are." He sighed. "Things changed over the generations. The priests began to forget their god and the prophecies were merely tools to gain riches. The church and the Sons of Ramrowan became one and the same, and the priests even bore their name. Eventually the great houses grew in unbelief until they only saw the priesthood as oppressors. The Sons of Ramrowan, who had grown fat and indolent, were no match for the brutal warrior caste they'd created to protect them. The great houses were so angry they destroyed the church and killed every priest they could find. The temples were burned and the statues were smashed. The Law was written to correct the excesses of the first caste, but it went too far. It declared there was no before and no after, so it only set in stone corruption . . . And thus our god was Forgotten."

"You claim to be of the old priesthood." Keta didn't know what to believe. "Why are you telling me this, Ratul?"

"Because the Protector of the Law isn't coming here for your pathetic rebellion, he is coming here for me."

Govind the net mender was at his left, and Baldev the stone lifter was at his right. Today they were not casteless net menders, stone lifters, or butchers, they were soldiers, and they were striking back against the house that had kept a boot on their faces their entire lives. Twenty more casteless were crowding against the doorway behind them, eager to begin.

This is what it must feel like to be a whole man.

The sound of woodcutters' axes falling on sleeping heads was far louder than expected. The warriors' barracks were coming to life. Men were springing from their beds—*the warrior caste got actual beds*—and taking up their swords.

"Kill them all!" Keta lifted his meat cleaver and hurled himself, screaming, at the nearest rising warrior. He lashed out and caught the warrior's wrist as he reached for his sheathed sword. The stump came back, pumping red. Keta snarled and hacked away. Steel parted flesh, opening the warrior's neck clear to the vertebrae, and he flopped back into this blankets.

Keta had never killed a man before, but he found they died not so different than butchering a pig.

Until they fought back...

The warriors collected themselves far too quickly and then their swords were slicing back and forth through the darkness. They stood shoulder to shoulder, each one knowing what to do because they'd practiced together for thousands of hours. A handful of assassins rushed them, and casteless blood splattered the walls and pumped out onto the floor as a result. Another group hit, but the warriors spilt the wave like a cliff rock.

They were a wall of steel. The warriors' backs were to a stone wall. Keta had expected this would happen. They needed to be pulled into the open, so Keta could surround and crush them with superior numbers. "Outside! Everyone run!" Keta slipped in a puddle, but then Baldev had him by the arm, hoisting him and carrying him back toward the door. "Run!"

Of course, the warriors gave chase, because that was what a predator did when its prey fled. Even naked and barely awake, the warriors didn't hesitate. They rushed out the door after the assassins, and right into the waiting spears and hurled rocks of a casteless mob. The pursuing warriors had not expected so many foes, and they died quickly as a result.

There were other barracks, but they were made of wood, so they'd been set on fire. As the coughing warriors tried to come out, they were shoved back with spears. Impaled or burned. The manner of their deaths didn't matter, Keta didn't care, only that they all died.

Keta climbed on top of a barrel so that everyone could see him. He waved his bloody cleaver overhead. "Tonight we show them we are whole men. To the master's house!" If everything had gone as planned, the master would already be dead, throat slit by a casteless pleasure woman who was part of the conspiracy, but Keta didn't want to dampen his new army's enthusiasm. "Onward!"

"Drag him from his hiding place and hang him on the punishment wall!" Govind bellowed as he brandished the dead overseer's whip.

The mob surged toward the master's house. Other warriors would be waiting, and these would be alert, ready, and possibly armored, but there would be no stopping the tide of blood tonight. Keta hopped down from the barrel.

A hand fell on his shoulder, so hard and strong that at first he thought it had to be Baldev, but instead it was the frail old Ratul, the supposed Keeper of Names. "What are you doing?" he demanded.

"Creating an army. Creating a future!"

"All the time I spent teaching you the old ways and you've learned nothing, hot-blooded fool!" Ratul pointed toward the gateway of the master's house. "You've doomed them all."

Shadows created by several torches bounced wildly across the stone walls. There was a lone figure silhouetted in the entrance, blocking the way. Keta had to squint to see. There was a man, tall, broad of shoulder, just standing there, without so much as a tremble before the rushing mob of furious bodies. He had a forward-curving sword in one hand, the tip resting on the steps. His armor was strange, and ornate, each piece of steel intricately etched and filled with silver. The stranger looked at Keta's army... and *smiled*.

It was the Protector of the Law.

"He's not supposed to be here yet," Keta stammered. "There's no way he can—"

The Protector stepped forward, directly into the mob. His movements were quick, difficult to follow, impossible to predict. Spears were thrust into the space he'd been filling and rocks were hurled uselessly through the air. The Protector took another step forward as the first wave of Keta's rebellion fell dead and dying behind him.

Only a few seconds had passed. The rest of the mob didn't even know that there was a nightmare in their midst yet, but then the screaming began, and blood sprayed into the torches and burned, sizzling with that familiar smell. Arms and legs were separated. Heads went rolling. And still, the Protector was untouched. Some tried to fight. All of them died. Others tried to run, a few of them made it.

It wasn't a sword. It was like a farmer's sickle. And the casteless were wheat.

He walked through the trailing edge of the mob, only it was no longer a mob, it was a mass of severed tendons and broken bones. It was like the floor of Keta's butcher shop on the busiest day of the year, magnified and spread over the entirely of the master's grounds.

Baldev was the strongest of them all. He roared as he swung his mighty hammer. The Protector stepped aside and let it shatter the stone where he'd been standing. With barely even a flick of the wrist, Baldev's guts were suddenly spilled everywhere in a tangled purple mass. Govind struck with the overseer's whip. It was clumsy, missing the snap of the overseer's skilled touch. The Protector merely caught the leather, tugged Govind toward him, and sheared the top half of the fisherman's skull off.

Calm as could be, the killer strolled down the path, silver reflecting the light of torches dropped from nerveless fingers. And at that moment, the uprising against House Uttara was broken. Keta's brothers dropped their tools and ran as if the sea demons had come to swallow their souls.

Keta would not run. This was his doing. He lifted the meat cleaver in one shaking hand. "Damn your Law!" he screamed at the Protector. "I will die a whole man!"

"No." Ratul pulled Keta around to face him. "Take this." He shoved a heavy bundle, wrapped tightly in oil cloth, against Keta's chest. "Keep it safe. Go south to the Ice Coast."

"I can't—"

Ratul shoved him away with surprising strength. "Flee, Keta the butcher. A new prophet has been called in the south to guide us. God will choose a general like unto Ramrowan of old to lead us. You will serve them both as they forge a true army. God will guide your path. I have seen it." Ratul reached down and picked up one of the fallen warrior's swords. He spun it smoothly once, as if testing the weight, and the old man did not seem unused to such an implement. Ratul began walking toward the approaching Protector. "It is time for our people to remember what has been forgotten."

Keta watched, horrified, as the Protector approached. He stopped several feet away from Ratul, and then did something that Keta had never seen nor imagined he would ever see from someone of such a high station. The Protector politely bowed to Ratul. "Greetings, Keeper."

"Good evening, Devedas." Ratul returned the gesture, as if he were an equal. "I'd always hoped it would be you."

The two lifted their swords, their stances a mirror image of the other.

Keta the butcher ran for his life.

He ran for hours, across rocks, down the beaches, through the tide pools shallow enough to be free of demons. When he didn't think he could run any farther, he ran some more, vomiting in the sand, but never slowing. When he thought his heart might burst, he still pushed on, terrified, afraid to look back toward bloody House Uttara. He tripped and gashed his head open on the rocks, but he never dropped the heavy bundle Ratul had given him.

When Keta could run no more, he collapsed into a quivering mass of burning muscle, crawled into the hollow of a tree, and pulled branches and leaves over his hiding spot as the sun rose. He'd sleep during the day and run at night. There would be a purge. There was always a purge when the casteless sinned against the Law. Everyone he had ever known was dead or would be soon.

When he awoke hours later, Keta found that Ratul's bundle was still in his hand. The oil cloth had been wrapped tight and cinched with leather straps. Curious, he carefully unwrapped the package.

It was a book. The thickest book he had ever seen. It was nothing like the plain things he's stolen from the master's library over the years. This was bound in a thick black leather, unbelievably smooth when handled one way, but sharp enough to draw blood if rubbed against the grain. He'd heard of such a thing. This was the supposedly indestructible hide of a demon. Keta opened it hesitantly. Each yellowed page was magnificent, packed with letters so small he could barely make them out.

They were names. The book was filled with names and numbers that had to be dates. Linking the names were lines. Page after page, there had to be as many names and lines as there were grains of sand on the beach. It wasn't that different from the ledgers he'd kept all his life, only these were people, not supplies or animals. The master had such a thing for his house, a wall painted with the names of fathers and sons, stretching back for generations. The master called it a genealogy, only that one had been insignificant in comparison to this.

One page had been marked with a folded piece of parchment. That page said *House Uttara* across the top, and it was dense with inked names and lines.

He recognized many of the names . . . These were *casteless* names.

But it couldn't be. Each entry had *two* names. Non-people didn't get two names. Only whole men had a family name. The Law did not allow the casteless to have families . . . Casteless were property. Not people.

Hesitantly, Keta traced his finger down the page until he found his own family name.

Ramrowan.

Heart pounding, hands shaking, he closed the book, then wrapped it tightly in the oil cloth, extra careful to make sure it was sealed and the straps were cinched tight.

Then Keta, Keeper of Names, began his long journey south.

Chapter 31

Dishonored Jagdish walked up to the gates of Cold Stream Prison, wincing as the stitches in his chest pulled with each step. He passed the spot where he'd stood in front of a wall of terrified flesh and sent half a dozen prisoners to the great nothing, and the place where the false Protector Lome had beaten him into the dust. It had rained the next night, so the red stains had been washed away.

Pakpa had warned him to stay in bed. She'd said he shouldn't be up yet. She said he needed his rest. But he knew she was only hoping he'd stay in bed until the crisis had passed, and hopefully Jagdish would be forgotten in the turmoil. Going out now would only draw attention, and the high-status warriors would need someone to blame for this failure. He'd not been summoned, so why go?

They'd only just found out Pakpa was with child. If Jagdish was to be executed for his failures, then his wife would be sent back to her old caste, and his son—for Jagdish was certain it was a boy—wouldn't get to be a warrior. It was best to stay, to keep his head down, to let this controversy blow over. Again he'd been wounded doing his duty, and wasn't that enough?

Pakpa was a good woman, but she'd been raised among the worker caste, so she couldn't understand that a warrior had no choice.

Guards were stationed along the walls, and they weren't his men. They'd seen him coming a long ways off and had warned the others. They met him behind crossed spears.

"I am Risaldar Jagdish."

The reply was stony. "We know who you are." But the spears parted and they let Jagdish through anyway.

It struck him as odd that the great gates were open. But why wouldn't they be? There were very few prisoners left to watch, and none of them would be out of their cells. Many had been slaughtered that night and more had escaped. Some had been recaptured and returned, but many more had just been executed when they'd been discovered by warriors eager to avenge the insult against their house. Jagdish entered the yard and looked around. Bodies were stacked in piles, awaiting cremation. Prisoners who had survived had been questioned, and the troublesome had been hung. Their corpses dangled from ropes, swaying in the breeze. Casteless were still gathering body parts to throw on the piles. Buzzards circled overhead, hopeful the humans would leave soon.

He was surprised to see that an old warrior wearing the insignia of a phontho, a commander of five hundred, was present. Someone of such high status wouldn't normally be inspecting a prison. He was accompanied by a masked Inquisitor. The two of them were studying a nearly headless body that had been dragged across the yard and hung on a pole. A tattered cloak snapped in the wind. All that was really left of the man's head was the lower jaw and some jagged gobs of meat, but Jagdish recognized the intricate armor of the man he'd fought. A soldier whispered in the phontho's ear, and the old man turned to regard Jagdish. His wrinkled face bore the scars of blade and burns, and this one looked to have earned his status through achievement rather than birth.

It hurt to bow, but Jagdish did, as contrite and low as his stiches and bruises would allow.

"Get up." The senior officer approached. The Inquisitor was like his shadow. "You were in command here?"

"I was."

"I read your report."

Jagdish had been questioned while in his hospital bed. "My testimony was as true and complete as possible."

"Then why are you here?"

"To help."

"To help?" The phontho laughed like that was the funniest thing he'd heard in a long time. The Inquisitor didn't make a sound. "To help?"

Jagdish swallowed hard. "Yes, sir."

"Every man under your command on the night watch died. Your responsibility was to keep these prisoners secure, and now most of them are rampaging across the countryside. Valuable hostages escaped, and rather than our collecting ransoms or swapping them for our own captured brothers, they're running for the borders. Worst of all, the most infamous criminal in Lok has escaped. Our Thakoor has been insulted and now he's crawling up *my* ass to bring back the Black Heart's head. Is there any possible way in which you did not fail, Risaldar?"

He pointed at the nearly headless corpse. "I fought that one."

The phontho nodded. "I see. And how many of your men were on duty here that night?"

"Eighteen, sir."

"And you consider eighteen to one a fair trade? Bad luck and bad at math. No wonder no other command wanted you."

That stung. Jagdish was a proud man, and he knew he was a good officer. It wasn't his fault that he kept ending up fighting supernatural menaces. "He was a wizard," Jagdish stated. "The other Protector turned into a great black bird and flew away."

The phontho's hard eyes narrowed dangerously. "I read that in your report. I was hoping that was just because the surgeons had given you some poppy to help you sleep. What you didn't see is that those Protectors swept through this entire place, slitting throats, and your men were so ill prepared and poorly trained that hardly any of them even managed to fight back. Pathetic."

It was one thing to be insulted himself, but to have his men questioned was intolerable. "They were good warriors. They did their duty, but how could they be prepared to fight against magic?"

"There's some truth to that, Risaldar." The phontho softened just a bit. "It's bad enough that once-great Protectors have turned to treachery, but witchcraft as well... These are dark times."

"I don't believe they were Protectors at all. I have fought a real Protector. These fought with trickery, not with real skill."

The Inquisitor spoke for the first time. "Twice now you've been shamed by Protectors, yet you still defend them? Curious."

It was difficult to keep his emotions under control. "This wizard didn't fight like a Protector, and I saw no sign of Ashok Vadal."

"Are you suggesting he's innocent?" The Inquisitor's question was flat and emotionless. "He certainly isn't here."

That was a trap. No matter how hotheaded a warrior might be, only a stupid one would verbally spar with an Inquisitor. "I only speak the truth. I don't interpret it." Talking back to that mask was asking for trouble, so Jagdish focused on the phontho, who at least seemed like an honorable member of their caste. "Allow me to join the hunt for Ashok. I have fought him."

"Many times, from what I've been told. You're dumb, but brave, I'll give you that. However, I believe when it comes to the Fallen, your reason has been compromised. I have an entire legion searching for him already."

"Then let me hunt down the wizards who I know are responsible for this."

"I'm afraid you don't get it, Risaldar. They are one and the same. Ashok and his Protector brethren also destroyed the garrison at Sutpo Bridge. Nearly an entire paltan, a workers' village, and a member of the first caste were killed. Men, women, and children, hell, even the horses and dogs, so many bodies hacked up and tossed into the river that they're still washing up in villages downstream. It wasn't battle, it was savagery. It was a message, a declaration of war against order and decency, and it was delivered by the Black Heart himself."

Jagdish couldn't believe it. "That doesn't sound like the work of Ashok."

"Five years ago I watched the Black Heart almost singlehandedly cut his way through a Makao legion, and afterwards I watched him carry out a judgment malicious enough to end a house war. Don't tell me what you think he's capable of, because I've seen it with my own eyes. He is the ultimate killer."

"Yes, but he's not without honor."

The phontho gritted his teeth. "Enough. You've survived the two most shameful, humiliating moments in our recent history. You allowed your Thakoor to die and now her murderer to escape. You're either cursed with ill fortune or totally incompetent. I don't want your help, Risaldar. No one does."

Jagdish's knees had gone weak. "My assignment then?"

"I'll have papers drawn up discharging your duties. Maybe

someday someone more merciful than I am will see fit to obligate you to some assignment again. Until then, there's nothing for you in House Vadal." The phontho spit on the ground at Jagdish's feet and then walked away.

He was unneeded...That was the worst thing that could happen to a warrior. No unit would have him. There would be no assignments, no opportunities, not even a stipend to live off of. How would he support his wife? His son? He would have to turn to mercenary work, selling his sword to guard merchants' goods or some other low-status behavior just to eat.

The Inquisitor had remained there, studying him through the narrow eye holes of his unnerving mask. "Other than luck or incompetence, there is a third possibility for your presence at these unfortunate events."

"And what would that be?"

"Treachery...A suspicious man might think that you were in league with these rebellious Protectors."

Was that meant to be a threat? "I am no traitor," Jagdish snarled.

The mask moved up and down in the semblance of a nod. "Of course. I was only trying to comfort you, for it's surely better to be thought of as stupid than a criminal. At least the stupid don't go beneath the hot knives. There will be rumors and some will surely say such unpleasant things about you, but if I thought you were in league with the Black Heart then we would be having this conversation in a *very* different setting."

How dare he? But Jagdish kept his emotions in check. "I will demonstrate my loyalty."

"Of course you will," the Inquisitor said in the most patronizing manner. "Farewell, Risaldar. I will be staying here until the Black Heart is found. Should you remember anything else of note, you may ask for me at the castle. I am Senior Inquisitor Taraba."

The Inquisitor left him standing there with Lome's battered corpse dangling over the courtyard, mocking him. He was tempted to draw his sword and hack the ropes, to drop the body into a rotting heap into the dirt, but that would only annoy the phontho further. "I will prove my loyalty!" Jagdish shouted to no one in particular. Lome could no longer hear him, and no lawful man believed in ghosts, but Jagdish whispered to him anyway. "Tell your wretched brothers I am coming for them, and that Jagdish the Warrior will kill them all."

Jagdish's hands were shaking as he stormed back toward the gates. This couldn't be. He was a soldier of Great House Vadal. He'd fought and bled for his brothers, and all of those accomplishments were being torn away. He ignored the sneers of the men at the gates and began walking back toward the city. His heart was heavy. He had no idea how he was going to explain this to his wife. She'd thought that she'd been marrying *up*.

More warriors were approaching up the road to Cold Stream. They were of his paltan, who had been lucky enough to have been on the day watch. They appeared haggard and exhausted, covered in dried mud and scratches. Of course, they'd probably been chasing escapees the whole time, and it looked like they'd had a bit of luck. They were leading several men in chains. One of the warriors saw him and exclaimed, "Risaldar Jagdish! You're here."

He lifted one hand in greeting. The men visibly cheered up. At least these warriors knew him for what he was. "I'm sorry," was all he could say.

But they would have none of it. These men didn't want apologies. They paid him respects and seemed overjoyed to see him. *Jagdish will know what to do.* They understood that it wasn't stupidity or dereliction of duty, but just a good soldier's fate that things randomly went bad. Even though they'd not been on duty that night, they'd been chastised too. The entire paltan had lost face, and low-status prison guards didn't have much to begin with.

"I'm afraid I'm not going to be your officer anymore," he told them. There was a chorus of groans and complaining, as was expected whenever low-ranking warriors lost a leader they actually had respect for. Still reeling, he heard their words, but his brain was having a difficult time understanding any of them.

Then Jagdish noticed who one of the prisoners was. "You..."

The large worker was even dirtier than the soldiers hauling him in. The other prisoners kept their heads down and their eyes averted, but this one stared right back at him with far too much pride, as if they were equals. He folded his thick arms, causing a *jingle* of chains. "My name is Gutch."

"Uppity worker-caste scum," a guard said.

"*Top* of the worker-caste scum," Gutch corrected. "Forge master smith of Vadal City before my unfortunate legal troubles."

"You killed the wizard Lome," Jagdish said.

"I never caught his name before I crushed his head. And you're welcome for that by the way." In the daylight Jagdish could see that the prisoner was even more imposing than he'd remembered. He had a chest like a barrel and a big square head. A cursory glance would lead one to think that he was a bit doughy, surprising considering he'd been living on meager prison rations, but having seen him hoist up the gate bar, Jagdish knew the man was as strong as an elephant. "How about by way of repayment for the favor of saving your life you have these guys look the other way and give me a ten-minute head start?"

Jagdish turned to the senior nayak. "What crime sent him to Cold Stream?"

"Trafficking in illegal magic. The Inquisition says he's still got a year on his sentence."

"Okay. How about a five-minute head start then?"

Jagdish walked over until he was directly in front of the prisoner. Now Gutch was wearing different clothing, far nicer than his blanket with a head hole, but he smelled like he'd spent the night hiding in a pig pen, wallowing in filth.

"Careful, sir. He's a clever one," the nayak warned him. "Don't let the appearance fool you. We found him hiding in the finest brothel in the city. It was only a day after the breakout and he already looked like a banker and had a wallet full of notes. The mess didn't happen until he leapt out a window and we had to chase him through the filthiest stinking canals in the city."

"And you slow bastards only caught me because I got stuck trying to wiggle through a sewer grate. Curse these broad shoulders, I know my mother certainly did when I was born—" One of the warriors helpfully thumped the prisoner over the head with the butt of a spear. "Ouch!"

Jagdish didn't ask the men where the prisoner's new money had gone, as men of their low status were paid stipends barely sufficient to live on, so they'd more than likely pocketed it, but he had a suspicion about how the prisoner had earned it so quickly. "The talisman you took from Lome, you sold it?"

Gutch snorted. "I'm not saying nothing about nobody."

"I don't give a damn about your criminal friends. That night, when you killed the wizard, you said you could sense magic..."

Gutch nodded. "Yeah, sure. I've always had the gift for that, like a bloodhound they used to say."

Jagdish stroked his chin thoughtfully. An idea was forming.

"Like a bloodhound...Stronger the scent, the easier the hunt, I imagine."

"Depends, but basically something like that."

"So while you were here with Angruvadal, surely you'd recognize its scent?"

"Of course! That sword is the strongest damned thing I've ever—" Gutch caught himself. "Hang on. I know what you're thinking...No! Oceans, no. All right, boys, lead me back to my cell."

According to the Law, Jagdish was still commander of this prison until the phontho's papers were filed, and that meant that its charges were his to do with as he saw fit. "Unchain him."

"No, really, on that whole head start thing I was only joking! I'm really not much of a runner."

"Sir, are you sure?"

"I'm taking the prisoner Gutch into my custody." Worst case scenario, the prisoner would escape again, but it wasn't like they could demote Jagdish much further than they already had. Or maybe the giant would smash his head like he'd done to the false Protector, but better a fast death than a slow, embarrassing one.

"What do you intend to do?" one of his men asked.

"I will find and kill those who murdered our brothers, and restore our name," Jagdish vowed.

The warriors cheered.

"Oh, hell..." Gutch muttered.

Chapter 32

Ashok spent a few days down in the dark hole. It suited his mood.

His quarters were a hidden compartment on the barge. It had been cleverly designed by criminals for smuggling goods and people. There was a trapdoor that opened directly into the river, for drinking, washing, and dumping waste, and plenty of air holes for just enough light to see by. Ashok wondered how many lawbreakers had escaped him over the years because of his hesitancy to go onto the water. It wasn't as if Protectors didn't know river traffic existed—it was vital for trade—but it was so distasteful that he'd always thought of it as business best left to the casteless.

The constant rocking still made him uncomfortable, but he was used to it by now. The wounds from the arrows had already healed. The poison had been purged from his system. He could have gone out into the daylight, but Ashok was content to stay in the hidden room, alone ... mostly.

Keta, the so-called Keeper of Names, had paid him a few visits. He'd spout some nonsense about praying for the Forgotten's blessings and mad prophecies, but Ashok ignored him until he went away. The woman brought him food consisting of rice and fish. He was casteless, so it was appropriate fare, but he gagged whenever he tried to put the ocean garbage in his mouth, and ended up picking the fish out. After the first few times she'd quit bringing him that unclean filth. Other than that the woman seemed content not to talk. He'd only learned her name—Thera—because of Keta's continual babblings. The barge was a large one, heavy with cargo, and he only knew the rest of the crew by the sound of their never-ending songs. The casteless avoided him. Whether out of fear or because they'd been ordered to, Ashok didn't know or care.

Days and nights bled together. Ashok didn't know how long he'd been on the river. It was like he'd traded one prison cell for another, only this one was humid and mobile. He had orders, straight from the Chief Judge, that he was to make his way to Akershan, but the barge was heading south, deeper into the interior, so even by sitting here he was still doing as he was told. The Law was still being upheld.

It was a strange thing, upholding the Law by breaking it.

One night someone opened the secret door and poked their head in. In the dark he could barely tell it was the woman, Thera. He still didn't know what she looked like. "Come with me."

He'd been ordered to obey the false prophet, not every petty criminal. "No."

"Fine, you smug bastard. We're landing soon. Stay down here and let the warriors find you for all I care." She climbed back up the ladder.

"Oceans . . ." Ashok waited a moment, and then followed her.

It was the first time he'd been outside since being pulled from the river. The night air was crisp and it felt good to fill his lungs with something that didn't stink of mold. Ashok glanced around. Lanterns were mounted on each corner of the barge, both to light their way, and also so other barges could see them. The casteless were still poling, though there was a stutter in their rhythm as some of them spotted him and stopped to stare. There were lights on both sides of them, small villages along the banks. The river was very wide here, which meant they had to be close to Red Lake. He'd crossed plenty of rivers in his life, but it was a little uncomfortable being on a few pieces of lashed-together timber in the middle of so much water. He couldn't help but reach for his sword to confirm that it was still there.

"Easy there, Protector. There's no demons below us. We're a long ways from the sea now," Thera said.

"I know where we are."

She was hunched over, rummaging through a crate. "Then you know we're getting off soon. No locks into Thao lands, and you can't hardly pole a barge up waterfalls. From here on, we ride, but we won't get anywhere with you looking like that."

The only clothing he had left was a burned, blood-stained pair of prison-issued pants. "I'm casteless. This is sufficient."

"Not carrying that sword around, it's not." Keta joined them. The Keeper of Names leaned on the railing next to Ashok, seemingly unafraid of falling into the river. "If we're to make it to Akershan safely, you'll need to blend in. Casteless can't have weapons and they can't freely cross house borders. Not to mention you'll get frostbite where we're going."

"I'll be fine, Keeper." The tallest mountains of Thao were hills compared to the Order's training grounds in Devakula, and really, who cared if an untouchable froze his nose off?

"No, you won't. We need you to avoid notice, Ashok. Can you do that for us, please?"

In truth, he had no more desire for conflict either. Ashok nodded. "All right."

"I have some things you can wear," Thera said as she shifted through the contents of the crate. "You're about the same size as this barge's last overseer."

"What happened to him?"

"One of your Order suspected him of smuggling and stabbed him in the heart."

"Was he guilty?"

"Yes, but that's beside the point. Here you go." Thera pulled out a bundle of clothing and handed it over. It was the first time he'd ever seen her in the light. Large, dark eyes in a face that was a bit too round to be considered beautiful among the first caste, but she was still rather attractive. *For a criminal.* "Don't put them on yet. You'll need to look casteless until I get our new papers."

Ashok took the clothes from her. They felt sturdy and well made. He held the long coat up to the torchlight. The canvas sleeves bore a green worker's insignia, specifically that of the merchant sub-caste. "I can't wear this."

"Sure you can." Thera touched the same insignia on her sleeve. For a woman, Thera's clothing was remarkably drab in color and cut. "I've got a man in Apura who can forge traveling papers to match, and even say you're authorized to carry a sword to defend yourself from highwaymen. Easier than trying to hide that thing, and sheathed it looks normal enough. I figure if you have to pull that evil creation out for the world to see, we've got worse problems than getting caught with fake documents."

"Fake documents…" Ashok trailed off. Forging an arbiter's stamp was punishable by death. It took all of his self-control not to strike her down on the spot.

Keta reached out to place a calming hand on Ashok's arm, but then he saw the dark look on his face, and must have thought better of it. Logically, Ashok knew that he was no longer of status, and that he and Keta were equal nobodies, but he wasn't used to being *touched*. The Keeper slowly withdrew his hand. "Please, Ashok. If you wish to meet the prophet, this is the only way. If you draw too much attention to my people, you will endanger them. I can't allow that."

"But this is fraud."

"What the hell is wrong with you?" Thera snapped, then, exasperated, she turned on Keta. "What's his problem?"

"It takes time to adjust to a new sit—"

"The problem should be obvious," Ashok said through gritted teeth. No barge-riding lawbreaker could possibly understand that lying left a taste in his mouth worse than the fish he'd tried to eat. "I'm an untouchable. I can't use forged papers. I can't wear the insignia of another caste."

"But you can slaughter whole villages? You can execute women and children!" she snapped. "A monster who can slice the limbs off the relatives of lawbreakers, just to send a message, can't wear someone else's shirt? To hell with your Law, Protector."

Ashok couldn't believe his ears. In his world, no one openly disparaged the Law. In his mind's eye he saw her severed head bouncing across the deck and into the river, but his mission required him to keep his anger in check, so he did. Thera remained there, glaring at him, strangely defiant.

"Thera, stop," Keta implored. "There's no need—"

"It is fine." Ashok took a deep breath. This was *so* hard. She had no idea how thankful she should be that he always followed orders. When it came to punishment, Omand was an artist. It wasn't just the big things, but the indignity of the simple. "Thank you for the clothing."

Thera stomped off without another word.

Ashok watched her go. Keta looked like he wanted to say something, perhaps make up some excuses, but he refrained, which was a good thing right then.

"What's her purpose here?" Ashok asked.

"She keeps me safe."

"Since she tempts me to kill all of you, she's very bad at it."

The city of Apura was the last Vadal holding before entering Thao lands. Borders shifted as the houses rose and fell in power, constantly struggling for land and resources. Before the Thao had claimed the hills to the south, the violent Somsak had ruled the region, and many battles had been fought against Vadal over ownership of Red Lake. The huge lake had earned its name centuries ago after a terrible raid had turned into a slaughter through the city and the Somsak had hurled thousands of corpses into the lake. It was said that they had spilled so much blood in the water that it had attracted demons all the way from the sea.

There could be no doubt that Bidaya's messy end and the shocking revelation that their bearer was an untouchable had weakened his old house, but for now Vadal remained stronger than their southern neighbor. However, seeing how tense the locals were indicated that something was going on. The soldiers patrolling the docks were nervous and numerous, as if they expected a raid at any time.

Ashok hadn't been keeping up on current events. Spending a year in prison had that effect on a man. He watched a squad of gray-clad soldiers jog down the cobbled street. They were wearing all their armor, but with none of the frivolous ornamentation typical of the warrior caste in peacetime. Their packs were heavy, as if they were expecting to be cut off from resupply and would have to make a go of it on their own for a long time. House Thao wasn't normally very aggressive, but Sarnobat and Vokkan were, and it wouldn't surprise him to see the poorer house try to take territory while Vadal was distracted.

"It smells like there's house war brewing. I suspect there are troops massing on the other side of the border," Ashok warned Keta as the two of them walked along the wooden planking of the river docks. "We should find out before trying to cross into the hill country."

"Thera knows who to ask. As a Keeper of Names, I'm supposed to be far beyond petty partisan politics." Keta sniffed.

"Don't start putting on airs. If I recall the history I was allowed to learn, wasn't the old priesthood cast down because they turned to evil and made asses of themselves?"

"Something like that. Pride leads to wickedness, even for those who start with the best intentions," Keta said pointedly. "But I was trying to make a *joke*. Come. Sit, we'll wait for her here." Ashok put down the box concealing Angruvadal, and the two of them sat in the shade of some ragged tarps, killing time until Thera returned with their fraudulent papers.

Apura was an old city, but it was a clean and orderly one. Since the fall of the Somsak it had become a bustling hub of trade. It was predominately a worker city, devoted to traffic and business, so it was crowded, loud, and busy. Most of the city's decoration came in the form of garish painted advertisements for goods and services. The two of them watched as hundreds of casteless moved cargo back and forth.

"I never understood raids," Keta said after a few minutes had passed. "You people are always attacking each other. The untouchables usually remain beneath notice. Their masters change, but the day-to-day misery of life goes on. I don't know why you bother."

"I suppose the warriors need something to do, but there are rules. The Law sets limits on the frequency and numbers involved. A house war is different. It is total war without constraint. Nothing is held back. If gains are to be made, then they must happen before the Capitol becomes involved. If Vadal is seen as weak or distracted, it wouldn't surprise me to see Thao try to claim this lake." Ashok waved his hand toward the multitude of barrels and crates being loaded and unloaded. "Then all the taxes on these goods would fill Thao's coffers instead of Vadal's. You only risk an unapproved war if the rewards are greater than the potential sanctions."

"Sanctions?"

"Protectors...No one breaks up a fight quite like my old Order."

"The firsters and their rules, even rules about murdering each other and stealing their land, well, as long as everyone remains polite about it, then, by all means, carry on."

Ashok was weary of killing his peers, especially when he didn't see a point to it. "We'll be careful. I've no doubt I could destroy a small raiding party, but you asked me to keep a low profile. I don't think you want me to cut my way through a legion."

"That's very considerate of you, but according to what I've heard since we've landed there haven't been any raids. Yes, Ashok, even the casteless can pay attention to politics when those politics mean their huts might get burned down." Keta gave a small nod toward where several soldiers were walking along the planks, examining the laborers. "I think all those extra patrols are looking for you."

With his hair long and unkempt and his beard grown out, it was doubtful anyone would recognize him. The only people who knew him well enough like that to give a good description would be Jagdish and the Cold Stream guards. "They'll have no luck with me looking like any other casteless scum."

Keta snorted. "Yes, because the casteless have such a problem being heavy with muscle from all that extra meat they've eaten over the years. You call yourself casteless, but you don't carry yourself like one. Considering your early years were spent as malnourished as mine, I'm amazed you're so tall."

"Yes. I am bursting with good fortune." Ashok continued studying the patrol until one of the warriors noticed the attention.

"Don't look directly at them! Are you trying to get caught? Casteless keep their eyes down when their betters are around."

It was difficult, but Ashok did so. One of the basic principles of combat was to always be aware of your surroundings. It was hard to imagine going through life staring at his feet all day. But perhaps it was for the best, because if the casteless got in the habit of looking around they might see something they wanted.

"Great. You got his attention," Keta whispered. Only a few steps away, Angruvadal was waiting for him inside a crate. It would be so easy to take it up and teach those warriors that he could stare at whatever he damned well felt like, but that was only the bitterness talking. The Law-abiding didn't deserve his wrath. "Look busy. Help me move these boxes."

Ashok turned from his sword and effortlessly hoisted up a crate full of ore.

"Act like that's hard, damn it. Malnourished casteless aren't supposed to have super strength!" Keta hissed. They went to work. Hopefully the actual owner wouldn't come across them messing with his property. The observant soldier watched them for a bit, until he was satisfied their guilty appearance was due to them being caught in a moment of sloth and not something more nefarious. The two of them kept moving boxes, pointlessly shrinking one pile and growing another, until the patrol moved on out of sight.

"Couldn't you have used your magic to hide us from sight, like the first time we met?"

"I'm no wizard. I just hired one to sneak me into the prison so I could see you." Keta wiped his brow and sat on the box he'd just moved.

"Oh..." Unlike many of his former brothers Ashok had never had the gift for sensing if someone possessed magic or not. "You are even less capable than I suspected then."

"Deceit doesn't come naturally to you, does it, Ashok?"

He pulled up a crate next to the madman. "I never saw the point."

The barge they had arrived on had left as soon as its new cargo had been loaded. Ashok had expressed concern that the casteless aboard might talk. After all, when he'd been enforcing the Law he'd never had a lack of informants willing to sell their loyalty for a handful of notes, but Keta had assured him they wouldn't speak. The Keeper had far more faith in the strength of casteless's tongues than Ashok did. Despite Keta's assurances to the contrary, he couldn't help but notice that many of the casteless were looking their way, as if they'd been recognized.

"I think your crew might have talked. You should have let me silence them."

"There was no need," Keta said. "They're all faithful believers."

"I've dealt with plenty of your faithful over the years. I've not been impressed."

"Oh, but you will be. Wait until we get to Akershan and you see the great and glorious future which is being constructed there. We've never been organized before. Things are changing. Trust me, those pole men won't tell anyone about you now, because in their hearts they believe that someday they'll be able to tell their children and grandchildren about how they once helped the great Ashok."

"Yes, I can imagine." Ashok shook his head. "Gather 'round, children, so I can tell you about how I helped a horrible criminal escape justice."

"Your existence gives them hope."

"Hope stirs them up to pointless rebellion, so they can die futile deaths."

Keta shrugged. "They've lived futile lives. What is some death in exchange for freedom? It is mankind's natural inclination to desire freedom, and the tyrant's natural inclination to control them. Your very existence gives hope to people who have had none. In you, they see someone born just like them, a non-person, but you took up the strongest magic in the world and ruled the highest levels of the Capitol."

"I *took* nothing. The sword picked me. And I didn't *rule* anything. I served. I had a place in the Law, just like every man should." That place was gone now. Now he was nothing. Just like the casteless.

"That's not how they see it. If you could rise up and do so much, why not them too? Why should they have nothing, just because of the status of their birth? You have demonstrated that they can achieve greatness, that they can be whole men too. Together, you, me, and the prophet, we will restore all that has been forgotten. We've been waiting a long time for you."

"Oceans, Keeper. Will you listen to yourself? That's nonsense. I'm the unfortunate byproduct of a lie, nothing more. Nobody's been waiting for me."

"The Forgotten spoke through our prophet and said that a great general would rise, strong as Ramrowan of old, to save our people from evil, build an army, and lead us to reclaim our birthright. He would be descended from the Sons and wielding a sword of black steel. That's why I sought you out in prison. I had to see for myself."

"You traveled a long way for nothing."

"No!" Keta shook his head vigorously. "The Voice of the Forgotten told me how I would know when I'd found the right man. When the rest of the vision is fulfilled, I'll know for certain, and *then* I can take you to the prophet."

The foolish priest just wanted someone with an ancestor blade to join their rebellion. Ashok was certain any bearer would have done. "So what else must I do in order to satisfy this vision? I'd prefer to just get it over with."

"Well, keep in mind the Voice can be a bit cryptic, because the visions only come when the prophet has fallen into a dream state, a trance if you will, where the gods take hold and speak through what the prophet experiences. So sometimes the prophecies may sound strange, but they always work out somehow. On this particular revelation..." Keta looked at his sandals, awkwardly trying to phrase it. "Well..."

"Spit it out."

The Keeper of Names sighed, obviously aware that Ashok wouldn't believe him. "We will know for certain who the Forgotten's chosen general is when the prophet and I witness him willingly sacrifice his life to protect the innocent, while fighting a mighty battle against a demon in the body of a man atop a bridge made of crystal."

Ashok laughed. "Let me amend my earlier statement. No one *sane* has been waiting for me."

Keta grew red in the face. "Ratul was."

That took him off guard. "What do you know about Ratul?"

It seemed Keta regretted saying that name. "I meant to tell you eventually. He was my teacher, the first who exposed me to the truth. It wasn't until later on that I learned what a great man he was. I know the Protectors like to pretend Ratul never existed."

How had Keta met *him?* Ratul was one of those who had a powerful gift for magic, but eventually it had driven him mad. He'd turned against all that was right and good and actively fought against the Law. Ratul had abandoned his obligation and fled, ranting about gods. The Capitol had simply been told that he'd gone missing and was assumed to be dead. It was a common enough fate for Protectors, and it had spared them the public embarrassment of having one of their leaders turn fanatic. "We don't like to speak about Lord Protector Ratul."

"I've been told that internally your Order called him the Traitor. I wonder if *you've* since claimed that title from him?"

Now the Keeper was just being spiteful. Ashok took a deep breath and held it until the urge to backhand Keta in the face passed. "Ratul was a coward and a liar."

"No, Ashok, I'd say it was exactly the opposite. He discovered the truth and had the courage to do something about it. Ratul was a wise man. When he learned that he'd been on the wrong side, he did what wise men do and tried to make things right. He sought out the records of our forefathers and helped keep the new prophet safe. He taught me about the Forgotten and showed me what to do. If it wasn't for him—"

"I would still have a place!" Ashok roared. Several casteless looked in their direction. The few who seemed to suspect who he was looked away fearfully, while the ignorant seemed distressed that one of their own would raise his voice in public. "Don't speak to me as if Ratul is some kind of hero. He could have ended my fraud when he first learned of it, but his greed allowed the lie to continue so that I could destroy the Order's enemies for him."

"If he'd exposed you, you would have been killed."

"Better to die like that than live like *this!*" Ashok gestured around the dock and its filthy denizens. Temper flaring, Ashok lowered his voice to a dangerous whisper. "How dare Ratul think he's better than the Law? Yes. I'm certain I've claimed his title. Through no fault of my own I became a traitor, but Ratul betrayed us willingly. He abandoned the Order in exchange for you delusional fools!"

"He turned to the Forgotten because of *you.*"

Ashok was so furious, that took a moment to sink in. "Explain yourself."

"Your Lord Protector studied the old ways, not as a believer at first, but so as to better understand his enemies. They were nothing but myths to him, until the day he found out an ances-tor blade had picked an untouchable child to be its bearer. Then Ratul realized the old prophecies were being fulfilled. It told him that great and terrible events were upon us. *You* are the reason he left your Order. Your calling by Angruvadal is the reason he abandoned your precious Law."

Ashok's anger was growing hotter. "No more of your lies. Ratul lost his mind and disappeared. He fell in with delusional fools babbling about false gods. Mindarin tried to reason with him, but he left and we never saw him again. Apparently he found some dumb enough to listen. Ratul was once the best of us, but now I hope he's living in some casteless shack, shoveling shit to earn his fish. Let him preach his nonsense for the rest of his pathetic life."

Keta gave him an incredulous look. "I can't believe this. You really don't know? The Protectors tracked Ratul down years ago."

"Impossible." Something like that would have been recorded and reported.

"Ratul died in Uttara at the hands of one called Devedas."

Angruvadal felt his rage, and was quick to respond. The sword called to him from the other side of the flimsy wooden box, eager to dispense justice. "Silence." Ashok lurched to his feet and took a few steps away, just far enough that the sword wouldn't tempt him. Devedas had never told him any such thing. If he'd found their old master, he never would have hidden it from the Order. "I'm done listening to your lies. Don't speak of this further."

Keta nodded slowly. Even the seemingly oblivious Keeper seemed to understand that he'd gone too far this time. Yet he finished what he had to say. "Believe what you want, but I was there."

At that moment, it was either walk away or kill Keta, and he still had orders to follow, so Ashok walked away. He went down to the lake and stood by the shore, close enough that he could retrieve his sword, but not so close that it tempted him to spill blood. At times it was as if the sword sensed his emotions and magnified them. Sometimes he didn't just have to deal with his own wrath, but also that of fifty generations of its bearers as well. He could feel the weight of their gaze upon him.

Why did you choose me? You foolish sword, why me?

The casteless moved their boxes, sang their work songs, and caught their dinner with hooks and strings. Ashok watched them, and hated them for his being one of them. They might be his people now, but that didn't mean that he had to *like* them.

Chapter 33

The three of them rode through the forested hills south of Red Lake. The only sound was the slow clomp of their oxen's hooves and the creak of wagon wheels along the rocky trail. The ponderous animals were annoyingly slow to a man who could outrun a horse over short distances. But merchants without merchandise were suspicious, so they had purchased the wagon in Apura.

Keta had not shown Ashok where he kept the notes hidden, but it was obvious he had a large supply of money. When asked, the Keeper had cryptically told him that the rebellion had many wealthy backers, even some in the Capitol. Ashok assumed that was an aggrandizing lie, and the money was actually the reward from some horrible criminal endeavor.

Keta was driving the team. Ashok sat on the bench next to him, and Thera was behind them, nervously watching the other travelers through slits in the canvas.

"They're crowding up ahead. This must be the checkpoint," Keta said. They couldn't see around the curve of the rocks until it was too late, and then they were stuck in a line of travelers waiting to have their papers stamped. This was an excellent spot to catch tax evaders, as there was no way to backtrack without being seen. With rocky hillsides and thick forest on both sides, it would take too long to turn a wagon around to flee, and there would certainly be at least one warrior somewhere nearby with a good vantage point watching for suspicious activity.

Ashok may have looked like a merchant, but he certainly didn't feel like one. Here he was, sitting instead of marching or riding, dressed in a warm coat instead of cold armor, bathed and groomed, yet he was far more uncomfortable than at any point of his training. He'd rather be a tired, freezing, starving, exhausted acolyte than a comfortable liar.

The checkpoint came into view. It was more of a shack really, with some simple wooden barricades that could be dragged across the road. Normally this out-of-the-way trail would only have a handful of low-status warriors garrisoned here, but several large tents had been set up in a field beyond the shack. At least a pal-tan of troops were encamped here. Their flags bore the symbol of a yellow sun rising over a red mountain.

"These soldiers are from Thao," Ashok mused. "This pass used to belong to Vadal. My old house must be even more vulnerable than I thought if they're losing ground to them."

"Yeah, you pretty much screwed up everything," Thera said.

He felt bad about that. Their leaders had committed fraud, not the people. Harta—the silver-tongued bastard who he'd once thought of as a cousin—would find some way to return Vadal to its prior glory... unless, of course, Ashok had the opportunity to take his life before then.

"Don't worry. These traveling papers are perfect. We'll be fine," Thera assured them.

"It's taking too long," Keta said.

Ashok called upon the Heart of the Mountain, this time concentrating on his sight. Distant objects came into clearer focus. Far ahead, the guards weren't just checking papers, they were also searching each wagon. Warriors were even crawling between the wheels and thumping the sides with a mallet, looking for hollowed-out smuggling compartments. As he watched with the eyes of an eagle, a man was led off to the side. That one was dressed in the cheap armor of a caravan guard and had a sword sheathed at his side. While several warriors watched, the sword was drawn and shown to an inspector. Satisfied that it was only steel, the guard put it away and was escorted back to his wagon.

Of course, very few people would recognize Ashok on sight,

but there was no way to disguise a terrifying black steel blade. He let go of the Heart and his eyesight returned to normal. "They're looking for Angruvadal."

"So now the other houses know you escaped," Thera muttered. "This complicates things."

There was no way Harta would have asked their neighbors for help, but if word of his escape had gotten out... Ashok couldn't guess at how huge a ransom could be demanded for the return of an ancestor blade. Worse, they could try to keep Angruvadal for themselves. Would it pick a worthy bearer from another house? Who knew? The inscrutable sword had picked a casteless last time.

Search complete, that caravan passed through the checkpoint. The line advanced. Their oxen had done this sort of thing so many times they didn't even need to be motivated to obediently trudge forward.

There was no place to turn the wagon without raising an alarm. Keta and Ashok had already been seen on the bench. If they got out and ran, they'd be spotted. Keta shot him a nervous glance. "What are we going to do?"

He saw no other options. They were trapped. The soldiers were going to have to die. He'd been doing his best to avoid killing, but he was incapable of not fulfilling his orders. He couldn't let these warriors stop him. More law-abiding men were going to perish because of Ashok's existence. Anger flashed, but it was aimed entirely at himself.

He put one hand on Angruvadal's hilt. Flickering images and bits of other men's memories filled his mind, as the sword analyzed the terrain and decided on the most efficient way to kill everyone. He counted the visible soldiers, but then he found his mind wandering, using that number to guess at how many widows he was about to create, and how many children would never know their fathers. What great deeds would these men have accomplished if they'd not had the misfortune of straying into his path?

"I'll take care of them," he whispered as he shook his head. It was not like him to lose focus. Ashok cursed himself for the momentary lapse, and refocused on the impending mass murder he was about to commit. The hard part would be killing all of them before they could send for help. They wouldn't have a runner that could escape him, but if their risaldar was smart, he'd have multiple messengers ready to go in different directions. Even as fast as Ashok was, he could only be in one place at a time. "I only see a few horses. If anyone goes for those, try to slow them. We can't let them get away or we'll have a whole legion descending on this pass."

"So much for your trying not to kill anybody," Keta said.

"Thank your false gods I have orders, because these soldiers' lives are worth far more than ours," Ashok snarled.

"Orders?" Keta asked.

The momentary distraction had made him slip. He'd said too much.

"Wait!" Thera had begun searching through one of their cargo crates. "I've got an idea. Stick with the plan. Try to act normal. Don't attack unless you have to."

The sword could find no memory where hesitation was the best option.

"Please." She sounded desperate as she pulled two large clay jugs from a crate. "Trust me. I can get us through."

Ashok let go of his sword.

"Thera, where are you going? Wait," Keta demanded, but she'd already slipped off the back of the wagon. She landed on her knees, and quickly rolled into a ditch. Thera scrambled forward, pushing the jugs ahead of her, and crawled into the brush. Her movements had been so smooth it was doubtful that she'd been seen. She was dressed in earth tones, and even the false merchant's insignia was dark, so she blended in with the fall foliage.

"She's quick," Ashok admitted.

"I just hope she doesn't get hurt." Keta sounded very concerned, and Ashok suspected it wasn't for himself. "We'll do as she said and wait."

Angruvadal didn't like it. The sword wanted to kill everyone *now*.

Several tense minutes passed as more wagons were searched and more armed workers were examined. There were several casteless walking behind one wagon, probably being transferred to a different house, and one of them must have done or said something that angered a soldier, because the non-person was dragged from the line by his long dirty hair and thrown down. The warrior gave him a savage beating with a stick he'd picked up from the side of the road until his arm got tired, and then he went back to his search, laughing.

"You see that, Ashok? That's your 'law.' That's what you've been defending."

"There's more to it than that."

"Not really."

"Shut your self-righteous fish hole. I'm trying to concentrate." Since he couldn't see Thera through the densely packed trees, Ashok had sharpened his hearing. Farther up the hill there was the scramble of boots finding purchase on loose rocks, scratching, and then a thump of something being put down. He had no idea what Thera was up to. There was the whisper like a knife leaving a sheath. Even with the Heart of the Mountain helping him, the next part was hard to discern, but there was a scraping noise—*a firestarter*—then a tiny crackle. Something was burning.

Another wagon passed through, and their obedient oxen lumbered forward. A female casteless and two small children had gone to the barely conscious untouchable lying in the weeds and dragged him back onto the road so they wouldn't lose their place in line. The current wagon was filled with non-people clad in rags, so it was easy to search. It didn't take too long before it was their turn.

A Thao soldier approached their wagon with a spear over one shoulder and a bored expression on his face. "Travelling papers?"

"Of course, noble warrior," Keta proclaimed as he produced the forged documents from inside his merchant's coat.

The warrior took the papers and scanned over the stamps. Wearing the insignia of a lowly junior nayak, he couldn't have been more than sixteen years old. The Thao tradition was to grow out long mustaches, but he barely had fuzzy hairs on his lip. Ashok knew that he would have to kill this one first. The warrior noticed Ashok's sheathed sword. "Step down from there and come with me."

Ashok didn't move.

"Forgive him, noble warrior, he means no offense. My bodyguard's not very bright and doesn't listen well. What do you need him for?" Keta asked innocently.

"A special inspection that's of no concern to you, merchant. Come on, dummy. Let's go."

There was a clatter of rocks as Thera slid down the hill. Now she was heading straight for their camp. He didn't need the Heart to help him hear what came next, because Thera began screaming at the top of her lungs. "Raiders! Vadal raiders are coming!"

The camp erupted. Warriors sprang from their tents and ran toward the commotion. A risaldar at the checkpoint began shouting orders.

Thera stumbled out of the woods, screaming. "Vadal raiders coming down the hill! Hundreds of them! Hundreds!"

The young warrior turned to see. Ashok thought about kicking a dent into his helmet, but he waited as he'd been told. There had to be more to Thera's plan than this. The soldiers weren't stupid. It would quickly become obvious that there were no raiders and then—

BOOM!

Part of the hillside disappeared in a spreading cloud of dirt. Thunder rolled across the checkpoint. The young warrior jumped back and crashed against one of their wagon wheels, covering his face as bits of rock and bark rained from the sky. The oxen lurched forward, bellowing in consternation.

"What was that?" the nayak screamed.

BOOM!

The second blast was just as big as the first. Whatever Thera had ignited on that hillside was rather impressive.

"Vadal battle wizards!" Keta pointed at the hillside as debris pelted their canvas. "Come to kill us all!"

A noxious gray smoke was rolling through the checkpoint. It burned the eyes and stung the throat. Within seconds Ashok could barely see past the oxen.

The warrior drew his sword and exclaimed, "Get out of here. We'll stop these bastards!"

Keta snapped the ropes hard. "*Yah!*" The oxen heaved and strained and the cart started forward.

They rolled through the stinking haze. Soldiers were running to engage the imaginary foe. There was some swearing and exclamations as untouchables and warriors both had to get out of the way of their oxen before being trampled. Ashok smiled. Every man had his place, but eighteen-hundred-pound beasts of burden didn't care what anyone's social status was.

Bowstrings thrummed as archers fired at shadows on the hillside. The risaldar was doing a very good job organizing a counterattack against their imaginary foes. A merchant's wagon not paying its toll was the least of their worries. They were most of the way through the encampment before Thera reappeared and caught the back of their moving wagon. She sprang up onto the boards and ducked under their canvas.

"How long will that smoke last?" Ashok asked.

"Not long."

Keta thumped the oxen again, not that the frightened beasts needed much motivation to get away from the thunder.

"What was in the jugs?" Ashok demanded.

"Fortress alchemy." Thera was breathless, flushed and excited. "This mix looks like coal dust but blows up like a volcano. Everything it sticks to burns and makes that nasty smoke."

He'd figured as much. Ashok had never dealt with such things himself, but some of his brothers had. They'd faced terrible fire and thunder, capable of ripping through armor like it was cloth. Between their strange powers and their island's location, Fortress was the only place in Lok that had never bowed to the forces of the Law. "Witchcraft."

Thera laughed. She was actually enjoying herself. "It's ground-up stink rock and salts and bird shit. There's nothing magical about it."

"Witchcraft . . ." he muttered to himself again.

Keta saw Ashok's dark expression. "Did you have to kill any of those innocent warriors today, Protector?"

"No," he had to admit. "No, I didn't."

It wasn't until later that Ashok realized that Keta had called him by his old title.

They'd not seen a warrior for hours. The roads had been empty as clouds had rolled in and a light rain had begun to fall. The slow bump and sway of their wagon gave them time to talk.

"So, you're the priest's bodyguard?"

"Something like that," Thera answered.

Ashok appreciated economy of speech as much as the next man, but she'd not answered his question. With nothing better to do, and many long miles ahead of them, Ashok decided to try again. "It seems strange to hire a woman to guard a man."

She was still trying to be evasive. "There's more to keeping someone safe than swinging a sword. I know my way around and I know the right people."

"Meaning you willingly associate with criminal scum," Ashok meant it more as a statement than an accusation, but Thera stiffened. She was sitting next to Keta on the driver's bench. It was hard to tell since every time he'd seen her she'd been wearing a cloak, hood, and scarves, but she appeared to be tall and strong for a woman, but even then, a very strong woman could be physically overpowered by an average man. Keta was a priest, and priests were supposed to be important. This rebellion couldn't have lasted as long as it did if they were stupid. "Do you have any other witchcraft?"

"*So anything you don't understand is witchcraft?* Then I've nothing of note to you, *Inquisitor.*" The way she spat the word left no doubt as to her feelings about that Order. Their methods were harsh and unforgiving, but there was no room for error when dealing with treason or forbidden magic.

"I was never an Inquisitor."

"But you killed people on their behalf."

Ashok didn't dignify that with a response. Of course he had. That had been his obligation.

"She's more dangerous than she looks," Keta supplied. "And I don't just mean the alchemy."

He couldn't tell if Keta was complimenting her because women were supposed to enjoy that sort of attention, and though the priest had tried to hide it, Ashok had seen earlier that he was genuinely concerned for her, or maybe Keta was being sincere and she actually was dangerous. Ashok decided to push her as a test. "She has no real magic and can't fight. What good is she?"

Ashok was riding in the back with the cargo, so for a moment couldn't tell if it was the oxen or the woman who snorted, and then he decided it was the woman. "I'll tell you, Ashok, I like to let the well-muscled fools like you stand there and hack each other to bits while I hang back and look nonthreatening. I prefer surprise—" Thera spun and lashed out with one hand. The knife flashed, flicking end over end. It would have stuck into the barrel next to him, making for an impressive display, except Ashok effortlessly snatched the knife out of the air before it could reach its target.

Thera was surprised by the inhuman reflexes. Her mouth hung open, and that expression gradually turned into a frown. "So much for getting the drop on the likes of you."

He tested the balance of the little blade. It was more of a spike, sharpened on each end, and heavy enough to cause a serious puncture wound at close range. He wouldn't want to catch one in the skull. "Very nice. I've been told the warriors of the Ice Coast like to play games with these." Then he tossed it back.

Thera caught it and quickly hid the spike inside one of her voluminous sleeves. "More practical than darts and keeps the forts free of vermin. A running rat is a much harder target than a man's throat."

"So you were born of the warrior caste." No house sent their women off to fight unless they were extremely desperate, but that didn't mean their women didn't know how to. It fell to the warrior caste's women to protect their lands from raiders when most of the men were off raiding other houses. So Thera would have at least had had some training, and depending on the house's traditions and her teachers, she might even be useful in a battle. "Good."

"I didn't say I couldn't fight. I'm just not an idiot about it. The last time some bandits threatened our good Keeper here, I pretended to be his wife and scared out of my wits. I let their leader drag me off by the hair thinking he'd have his way with me, but it doesn't matter how much stronger you are when the knife you didn't see cuts off your cock."

"True." Keta shuddered. "Seeing that unnerved me, and I was a butcher."

"Then we dropped the other two while they were distracted by his screaming," Thera proclaimed, obviously proud of her work. "If my enemy sees me coming, then I've not done my job."

In combat you needed to work with your strengths and avoid your weaknesses. Thera was pragmatic. Ashok approved of such philosophy. "You must have belonged to a house once. Why would you leave it to become a lawbreaker?"

"If I wanted to be interrogated I'd turn myself over to the Inquisition."

"I'm sure they'd enjoy that, but you don't seem naïve enough to believe in these fools' false gods."

"False?" Keta sputtered. "They were real enough to guide us to you in time to save your ungrateful life!"

Thera laughed. "Calm down, Keeper. You'll spook the oxen." She turned back again, this time with a malicious gleam in her eye. "I'm not insulted, but as for the Forgotten? Keta will talk your ears off on the subject if you let him, but I pay him no mind. I don't believe in such things."

Perhaps it was the flick of her eyes to the side as she said it, or something else that gave it away, but she was lying to him. He had interrogated far too many criminals not to sense it. He just wasn't sure if she was lying to him or to herself on this particular topic, so he let it go. "Then why join with the rebels?"

"I'm not inclined to believe in things I can't see with my own eyes, but this invisible god's rebellion has money to spend, and money buys power."

"And what does power buy?"

"Revenge." Then Thera paused, scowling, as if she'd realized she'd said far too much. She turned her attention back to the road.

Keta was studying her as well with a strange look on his face, and those were emotions that Ashok couldn't decipher. But Keta composed himself and said, "Personally, I believe the best thing power can buy is *freedom*... What do you say, Ashok? With that sword of yours you've got more power than any of us. What do you hold dear enough to purchase with it?"

Ashok had no answer.

Chapter 34

Ashok lay on his blanket, looking up at the clear night sky and its millions of stars. The others thought he was asleep, but in truth he was eavesdropping on Keta and Thera's whispered conversation. The two of them were on the far side of the wagon, out of range of normal hearing, but with the Heart of the Mountain aiding him could still make out their words over the crack and pop of their fire.

"Are you certain?"

"Yes," Keta hissed. "In the heat of the moment, Ashok mentioned having orders. I'm surprised you didn't catch that."

"I was a little preoccupied trying to pick out the right jugs. It isn't like we label our contraband, and some of those detonate the second they catch fire. Blowing myself to pieces might have still made a great distraction for you two, but for me that plan had a few drawbacks...What kind of orders?"

There was a long pause. Ashok assumed Keta was shrugging or giving a perplexed look.

"I'll tell you what his orders probably are," Thera stated. "Destroy the rebellion. Bring back the prophet's head in a sack... Don't look at me like that, Keeper, you know I'm right."

"But the Voice of the Forgotten was clear—"

"*Clear?*" Thera raised her voice in anger, then quickly lowered it so that Ashok wouldn't hear. Not that it mattered, though she had no way of knowing that. "There's nothing clear about that thing. Assuming the Voice isn't just the result of some crazed fit from an addled mind—"

"Thera, please," he pleaded. "I've heard it. If you could hear it yourself, you'd know too. Don't let the words of the doubters shake your faith."

"So let's say you're right, and it is the Forgotten taking hold and speaking. It didn't come out and call Ashok by name. If you're wrong, you're endangering everything you've accomplished in Akershan. You've created something great. True or not, the people listen to you, and they're changing the world. Are you really going to lead a monster right through the front door to threaten everyone you love?"

"I *will* keep you safe," Keta vowed.

For some reason, despite knowing it was correct to maintain every tactical advantage, listening in on this particular conversation made Ashok feel dishonest. He tracked the path of the smaller moon, Upagraha. The small bright dot moved leisurely along its regular nightly trajectory as Ashok waited through their awkward silence.

Thera sighed. "He's not taking orders from the Forgotten, Keta, but he's certainly taking them from someone. I'm not saying we have to kill him or anything like that, but the next city we reach, it would be really easy to just disappear. Ashok would never find us. Then we can go where the Inquisition can't catch us. No more of their castes, no more of their Law... You've carved out a home, why not go back?"

"How long will that home survive, Thera? The Law will never rest until it has control of everything. It can't abide even a taste of freedom. We've drawn the Capitol's ire, and they'll find our people eventually. The Voice can guide our spirits, but it falls to us to protect our flesh and blood. We need a general to lead our rebellion or we will fail. Finding him is my responsibility. *Mine.*"

"You're blinded by your own stubborn belief. If you're not going to listen to me, why should I even bother being here? Maybe I'll just sneak off at the next town and leave you and the Protector to continue on your merry journey. Then when he slaughters all of you like pigs, it won't be on my head."

"You can't. The rebellion needs you. *I* need you. You're too important. You may doubt the gods, Thera, but they believe in you."

"If we're both so special, then maybe I should wait until you aren't paying attention, then set another one of those Fortress bombs on fire and roll it over to Ashok's bedroll. Then we'll see which one of us your gods believe in more."

Before his fall, he wouldn't have cared what they thought of him. For some reason, now they actually mattered. Plus, Ashok didn't like the idea of being blasted into a cloud of bloody chunks in his sleep. It was time to deal with this foolishness. He got up, walked around the wagon, and approached the campfire. The two conspirators were sitting next to each other, wrapped in wool blankets to stay warm.

Thera saw him coming. "You're awake."

Keta couldn't help but look guilty. "We were just—"

"Talking. Yes." Ashok sat on another fallen log and studied his companions. "About my orders."

They shared an uneasy glance. Thera shifted beneath the blanket, probably to put a hand on one of her many concealed knives. "Oh?"

"I like your bomb idea. Pragmatic, but unnecessary." Ashok forced himself to smile, but from their reaction that actually made things worse, so he stopped. "You are correct. I was given orders as punishment for my crimes, but I am forbidden from ever speaking of them."

"Convenient," Thera said.

"I keep my vows. On the barge I made an agreement with the Keeper, and I am just as bound by that agreement as any that came before. You have my word that I intend no harm to you, your compatriots, or your prophet. I will not expose you nor will I hinder your goals."

"That's an easy thing to say," Thera muttered.

Ashok met her gaze and locked onto her eyes. "Do you doubt my word?"

She didn't look away. There was strength there. Very few people could stare down a Protector, but she watched him for a long time, surprisingly defiant. Finally she admitted, "No...I don't."

"Good." It made him wonder just what kind of life Thera had lived to be able to stand up to him like that. She was angry, but she'd found power in it. He continued looking at her until the wind shifted and the smoke stung his eyes. "If you don't believe me, then use that knife you have in your hand and drive it into my heart now. I won't stop you."

Keta cleared his throat. The Keeper had almost been forgotten in the exchange. "Ashok, may I ask—"

"No."

"What do you intend to do when you meet the prophet?" Thera demanded.

"Offer my allegiance. If accepted I will serve to the best of my abilities for the rest of my days."

"And if denied?"

"Then I will leave my ancestor blade on the shore and wade into hell."

"For your sake, I hope the gods are less suspicious than I am."

"I'm certain that an inspired judgment will be made once we reach Akershan," Keta interjected.

Thera nodded slowly. "I'm sure it will." Beneath the blanket, Ashok could tell that Thera let go of her knife.

Ashok felt like they'd come to an understanding.

Chapter 35

It was a strange sensation being the bait in a trap, terrifying, yet exhilarating at the same time. As Rada walked through the busy streets of the Capitol, she knew she was being watched by Inquisitors. Rada would not have agreed to this if she'd not had complete faith in Devedas' promise to keep her safe.

The large man next to her was supposed to be her slave. His thick arms were loaded with books taken from the library, none of which were special or of any real value, but the men tailing her wouldn't know that. All they would see is that the archivist they'd warned to remain silent was approaching the estate of the presiding judge in broad daylight, without having been summoned, carrying lots of evidence. Devedas had told her that the conspirators would assume the worst—that she was about to present the true report on the casteless question—and try to stop her. That had not been very reassuring.

It was early morning. The streets were crowded this time of day, as everyone tried to get their business done before the desert became too hot. A network of massive aqueducts divided the Capitol into six different districts, and Rada was walking toward the richest one, where the estates made her father's house look tiny and poor in comparison. By now the men following her would know that there was only one possible place she could be going and they would be prepared to act. Rada paused under the shade of a great stone wall to collect herself. If everything went according to plan, within a few moments someone would try to murder her.

"Are you all right, Senior Archivist?" her *slave* asked.

"I'm fine, Karno," she assured the Protector. In humble gray robes and a wide straw hat, he was not nearly so intimidating as when they'd first met. He might not have been carrying that ridiculous hammer, but by the way he'd hauled such a heavy stack of books all this way without ever so much as the slightest sign of exertion or so much as a bead of sweat on his face, she could only assume he didn't need a hammer to hurt anyone.

"It's fine. You'll be safe," Karno whispered.

"Will they really think I'm this stupid, this naïve, that I'd thwart them so brazenly?"

"They'll expect no subterfuge from a bookworm," the big man explained patiently. "I mean no offense."

"The library is the noblest calling in the Capitol, why would I be offended?" Rada looked around the jostling mass of humanity she'd have to pass through, men, women, young and old, of three castes and their slaves, any of them could be an Inquisitor waiting to drive a poisoned blade into her as she passed by. There was no way to recognize them without their masks. "There's just so many of them."

"Only a few will be assassins."

"That's not helping."

"Devedas is near. Do you trust him?" Karno asked.

More than she'd ever trusted any man. She didn't know if that was a side effect of being in love for the first time, or if he really was as capable as she believed him to be, but Devedas had said he'd needed her help, so she'd agreed to be a target. She didn't understand the political nuances of everything that was going on, but the rebellion in the south was causing a lot of trouble, fragile alliances were being strained, and there was a power struggle going on between the righteous Protectors and the insidious Inquisitors. Her father had warned her to stay out of it, because no matter who won, the library would still be there. But he didn't know she was sleeping with the Lord Protector either.

"I trust him." Rada's mouth was suddenly very dry, and her

legs didn't want to work, but she continued into the judge's district anyway.

Her nerves were twitching, but she tried not to flinch as the crowd pressed around her. Rada did her best not to show her fear, but she didn't know how the warriors did it, somehow keeping their emotions concealed while threatened. People bumped into her. Normally everyone avoided colliding with a member of the first caste, but most of these were first caste, functionaries who worked in the various bureaucracies, and she was nothing special here. A woman was coming right at her. Rada almost shrieked when she saw the woman had a mask, but then she realized it was only a veil over her face in the Zarger style. Before she could brush against Rada's arm, Karno bumped into the woman with his stack of books and knocked her aside.

"Watch it, oaf."

"Apologies," Karno said as he bowed his head submissively.

"You should have your slave whipped for his clumsiness," the woman spat as she continued on her way.

"I will. Bad slave!" Rada exclaimed.

Karno was right next to her as they walked. He seemed perfectly calm, but his eyes were darting back and forth as he absorbed every detail of the people around them. They were surrounded by bodies, so close that Rada could smell their perfume or what they'd eaten for breakfast. Then she realized that Karno wasn't just looking side to side, but upwards as well, checking the windows and roof tops. There were flags, colorful banners, and curtains rustling in the breeze. The lower rooftops were shielded from view by lattice walls woven with vines. An assassin could be hiding behind any of those things. She'd not even thought about being shot with a poison dart. The assassins in the adventure books she'd read always used blow guns with poison darts! The buildings were three and four stories tall here. That was a *lot* of windows. It was still a mile to the judge's estate, but she was so nervous she didn't think she'd make it that far. Another minute of walking and being brushed up against by several strangers and Rada was sick to her stomach, flushed, and sweating.

Luckily, she didn't have to go very far before they struck. In fact, she'd have been dead twice before she'd even realized she was under attack if it hadn't been for Karno.

Suddenly, he dropped all but one of the books. Rada turned to see what was the matter, but the big man reached out, lightning quick, and shoved the book right in front of her face. *Thunk*. At first she'd thought the blur had been a flying bug, but then she saw the fletching and realized an arrow had been stuck deep into *Urag's Compilation of Trade Regulations*.

An instant later Karno had turned away to intercept a plain-looking worker. It wasn't until Karno had grabbed onto him that Rada realized the worker was holding a knife in his hand, hidden low at his side. It was hard to tell what happened because it was all so fast, but Karno twisted the worker's arm in a direction never intended by nature. The man snarled, struggled, then cried out in pain as Karno levered him around and snapped the bones of his arm. Karno took the worker's knife away and stabbed him in the stomach so hard that it lifted the worker from his feet. Karno twisted and the man screamed. A blob of blood fell and burst on the stone. Droplets hit Rada's shoes.

Shocked, she looked up to see that several warriors were pushing through the crowd straight toward her. The violence had all happened so fast that it made no sense that their swords were already drawn. "Get down," Karno told Rada, as he lifted the impaled man to shoulder height, then *threw* him at the warriors. The impact swept people from their feet, and from their shocked and indignant reactions, most of them weren't assassins. But the warriors kept on coming.

As Rada ducked behind a noodle cart, Karno spread his arms and calmly waited for the warriors to approach. There were four of them, wearing the insignia of Capitol guards on their chests. As people realized the cries were coming from a man who'd just been disemboweled by an unruly giant slave, and swords had been drawn, the crowd retreated. Members of the first caste might have been fans of watching bloodshed, but they didn't enjoy being participants. The warriors spread out, swords pointed at Karno, but Rada realized they were eyeing her, seeking an angle past the giant.

"Archer on the second floor of the building with the red pillars," Karno stated, and that seemed like an odd thing to say to his assailants, until she realized that instead he'd meant the message for the cloaked figure who had suddenly appeared through the fleeing crowd.

A warrior turned just in time to catch Devedas' curved southern blade through his neck. The blow was so quick, so smooth, that

Rada hadn't even realized the warrior's head was now travelling in a different direction from his body.

Devedas tossed something toward Karno, then he turned to face the other warriors. Karno caught the hammer—this one far smaller than the one he'd threatened her with—but rather than join in the fight, he went to the noodle stand and protectively placed his bulk in front of Rada, shielding her from harm.

"What are you doing? Help him!"

"My orders are to keep you safe. He's got this," Karno stated as he searched for other threats.

The three warriors approached Devedas. He lifted his curved blade in both hands, shoulder high, and waited, seeming as still as a statue. Devedas was in danger. If Karno wouldn't help, then she would! Rada drew her ceremonial dagger.

"Calm yourself and watch," Karno said.

The warriors lifted their swords, screamed, and charged Devedas. The Protector moved with such inhuman grace that it was like nothing Rada had ever seen. The odd southern blade took off a warrior's arm at the elbow so smoothly it was like watching a gardener prune a tree. Devedas moved around the disarmed warrior, slicing him open from belly button to spine, and then immediately swung at his companion, hitting him in the hip so hard that the warrior went spinning away, flinging blood like a fountain.

That injured warrior stumbled toward the noodle cart, but that must have been too close for Karno's comfort, because the big Protector surged forward, and embedded his hammer in the man's skull. *Crack!* He wrenched the hammer out and stepped back in front of Rada before the limp body had even hit the ground. Rada realized there was hair and... stuff... clinging to the hammer and dripping down the handle onto his meaty hand. Karno didn't seem to notice.

The last warrior took one quick look at his dying allies, then at Devedas, and decided to flee. He made it all of five feet before Devedas intercepted him, caught him by the uniform, and slung him hard against a sandstone wall. The warrior desperately swung his sword, but Devedas parried it, then kicked the warrior in the knee. He toppled, but Devedas dragged him back by the hair, and smashed the man's nose with his knee.

"I recognize your pathetic fighting stance. The Inquisition's training is inferior, but I suppose an order doesn't need to spend much time on sword training when they mostly fight unarmed women," Devedas said as he shoved him away.

"You," the assassin spat as he recognized the scar across Devedas' face. He tried to lift his sword, but Devedas effortlessly delivered a cut so deep that it severed the tendons and left the warrior's arm dangling useless. He let out a terrible wail that made Rada flinch.

Devedas kicked the sword from his limp fingers. "Who sent you?"

"You know," he gasped.

The Lord Protector nodded. "Of course." Then he kicked the man in the ribs. "How is the Grand Inquisitor?"

There was shouting. Rada looked up to see another group of warriors pushing their way through the stunned witnesses. Karno stepped forward, lifting a chain from beneath his rough-spun slave's shirt. "Don't worry, Archivist. These guards appear legitimate." The symbol of the Protector Order swung from the chain as Karno held it high. The warriors made their way into the opening created by the fight, saw the dead and dying, then they saw the swinging gold token. "Protector business," Karno warned them.

The real warriors froze. Their officer swallowed hard. "Do you require assistance, Protector?"

"Continue your patrol elsewhere."

The guards seemed really happy to hurry away.

Rada turned back to Devedas. He was standing over the survivor, sword placed against the man's throat. Blood was running from the assassin's nose and dripping onto the gleaming steel. "You were supposed to be confined to your compound."

"No one *confines* me." Devedas lifted his sword, placed the tip beneath the man's ear, and *sliced it off*. The man screamed. Rada had to cover her mouth so she wouldn't. "I will spare your life so you can send a message to the Grand Inquisitor. Oh, quit your weeping. You can always hide the stub beneath your mask."

There was a lot of noise, and incoherent sounds before the man was able to beg, "Mercy, Protector!" as he flopped about.

"Yes, yes, losing an ear truly damages one's balance, but you'd think someone so used to applying torture would be able to withstand a bit of it himself. Show some dignity. Can you hear my message now, or must I speak into your good ear?"

"Yes, yes!" the man wailed. "I'll give it."

"Tell Omand Vokkan that we must speak. Tell him I know. The way he has poisoned the Capitol against my Order is clever, but it will not stand." Then he bent over and struck the man in the face with his fist, once, twice, three times. Each impact hit with a meaty thud that made Rada wince. Devedas stood straight as the assassin rolled over, coughing up blood and teeth.

There was blood everywhere. She'd never seen anyone die before.

Devedas looked over his shoulder and saw Rada staring at him. For just a moment, he seemed ashamed, as if he'd never intended her to see this side of him, but then his face darkened, and he turned back and kicked the assassin one last time. "And tell him that the librarian is off limits."

Chapter 36

"You know, a warrior like you could make a lot of money, Risaldar," Gutch told Jagdish one afternoon. "With the folks I know, and the things they get into, they're always looking for somebody handy with a blade. People are willing to pay good notes for magic bits off the Inquisition's books, but such a trade tends to attract shifty types. A right honorable fellow like you who's solid in a fight could command a decent wage."

Jagdish had mostly ignored the big worker over their long journey, but Gutch rarely shut up. "Lots of *honorable fellows* in the criminal smuggling underworld then?"

"We're lousy with them!" Gutch had a loud bark of a laugh. The first few times he'd done it the noise had startled his horse so badly it had nearly bucked him off, but after several days his poor bedraggled mount had either gotten used to it or gone deaf. "Keep in mind, honor is a relative term, Risaldar."

"No, it isn't," Jagdish said. They were approaching another fork in the road. One path would take them toward Thao, the other toward Sarnobat. Assuming that Gutch hadn't been lying to him the whole time, Angruvadal had been moving south. It wasn't like following a trail, as they weren't on the same path, but more like following a compass with a twitchy needle. "Which way now?"

Gutch got off his horse, walked to the middle of the road, and spread his arms, slowly turning. Jagdish figured that whole twirling bit was for show, and Gutch looked like a fool for nothing. He had originally started doing that as an excuse to get Jagdish to remove his manacles and chains. After having to stop and reorient himself several times a day, Jagdish had just given up and started leaving the chains off while they traveled. It was probably just a matter of time before the prisoner tried to escape.

Jagdish tried to prod him into getting the show over with. "Surely, you can't be the only person in Lok with the gift of tracking magic. Perhaps you could refer me to one who works quicker?"

"My talent is extremely rare. If it were a common gift, I wouldn't have been given absurdly heavy bags of notes to help illegal magic smugglers gather the stuff. There are always dead demon bits washed up on shore, or old fragments of black steel to be stol—er...found. There's quite a good trade in such things that are off paper for those who want to use magic without the Inquisition sticking their masks in your business. I'll tell you, it was enough money to tempt even a brilliant artist such as myself from honest labor into terrible criminal misdeeds...Now, please, Risaldar. I'm trying to concentrate."

After a few minutes of spinning about and humming, Gutch began to speak. "I can feel it...The magic calls to me! The terrible black steel craft alters the very fabric of the world around it!" Gutch put one meaty hand on his forehead and grimaced. "But Jagdish the Warrior would never know this without the faithful service of humble Gutch that mighty Angruvadal is..." Gutch stopped spinning and pointed. "That direction." He opened his eyes, found the sun, and confirmed it. "South!"

At least he was consistent. "Thao then." Jagdish was beginning to suspect that his prisoner was full of fish, but at least he hadn't pointed them toward Sarnobat. Because of the recent raids back and forth, if they discovered Jagdish was from Vadal he'd likely be taken hostage. Then he'd get to experience prison life from both sides, only nobody in Vadal would pay a ransom to have Jagdish returned. "You'd better not be putting me on."

The big man climbed back on his horse. "Of course not, Risaldar. You have my solemn word as a forge master—well, temporarily retired forge master at least—that I'd never lead you astray."

Or run off when I'm not looking or murder me in my sleep, Jagdish mused. But Gutch hadn't fled yet.

The big man talked nonstop the rest of the day as they rode through the forest, but Jagdish couldn't shake the feeling that he was going to try something. So a few hours later when they'd stopped to camp for the night, Jagdish locked the manacles onto Gutch's wrists and looped the chain around a stout tree.

"This is hardly a comfortable position to sleep. If I don't get enough rest, it might affect my tracking ability tomorrow. If my keen magical senses are worn out, I might accidentally lead us astray, Risaldar. We could lose Angruvadal."

"Uh huh..." Jagdish said as he put together their campfire.

"What if I need to piss?"

"Hold it until morning."

"What if in the middle of the night we get attacked by wolves? Or bandits?"

"Try not to wake me."

"Oh." Gutch leaned against his tree. "Bark makes a terrible pillow."

Jagdish got a strong fire going. They'd been climbing all day, and nights were cold in the foothills. Satisfied that it wasn't going to go out, Jagdish began preparing their food. Thankfully, Gutch was silent for a few minutes while he did it. Once he had the kettle on, Jagdish took out his pocket watch and wound the spring. The marvelous little thing was still working, long after its previous owner had been murdered by wizards. He felt it whir and tick in his hand, and regretted not leaving it with Pakpa.

He missed her already. It was an embarrassment for a bride to have to go back to her parents' house, but his name had collected so many embarrassments at this point that what was one more? They may have been of different castes, but his loyal soldiers had promised to watch over Pakpa's family household while he was away, an act of such unselfish kindness that it had left Jagdish humbled.

"Do you mind if I ask you something, Risaldar?"

"Me minding hasn't stopped you once yet. What?" Jagdish muttered, but then Gutch was quiet. He looked over to see that the worker was studying him intently. There was a lot more intelligence behind those beady little eyes than the big man let on. "What do you want to know?"

"Why are you doing this?"

Jagdish assumed he wasn't talking about fixing supper. "I have to. I've got nothing else."

"I noticed your wife see you off at the gates of the city. Hardy worker stock by the looks of her. Maybe we're distant cousins? But a beautiful girl, and it was plain as day how she feels about you. Can't hardly call that nothing."

"We both know Ashok wasn't the one who attacked Cold Stream. I can't let that stand."

"And when you catch up to him, you're going to do what? Are you going to have him sign a testimony? *I hereby swear I didn't murder everybody.* Now I'm no judge, but I figure they might be a little leery of taking him at his word."

"I'll think of something," Jagdish said.

"Do you think you can duel him and take his sword? My cell had a crack in the wall. I got to watch how your sparring sessions went. If you think that's going to happen, you're delusional."

"Damn it, Gutch, I don't care about the sword. I care about the truth. My name has been dishonored. That's . . ." Jagdish sighed. "You're not a warrior. You wouldn't understand."

"I'm a different caste, not a different species. I know what it means to have a name." That hung there for a while as Gutch continued studying him.

"Perhaps." Jagdish looked back down at the pocket watch. "You've seen this device?"

"Yes. Impressive little thing. While your caste spends its time hacking each other to bits, my caste improves our lives through labor and miraculous invention. You're welcome."

"I should have left it home. If I don't come back, I want my son to have it."

"Then return it to him."

"Only after I prove who really killed my men and my charges. They may have been prisoners, but they deserved better, and their safety was my responsibility. I will avenge them. I will kill these wizards. Then I'll return, with my name and my honor intact. A warrior is only worth his name."

Gutch nodded thoughtfully. "You actually believe all that stuff?"

Jagdish put the watch away. "I have to."

The next morning Jagdish turned over in his blanket and realized that his prisoner had escaped. The chains were lying

discarded at the base of the tree he'd been tethered to. The
manacles were still there, but somehow opened. "Oceans!" He
threw off the blanket and reached for where he'd left his sword,
but his hand hit nothing but pine needles.

"Morning, Risaldar. Did you sleep well?" Gutch was sitting
on a rock a few yards away. Jagdish's sword was next to him,
still sheathed. The prisoner seemed not only calm, but in a
good mood. He gestured at the small cooking pot on the fire.
"Breakfast?" Then he made a big show of glancing down at the
sword. "Oh, this? I thought you might wake up cranky and I
know how you warriors like to cut folks down without thinking things through first." Gutch lifted the still-sheathed sword.
"Now that you've taken a moment to wake up and realize that I
refrained from doing anything bad to you, hopefully you won't
be an ass about it and will grant me the same courtesy." Gutch
tossed the sword over.

Jagdish caught his blade, but left it sheathed. "You could have
murdered me in my sleep."

"I'm not that sort of criminal."

"How'd you escape?"

"A piece of wire, some mechanical know-how, and nothing
else to do all night but work at the tumblers because my pillow
was a *tree*."

"I'm sorry, was I supposed to have fluffed it for you?"

Gutch laughed. The booming noise echoed through the forest
and caused their horses to snort and pull at their ropes and a
flock of birds to leap into the air. "So now that we've established
I'm not going to murder you or run away even when granted the
opportunity, let's reexamine this working relationship of ours. In
my caste, we do business willingly, entering pacts based on trust
and respect, not threats...Okay, some threats, but only on special
occasions. No more chains and in fact, no more of this prisoner
nonsense. To hell with the Inquisition, this journey counts as time
served. No ordering me around. I'll keep helping you, but once
you've murdered all these wizards and restored your honor and
whatnot, I'm going to collect their magic fragments, sell them, and
buy myself a palace. You strike me as a dedicated enough man
to pull it off, and I've always wanted a palace...and a harem. A
palace with a harem sounds reasonable. Partners?"

That seemed like a very worker way of going about the

endeavor, but Gutch's demonstration had been rather effective. "I agree with your terms."

"You seem to take it so damned seriously. Give me your word."

"Very well, you have my word as a warrior. Help me, Gutch, your sentence is served, and afterwards loot the wizards as you see fit, I don't give a damn." The he realized that a length of cord had been run through his sword's scabbard and tied around the hilt. If he'd tried to draw, it would have slowed him. "What's this?"

"A test of politeness." Gutch reached behind his rock and picked up a stout tree branch. In those massive hands, there was no doubt the improvised club would be extremely lethal. "If you'd tried to pull on me—despite my exceedingly reasonable proposal—I'd have caved your head in."

"Clever."

"Thank you. The sword you're looking for is . . ." Gutch frowned for just a moment, then pointed. "That way. The feeling is faint, but when Ashok uses it again I'll be able to tell you approximately how many miles away it is."

"No more spinning around and carrying on then?"

"Nope. I'm too big to keep prancing about like that. Some traveler might see me on the road twirling and tell their friends. Talk about damaging your reputation! Breakfast?"

Chapter 37

The mountain passes were their most direct route south, but at this time of year, crossing was questionable. The lands that had formerly belonged to House Somsak were treacherous in winter. It wasn't nearly as rugged, high, or cold as the ranges to the south, since the snow here was usually measured in inches rather than feet, but sudden storms came often enough to block the high passes for days at a time. Regardless of how much snow fell, Ashok knew he could make it, but the others would more than likely perish, and without Keta, he wouldn't be able to fulfill Omand's order. He'd offered to carry Keta across the mountains on his back, but the Keeper had declined the offer.

So they stuck to the hill country and the lower mountain valleys. The trade roads were well maintained. The going was easier, but the weather was still unpredictable. It was common to wake up to a dusting of snow, have the sun melt it by noon, and then get rained on for the rest of the day. However, Keta had money, so they were able to sleep at inns most nights. Ashok remained with the team, avoided speaking to the locals, and Keta or Thera would bring him his food. He slept beneath the wagon every night, ostensibly to protect their goods, but mostly to stay out of sight. Many years before he'd worked in these lands and didn't want to be recognized.

Each morning they set out again, bright and early, and every day brought them a little closer to his final condemnation in Akershan.

Ashok tried to give Thera her privacy. She was a woman, and his limited social knowledge had taught him ladies deserved their privacy. He wasn't sure if that applied to profane fugitives from the warrior caste as well, but it seemed reasonable.

One night, Ashok learned that Thera was not in good health. There was no inn, so they had made camp beneath the stars. Whether from the influence of the Heart of the Mountain, or just practice, Protectors were notoriously light sleepers, and he had been awoken by the sounds of thrashing. Thera was convulsing in her bed roll, muscles contracting violently, eyes rolled back up in her head, seemingly awake, but incoherent and speaking nonsense words.

When he'd gone to her, Keta had stopped him, warning him that Thera sometimes had these fits, and there was nothing that could be done for her. The Keeper stayed with her, her head in his lap, whispering calming words as Ashok had stood there uselessly. The fit had passed shortly, and she'd fallen into a deep sleep, as if nothing had happened at all.

Keta said such events were rare, and it was best to not speak of them to her at all, to avoid embarrassment. Ashok had heard of such a twitching sickness among members of the first caste, but he was surprised that it existed among the hardy warriors as well. The next day, Thera made no mention of the event, if she even remembered it at all. He was happy to keep avoiding her.

In truth, Ashok hadn't spent much time interacting with women. He was no stranger to them, but visiting the pleasure women or being gifted slave girls for the night—great houses tended to be *very* hospitable to Protectors—was drastically different than actually *speaking* with one.

He'd been of the first caste, where women were allowed to hold offices and obligations, but it wasn't as if Protectors spent much time in the courts of the Capitol or the great houses. Their time was spent in the jungles, mountains, slums, and forsaken places abandoned to the criminal element. They were outsiders in the society that their actions made possible.

Emotional attachments were discouraged. Such things made it difficult to enforce the Law in an unbiased manner. Some

Protectors were more rigid about that tradition than others. When the terms of their obligation were up, then they'd be assigned a wife. Other than mandatory social niceties and politics, there really wasn't much reason to speak with a woman before that. At least most Protectors had grown up around others, but all Ashok had for a childhood was a lie of memorized statutes and governing-caste etiquette painted over the casteless dog beneath.

In the only world he understood, everyone had a place, and how you treated them was based upon whether they were higher or lower in status, and by how much. Here, they were all equally nothing, which was very confusing. So Ashok avoided Thera. He figured that was for the best. She had yet to roll a bomb under the wagon while he was sleeping as she'd threatened, so their terms must have been acceptable. Except for the times he caught Thera watching him suspiciously, she mostly seemed content to ignore him as well.

With Keta, on the other hand, he wasn't so lucky, because the Keeper was incapable of shutting up about his damned Forgotten. During the days he would try to tell stories of the old times, legends mixed with real history, about demons that fell from the sky, and a heavenly hero who followed them, forging swords that could smite through demon hide from the hull of his black steel ship, and about a people who had risen, then fallen, but who would rise again. As the days passed, Ashok discovered he was less inclined to murder the strange little man. Keta might have been totally delusional, but at least he was passionate about it.

One morning Ashok was walking along, trailing after the wagon as their oxen lumbered up a steep hill. It was that much less weight for them to pull and it felt good to walk anyway. The terrain was rolling and covered in tall brown grass that swayed in the cold wind. Across the hills, fat gray mountains loomed, their tops cloaked in white clouds. It pained him to admit it, as much as he deserved otherwise, but it felt good to be out of his prison cell.

To the side, Thera came out of the tall grass, carrying a small bow and a few arrows, her cloak and hair whipping in the wind. He was no longer surprised at how stealthy she was when she set her mind to it. She probably would have made a fine border scout.

"No luck?" Ashok asked.

"I was hoping to see a rabbit or something. I'm getting sick of jerky and rice. That's the last time I let Keta be our pretend merchant and buy stock for our pretend wagon. Never let a man who grew up on gruel and slop choose your rations."

If he wasn't worried about witnesses, he could have chased down an elk on foot and carried it back over one shoulder. Ashok extended his hand toward the bow. "I can try."

"You know how to shoot a bow?"

It was a weak bow with a light pull weight, not a proper fighting bow at all, thus legal to own, but sufficient for a worker to hunt small game. "If it's possible to kill a man with a device, then I've been trained how to use it."

Thera began to laugh, then realized Ashok wasn't making a joke. "Oh..."

She didn't give him the bow, but surprisingly, she didn't walk away either. Instead she fell in beside him and the two of them followed the slow-moving wagon together. They climbed in silence for a time, listening to nothing but the whistle of the wind through the tall grass and the creak and rumble of their wagon. For just a moment, he could imagine that they were just a man and a woman out for a stroll on a beautiful winter day. Was this what it was like to be *normal?*

"How have you taken to Keta's sermons?"

"Is that what those are supposed to be?" Ashok asked.

"I think so. I've heard them all. I think he practices on me before he tries them on the masses. You should see him work a crowd. He's so enthusiastic that by the time he's done people actually believe."

"Preaching is dangerous." Strangely enough, Ashok actually found himself respecting someone for having the courage to do something *illegal.* "He's an odd, but brave little man."

"Yes, I think so." It was a rare sight, but she had a very genuine smile. It was one of the few times he'd seen her without her hood up, and because of the wind, for just a moment he caught sight of a terrible scar running along the top of her head. Normally it would be hidden from view by her long dark hair. Thera caught him looking and self-consciously put her hood up to cover it.

Ashok was no stranger to injuries, and it was odd to see anyone heal from a head wound that extensive. That hadn't been some superficial cut. That was a skull being put back together.

He'd known a few warriors over the years with marks like that, saved by surgeons, but they were usually fools, their brains left dimwitted and damaged from the impact, but Thera's mind seemed as sharp as her many knives. It certainly explained the strange convulsions he'd witnessed. "What happened?"

"I was only a child. Something fell on me and I nearly died."

"What was it? An axe?"

"I don't want to talk about it."

He'd been told that women were sensitive about such things, as if a scar could somehow ruin their beauty, but scars were just stories told in flesh. "There's no need to hide it. It gives you character."

"Was that meant as a compliment?" she asked, incredulous.

Ashok shrugged. "I tell the truth. Take it or leave it."

"Well, there is a need to hide the mark. I'm a criminal, remember? So I'm not in the habit of displaying any distinguishing features that might show up on a wanted poster...But thank you."

"You're welcome."

They continued on in silence for a time, neither of them in a hurry to catch the wagon. "So why are you out here, Ashok?"

"I'm avoiding another sermon."

"Which one?"

"He started talking about an ancient hero being sent by the gods to chase the demons into the sea."

"Ramrowan," Thera said thoughtfully. "That's one of Keta's favorites, the greatest warrior who ever lived."

"Keta has not seen me fight."

"Wow, our Protector is humble too."

"It is not bragging if you can perform on demand. And do not call me Protector."

"Ramrowan, the first king. By the time Keta gets done telling that story to a barracks full of casteless, they're believing that they're so destined for greatness they're usually ready to rebel on the spot."

"Cruel foolishness," Ashok muttered. "Nothing good comes from a casteless thinking they can achieve anything. I once met an untouchable on a beach in Gujara. He'd found a spear. He was very proud of it, and he even used it to try and save his family from a demon."

"That's brave."

"No one realizes how hard it is to stand against a demon. I've seen the mightiest warriors flee in terror when faced with such things, but this old untouchable wouldn't budge. After, when he wouldn't put the spear down, they killed him with an arrow without so much as a second thought. So much courage, but they just left him there on the sand for the tide to take out and the demons to eat." Ashok hadn't thought of that incident in a long time. "I buried him myself."

Thera seemed surprised. "Why would you bother?"

"It seemed like the thing to do." Perhaps there had been cracks in his foundation of lies even before Mindarin's revelation, but he didn't like to dwell on such things, so Ashok changed the subject back. "Maybe someday Keta will use that story in a sermon, like this fabled hero from the sky."

"I've heard that story so many times now. After the demons were cast from the heavens and went about destroying the world, the gods took pity on us and sent their champion to save mankind. Ramrowan fell from the sky in a ship made from black steel," Thera recited from memory.

"Landed in the desert, rallied the survivors, gave us magic, and man chased the demons into the sea. Yes. That's the one. Keta seems fond of it." He had heard a lot of theories as to the origins of the ancestor blades over the years, and that story was as ludicrous as all the others.

"Keta likes to share the heroic parts to get the casteless riled up, but he doesn't tell them the sad part of the story that comes next."

"There's a sad part?" Ashok asked, intrigued. "He must have been saving that for after my miraculous conversion to fanaticism he keeps hoping for."

"Yes, very sad. A parable about how men are stupid. He took all the tribes of Lok, united them into a single kingdom, and won an impossible victory. Yet the demons were supposed to invade the land again someday, and only his bloodline would be able to stop them. So protecting royalty became the most important thing in the world. The age of kings was glorious for a time. Keta says they were blessed because the people heeded their gods, but eventually the Sons of Ramrowan got too proud for their own good."

Ramrowan. Mindarin had once referred to the Heart of the Mountain by that name. There was usually some element of truth to even the strangest of myths, so this supposed champion had probably actually existed. As for the rest, Ashok had no trust in fables.

"His descendants got greedier and greedier. Keta's books say the Age of Kings fell apart because they forgot their gods and just used their church as an excuse to steal whatever they wanted, but the way I see it, if the whole world kisses your ass because they think you're the only one who can save them, of course you're going to get cocky. But that only lasts as long as the people still believe."

"If authority is not respected, authority is not retained."

"Exactly. A few hundred years later, the idea of demons coming inland was seen as a trick, and the church just a prop to excuse the kings' whims. Once they got sick enough of their tyranny, the warriors rose up and destroyed them. The kingdom broke into the houses. The royalty and priests who survived became casteless. That's why, no matter what, the Law keeps the casteless around, just in case the old stories are true. Only the bloodline of the first king can stop the demons."

Ashok had actually fought demons. Regardless of Keta's myths, if an army of demons was to crawl out of hell and invade the land, all of the casteless in the world would be nothing but a snack.

"Everything changed because of the excesses of the Age of Kings. Religion was banned, and we ended up with the Law instead. Fat lot of improvement that was."

Ashok gritted his teeth. Insulting the Law was like insulting *him*. He knew now that was Kule's doing, but it was still so ingrained in him that such slights made him angry.

Thera caught his reaction and paused. "Don't take it personally. I meant no offense."

He'd not expected an apology. They followed the wagon quietly for a time while he tried to come up with a polite response. "I suppose if I'm going to spend the rest of my life a criminal, I'd best get used to such talk."

"We don't hate law, Ashok. We're rebelling against the unjust parts of it, not the whole thing. You'll see. Keta has built something remarkable in the south."

"You always speak of Keta's accomplishments, but never his prophet..." Ashok mused. "Do you think he's a charlatan or a just a madman?"

She paused for a moment, unsure how to answer. "Neither. Both." Thera shrugged. "It doesn't really matter, does it? If it is really the Forgotten speaking or just some poor deluded fool hearing voices, people will fight as long as the Law is unjust."

"The Law is by definition justice."

"Saying something over and over doesn't make it true. Wrong is wrong. Like declaring some men whole and others barely more than animals, or where the innocent can be punished on a whim, or where we're deprived of our ability to believe in something more."

"But you don't believe."

"I want the *freedom* to choose for myself."

"So that is why you fight? For some nebulous concept?"

"Freedom isn't nebulous once you've lived it, Ashok."

A couple of weeks south of Apura and skirting the base of the Somsak Mountains, the sky had darkened as terrible storm clouds rolled in. The weak rain turned into a torrential downpour, followed by thunder louder than Thera's alchemy. The wind threatened to rip their canvas cover off. Within minutes the poor oxen were having a terrible time of it as the road melted into mud and ruts.

"The water is particularly evil today," Ashok said after a horrendous crash of thunder.

"Water doesn't have intent!" Keta shouted back. "That's just superstition."

"Water is the source of all evil and the home of Hell."

"If water is so evil, how come we make beer out of it?"

Ashok found it ironic that he was being lectured about superstition by a man who believed in prophecies. "Malevolent or not, if we don't get out of this soon we'll get stuck or lose the animals."

"That would be awful," Keta agreed.

"Yes. It would look suspicious if I had to pull the wagon the rest of the way myself," Ashok said. The Keeper gave him an incredulous look, trying to decide if Ashok was trying to be funny or not. Ashok let him wonder.

As the rain increased in intensity, they found a road sign pointing them toward the next settlement, only a mile away. The temperature continued to drop and darkness fell long before sundown. Ashok had gotten in front, taken hold of the yoke and half guided, half dragged the blind and scared oxen up the hill and into the relative shelter of a rocky canyon. At times the wagon would stick, and Ashok would go around to the back and push. A journey that should have taken minutes took hours against the wind and building muck. By the time they reached the settlement, tiny streams had grown into vicious rivers that threatened to tear away the small bridges leading into the village, and Thera was doing everything she could to keep their canvas from being torn off in the wind.

The village was called Jharlang. It looked like all of the other minor places they'd passed through recently. Ashok counted the lights. There were maybe a couple hundred workers' houses, some other miscellaneous buildings, and a casteless quarter on the other side of a now flooded irrigation canal. There was a single inn, but thankfully it had a barn large enough to fit their wagon.

Keta leapt off the wagon and ran for the inn while Ashok led the team toward the barn. Whether there was room or not, he was going to make room. He was glad to have some structures taller than the wagon around. He had no idea if the Heart would sustain him through a lightning strike, but if Thera had any more jugs of her Fortress powder stashed, the resulting explosions would probably get him for sure.

Luckily, there were a couple of young casteless huddled in the barn, shivering in their rags and watching the fury of the storm through the slats. They saw him coming and prepared a spot. Ashok kept his face down as he ordered them to tend to his animals. If he was recognized, they'd surely sell him out. Or worse, start worshipping him like the fools on the barge.

Of course, when he looked, Thera was no longer in the back of the wagon. She had a way of slipping off unnoticed to scout whenever they entered civilization. One of the children cared for the oxen while Ashok leaned against the wagon and waited for his companions. Now that they thought a worker was present, the casteless could no longer enjoy watching the storm, and had grudgingly gone back to mucking out stalls. Rain pounded on the roof and leaked through dozens of cracks, forming puddles in the old straw. The entire place stank of mold and dung. He'd slept in worse.

Thera joined him half an hour later. The wind had blown her hood off, her black hair was sodden and hanging over her

face, and she seemed angry. She had two things for him, a bowl
consisting of sausages and some unidentifiable vegetable mush,
already turned into a cold soup by the rainy walk over, and a
piece of paper. A single cheap lantern was the only source of
light in the entire barn, so Ashok had to call upon the Heart to
strengthen his eyesight enough to clearly see what was on the
damp, ruined notice she handed him. Even then, the ink had
run so much that it was hard to read.

*The Somsak will pay a ten-thousand-note bounty for informa-
tion that leads to the death of the fallen Protector Ashok Vadal.*

"I never really had to concern myself with money, but that
seems like a lot."

"For that much, I should kill you myself," Thera hissed. "You
didn't tell us the Thakoor of this territory burns with a special
hate for you."

Ashok shrugged. "I smote the tongue from the man's mouth
in a duel. He was so foul and insulting he's lucky that's all I
did to him, but Nadan Somsak does seem petty enough to hold
a grudge."

"You cut off his *tongue?* And now we're riding across his
lands. You didn't think to tell me this before?"

"If I made a list of all the men who wanted me dead for
one cause or another, it would be a very long list." That wasn't
a bad idea. Maybe by the time they reached the Ice Coast he'd
be finished. It would give him something to do to pass the time.

"I expected wanted posters for you at some point. That's no
surprise, but not for that kind of fortune." Thera looked around,
making sure that the casteless were too occupied to hear her.
"Inside the inn all the travelers are telling stories about you.
They're saying the Black Heart recently killed an entire prison,
then murdered half a legion on a bridge, before burning a village and throwing all the women and children in the water to
be eaten by demons."

"None of that's true."

"It doesn't matter. The people here think it's true. You'll find
no friends in these lands now."

"Good. Criminals shouldn't have friends."

"It never ceases to amaze me that someone who has seen so
much of the world could be so oblivious to it. We *had* friends.
Now, they'll give you up to this Somsak without a second thought.

Most warriors here would avoid you because some Vadal criminal isn't worth dying over, but this particular Thakoor would swim the ocean to rip out your guts, so now they'll be motivated. You should have told me."

Thera was glaring at him, and for whatever reason that made him want to apologize. "In the future I'll try to notify you of things like this. I am sorry."

That seemed to mollify the warrior woman a bit. She pushed her wet hair away from her eyes, absently making sure her scar was hidden. "There's no indication he knows you're here. This is just grasping at straws. If he's willing to offer something like this, just in the off chance anyone sees you, I can't imagine what kind of ransom Harta Vadal must be willing to pay for that sword."

It was hard to imagine Vadal—the strongest of them all—experiencing the same fate as a tiny, poor house like Somsak or Dev, but Harta was no fool. He would pay a fortune to get Angruvadal into the hands of a new bearer. Until that happened, Vadal would be vulnerable. Ashok wasn't sure who Omand was punishing more with this ridiculous endeavor, him, or all of Great House Vadal. It was especially cruel either way.

"I'll be careful," Ashok assured her.

"You'd better. There're a lot of people like me on these roads, sharp-eyed and always looking for an angle, a whole world beneath your shiny law-abiding one. Those are the folks I would have used for checkpoints and new travelling papers, but ten thousand notes would set them up for life. Our Keeper has some money from the rebellion's backers, but nothing that can compete with that. If I'd known you were this popular I never would have agreed to this. Freeing a lunatic from prison and getting him from one end of Lok to the other without killing half the countryside in the process, no problem, I thought...I'm such a sucker." Thera shook her head, annoyed. "You're lucky I stick to my contracts."

"You underestimated the difficulty, but still honor your agreements. It is the difficult tests in life that demonstrate a person's true character." He'd never thought he'd someday be impressed by a criminal's dedication. Ashok gave her a respectful bow. "Thank you."

Thera seemed a bit taken aback by that. Surprise turned to annoyance, almost as if she thought Ashok was being insincere. "Fine. Whatever. I'm soaked and freezing. I'm going to get some of that slop for dinner and warm myself by the fire in the company of my fake husband."

"Do you not have a real one?"

"I used to...But if I ever wanted another I've met many who'd make for far worse company than Keta. I'd better go before he starts spouting off revolutionary nonsense to the locals."

"Good night."

She began to walk away, but before Ashok could begin eating, Thera turned back. "It's so cold. Will you be all right out here tonight?"

"I'll be fine."

"That's right." There had been genuine concern there, but now she tried to be nonchalant about it. "I suppose your kind don't feel things like the rest of us."

Ashok shook his head. "We still feel. We just learn not to want the things we can't ever have."

Thera tilted her head to the side, a curious look on her face, as if she wanted to say something else, but then she must have decided against it because she put her hood up and ventured out into the storm.

Finding a spot that wasn't under a roof leak, Ashok sat down and leaned his back against a wagon wheel. The food was bland. A minor inn in poor lands couldn't afford much in the way of spices. The sausage was mostly blood and fat, and from the flavor he couldn't even tell what kind of animal it had come from, but he was so hungry it didn't matter, and he chewed it anyway. The fat coated the roof of his mouth and teeth and clung there, greasy.

One of the casteless was staring at him through the slats of a horse stall, looking more like a filthy wild animal than a child. He couldn't have been more than nine or ten, but it was hard to tell since he was so thin and sickly. His clothing was nothing more than a mismatched tangle of old rags, knotted together in a heap for warmth. *Is that what I looked like?* The boy was neglecting his shoveling, and for a moment Ashok was concerned that he'd been recognized, but then he realized the boy was only staring hungrily at his dinner.

Ashok looked down at the bowl, then back at the starving child. He stood up.

The boy instinctively cowered and the other casteless rushed over to protect him. Ashok was so used to not paying attention to their kind that he'd not noticed this one was a girl, a few years older than the boy, and in just as sorry a state. She dropped her shovel, grabbed hold of the boy, and began dragging him away. "So sorry! So sorry!"

"Stop," Ashok ordered.

The girl did so, but she was shivering uncontrollably. As she stared at her bare, blackened and filthy feet, she stammered "Brother didn't mean to look at you, worker sir. Please don't beat him."

She was honestly terrified. Ashok had seen such quivering fear before, but normally only on battlefields or before an execution. Her fear was contagious enough that it was making the horses and oxen shift nervously in their stalls. "Be calm. I'm not going to beat anyone." He set the bowl on the fence. "Here."

"Oh..." The girl looked at the food with a nervous, pained expression, but didn't approach. On the other hand, her brother must have had more hunger than fear, because he snatched up the bowl and ran away. He crouched in the corner and began to eat. The back of his rag shirt fell open, revealing that his skin was covered in old lash scars and fresh purple bruises.

"When was the last time you were fed?" Ashok demanded.

"A few days. I will trade for the food." Resigned to her fate, the girl seemed to melt in defeat. The fear had been for her brother, not for herself. "Do what you want to me, but please don't hurt me too much, because I still have more stalls to clean."

"What? No." Ashok felt like someone had just slapped him in the face. "That's...No. Nothing like that. There's no trade. The food is yours. It is a gift."

She clearly didn't understand the concept.

"You did a good job caring for my oxen. Just go eat." Suddenly flushed and unexpectedly angry, Ashok went back to his wagon.

The girl fled.

Ashok watched the casteless children eat the vile slop as if it was a great hall feast. Their overseer was obviously neglecting them, but that wasn't against the Law if they were doing a bad job. Starvation was a legally acceptable punishment, and he'd never really thought about it before. Ashok had experienced the weakness and pains of hunger, but nothing like this. He spied a pile of old grain sacks and some flea-ridden blankets and realized that was their bed. These two didn't even rate a place in the casteless barracks.

You see that, Ashok? That's your law. That's what you've been defending.

"Shut up, Keta," Ashok muttered to the priest who wasn't there.

There were almost no memories left of his life before Angruvadal other than scrubbing blood from a stone floor, but he remembered that he'd had a mother who had loved him. These children didn't even have that. The entirety of the Law was memorized, imprinted deep into the fiber of his being, and he could cite nearly any line, so he knew there was nothing technically illegal here, yet it still seemed... *unjust.*

And that gnawed at him.

Mind made up, Ashok got into the back of the wagon. He had a thick wool blanket that made sleeping beneath the wagon bearable. He took the blanket, a sack of dried fruit, and another of jerky, and carried them over to the children's sleeping area. The untouchables watched him, nervous, as if he was going to loot their pathetic belongings. Instead he dropped the goods there, walked back to his wagon, found the driest spot possible beneath the wagon, and tried to go to sleep.

Chapter 38

~~~~~~~~

Ashok woke to the sounds of children screaming.

He may have been an outcast, but a man didn't just forget twenty years of training. Protectors always ran toward the sounds of trouble. With a reaction that was automatic and unconscious, he rolled out from under the wagon, buckling his sword belt as he went. The animals were all looking in the same direction, ears erect and curious. The noise was coming from outside the back of the barn. Ashok threw open the double doors and walked into the freezing light.

The first rays of the sun were just intruding into the canyon, but the reflection was stark and bright. It must have dropped far below freezing during the night because the torrential rain had begun freezing as it struck, building in ever increasing layers, until the entire valley had been coated by the ice storm. Everything was frozen and slick. Beautiful clusters of ice hung from branches, so heavy that the trees were bowed and lopsided. After the freezing rain had tapered off and the ice world had been dusted with fresh snow. Having left his boots beneath the wagon, his bare soles crushed the snow and stuck to the ice. His toes began to sting with the cold.

There were six people there, but the screaming had stopped, apparently because a man was holding the noisemaker's face down in a water trough. From the ragged clothing and rail-thin limbs, it was the casteless girl who slept in the barn. She was struggling against the attempted drowning, thrashing against the strong hands mashed against the back of her head. The casteless boy was there as well, calling out for his sister and struggling against the men holding him back. The boy was silenced when one of the men grabbed a handful of rags and hurled him against the wooden fence. The boy collapsed, sobbing.

The four men were worker caste, mostly young, all large and strong, with big arms, callused palms, and thick necks. Three of them were wearing the insignia of the miner subcaste, and the big knives on their belts were considered *tools* rather than *weapons*, but they'd open a man's guts either way. The last was the oldest, with hair that had gone white and muscle that had turned to fat.

Ashok analyzed all that in a heartbeat then demanded, "What's going on here?"

"This is my inn, and this little fish-eater stole from one of my guests," the old one shouted to be heard over the gurgling and splashing child. "Drowning her should send a message to the rest."

He wasn't a Protector anymore. This was none of his affair. He had orders from the highest levels of the government. Getting involved here would only draw unwanted attention. The correct thing to do would be to walk away.

"Let her up."

A miner pulled the girl back by the hair. She heaved and gasped. The trough had been frozen over too, but from the fresh cuts they'd broken through the ice with her forehead. Diluted blood ran quickly down her face. The boy called his sister's name, but a miner shoved him over with his boot, sliding him across the ice.

"My apologies for waking you up with all the noise, honored guest." The innkeep didn't want to chase off any customers, but a man in the mood to murder had very little patience. "But she's mine and she stole. Law says I can do what I want."

The Law didn't care what anyone *wanted*. "What did she steal?" Ashok asked, already suspecting the answer.

"A blanket and some food. We caught her round back passing out good meat to some of the other fish-eaters. You'd best check your wagon, merchant." One of the miners laughed. "They'll rob anything not nailed down."

This altercation was his fault. "There's been a misunderstanding. Those things weren't stolen. I gave them as a gift."

"The hell you did. Who gives away good stuff to untouchables?" The innkeeper yanked the girl around by her wet hair. She fell hard, curled into a ball, and covered her face. "Ah, trading a little skin on the side now, are you? I'm surprised you thought this one was worth that much. Well, she's mine, so I should have gotten paid for that, not her. Not passing it on? Law says that's stealing either way."

Ashok ground his teeth together until the muscles of his jaw ached. Sensing his mood, Angruvadal didn't even bother suggesting how to kill these fools. They weren't worth the sword's effort. "Don't try to quote the Law at me, you ignorant swine."

The miners shared nervous glances. They'd just come out here to participate in the fun of drowning a disobedient untouchable, and hadn't expected a fight. "Easy, friend. No need to get riled up over the likes of these," the youngest of them said.

"You want to speak of Law?" The cold air did nothing to calm Ashok's anger. He crunched across the ice, heading toward the innkeeper. "The Law says overseers are supposed to provide adequate sustenance. They're nearly starved to death, with a fat ass like you in charge that tells me you've been stuffing your face with their rations. These untouchables belong to your Thakoor, who places them as he sees fit. They're owned by your house, not you. They're not to be used up and thrown away stupidly by some pathetic scum like you."

"You keep running your mouth, you're likely to get hurt," another miner warned. Technically, a merchant was of higher status than they were, but they were in a backwoods village, in the middle of nowhere, behind a barn, with no witnesses. Status didn't mean much in such situations. They'd seen he had a sword at his side, and were eyeing it nervously, but there were four of them, and one of him. And after all, it wasn't like anyone expected a merchant to really know how to use a sword.

He stopped right in front of them, knowing what was coming because he could feel it in the charged air.

A miner swung a fist at Ashok's face. He caught it in the flat of his palm and *squeezed*. The miner shrieked as fingers broke. That startled them. Ashok twisted the arm, levering him around, and hurled him into the next miner, sending them both sliding into the fence. The third lumbered toward him, but Ashok blocked that arm, and used the miner's momentum to roll him over one hip and toss him to the ground.

"Stop before I hurt you," Ashok warned as the miners got up and surrounded him. They were red-faced, furious, feeling the blood rush of impending violence, their breath coming out in fast gouts of steam.

A knife was drawn.

Ashok spun around the thrust, snapped that wrist, and sent the knife flipping high into the air. He swept the miner around, and flung him headfirst into the fence, breaking boards. The next was caught on the way in, and Ashok's elbow shattered his jaw. The last miner's clumsy attack was intercepted, and Ashok threw him against the trough hard enough to break both it and several bones. A hundred-gallon flood of water and ice chunks spilled out, washing over Ashok's bare feet.

The innkeeper took a step forward. Ashok kicked him in the chest and sent him ten steps back.

Thump. The knife landed in the snow.

Ashok hadn't been this mad since the night he'd confronted Bidaya about the truth. He walked through the slush toward the panting, heaving innkeeper. "The Law doesn't exist to satisfy petty greed." The soles of his feet were sticking to the ice, and each step tore at his skin. "It isn't about justifying your stupid desires. What you want is irrelevant. The Law is supposed to be *more*. It's supposed to be greater than any of us. It isn't some club for you to beat your inferiors with. I'm sick of people like you."

"People like me?" the innkeeper squeaked.

"Those who pervert the Law and use it to justify their whims." Ashok reached down, grabbed the innkeeper's ear, and pulled. It didn't take much to convince the man that regardless of the newly broken ribs, he'd best stand up. "You don't have the right to execute someone without evidence."

"But they're not people!" the innkeeper squealed.

"Who are you to decide?"

"The Law! The Law says they aren't people!"

He was right. Ashok looked down at the girl. She'd been swept away by the water, and was lying there, shivering, bruised and bloodied from the beating the workers had administered. The boy was crawling toward her, leaving droplets of blood on the white behind him from a leaking cut over his eye. They were

weak and frozen and suffering and malnourished and afraid...
but they weren't *people*.

How could I forget?

The disconcerting thought shook him to his core. He stood
there for a time, rattled by his own weakness. He might have even
forgotten the innkeeper if he'd not opened his stupid mouth again.

"Please, don't murder me over some non-people, merchant. I
didn't mean no offense to you."

"But offense was given, and offense was taken. I said I gave a
gift. You should have taken me at my word." Ashok let go of his ear.
"You're unfit to be an overseer. You'll never lay a hand on either of
these again. Understand?" The fat man nodded vigorously. Ashok
turned to go, then thought better of it, turned back, and punched
the innkeeper in the face, smashing his nose flat. The fat man lay
down, whimpering and bleeding. "Be glad that's all you get."

Ashok turned to walk away. The best thing to do would be
to fetch Keta and Thera, and then get out of town as quickly as
possible. He cursed himself for his foolishness. Outlaws couldn't
afford the attention. He walked around a moaning worker, but
paused when he heard the girl's weeping. Once these men talked,
the villagers would be outraged, and someone would have to pay.
Casteless were routinely executed for far less.

What did it matter? The innkeeper was right. They weren't
really people...

He went over and took the girl by the arm. "Stand up." She
flinched away from him, but Ashok pulled her to her feet anyway.
"Come on. You too," he snapped at the boy.

"I'm sorry," she said through shaking, blue lips. "I shouldn't
have shared. The master wouldn't have seen. It's my fault."

"When these get up, they'll be mad, and I won't be able to
help you if a mob of workers comes looking for revenge. Do
you have a place you can go in the casteless quarter? Is there a
barracks that'll take you in?"

"I think so." Blood dripped from her cuts and spattered on
Ashok's fine merchant's coat. "Maybe."

"Go there and hide until this calms down."

Her legs were visibly trembling. He could feel the vibration of
her thin bones in the palm of his hand. "I don't think I can walk."

As he carried both children away, Ashok looked up at the
bright blue sky. Far above a single hawk circled.

Chapter 39

"Are you certain it was him?"

"Positive, Sikasso. It is either the fallen, or the swiftest warrior who has ever lived is in Jharlang dressed as a merchant. He just dropped four men..." Bhorlatar drew one of his many daggers, held it out, and then let go. It stuck point down in the dirt between them. "In the time it took a knife to fall."

None of his men were given to much exaggeration, and Bhorlatar's magical constructs not only looked like hawks, but they had the vision to match. "Very well," Sikasso nodded. "That has to be him. I don't know Jharlang. Where is it?"

Bhorlatar unrolled his map and pointed at an area in House Thao lands. "About here, in a canyon off the trade road."

The fallen wasn't that far away, especially to those who could soar above the mountains. Sikasso glanced around the camp. There were four of his men here. The rest of them were spread out across the other houses that bordered Vadal, all on the lookout for their target. Now that Ashok had been spotted, they could track him as the Grand Inquisitor had commissioned them to, and make sure there was sufficient carnage left in his wake.

"Do we follow him?"

"That's what we've been hired to do."

However, if they waited like they were supposed to, there was always the risk that the precious sword would be lost, or worse, fall into the hands of rival wizards. The Lost House had big plans and needed that black steel. It was always better to have such things sooner rather than later.

His subordinate knew what he was thinking, and Bhorlatar was just as eager to get that sword as he was. "The fallen has proven to be a slippery one, but he'll be stuck in Jharlang for a bit. I doubt he knows it yet, but a flash flood wrecked the bridge back to the trade road last night. The only other clear path is up the mountain toward the Somsak homeland. Unless he wants to try climbing up canyon walls covered in ice sheets, he'll be there until it melts some."

"How big is this place?"

"Maybe a thousand people, a handful of warriors, and I didn't see a single banner of the first caste. If it wasn't for a favorable mountain wind I never would have seen the place at all. No one will miss it."

"I doubt any of these poor mountain folk are personally acquainted with the Grand Inquisitor," Sikasso mused. "You make some good points, Bhorlatar."

"Dead now, dead later, really, does it matter as long as the work gets done?" Bhorlatar had a savage grin. "Come on, you know you want to kill this bastard and be done with it. Do you really want to waste our time following the Black Heart all over Lok? And what happens when he realizes he's being followed? Better to strike while he's unaware. Omand never has to know."

The others had heard the conversation and stopped their meditations to listen. They were all looking to Sikasso for permission. Their hungry expressions reminded him of the poppy addicts he'd seen in the hidden smoke dens of the Capitol. His men were desperate for new magic. If he didn't allow them to strike now, it was only a matter of time before one of them stepped out of line and made a move on his own.

Sikasso walked to the edge of the cliff and looked across the ancient mountains of Thao. The view was breathtaking, displaying miles and miles of new ice and rising steam. The five wizards had made camp perched high in the peaks, because how could anyone hide from you when you could see the whole world?

For five generations his people had remained hidden. In the official histories, his house was listed as extinct, their bloodline extinguished, and their heritage erased. They had once been the greatest wizards in the world, so mighty that they had threatened to upstage the Law itself, so the Capitol had crushed them. The survivors had pieced together an existence, selling their skills to the highest bidder, but never forgetting what they'd learned. All those generations in the darkness they'd waited, knowing that if they reclaimed too much magic at once it would attract the full wrath of the judges, but here they were today, with the Inquisition practically giving a whole ancestor blade worth of black steel to them as a present. Houses had risen and fallen over far less.

And if he could take Angruvadal *whole*... That would change everything.

From Sikasso's lofty vantage point the terraced hills of the Thao farm country seemed unnatural, far too orderly and sculpted to exist in such a rugged place. His eyes followed the mountains until he found the steep canyons where Jharlang lay hidden. Something on the mountainside above that was reflecting the sunrise, glass or polished metal perhaps. There was no way to tell from here. Sikasso glanced at the map again and traced the dotted lines. That shining beacon he was seeing had to be the old Somsak fortress. Like all rational men, Sikasso didn't believe in gods, but if he had then he'd have known this was a sign.

"Five against one is good, but an army against one is better. Bhorlatar!"

"Yes, my Thakoor," the wizard approached, eager to hunt.

"Fetch my bag of body parts. I need to give someone a gift."

The reflection had come from a massive steel shield, polished mirror smooth and set on top of the tallest tower of an ancient keep. Even the backwoods mountain folk liked a bit of flash.

Sikasso brazenly landed in the field in front of the stone fortress in the form of a great black buzzard, changed back into a man, and then walked right up to the front gate. Several crossbows were trained on him the whole time. He spread his arms wide and opened his hands to show that he was unarmed, not that such a thing mattered to someone who was obviously a wizard. "I come in peace and bearing gifts for the terrible and mighty Somsak." There was shouting from the walls as a guard found someone of high enough rank to decide whether to open the gate or not.

Curiosity must have outweighed their superstition. Chains rattled and the way was opened for him. Ten warriors marched out, dressed in mismatched hand-me-down armor, and surrounded him with drawn swords.

"Who are you, wizard?" the one with the most tattoos on his face demanded. That must have been how the Somsak denoted rank. Assuming the more ink the face had, the more status, this one must have killed scores of men in his day.

"I am Sikasso of the Lost House and I bring an offer of alliance and gifts of friendship for Nadan Somsak."

Wary glances were exchanged. They'd heard legends of the Lost House, dark and powerful. "The Thakoor does not speak to uninvited strangers."

"I've been told your Thakoor doesn't speak to anyone since the Black Heart chopped off his tongue and left him a crippled mute." The circle of swords closed in at the insult. The Somsak used a straight, two-edged blade, and they were close enough now that Sikasso could see the quality of their steel. The blades weren't up to his exacting standards, but still sharp enough to hack him to bits. "One of the gifts I bear will cure that condition and give him back his speech. The other will grant the Somsak their revenge."

"Your words interest us." The officer nodded, and a runner was dispatched into the keep. While they waited for the response, the swords barely wavered. The mountain folk had strong arms, that was for sure. "You'd better not be wasting our time. Our Thakoor is not a patient man."

From what he'd heard from his sources, ever since losing his duel their Thakoor had alternated between bouts of impotent rage and suicidal depression. After his defeat, he'd taken out his rage on his holdings, raising taxes, and executing anyone who questioned the sanity of having a ruler who could no longer speak. Rumor suggested that the leadership of Great House Thao was growing tired of their subordinate's petulant anger, so it would surprise no one if they ordered him to be retired, banished, or even executed. So Nadan Somsak had absolutely nothing to lose.

Sikasso gave a polite bow. "Of course."

A few minutes later the runner came back and whispered something to the officer. He seemed surprised, but gave a signal and the sword points pulled back enough for Sikasso to pass. "I thought for sure he'd have us hack you to bits, but he will see you. Follow."

Sikasso was escorted into the keep. Compared to the nobility of the other houses or the opulence of the Capitol, the Somsak keep was like stepping back into a more barbaric time. This must have been how the warriors lived back during the Age of Kings, when the houses were little more than subservient tribes. Scores of men watched him suspiciously as he passed. They wore rough leathers and chainmail shirts that had been continually repaired and passed down for generations. Their decorations tended toward crow feathers and slapped-on paint. The once proud Somsak were little more than thugs now. They were a vassal house in name only. Letting them collect taxes from the terrace farmers kept them from turning to banditry, and whenever there got to be too many of them, House Thao would simply rent out their savages as mercenary raiders to their neighbors.

From the large number already gathered here and outfitted for war, it looked as if the Thao had been about to send them on a raid anyway, probably into Vadal lands to take advantage of their misfortune. They appeared ready to strike. Today was Sikasso's lucky day.

Their great hall stank of sweat and smoke. Massive war dogs were gnawing on the bones left over from the warriors' breakfast. A muscular, scarred man sat on a massive chair decorated with antlers, coldly studying Sikasso as the wizard entered. His cheeks had been roughly stitched back together from where Angruvadal had split open his face. The artistic tattoos there had been ruined by the black steel's passing. The wizard gave a very respectful bow. "Thakoor Somsak, I am Sikasso."

Nadan didn't so much as nod. He growled some unintelligible command, but the warrior escort seemed to understand, since they all turned and left the hall, leaving Sikasso alone with their master.

The two men measured each other up. Nadan was as imposing as Sikasso was unremarkable. Most of his exposed skin was covered in tattoos that told the story of his many raids and victorious duels, but his eyes told a much different story, one of defeat and shame, and as Sikasso peered through the Somsak leader he saw a desperate killer teetering on the edge of madness.

Perfect.

"Curious. A Thakoor who allows an illegal wizard in his presence without his guards," Sikasso said. "You understand, then, that anything I have to offer would be outside the Law."

"*Core!*" Nadan shouted, banging one fist against the arm of his antlered throne.

"That's right. I did speak of a *cure* for your condition. What good is a war leader who can't give understandable orders?" Sikasso reached into a pouch on his belt and removed a small wooden box. "Inside this box is a severed tongue. Awakened with my magic, it will replace yours." Sikasso opened the lid and held it up so the crippled Thakoor could see. "But it comes with a price."

The dried piece of meat was forked and black. Nadan's brows crinkled together. The tattoo lines accentuated his anger. "*Emon?*"

"Correct, Thakoor. This is a demon tongue, taken from a fearsome beast that was slain in Gujara last year. It cost me a fortune on the black market, but that fortune is nothing compared to the value of our friendship."

"*Ost?*" Drool spilled from the gaps in Nadan's cheeks.

"The cost is simple. Place this in your mouth and it will attach to the stump and become one with you. Demon blood will mix with your own. You'll immediately gain their speed and resilience, but with it comes their hunger for blood. It is a small price to pay, if you ask me, to make you strong enough to defeat the bearer of Angruvadal."

"*Ock!*" He stood up so quickly that the antler throne crashed onto its side. The war dogs cowered beneath the table.

"Ashok is here, within your borders. If we don't hesitate, I can show you the way and deliver him into your hands, before he escapes." Sikasso smiled. Nothing was more important to the Somsak than revenge. Even after hundreds of years united beneath the Law, those who lived on the ragged edges of civilization still retained some of the savagery of the tribes they'd descended from. "Ashok must pay. I too, want the Black Heart punished for his wickedness, but I am too weak to defeat him. But you are strong. And with this, you will be even more powerful."

Nadan strode forward and picked up the box. He plucked out the forked tongue and held it up to the beam of sunlight coming through the tall window. The desiccated flesh seemed to soften around his fingertips, becoming as vibrant and slick as when it was still alive. "*As-ohn-ee.*"

That was incomprehensible, but Sikasso guessed he was speaking of *blasphemy.* "The Law frowns upon such things, but once you take Angruvadal for yourself, you can make your own law," Sikasso lied smoothly. He had no intentions of letting the precious black steel fall into the hands of this barbarian. "Who could stop you? Who could stand before the Somsak if they had an ancestor blade once again? I offer you your speech back, the fearsome physical power of a sea demon, and an opportunity for vengeance. The entire world will speak of your victory. What you do after that is up to you, great Thakoor."

Nadan Somsak placed the demon's tongue into his ruined mouth.

Chapter 40

There was a wide drainage ditch cut through the town, separating the casteless quarter from the homes of the whole men. The ditch had been filled by the torrential rains and partially iced-over during the night. The only way across was an old stone bridge that was completely covered in thick ice. Ashok crossed with an untouchable child cradled in each arm, and his bare feet leaving a smear of blood with each step. The girl had passed out. The boy was still crying. They weighed nothing.

All of Jharlang seemed dirty and run down, but this quarter was far worse. The workers' roofs were made of shingles, the casteless's of straw. There was no order here, just haphazard buildings stacked deeper and deeper, until there were only narrow channels for bodies to pass through. The workers' main street was paved with stone, the casteless didn't have an open space wide enough to call a street, and the path Ashok found himself on was nothing but ruts and frozen mud puddles.

Always on the lookout for trouble, the casteless had seen him coming and gone into hiding. They probably didn't know what to make of a whole man in a fine merchant's coat carrying two of their own, so they'd retreated. He saw frightened eyes peeking out from behind slats. "Who is in charge?" Ashok's shout broke the early morning stillness. The sound startled a stray dog from beneath a pile of rotting timbers, and it ran away, tail between its legs. "Come out."

He continued through the maze, shouting. If they didn't answer soon, he'd pick a shack and leave the children inside. That thought angered him, and he wasn't even certain why.

The barracks didn't have doors, just curtains made of hide. One of those curtains parted and a hunched-over old female came hobbling out, using a knotted old stick for a cane. Her hair was wild and white, her skin was yellowed and had the same texture as the leather curtains. She stopped a few feet from Ashok, and he thought that she looked so brittle that if a strong wind pushed her over she might shatter.

"These folks heed me." Her voice was stronger than her appearance suggested it would be. There was something too proud about this one. She wore her rags like a Thakoor would wear their finest silks. "I'm Mother Dawn."

"Casteless don't have titles."

"Mother is more of a nickname than a title." Her eyes were so clouded and gray that Ashok thought she might be blind, but then she looked right at the children in Ashok's arms. "Poor little things."

"I saved these."

"How unexpectedly kind of you."

Ashok had never been accused of kindness before. "Take them."

Then she put her fingers to her lips and whistled. It was a surprisingly sharp noise. Another curtain opened and two casteless women hurried over to Ashok and relieved him of the bodies. For a reason he couldn't begin to understand, he was hesitant to let go.

"I assure you they'll be tended to."

He relented, and the meager weight was lifted from him. Ashok watched as they were taken inside a barracks and the curtain closed. It was over. Ashok owed the casteless no explanation and turned to go.

"We've been expecting you."

Ashok kept walking. "You know nothing of who I am."

"You are Fall."

He paused.

"All of the youngsters speak of you, at night, in the barracks, where their overseers can't hear. Some don't believe, but others do. It has been a long time since we've had a hero."

"Hero is an inappropriate description. Command them to stop."

"I'm not talking about these here, but *all* of us. Word of your existence has traveled across all the houses to every barracks and slum. It is good to have a new story! The few of us who've lived long enough to get old have been telling the ancient stories, hoping the day will come, and if we hope hard enough, sometimes the Forgotten shows us things. He showed me you would come here."

Ashok's curiosity got the better of him. "What did your false god have to say about me?"

"Say?" The crazy old casteless cackled. "I'm no Oracle."

"I don't know what that is."

"A title from the old days. *Prophet* I suppose they call it nowadays, though I think that's just inexperienced Keepers mixing up jobs. I've not heard the Voice. I don't get the words! Couldn't write them down even if I did, so why waste perfectly good words on someone who can't read or write, like me? I got no Keeper here to scribble them down! Everybody knows an Oracle always has a Keeper in tow. How else would the Forgotten's words get recorded for his people?"

He shrugged.

"But I *saw!* The gods showed me two paths. You take one, we all die. You take the other, we live—for a bit—but you might not. It weren't clear."

Ashok studied the crone's milky eyes. "No wonder."

"Two paths before you, Fall. Before you pick, know there are five hundred of our kind here, innocent, and we'll all be punished for what you done. Our only use in Jharlang is to work the terraces. Everything else is above us. No terraces to work during the winter, but we still eat up the food stores. Only this was a poor year, and there's not enough food. The workers don't like going hungry to keep us around. Spring's a way off still. Winter's long. They won't need much other excuse to kill off most of us, and you just gave them one."

There was shouting on the other side of the bridge. He called upon the Heart to focus his senses. Some villagers were telling the tale of the beaten workers, trying to rile up the others. Angry cries echoed through Jharlang.

"It is not right for them to punish you for something I did," Ashok muttered.

"We are all still being punished for something our ancestors did hundreds and hundreds of years ago. This comes as a surprise?"

There was a *clang clang clang* noise as a villager began beating on a kettle. That would serve as their alarm. Retribution had to be sought. *Justice demands blood.*

"These two paths you saw, where did each one lead?"

"Both end in blood. You were born into this world to kill. That can't be helped, Fall. The question is, whose blood will you spill *first*? Gather your friends and flee, or stay and fight? Will you help your brothers and sisters here live, or will you abandon us to the mob so that you can continue to pretend to be something you are not?"

"I don't want to hurt these workers."

"Workers?" The Mother tilted her head to the side. "If only it were so easy! We can hide from workers until their rage cools. We have far more patience than they do. No, Fall, I was shown that something much worse is coming. The Forgotten doesn't care how many innocents must perish to convince you, only that you are convinced. Of the many different gods the tribes worshipped back in the old days, I've been told that some of them were merciful, even kind and loving. The Forgotten was not one of those."

More noise was coming from the worker side of the village. Angry cries for vengeance were answered. Clubs banged a rhythm against walls. They were coming.

The Law demanded that he continue on his way. He may have made a foolish, emotional mistake getting involved earlier, but orders came first. Now he had time to think clearly, and knew he had to get to Akershan and find the prophet. But Ashok couldn't move, torn between duty and something else. *Shame? Doubt?* He didn't know what to call it, but the unfamiliar emotion gnawed at him. He looked around the humble casteless quarter, and knew that if he did what he was supposed to, this place and its inhabitants would be reduced to ash.

"Yes, Fall, life would have remained simpler if you would've just let those children die."

"Only I didn't." He started for the bridge.

She called after him, "The Forgotten didn't show me that he'd pick someone too dumb to wear shoes after an ice storm!"

"I was in a hurry."

Chapter 41

Keta had been awake long before sunup, nervously watching Thera sleep. Though they pretended to be husband and wife when they stayed at inns, they had never shared a bed. Suggesting otherwise was likely to get him knifed, so the Keeper of Names always insisted upon sleeping on the floor. He was, after all, extremely used to it.

It wasn't like Thera to sleep in this long. Normally she was alert and sharpening something by the time Keta stirred, and it wasn't as if someone who'd once been a hard-working butcher was prone to slumbering long past sunrise. Regardless of how poorly she slept, they needed to discuss this new complication. "Thera?"

She immediately snapped awake and pulled a dagger from beneath her pillow. She lowered it when she saw it was only Keta. "What?" she asked, rubbing her eyes, then she must have noticed the concerned look on Keta's face. "Oceans... Was it the Voice again?"

The Keeper of Names gave her a sad little smile. "I'm afraid so."

"There's no escaping that damned thing!"

Then he averted his eyes as Thera climbed out of bed, heedless of his presence, and began throwing her clothing on. The warrior caste didn't get too hung up on modesty. It wasn't as if

343

someone who'd grown up living in crowded casteless barracks worried about such things either, but looking away seemed the polite thing to do. "The message was short."

"Damn it, damn it, damn it," Thera muttered as she pulled her shirt over her head. "What did it say this time?"

As was required, he'd written it down, but there was no need to get the paper out. He remembered exactly what it said. *"Here the path is set. Let my general begin his war. The world must remember what has been forgotten."*

"What does that mean?" Thera lashed a small knife to the inside of her wrist and hid it beneath a sleeve. "Bunch of cryptic nonsense is all. That's it?"

"That was all." Keta lied. He'd written down two more lines, but he couldn't bring himself to tell Thera about it yet. This was not the time to have a crisis of faith, but Keta was afraid to tell her the rest.

"I've got a bad feeling about this. You should have woken me sooner. Let's grab Ashok and get out of here."

There was a commotion outside of their room and shouting downstairs. Someone ran down the hallway, passed their room, and thundered down the stairs. Keta listened closely as the panicked messenger's noise woke the entire inn.

"Did I hear that right?"

Keta hadn't been sure himself. "I think he said there's a *riot*." The Keeper got off the stool, carefully tucking the piece of paper containing the transcribed holy vision into a pocket and went to the window. The inn was too poor to have glass, so he had to untie a thick cord before he could pull the insulating curtain open. A harsh winter chill rolled into the room as Keta threw open the flimsy shutters.

The world was blinding and bright. The early morning sun was reflecting off of every iced-over surface. He'd heard of ice storms, but they didn't have such things where he was from. It was rather impressive in person. Keta lifted one hand to shade his eyes. The people of Jharlang were gathering in the streets as excited runners went from house to house, proclaiming news of some injustice. Workers rushed past below, carrying axes, hammers, and pitchforks. Some fool had begun ringing a bell. In the distance he could see a much larger group forming.

Thera joined him at the window. "Looks more like an angry

mob than a proper riot, but workers tend to exaggerate. I scouted around last night. That's the casteless quarter they're heading toward. Looks like some poor untouchable slob is about to get executed."

He'd personally witnessed that sort of thing a few times over the course of his life. That many angry people meant that the crime had been something serious, and infuriating enough to not wait for a proper judgment. He'd heard of whole casteless barracks being burned down with all of their inhabitants inside to avenge the murder of a single worker. The casteless quarter was nearly as big as the rest of the village, and was kept separate by a wide irrigation ditch spanned by a single bridge. They were agitating about in front of it, but for some reason the mob hadn't crossed that bridge yet. Keta squinted and tried to make out what was going on.

There was a lone figure blocking their way.

Chapter 42

Ashok stood alone before the angry mob, Angruvadal still sheathed and hidden beneath his long coat. He held a miner's pick in one hand. The worker he'd taken the pick from was crawling away with a broken elbow. That's what the fool deserved for taking a swing at him.

"I warned you," Ashok told him as he tossed the pick onto the ice, before turning his attention back to the assembled villagers of Jharlang. They'd seen him mercilessly incapacitate two strong men so far, and it appeared that nobody wanted to be the next to try. "Leave the untouchables be."

"Stand aside, merchant! They murdered one of ours!"

Ashok frowned. He'd not meant to kill any of them. Perhaps the one he'd put into the fence had broken his neck? Either that, or rumors flew faster than truth, and later they'd find that no one had actually died at all, but by that point the quarter would be in flames. "These casteless didn't kill anyone. I'm the one who fought those men."

The crowd began to shout, some for him to be arrested, others to have him killed. The local warriors hadn't arrived to restore order yet, and the workers were mad *now*. The people here were poor and lived a hard life, but they were proud, and the proud didn't take insults well. The roar began to build as those in the back—who hadn't seen how quickly he'd eliminated the last who'd tried to cross the bridge—pushed their way forward. The anger was building. Soon it would overcome sense and he'd have no choice but to really hurt them.

"Turn back. This isn't justice," Ashok shouted to be heard over the rumble.

"You're no judge! Kill him!"

"Break that barefooted outsider's skull!"

Their temper was as hot as the morning was cold. Ashok didn't know much about the life of a poor worker village, but an ice storm couldn't be good for their livestock. Life here was harsh enough anyway, but this village had woken up in a bad mood, and the first news they'd heard was that some of their own had been beaten by casteless. Of course they were upset, and they were going to take their frustrations out on someone.

No matter what, Ashok wasn't going to let them through.

Behind him the casteless were either hiding or gathering their meager belongings and fleeing into the terraces. Had his people tried to run when Bidaya had sent her warriors to eliminate them? Were they as frightened as these casteless were now? Or had they been taken by surprise, when Vadal troops had set their barracks on fire and erased everyone he'd ever known?

Such thoughts put him in a foul mood. "Return to your homes."

A miner ran forward and hurled a rock at Ashok's face.

Ashok caught the rock in one hand. It stung his palm. The miner had a good arm. But he immediately launched it back twice as fast. The rock struck the worker in the forehead with a sick crack, bounced off, and he collapsed unconscious into the snow. That gave them some pause, but more rocks were being pried off the frozen ground.

"Who are you to tell us what to do?"

Enough of this nonsense.

"Who am I? I am Ashok Vadal." He opened his coat and drew his sword. Somehow the air became even colder. The villagers gasped in fear as the unmistakable black steel seared their eyes. "And the casteless are under my *protection*."

The men of Jharlang began to flee, crashing into each other, slipping and sliding across the ice, trampling their neighbors in order to get away. They were in such a hurry that they left their injured men behind.

"That's better," Ashok muttered as he put his sword away.

Despite the Mother's predictions of inevitable bloodshed, it seemed that he'd solved this issue without murdering anyone. It was shaping up to be a successful morning.

"You told them who you are?" Keta shouted. "Are you insane?"

After he'd found the others, the three of them had retreated back to the barn to hide and plan their next move. Keta clearly didn't approved of Ashok's actions, but to be fair, Ashok didn't approve of what he'd done either.

"If I hadn't said who I was, eventually I would have had to kill some of them." Ashok was sitting on the back of the wagon, and winced as he shoved his bloody foot into its boot. If he'd had more time he'd apply a clean foot wrap, but they needed to get out of town fast. "I had to let them know that their behavior wouldn't be tolerated."

Keta was clearly agitated. The Keeper had been patient and helpful this whole trip, but this had pushed him over the edge. "I asked you to avoid notice!"

Thera seemed annoyed, but she was being a bit calmer about the whole thing than the Keeper. "Why?"

"Why what?"

"Why spare the lives of workers? Since when do any of those lower types matter to you?"

"They still don't." But that was no longer quite true. He thought about it while he pulled his other boot on. The ice had removed a lot of skin, leaving the soles of his feet bright red and burning. It was a good thing the Heart of the Mountain would keep the wounds from corrupting and rotting his feet off. "I don't know."

"You put us all at risk, and you don't even know why?" Keta shouted.

He really didn't, and that was truly bothering him to the core of his being. "I just couldn't abide it."

"You have no idea how important our work is, and this foolishness jeopardizes everything! You had no right to endanger our lives."

Keta was correct, but that only made Ashok angrier. "*You* supposedly speak for the untouchables, Keeper. You should be filled with joy. Is your false god not pleased that I saved a few?"

"I don't know why the Forgotten chose you, yet still tolerates

your constant mockery. Your pride threatens our entire movement, everything we've accomplished. You have to understand—"

"You claim to want rebellion, Keeper, so there was a taste.
Or was all that just talk?"

That seemed to hit Keta hard. All during this journey he'd
preached about his people remembering their gods, rising up, and
stopping their oppression. He seemed truly chastised by Ashok's
harsh words. He took a deep breath, and when he exhaled, the
small man seemed to deflate a bit. "I may not understand it, but
the Forgotten has a plan. There is a time and a place for everything. I'll be happier to stir up a revolt when we've got an army
of faithful at our backs and we're not surrounded by enemies."

"When you declare war on the Law, you'll never lack for
enemies." Ashok hadn't meant to give offense. Keta may have
been delusional, but his delusions had integrity. Calling Keta's
honesty into question was a terrible insult. He dipped his head.
"I didn't intend to endanger either of you. I'll try to do better
in the future."

"We should leave before the local warriors find their courage
and come looking," Keta muttered as he went to the stall holding their oxen. Something else was bothering the Keeper as well,
but he must have not wanted to speak of it in front of Ashok.

"Leave them. The wagon's too slow," Thera said. "The ground
is iced over now, but it'll be nothing but mud in a few hours
and the wagon will be useless. We've got to make distance before
word spreads. Let's take their horses."

"Good idea," Keta said as he went to a different gate.

"That would be stealing," Ashok pointed out.

Thera was incredulous. "You inconsistent bastard, one minute
you're beating workers senseless in front of hundreds of witnesses
and the next you won't steal a horse!"

"That was different."

"Just when I'm beginning to think there's actually a normal
person lurking inside of there, you have to go and prove me
wrong." She sighed. "What if we consider our abandoned wagon
a trade? The value of the goods inside far outweighs the value
of these sad excuses for ponies. Does that work?"

That was actually a very pragmatic and just solution. "Very
well." He slid off the back of the wagon, and white-hot pain
slapped the soles of his feet. Ashok ignored it.

"I wouldn't worry about the warriors too much. I saw their barracks when I was scouting last night. It's tiny. There are probably only a handful of them in the whole village. They're not going to cross that sword." Not that Thera was arguing against leaving, since she'd already gone about stealing a local's saddle. "I'm more worried they'll be riding to tell the Somsak we're here to try and collect that bounty."

A sudden discomforting sensation moved down his spine, causing an involuntary shiver. Angruvadal was warning him of an impending threat. The sword could sense far more than he could, so Ashok went to the barn doors and peered outside. He couldn't see anything yet, but when he focused, called upon the Heart, and laid his hand on the wall, he felt the vibration of hundreds of distant hoofbeats thrumming through his palm. "We're in danger."

"What is it?" Keta joined him at the door.

"Horses." They were coming down the mountain like an avalanche. He nodded toward the west.

"That's the route to the old Somsak house," Thera said. "There's no way a messenger made it there and back so fast, especially not in this weather. Must be a random patrol."

"That's no patrol." There were so many hoof beats he couldn't even calculate how many of them there were. "It's an army."

It was their doom.

"A raid on the way to Vadal?" Keta asked hopefully.

"Regardless, when they're told I'm here, they will strike." Angruvadal was warning him there were far too many to fight at once. A direct confrontation would likely result in his death. Ashok turned to his companions. They were looking at him wide-eyed and fearful. Everyone in Lok had heard the stories about Somsak depravity. Even the Protectors respected the mountain folk for their brutal thoroughness. As he concentrated, the sword was helping him calculate the speed, direction, and numbers of the threat. For a thing with no eyes or ears, it always seemed to have an excellent grasp of what was going on around it. Small groups of horsemen had broken off, and from the echoes on the canyon walls, they were taking the high ground. Anyone fleeing the village would be spotted and intercepted. "No . . . They're not passing through. They're spreading out. Jharlang is their objective."

"Come on!" Thera rushed to the wall and desperately began

pulling dusty leather tack from the hooks and tossing it on the straw at Keta's feet. "We've got to hurry."

She had no way of knowing that her actions were futile. There was no way out. Ashok knew he could fight his way through, then he could likely evade pursuit on foot by sticking to the roughest terrain possible, but the other two would slow him down too much. They couldn't follow where he could go. To have any chance at all he would need to abandon them. Only the villagers knew Ashok wasn't travelling alone, and Thera and Keta were outsiders. If they hid, the Somsak would go door to door until they were found. No one would claim or hide them. They would be caught, questioned, tortured, and executed.

"There is no escape," Ashok stated.

Keta rushed to the wagon and pulled out a meat cleaver that had been hidden beneath the driver's bench. "We'll fight!"

Ashok glanced at the cleaver and raised an eyebrow. "If it comes down to you using that against a few hundred Somsak, Keeper, better to cut your own throat with it than to let them take you alive."

Keta was terrified as the bleak reality of the situation took hold. "What do we do?"

For them? There was nothing they could do. For him? Escape, evade, and live to fulfill his orders. It was cruel, but Angruvadal's calculations were never wrong. There was no option for victory, only retreat or dying in a futile defiant gesture. Ashok threw the barn door open. The path was open before him.

Damn it . . . He was a man without fear, but not entirely without conscience. Dying was easy. Failing was hard.

"I am sorry," he said.

The Grand Inquisitor had spoken for the judges, and their orders were more important than any handful of lives. His guides would perish, but Ashok would find another way to complete his mission. He always did. Logically, he should have as much loyalty to a criminal and a fanatic as they did to the Law. The Capitol's demands outweighed any personal feelings he had. His entire existence meant doing that which was expected of him. Any other time in his life, the decision would have already been made, but the last year had left him broken, his foundation cracked.

Ashok looked back at his companions. Keta was still scrambling, trying to think of something, but Thera was watching him, almost detached. Like she understood exactly what was coming. Their eyes met, and she knew the truth. There was no time to explain that he had to put his mission first, or to apologize for abandoning them. She was strong, raised in the warrior caste, so she would understand. Relentless death was coming for them and Ashok wouldn't be there to stop it.

Ashok turned away.

"Do what you have to do," Thera whispered. "We'll find a way to survive without you." She was enough of a survivor that she may have even believed her own words. He took a step, but couldn't bring himself to take another.

The choice was clear, obedience or rebellion.

Ashok's hands curled into fists. That morning he had rashly chosen mercy over the Law, but it had been in a heated moment, without thought. Now with perfect clarity, he faced two paths.

This time, I do not obey.

Decision made, he spoke quickly. "Listen carefully. I'll challenge the warriors. Wait until they're all concentrating on me, then ride."

Unaware that Ashok had just made the most selfish, and selfless, decision of his entire life, Keta kept saddling the horses. Thera, however, understood what was going through Ashok's head and approached him. "You can't protect everyone."

"See to your duty and guard the Keeper." He began walking toward the sound of hooves.

She grabbed onto his coat sleeve to stop him. "You'll die." She actually sounded like she cared.

"More than likely." He was one of the greatest combatants in the world, but Angruvadal was telling him that these numbers were too many, the odds too drastic. Death was certain. *But was that truly a bad thing?* Better to end it now than to drag out Omand's terrible punishment. It had felt *good* to tell the villagers his name. "I should have died a long time ago."

"What about your mission? What about finding the prophet?"

"Keta can tell him that I tried." He took her hand and gently removed it from his coat. "Goodbye, Thera." Already he could hear the first of the Somsak riders entering the canyon. He walked into the sunlight to meet his fate.

Ashok didn't look back.

Chapter 43

At first the villagers of Jharlang had mistaken them for raiders from another house. It was an understandable error. At most, these workers had met a few Somsak at a time when they'd come to collect their rightful taxes. It had been generations since Jharlang had seen so many Somsak at once, and those had been raiders, in the days before the savage mountain people had been defeated and made vassals to a bunch of farmers. How were they supposed to know the hundreds of terrifying warriors rapidly converging on their little village were of their same house? They'd meant no insult when they'd fled across their frozen fields.

Only Nadan Somsak didn't see it that way. He took offense, and he was not the sort of man you wanted to give offense to.

A few Thao warriors from the tiny local garrison were brought forward, and shoved down in front of the line of stamping horses. The Somsak were truly frightening when they rode to battle, dressed in dyed furs and crow feathers tied over their gleaming mail. *"Where is the fallen?"* Nadan Somsak demanded. His words were nothing but a hissing whisper because of his new demon tongue. *"Where is Ashok Vadal?"*

"I don't know, mighty Thakoor." Oh, how they recognized him now.

Nadan made a growling noise that reverberated inside his helmet. *Wrong answer.* He lifted his powerful crossbow. The bolt was so quick that it was almost as if feathers sprouted from the warrior's eye socket. It only pierced the side of his brain so death wasn't immediate. He rolled onto his back, grasping at the shaft, kicking and screaming as he tried to pluck it from his head. Nadan passed the crossbow over to one of his men so it could be reloaded. The Somsak crossbows were unwieldy things that required a lever to draw back, but they were extremely powerful. *"Where is he?"*

The next Thao warrior in line wasn't eager to die. "Last I saw he was at the bridge, defending the casteless quarter."

"If you knew it was the fallen, why didn't you capture him?" Nadan asked as one of his soldiers passed him another loaded crossbow. The Somsak's horse stomped nervously as blood stink hit its nostrils.

The warrior was choking on the words, struggling to get them out in time. "He drew that magic sword, Thakoor." He hesitated, probably trying to think of a response that wouldn't incriminate him as a coward. His eyes flicked over to his thrashing compatriot. "We had no—"

Since his head was turned to look at his dying companion, Nadan shot that one through the ear canal. This time death was instantaneous.

Sikasso shook his head at the display. Theoretically they were of the same house, and the Thao were of higher status, but the tattooed mountain thugs didn't see it that way, not today at least. Perhaps it was the boiling hatred that came from the demon blood now coursing through Nadan's veins, or perhaps he was just always that much of a barbarian at heart, but Sikasso could already tell that the day would end in slaughter.

"Ashok defends the untouchables here. All he defends, I will destroy. Fourth paltan, burn the casteless quarter. Kill them all. Third, search the workers' homes in case this coward was incorrect. The rest will remain with me. As soon as he is found, alert me," Nadan ordered as he was presented another loaded crossbow. *"Go."*

His damaged tongue didn't carry his words far, but his officers repeated them down the line until the units broke off, riding through the icy lanes. The majority of the Somsak remained just outside the village, ready to swoop in the moment their target was seen. Sikasso noted that Nadan had sent off the unseasoned and restless youths to cause trouble, while keeping the obviously experienced veterans close. A wise move. He watched the warriors. Most of them seemed ready for a fight, almost as eager as their Thakoor. There was a lot of stored aggression in these mountains, and for too long the Somsak had been vassals to a house that they secretly considered to be their inferiors. Before they'd ridden forth, Nadan had addressed his officers, speaking of how it was time for them to gain a new ancestor blade and become a great house again. They had heard their Thakoor's new voice and thought it was a miracle. At Sikasso's suggestion, he'd not let them see his face.

Most were thankful for this miracle. Sikasso had noticed a lot of superstitious glances in his direction. Not all of the Somsak were bloodthirsty fools, and the observant already sensed that there was something seriously wrong about their Thakoor. No matter how great Nadan was in battle, once they discovered the truth of their leader's miraculous healing, there would be violence. Even the most pragmatic warriors would never accept a Thakoor tainted by forbidden demon magic. If Sikasso was going to be among these people, he'd have to watch his back, because it was easier to lash out at the wizard who'd corrupted your Thakoor than the beloved and extremely deadly man himself, but he doubted their alliance would last long enough for it to be an issue. The wizards of the Lost House were already perched like falcons in the rocks above, ready to swoop in and secure the sword. Whatever Somsak were left when Ashok was done with them, his men would dispose of, and then the Lost House could disappear back into myth and legend where they belonged.

There was quite a bit of screaming coming from the workers' homes. Apparently to the Somsak the command *search* was a synonym for rape and pillage. Thankfully the warrior who'd been shot in the eye had quit his crying and bled to death. The horses were agitated and Sikasso had to struggle to control his mount. Even the hardy mountain animals were struggling on this ice. They'd been in such a hurry to get here that one rider had tumbled over a cliff, and there'd been a few other slips, crashes, and broken legs, but most of them had made it. Their horses were such an agile breed that the Somsak must have crossed them with mountain goats, but they still weren't real war horses, trained to crash into combat, so the smells and noises were frightening them. He got the animal calmed down and went back to surveying the humble village.

Once he had a moment to collect himself Sikasso began to feel a vibrant energy in the air. There was *strong* magic here. At first he thought it had to be Angruvadal, but there was something else, something different. He'd been near Angruvadal before, and while it was truly a masterpiece, this was an entirely new sensation. It was very different than demon and didn't feel quite like black steel. It was unlike any magic he'd ever felt before, and it was so powerful it made the hairs on his arms stand up.

There was something strange going on in Jharlang, and Sikasso vowed to get to the bottom of it. As soon as he could slip away, he'd inform his wizards to search for whatever was causing that sensation. *What luck.* He'd come here for Angruvadal, but if they could capture it along with something else... Sikasso grinned at the thought. That morning he'd thought of his men as addicts, and there was nothing more exciting to an addict than a new drug.

Nadan Somsak was eyeing the village. His helmet was an armored bucket with vision slits and elk antlers, which was good, because Sikasso wasn't sure how his flesh would react as the demon took it over. Nadan put his hands on the helmet and began to lift. "I would caution you against taking that off, Thakoor," the wizard said.

"*My throat burns. My guts churn. All I can taste is metal.*"

"It takes time for my magic to work. You will look like your old self soon enough, but right now, your appearance may be unsettling to your men." In truth, Sikasso wasn't sure what it was going to do to him. Every man's reaction was different when the demon got into their blood. Usually it took a day or two before the user became *too* hideous to pass for human, but for someone who barely qualified as human to begin with, perhaps the transformation would go much quicker.

"*What have you done to me?*"

"I've given you the strength to crush Ashok Vadal like a bug."

Chapter 44

Ashok walked around the corner of a house and right into a group of Somsak. They were distracted by all of the screaming and carrying on as panicked workers were being dragged outside and their homes looted. They were violating the Law concerning the conduct of a raid, acting as criminals. *Good.* That made this much easier for him.

The first one he killed never even knew Ashok was there. There was a black flash and then a severed head was rolling through the snow. The head hit another Somsak in the foot. He looked down, saw his companion's face, and then promptly lost his own. Ashok slid past, gutting a third, then spun and removed the arm from a fourth. That last one began to scream.

Several warriors turned toward him at once. Ashok stood there, black blade dripping, as the bodies collapsed around him.

"I am here."

He had never been gifted with subtlety.

Bellowing, they lifted their weapons and rushed forward. Ashok stepped into them, turning aside steel and parting flesh in return. With Angruvadal whispering how to move, where to place his body, and warning him of incoming threats that he couldn't even see, the Somsak weren't just fighting Ashok, who on his own was one of the greatest swordsmen to ever live, they were fighting every man who'd ever wielded Angruvadal, and it showed in the bloody results.

Ashok parried, dodged, leaping side to side, until he was in the middle of the pack, and then he went to work. Every movement resulted in serious injury as Angruvadal split chain and cleaved through bones. Angruvadal didn't cut like sharpened steel, but like a bolt of lightning blasting a tree into splinters. Warriors stumbled away, missing limbs or gushing blood, crying for help, or to be avenged, or for their mothers.

Within a span of a few heartbeats, the surprised group was broken. Every last one of them was dead or crippled.

The rest would not be so easy.

He set out at a run. The odds were still against him, but better in the chokepoints and narrow alleys of the town than out in the open. He had to keep moving. If the Somsak could bring the full weight of their numbers against him at once, he would perish. There was shouting behind him, so Ashok moved between the houses, pushing past chicken coops, iced-over gardens, and pig pens, until he came out in the next lane. A Somsak was coming down the steps of a fine estate, carrying a crying woman over one shoulder, so Ashok hacked through his knee without even slowing. He fell with his would-be victim on top of him.

More warriors were on this lane, but rushing in the direction he'd come from, so Ashok crashed right into them, swinging. He hit a Somsak in the back, slicing through furs and piercing his spine. His appearance was so sudden that the others slipped and fell on the ice, scrambling to get out of his range. Ashok followed one of them as he was sliding away, and the only thing he could reach was his foot, so he lopped off the end of his boot and a few toes out of spite.

There were mounted soldiers at the end of the street. They began firing their crossbows. With their horses dancing about nervously their accuracy was terrible, and the only thing struck was an innocent worker running for cover. Bolts spent, they kneed their mounts and rode off, shouting for help.

The warriors were trying to push back. His location was known and orders were being relayed. They were coming from all directions now, converging on his position. He had to keep moving; being surrounded meant he was finished. A spear was thrust his way, but his strong response splintered the shaft. Before the warrior even realized he'd lost his weapon, Ashok had driven Angruvadal through his chest and out the other side. He slammed his shoulder into the dying man, lifting him off the ground and pushing him back through the crowd. He was nicked and cut as he passed, but Angruvadal warned him of the dangerous swings so he was able to avoid those. Crashing into the next alley, he jerked his sword free and retreated, walking backwards as the Somsak pressed into the narrow space after him. He lunged forward and sank the tip of the blade into a thigh, then fell back as the warriors tripped over their injured.

The Somsak had no cavalry tradition. They didn't fight from horseback. They rode to where they were going to fight then got off. There was no room for elaborate maneuvers on the trails and canyons they normally fought in. Their methods tended to be direct. No historian had ever accused them of being tacticians. They did not train as a group, but as individuals, overwhelming their foes with speed and violence. Each one was more focused on gaining individual glory than achieving a united goal. They were fantastic raiders and terrible front-line combatants. He would use their own traditions against them.

This spot would do. He was between two solid homes. Ashok let the soldiers pile into the narrow gap after him. Two strong men, shoulder to shoulder, barely fit. Clever warriors would have boxed him in with spears on both sides before filling him with arrows and bolts, but these were too eager to prove themselves, and they got in each other's way in their rush to be the one to strike him down. He let them build up, their overwhelming numbers giving them courage even in the face of black steel.

Once there were too many of them pressed in to escape, Ashok attacked. He cut into them like a tornado, a whirling, never-ending flurry of deep slashes and splattering blood. They tried to fight, but the close confines caused them to get in each other's way. Arms were retracted to strike, but elbows ran into the man behind, feet were tripped over, and hands were bumped as Ashok turned the first rank into red fountains. He climbed over the dying and launched himself into the rest, wishing he still had his old suit of armor, because then he could have done so with even more abandon.

Realizing they'd walked into a trap, the Somsak tried to fall back, but crashed into their fellows. Ashok kept pushing as men slipped on ice or blood. The wooden beams were painted red. Angruvadal warned him that the other side was filling up as well, and he turned just in time to dodge a spear that had been hurled at his back. He kept pushing through, his movements so inhumanly fast that surely some of the Somsak thought they were fighting a demon.

Then he was out of the alley and back in the open. Sliding, trying to find traction, Ashok kept running. Vaulting over a railing, he landed in a crouch as crossbow bolts embedded themselves in the porch around him. He lowered his shoulder and crashed through a worker's front door.

Ashok rolled across a woven rug and back to his feet. It was a nice home, with wooden floors instead of dirt, and warmed by a roaring fire in a great stone hearth. The family who lived here was hiding, terrified, beneath a table as a battle raged across their yard. He was no longer of status. He couldn't just barge into the homes of whole men. That was trespassing. He started to apologize, but the Somsak were already following him inside, roaring like madmen. Ashok ducked beneath the first's wild swing, stabbed the second through the door between the ribs, then kicked the first in the ass, launching him head first into the fireplace. Another followed, but he made the mistake of lifting his blade for an overhead swing and stuck it into the roof beams. Angruvadal tore across his stomach, spilling his guts across the nice rug. Ashok shoved him out the door, into his brothers, and several of them tripped and fell down the icy stairs.

"I am sorry for invading your home," Ashok told the terrified workers between the screams of the burning warrior. That one had gotten up and was thrashing about, fur and feathers aflame, so Ashok ran him through, and knocked him onto the stones so he wouldn't burn the whole house down. "Should I live long enough, I will return and pay for the damage to your property." Then he headed for the back. There wasn't another door, so Ashok kicked out the shutters and climbed through.

He fell on the ground, and since the runoff from the roof had collected here, the ice was so thick and slippery it took a moment to find his footing. By the time he was up, more Somsak were already sliding around the corners. These warriors had learned a valuable lesson from the many dead and wounded he'd left behind and they approached with far more caution.

The smell of smoke struck his nostrils. He glanced over and saw a black pillar rising from the casteless quarter as it was put to the torch. Earlier, he'd declared that those untouchables were under his protection. That was *unacceptable*.

Ashok broke a sword, cut its owner's throat, and set out toward the flames.

Chapter 45

Judging from the incredible racket, Ashok had certainly made himself known. Even though they were only fighting against one man, it sounded to Keta like a mighty battle was being waged. A never-ending stream of horsemen had thundered past the inn, yelling their battle cries. But Keta really doubted the Somsak knew what they were getting into. He had once seen a Protector singlehandedly crush a rebellion, and that one hadn't been armed with an ancestor blade.

"Now's our chance," Keta said as he led his stolen horse from the barn. They wouldn't mount up until they were out of town. The ground was still too slick and the sun hadn't melted much of the ice yet. The horses would have a hard enough time not falling down even without riders on their backs, so better to save them for later, when they'd have to run for their lives across the hills.

After Ashok was dead and the Somsak could afford to turn their attention elsewhere.

Keta silently cursed himself as a coward, but what did the Forgotten expect him to do? The gods hadn't made him strong. What little magic he'd learned was as pathetic as his martial skills, and he had no black steel to call on anyway. His faith was weak. Keta was a bookkeeper. He was a glorified scribe for a prophet without faith.

What would you have me do?

"Come on, you damned stupid thing." Thera was tugging on the reins, but her horse wasn't cooperating. All of the crashing, banging, and screaming throughout the town had terrified the poor animal. She smacked it to let it know she meant business. It tried to bite her, so she punched it in the snout. "I'm not going to get caught over the likes of you."

"Shhh..." Keta saw movement on the other side of the inn. Not all of the Somsak had moved on yet. A few were more interested in terrorizing the locals and stealing their valuables than in seeking glory for their name against the legendary Black Heart. Soon enough, those moved on and the road was clear.

Thera's horse began cooperating when it realized she was leading it in the direction away from the scary sounds. They started down the road. Luckily it wasn't too steep, otherwise they might have slid all the way to the bottom of the mountain. It was terribly cold, but Keta was so flushed with fear that sweat was pouring down his face. They took one of the narrow paths through the tall rocks. With such a battle raging, all the Somsak would be distracted, so this was their best chance. The way back to the trade road appeared to be clear.

Ashok has wanted to die all along. Who am I to try and stop him? Keta thought bitterly.

"So much for him being our general. Can't lead much after you've been hacked to pieces." Thera kept her voice down. She was trying to sound tough, but Keta could tell she was moved by Ashok's sacrifice. Despite her callous act, she cared far more for others than she let on. "Ashok might not realize it yet, but I think I know why he saved those kids."

It was probably best not to talk at all, but that was easier said than done when they'd just abandoned someone. "What do you mean?"

"The old Ashok, the one they built made out of lies and law, is starting to crumble. He's starting to see for himself, to be what he's really supposed to be. Or maybe I've been right all along, and your Forgotten is full of it."

Or maybe I'm a coward who lacks the faith to do what must be done... "Don't talk like that. If anyone shouldn't talk like that, it's you."

"Fine, you're the Keeper." Thera threw her hands up in frustration. "You're the one who's supposed to know what the words mean. You're the one who's supposed to testify and all that nonsense."

That's right. I am.

He'd always been a dreamer, but those dreams kept on getting crushed. For his dream to succeed, for his people to be free, someone had to be willing to make the ultimate sacrifice.

"Keta, what's wrong?"

He hadn't even realized he'd stopped walking. *Grant me courage,* he prayed. "I have to go back for Ashok."

"Are you mad? You're no warrior!"

"No . . ." Keta understood exactly what he had to do. "I'm the Keeper of Names."

"So that means you need to die for no reason? I don't believe in your gods, but I do believe in your goals. So you picked the wrong man to be your general. So what? You'll find another. You'll make it work just like you always do." She tugged on her horse and this time it was smart enough not to trifle with her. "Now shut up and keep walking."

But Keta couldn't move. Thera deserved to know the truth. "I lied to you about last night's revelation from the Voice. There was more." He reached into his coat and pulled out the transcript.

She snatched it from him. "Where do you get off hiding that from me?" Thera read.

Here the path is set. Let my general begin his war. The world must remember what has been forgotten. My faithful servant will be sacrificed, a martyr. The testimony sealed in blood.

She frowned. "I *hate* the Voice."

"I'm sorry. I was trying to protect you. Don't you see, Thera? We're the servants. Me, you, and Ashok. One of us is supposed to die here today. It can't be you or Ashok. You're both too important to the work. It has to be me. I've got to go back."

Thera was staring at the paper. She looked like she was about to be ill. "You're certain this is exactly what the Voice said?"

"I'm positive. There are no mistakes."

"And you just decided that one of us is supposed to die, and that's why you didn't try to stop Ashok. How is that your decision to make?"

"I was scared, and he volunteered."

"And you think the gods would describe *him* as faithful?"

"It has to be me," Keta said. The gods would choose a new Keeper of Names, but there was no one else like Ashok. Keta had to be prepared to die for his beliefs, like Ratul before him. "I'm going back."

Thera stared at him as she realized their long journey together was coming to an end. She was a fighter, and so her first inclination would be to fight him over it, but there was no time. She didn't even dare raise her voice too much. "You're a stubborn fool." She shoved the paper roughly back at Keta. "If this message is so damned important, Keeper, make sure it ends up in your book with the rest of your god's nonsense. I'm getting out of here." Thera stomped off, heading further down the hill.

She might be furious at him now, but he was glad to see her leave. Thera had to escape. She was the most important of them all. Someday she would understand and believe. "May the Forgotten watch over you and keep you safe," Keta whispered as he prepared to go willingly to his death.

But Thera reached the edge of the bluff and stopped. Below her would be the bridge and path back to the trade road. He was unsure why she paused. Keta could barely hear her as she muttered a long string of curses against Keta, his ancestors, and his god. Then Thera pulled on her horse and turned the reluctant animal back toward the village. She began walking uphill. "I'm going back too," she snapped as she passed him.

"What! Why?" He watched her, incredulous, as she struggled up the icy slope toward where hundreds of blood-crazed Somsak were rampaging. "I'm the one that should be martyred. You need to stay alive!"

"I know that," Thera snarled. "I'm going back because the damned bridge washed out during the night. The river's too full, fast, and filled with ice chunks to cross. Feel free to stand here in the open until some tattoo-faced maniac puts an arrow in you. I intend to find another way out of this canyon."

Chapter 46

He'd swung Angruvadal into armor, shields, and bodies until a normal man's arm would have given out, but Ashok called upon the Heart of the Mountain and continued long past human endurance. That path he'd taken through the village was clearly marked in red. His long merchant's coat hung in bloodsoaked tatters. He'd been wounded several times, but none deep enough to be of concern.

Angruvadal seemed to be enjoying itself.

Ashok ran toward the open square where he'd turned aside the mob earlier. Large groups of horsemen were riding parallel to him. The townsfolk were trying to stay out of the way and were being ridden down for their trouble. Some of the Somsak had taken to the rooftops and were launching crossbow bolts his way. The ice made everything treacherous. One slip, a moment on the ground, and Ashok would be pinned there to die, but his opponents were only men, and so were far more vulnerable to the bad footing than he was. A few crossbowmen lost their grip and slid helplessly from the roofs.

When he reached the square, he had to pause and take stock. The Heart was being used to maintain his physical strength so he couldn't call upon it to augment his senses, but he didn't need supernatural perception to know that he was horribly outnumbered, and crossing the open space toward the casteless quarter would put him in grave danger. Angruvadal warned against it. Between the homes he had some chance of outlasting the Somsak, but in the open there was only death.

Ashok welcomed the idea.

The first warriors he'd faced had been inexperienced, probably the young and the foolish, sent out to shake the trees to flush their quarry. The men who were waiting for him in the square appeared to know what they were doing. The Somsak had no standardized uniform, but these were wearing more armor, and their weapons appeared to be of higher quality. Most importantly they seemed confident without being incautious. These were experienced combatants, and they were all that stood between him and the burning casteless quarter.

Swatting incoming crossbow bolts out of the way, Ashok charged.

Even though they were veterans, these Somsak were still raiders at heart, and working together didn't come naturally to them. Very few of them were carrying shields, and those who were had no formation to speak of. Ashok crashed into the men, Angruvadal slicing back and forth. Those who tried to parry, he swatted their blades aside and struck them down. He smashed shields out of the way and hacked at their limbs. Men fell, but more took their place.

The warriors surrounded him. He was stronger and faster than they were, but there were just too many. Angruvadal warned him of incoming threats and Ashok turned as fast as he could, meeting each attack, dodging or turning it aside. A spear sliced across his calf. A sword nicked his back. He killed each one in turn. Bodies fell in gushing heaps. Normal men would have run, but the Somsak were not normal. Their courage verged on insanity.

An extremely good swordsman had survived several furious exchanges with him and was still standing. Though his expression was a mask of concentration, the tattoos on his face transformed it into a perpetual leering grin. Annoyed, Ashok swung with all his might, and the stinging blow ripped the sword from his opponent's hands, but before he could finish that one, he had to turn to catch a descending ax. Angruvadal warned him that the talented swordsman had drawn his knife, but it was too late.

By the time he threw down the man with the ax, the blade was driven deep into his back.

Ashok turned, swung from the shoulder, and took the top of the leering man's skull off, but the damage was done. Hot blood was pouring from the hole and rolling down his back. He lurched to the side. The crowd parted a bit as the Somsak sensed the sudden weakness and were confused by it. Ashok reached up with his free hand, over his shoulder, and found the dagger's hilt sticking out. He tried to pull it free but couldn't get a good angle.

Now the Heart of the Mountain—rather than lending all its strength to his limbs—had to concentrate on keeping him alive instead. The bleeding stopped, but now his arms felt heavy and his legs burned.

The veteran Somsak realized that a terrible blow had been struck and the circle closed as Ashok finally got a grip and yanked the blade out of his back. He planted the dagger in a warrior's neck and returned to the fight.

The roar of the flames was his beacon, and Ashok tried to steer the crowd in that direction. A few brave men hurled themselves at him, trying to entangle him, but Angruvadal saw that coming. He would not die crushed under a pile of bodies, and everyone who tried to lay their hands on him left those hands in the snow.

They'd neared the drainage ditch. Ashok kicked a shield and knocked the warrior holding it into the freezing water. From the way the man disappeared, thrashing beneath the slush, it was deeper than it looked. The ditch was fifteen feet across. Too far for even a strong man to jump across without a running start. With a roar, Ashok lashed out, swinging Angruvadal in a wide arc, trying to force his opponents back, and as soon as they gave him the tiniest bit of distance, he turned, called upon the Heart to give him strength, and leapt.

He nearly made it. Ashok hit the bricks on the far side with his chest. His lower body landed in the freezing water. It was an incredible shock to the senses. Scrambling for purchase against the ice, Ashok tried to pull himself out. He rolled to his feet, scattering bits of ice and fresh blood. Concentrating on his strength had caused the wound in his back to open again. He lifted his sword just in time to knock aside a hurled spear.

One of the Somsak tried to leap across after him. He made it half the distance and hit the icy water with a splash. The others gave him rude gestures and shouted insults as the soldiers armed with crossbows pushed their way through the crowd to take a shot. Ashok had no time for their foolishness and continued on toward the casteless quarter.

He was freezing. His clothing was soaked. Blood was sluggishly leaking from a dozen wounds, and Ashok cursed himself for using up so much of the Heart's precious magic on someone so terribly unworthy. After passing through the swirling smoke what he saw on the other side came as a shock. He'd expected to find a slaughter, and that much was true, but the bodies he stepped over belonged to Somsak raiders, not untouchables.

The raiders on this side hadn't seen him arrive because they were fleeing back toward the bridge. They had been beaten by makeshift clubs, stabbed with pointed sticks, and struck by thrown stones. The Somsak were fierce, but they'd not been expecting resistance, and they'd walked right into a maze of barracks and shanties where they were outnumbered ten to one, and set the place on fire.

There were at least a dozen dead warriors, and two or three times that many casteless bodies in view. Yet from the way the casteless were celebrating, dancing about and showing off looted weapons, they were considering it as a great victory. Little did they realize there were many more raiders on the other side of the bridge, and they'd be coming back, prepared and in force. Everyone here would be made to pay for this transgression.

"What have you done?" Ashok demanded. The casteless didn't stop their celebrations, not for questions, and not even to battle the fires that were spreading through their quarter. "*What have you done?*"

They heard him that time; a few stopped, but most were too caught up in the moment. It was like a fervor had come over them. When they actually saw who it was they began to cheer. *Fall. Fall. Fall.* It sickened Ashok to the core of his being, these scum chanting his birth name while they desecrated the corpses of their betters.

Mother Dawn hobbled up to him, wearing a Somsak helmet backwards on top of her frizzy mane. "You had to pick your path, Fall, and we had to pick ours."

"You had no right to kill them."

She looked at him, coated in blood and filth, and judged him a hypocrite. "But you do?"

"I'm already condemned. An uprising is the gravest breach of the Law."

"Have you come to punish us then, Protector?"

"That isn't my place anymore, but it doesn't make you any less wrong." A young casteless man was crouched next to one of the dead Somsak and had taken a rusty old saw to his neck, intending to take a trophy. Ashok walked over and kicked the boy away from the body. "Leave them be." The boy scrambled to his feet and ran away.

"Whenever we do wrong, they take our heads and stick them on poles as a warning to the rest," the Mother explained. "Seems fair to give a warning back now, don't it? Didn't you used to do that yourself on occasion?"

Killing a man was one thing, but ruining his body out of spite so that his people couldn't honor it later was different. Ashok had never cared for how they'd left the bodies of witches and traitor on the Inquisitor's Dome to be torn apart by vultures either. "There will be no more of that."

The Mother gave him a little bow. "We'll do as you command."

"Then run." A horn blew on the other side of the fire. "The warriors are coming back and this time they'll be ready. Is there another way out of this canyon?"

The old woman nodded. She nearly lost the helmet. "Our kin have lived here for generations, and unlike the workers who live harvest to harvest, our memories are long. Some of the old mines pass through the hills. There is a way."

"Then take it." He had no idea where these casteless would go, but the non-people were turning out to be full of surprises. He'd brought this suffering down on them, so it was his responsibility to make it right. He didn't know why he cared, but he wanted to know. "The children I brought you?"

"Taken somewhere safe."

"Good. I'll hold them at the bridge."

"You might stop these here, but the rest won't ever stop now, Fall. Oh no. You've started something great. This has been a long time coming. There's those in the Capitol who want every last one of us gone for good. There's plans, and schemes, and plots, all waiting on what you do here today, and before the ashes even cool, the whole world will change. Once the boulder starts rolling down the hill, it won't stop to heed the pebbles."

There was no way some casteless crone from a mountain farming village in the middle of nowhere understood the will of the judges. "What are you?"

She gave him a toothless grin. "I'm merely an old lady more interested in the near future than the distant past."

The horn blew again, two sharp, short blasts. The Somsak were coming. "Take your people and get out before I change my mind."

Chapter 47

Keta peeked around the corner of the storehouse. The only people he saw moving were worker caste, and they were concentrating on putting out fires or caring for their wounded. There weren't any warriors in sight. Not that either group wouldn't murder them if given the opportunity, just that one would be a lot better at it.

Thera was at the other corner, trying to be discreet, but that was difficult when your stolen horse kept stomping and making noise. "Maybe we can take the mountain path the Somsak came down?"

"And go where? Deeper into the homeland of the house that's trying to murder us?"

"Maybe there's another trail that branches off that'll take us back to the trade road. If you've got a better idea, I'd love to hear it."

They couldn't swim an icy river. Waiting around until that was doable would get them killed for sure. From the smoke rising from the casteless quarter, the only residents who might have been inclined to hide them were under attack. The workers would turn them over to appease the raiders. "I've got nothing."

"Then let's go. From the sound of it, Ashok still has their attention."

Even with everything he'd learned about Protectors and bearers, it was a little astonishing that a lone man could fight a whole army for that much time, and for just a moment Keta felt a little flicker of hope, that maybe this was all going to work out after all. If the Forgotten truly wanted Ashok to be his general and lead his people to greatness, then the gods would surely provide a way.

Except the Voice had already spoken, and it seemed like the way provided ended in martyrdom and death. Maybe the Forgotten had only given Ashok the strength to last this long so that Keta had a chance to overcome his fear and fulfill his destiny? As usual the Voice's prediction had been cryptic, and only available at the most damnably inconvenient of times, but for the things that had come to pass so far it had never been wrong.

But what if it wasn't perfect after all? He'd written down several pronouncements that hadn't happened yet, and he'd always just assumed those things would happen in the future. What if the Voice was wrong? What if Thera was right and the ones that had happened had been lucky guesses? If that was the case then all of his work—and all of Ratul's work before him—meant nothing. He truly believed the Forgotten existed because he'd seen the miracles with his own eyes, but if the Forgotten was fallible, was he really a god at all?

They put their hoods up and kept their faces down low as they moved past the distracted workers. Some of them were crying over dead loved ones or wailing as their homes burned to the ground right in front of them. The raiders had truly made a mess of things, and it reminded Keta that his people weren't the only ones suffering injustice in this world. The whole men of Jharlang made their living from the dirt, and being unlucky enough to live in a place a fugitive had hidden was their only crime. Such destruction was uncivilized. The raiders were violating the Law, and they'd surely be punished for it eventually, but no fines, or executions, or prison sentences administered afterwards would help Jharlang today.

There was a crowd of villagers at the end of the road, but they were all looking the other way, watching as events unfolded in the square. Only an hour ago many of them had been part of the angry mob that had formed on that very spot, but now they were only helpless observers. *Well, not too helpless*, because if they realized Keta and Thera were travelling companions of the man who'd brought all of this misery to their sleepy village they'd probably rip them limb from limb. As they got closer Keta caught glimpses of what had the crowd's attention. There were bodies strewn all over the open area and a huge group of Somsak warriors were converging on the bridge to the casteless quarter.

"There's Ashok," Thera said. "I can't believe he's still standing."

Keta had to shield his eyes. The angle was such that the reflection on the ice from the climbing sun on the ice was blinding. The bridge seemed to glow like molten gold in the morning light…

It couldn't be.

He had to see. Heedless of danger, Keta began pushing his way through the workers. "Please, get out of my way." He tried to force his way through, but everyone here was bigger and heavier than he was. The damnable bunch of pick swingers didn't realize that they were preventing a Keeper from seeing a prophecy fulfilled. Growing frustrated, Keta shoved someone. "Move!" The worker turned and shoved him back. Keta balled up his fist and punched him in the stomach. The man went down, groaning. "I must see this!" Keta got to the front of the crowd.

Ashok held the bridge. In one hand was the furious Angruvadal, a swift black arc of destruction, and in his other hand was a Somsak shield, riddled with crossbow bolts. The bridge wasn't very wide, so soldiers could only come at him two or three at a time, and Ashok kept forcing them back or over the side, sometimes in pieces. As Keta watched, the fallen Protector beat soldier after soldier, while behind him scores of casteless could be seen running through the smoke, all fleeing down a path to the north. The bridge seemed to glow with reflected light.

Or as the Voice had described its vision, the Forgotten's chosen general stood on a bridge made of crystal, sacrificing himself to save the innocent.

Keta's heart was suddenly so filled with hope that he thought it might burst.

The workers around him were quivering with fear, knowing that when the Somsak finished their work, all they could do was beg for mercy for unknowingly harboring the infamous criminal. They didn't realize that something amazing was happening right before their very eyes.

"It's true. Don't you see, it's all true!" Keta told the workers.

Only there had been more to the prophecy. It had said that general would have to fight a demon in the body of a man, and as soon as Keta had that thought, he knew exactly which one it had to be. A lone Somsak was slowly lumbering toward the bridge while the others hurried to get out of his way. His intricate armor was painted black and there were antlers on his helmet. There was something alien about his manner, an eerie impression that caused Keta's skin to crawl. The Keeper knew somehow that this man's very existence offended the gods. His sword was a long, fat chunk of steel, the sort of heavy, clumsy thing only used for executions, and from the way he was carrying himself toward the bridge, that's exactly what he expected this fight to be.

As the Keeper of Names, Keta was compelled to testify to the world. He turned toward the crowd and shouted, "*Behold!* The Forgotten has called Ashok Vadal to be his general. He is the one who will free you from tyranny!" They were all looking at him now. He'd never preached to a big group of whole men before, but when Ramrowan had fallen from the sky he'd protected *all* men from the demons. Thera was behind the workers, waving her arms to get his attention. She was mouthing the words *shut up* repeatedly, but she couldn't understand that Keta's faith had just been reaffirmed and that a fervor had come upon him. It was his duty to spread the truth, no matter the costs.

"Listen to me, people of Jharlang! If you help protect his general, the Forgotten will save you from these raiders. The gods are on our side. Heed my words, the Law cannot protect you now, only Ashok can!"

He turned back to see what would happen next. Sadly, before he could watch the duel between Ashok and the demon in the form of a man, someone wacked him in the head with a rock. Dazed, Keta landed on the hard ice and tried to roll over. Between kicks to the ribs and blows to the face, Keta realized that maybe this testifying thing wasn't all it was cracked up to be.

Chapter 48

~~~~~~~~~~~~

The warriors had retreated, leaving Ashok momentarily alone, exhausted and shaking. So much blood had been spilled on the bridge that it had melted the ice beneath him into a pink slush. The ditch was filled with floating bodies. More had rolled down the bridge to collect at the base. He wasn't sure why the Somsak were falling back, but he was thankful for the chance to catch his breath. At this point the Heart of the Mountain was doing everything it could to keep his body functioning despite the many wounds he'd received. Sensing danger, Ashok casually lifted the Somsak shield and let another crossbow bolt strike it. *Thwack.* There were so many bolts embedded in the wood that it was far heavier now than when he'd first taken it off a warrior foolish enough to stick it in his face.

He glanced across the waiting army. *How many of them have I killed so far?* There had been no need to turn in an after action report to the Order, so he'd not bothered to burn each wound he'd administered into his memory. They'd all blurred together into a never-ending stream of tattoo-faced maniacs, spitting up blood and organs. Ashok looked at the sun. How many hours had he been fighting? He wasn't sure, but one way or the other, it would be over soon.

A Somsak in finely crafted heavy armor was approaching the bridge alone. That would be their champion. The rest had worn him down in body and spirit, and now the best among them would finish him off. When the warrior carelessly stepped on the bodies at the base of the bridge, one of them turned out to be unconscious rather than dead, and woke up screaming when his champion's boot spread his wound. The champion paid him no heed and the helmet's narrow eye slits remained focused on Ashok. The wounded soldier lingered for another few seconds before fading away. The champion continued his advance. He carried a huge steel shield and had a large sword resting over one shoulder. It was more of a sharpened steel bar than a proper sword. The warrior was either incredibly strong or incredibly foolish to choose such a cumbersome weapon.

The champion walked up the bridge until they were only a few strides apart.

"Remember me?"

It was a different voice, but he knew it was the same man. Ashok gave him a slow nod. "Nadan Somsak. I didn't recognize you without the swagger."

"I've come for my revenge and to claim my new sword, Protector. When I'm done here, none of you will go to waste. After I'm done raping your corpse, I'll make a mask from your skin, feed your flesh to my hounds, and use your skull as a bowl. I wonder who it is you defend across this bridge? Know that no matter what, I will find them, and when I'm through with them they'll beg for death and curse your name."

The dry rasp of his words was somehow familiar. It reminded Ashok of the sea. "I took your tongue. How can you speak?"

"A wizard fixed me."

He'd never had the gift of working magic, but even Ashok could sense the demonic corruption in the air, like a faint scent oozing through the cracks in the black armor. Nadan Somsak was now the foulest sort of lawbreaker. Ashok wasn't a Protector of the Law anymore, but he'd destroy such a thing on principle. Normally, he would have struck down a hybrid abomination immediately, but he was glad for the chance to rest for a moment. The longer Nadan talked, the better the Heart could knit together his many wounds. "So you found a new tongue. Too bad it's as foul and stupid as the first one."

"You're already beaten. You're weaker than last time, and I'm far stronger."

"Good. Our last duel consisted of me drawing and striking once." ‚

Ashok had never fought one before, nor had any of Angruvadal's previous bearers, but Mindarin had taught him that hybrid abominations were always unpredictable and more powerful than either of the species they'd been spawned from. They were among the worst things that could happen when someone toyed with illegal magic, and their existence was the Inquisition's single greatest fear.

"Things are different now, Ashok. Once you're dead, the sword is mine."

"You may kill me, but Angruvadal will never accept you."

"It will have no choice. Why aren't you afraid, Ashok? You know you should be. You know what you face, so you should be begging for a quick end... No, the rumors are true. You're not brave at all. You're nothing more than a wizard's broken toy. You're no hero. You're a puppy tricked into thinking it's a wolf."

"We're both abominations, but unlike you, I had no choice." They had the small bridge to themselves, but the Somsak troops were crowded around the base and the sides of the ditch, eager to watch the duel and struggling to hear their Thakoor's whispers. Ashok ignored Nadan and loudly addressed his men instead. "I commend you, warriors. You've fought hard. I've travelled across all of Lok and I've never met anyone with more courage and dedication than you've shown here today."

They seemed confused at the compliment from a man who'd already struck down so many of them. There were angry murmurs as Ashok's words were repeated and relayed through the assembled Somsak.

"I wonder, with men so valiant, surely they must not know what kind of creature they're serving? Your Thakoor's speech is no miraculous healing—"

"Silence," Nadan Somsak demanded as he took a step forward.

"Nadan Somsak's blood mingles with corruption. He's made a pact with demons."

There was no time to see the warriors' reaction, because the executioner's blade came crashing down. The attack was so incredibly fast that Ashok barely had time to move aside before it shattered ice and pulverized the stone beneath. Ashok lunged, driving Angruvadal toward the Somsak's breastplate, but somehow the heavy shield was there in time, knocking his attack aside. The giant sword rose, far too quickly, bits of stone and dust raining from it, and then it was moving in a terrible sweeping arc. Ashok ducked beneath as it whistled overhead. Crouched, he hacked at Nadan's legs, but the Thakoor lowered the shield and Angruvadal struck a gash in the steel instead. Nadan was able to step back unharmed.

The Somsak Thakoor was moving with a demon's speed, only he'd retained his warrior skill. Nadan launched another mighty overhand blow. Ashok intercepted it with his shield. There was a horrendous *crack* as wood splintered, leather split, and a terrible shock traveled down the bones of his arm. *Strong as a demon too.* Wasting no time, Ashok went after his opponent, striking repeatedly, thrusting and cutting, but Nadan wielded the heavy blade like it was a fencer's toy and stifled his attacks.

Ashok struck with all his might, bringing his indestructible sword down against Nadan's blade, a move that might have bent or broken a normal sword, but all it did was chip it. That thing was more like a sharpened piece of farm equipment than a mortal's weapon. Nadan intercepted Ashok's following attacks, then slammed his shield forward. Ashok caught it with his own shield, but it was like hitting a brick wall, and Ashok slid back across the red ice.

They parted and circled. Ashok watched his opponent, how he stood, how he put his weight down on the slippery bridge, how he held his shield and shifted his heavy sword, and could discern no weakness. Ashok took the initiative and made an aggressive move to the side, trying to strike over the top of the shield, but Nadan caught it, and then the two were trading blows back and forth. They broke apart again, with Ashok breathing hard and arms burning, but with nothing to show for it other than several new dents in Nadan's shield.

Nadan came at him, swinging high, trying to force him to the edge of the bridge. Ashok struck his flat with the edge of his own blade, disrupting the attack, and then he drove his body forward, crashing into the shield and trying to knock it out of the way. Nadan lifted an armored knee and struck Ashok in the side hard enough to lift him into the air. The helm dipped forward suddenly, and an antler struck him in the head, splitting open his scalp. Ashok accepted the hit and kept pushing. It took more than that to rattle a Protector's brain. They were too close, neither could get their swords in, so instead Ashok swung his shield, turning it and slamming the edge into Nadan's helmet. That staggered him. He kept swinging, hitting him over and over. A deer antler snapped off and flew into the air. The steel deformed, but with a hiss, Nadan brought his sword up and the flat caught Ashok in the chest.

Ashok fell, sliding and rolling down the bridge, not stopping until he hit the warm softness of a corpse. The air filling his lungs tasted like fire and blood, but Ashok sprang right back up. His shield was nothing but useless splinters dangling from frayed straps, so he flung it away. Nadan was coming down the bridge toward him, massive sword cleaving downward, and at the last instant Ashok noticed that the right side of Nadan's helmet had been so deformed by the repeated shield strikes that one eye slit had been crushed nearly closed.

Ashok flung himself that way as the executioner's blade cleaved the dead Somsak soldier in half. Nadan tried to turn, but Ashok was already circling on his blind side, looking for a vulnerable point. Finding a narrow gap at the waist, Ashok struck. Angruvadal hit cleanly between the plates and he pulled into the cut with all his might, letting the black steel edge eat its way through. Mail and quilting split and the ancestor blade bit deep into the flesh beneath. Nadan let out an inhuman shriek.

The huge shield flew around and hit him. It was like being rammed by an elephant, and the blow knocked Ashok clear back to the bottom of the casteless side of the bridge. He lay there for just a moment, figuring out which muscles had torn and which bones had cracked, but knowing it was worth it since he'd struck a mortal blow. You couldn't cut up as many men as Ashok had without gaining nearly a surgeon's knowledge of anatomy. He was certain he'd just sliced Nadan Somsak's kidney in half.

But the warrior was still up and coming his way fast. He rolled out of the way as the giant sword smashed more of the bridge into dust. Nadan should have been dying, but he wasn't even slowing. If anything he was moving even faster than before. Just as the Heart of the Mountain kept him alive, the demon's tongue must have been doing the same for Nadan.

Since Angruvadal had battered his shield into deformed scrap, the demon-man threw it down in disgust and took up his huge sword in both hands. Getting to his feet, Ashok was barely able to stay ahead of Nadan's blade. Blood and *something else* was pouring out of the terrible wound in Nadan's side. There were two streams, one red and the other white as milk, almost as if there were two separate beings living inside the Thakoor's armor.

Gritting his teeth, Ashok vowed to destroy them both.

They were on the casteless side now. Ashok backed away slowly as Nadan stalked him. The warriors were following them across, eager to see their house regain its former greatness. Ashok hadn't been exaggerating when he'd spoken of their courage and dedication. They may have been brutes, but they had honor of a sort. The Somsak deserved to know the truth before it was too late.

"You want to claim Angruvadal?" Ashok spread his arms wide. "Then this duel must be legal."

"*Insufficient,*" Nadan hissed. "*I grant you nothing.*"

"Not for me. This duel is unfair to you. Your vision is impaired. I'll wait while you take your helmet off."

Nadan may have been a hotheaded fool, but he wasn't stupid. Either he knew drawing on the demon's power was twisting his body into something else, or he at least suspected it enough not to take the chance. Nadan leapt forward, covering far more ground than even a Protector could have at his best, and then the executioner's blade was flashing back and forth again, nearly too fast to follow.

The combined instincts of fifty generations were the only thing that kept him alive. Faster and faster the two foes moved, striking and countering, hitting with blows that would have snapped regular blades or left them bent and useless. Another mighty attack came flying downward. Unable to move in time, Ashok raised Angruvadal in both hands and intercepted it. The impact felt like it would rupture every joint in his body. They clashed and locked there, with the far stronger demon pushing hard, sliding Ashok across the ice. The black steel blade was shoved inexorably downward. If he faltered, he would die.

Angruvadal warned him of the incoming danger, but there was nothing he could have done, nowhere he could have moved to, so all he could do was grimace as the crossbow bolt embedded itself deep into his abdomen. Razor-sharp steel pierced his stomach. Ashok gasped.

Nadan saw it and laughed in his face. *"Excellent!"* Ashok had already killed too many of their brothers for all of the Somsak to be concerned about the sanctity of a duel. Several others launched their bolts as well. Most missed, but another flew cleanly through his calf, severing strands of muscle and exiting in a fat shower of blood. His leg collapsed useless beneath him and Ashok fell. Nadan's sword embedded itself into the ground inches from his head.

"Enough! The Black Heart's mine to kill! Not yours!"

Rolling over, Ashok had to stick Angruvadal into the ice so he could lever himself back to his feet. One knee kept buckling, so he balanced on one foot until the Heart of the Mountain forced the damaged muscles to work again. All of his strength was flowing out of his stomach. His extremities felt cold, clumsy, and dead. Nadan watched, mocking him, but Ashok couldn't make out the words over the ringing in his ears.

There was no crime greater than consorting with demons, and no army was that loyal to their champion. If he exposed Nadan's transgression in time, then Jharlang might be spared from the Somsak's further wrath. Desperate, Ashok made his decision. The sword warned him the risk was too great and that escape was still possible.

Forgive me, Angruvadal. Let my death have some meaning at least. He would do this one last thing to uphold the Law and then go into the endless nothing, content.

Are you certain?

In all the years he had carried it, even in the times when it had been his only companion, the sword had never used words before.

"I am," Ashok whispered past the blood spilling from his lips.

Ready to die, Ashok slowly limped toward Nadan Somsak, intent on removing that helmet. He sincerely hoped that Thera and Keta had escaped. Omand and the judges would be so disappointed to hear that he'd not perished like a criminal after all. Ashok peered into the black steel resting in his hand. *My final hope is that your next bearer proves to be more worthy than I have been.*

Nadan Somsak saw him coming and laughed. They both knew this was the end. The army held its breath as their demonic champion lifted his sword in both hands. The executioner's blade flashed, but rather than avoid it, Ashok suddenly stepped *into* the killing arc, driving Angruvadal upward, directly into his opponent's helmet.

Angruvadal exploded.

Chapter 49

Keta saw it all.

Angruvadal shattered like a piece of glass.

Only instead of falling, the pieces seemed to hang there, suspended between the two frozen combatants, but time stalled only briefly, because there was a blinding flash and a roar of thunder that filled the whole world.

Keta had struggled up through the fists and boots of the angry villagers until he could watch. The Forgotten must have given him the strength to do so because it was his duty to be a witness. They'd still been trying to pull him down when the burning wind rolled through them and knocked the workers down.

The entire village was plunged into a searing furnacelike heat. The ice immediately began to melt and run. Where Ashok had been standing, there was a black spot floating in the air, almost like a hole had been burned into the world, but then it slowly faded, leaving nothing but a painful sting in the eye.

After the thunder, it was eerily still. A hushed silence fell over the entire village. The painful heat began to dissipate. Slowly, the Somsak warriors and terrified villagers lifted their heads, trying to figure out what had just happened.

The two combatants had been flung apart. Ashok was lying there, unmoving. Their demonic champion had gone down as well.

But slowly, the demon rose.

His helmet had been swept away, revealing the evil beneath. That face may have belonged to a man once, covered in scars and intricate tattoos, but there was a new art drawn on it in corruption. Beneath the ink and skin was a map of twisting, pulsing veins, white and thick with pus. The horrible being turned toward his army, lifted his arms triumphantly and shouted, *"I am victorious! Somsak!"* He pumped his gauntlets in the air. *"SOMSAK!"*

The warriors didn't cheer. Instead they recoiled in horror when they saw the forked tongue roll past their champion's jagged black teeth.

Keta was more concerned for Ashok. Pushing through the stunned workers, Keta stumbled toward the bridge. The Somsak didn't try to stop him. On the other side of the ditch, Ashok still wasn't moving at all. He didn't appear to be breathing.

Then Keta heard the *Voice.*

The path is set.

The Voice was difficult to describe, and he'd already heard it many times. It wasn't in your ear, but rather inside your head, crashing about the interior of your skull as subtle as a drum. When the prophet spoke to you with the Voice of the gods, there was no way not to hear it.

My faithful servant has been sacrificed.

And now the Voice was speaking to everyone in Jharlang. Most of the villagers were cowering and covering their ears, though Keta knew from experience that would do them no good. Nothing could keep out the Voice. Even the terrifying Somsak were confused and afraid.

Heed this warning. Soon, the demons will rise from the sea.

The rising clouds of steam began to coalesce into a gigantic man-shaped figure that loomed over the square. Warrior and worker alike recoiled in terror.

The Sons of Ramrowan must defeat them.

The Voice had never taken form before, yet beneath the glowing fog was a single person, tiny in comparison to the giant.

Today's testimony has been sealed in blood.

The prophet stood inside the glowing giant, hooded head bowed, swaying and arms dangling, most certainly unaware of the cryptic words being channeled through her. Keta felt both envy and pity when the trance of the gods fell over her. She would remember nothing afterward. It was the Keeper's job to record and remember.

There will be much more before all the world remembers what has been forgotten.

The glow faded. The fog collapsed and rolled away, leaving Thera standing there alone.

Keta's sense of duty told him to stop and write down the words, but he kept pushing toward the bridge instead. It had said the faithful servant had been sacrificed, and Ashok appeared to be dead. Keta looked back toward his prophet. Poor Thera was snapping out of her trance, looking around, bewildered, confused why she found herself with an entire village suddenly staring at her, shocked and afraid.

Thera lifted her hands imploringly toward the cowering villagers. "Please, don't be scared."

"Witchcraft!" a worker screamed.

Thera seemed to shrink, instinctively making sure her hood was up, hiding the scar from where the bolt from the heavens had smote her. The Voice had lived inside her ever since. Her house had been so terrified that they'd tried to hurl her into the sea. She'd spent most of her life running, constantly pursued by the Inquisition. It was Ratul who had recognized Thera for what she really was.

"She is the prophet, the chosen of the Forgotten!" Keta shouted. Then something caught his eye. High above, vultures were circling. A few of them were descending, far too rapidly, growing larger and larger, until Keta realized each was as big as a man. They were heading straight for his prophet. "Thera, look out!" But as Keta watched, horrified, the unnatural things landed, encircled her, and attacked.

Chapter 50

The little casteless blood scrubber boy looked up from the red puddle. He was on his knees on the cold stone floor of the main hall of Great House Vadal. There were two objects lying before him. At different times both had been his most precious possession in life, mighty Angruvadal and a humble wash bucket. He looked at his hands, a child's hands, tiny, torn, and rubbed raw from pushing a rag and wringing it out hundreds of times. Then he looked up to see that there was a lone figure watching him, dressed in a suit of armor, far different than any he'd ever seen before, yet somehow still familiar.

"There should be nothing after death. The Law promised nothing. This is *not* nothing."

"Your Law was an attempt to make things right, and in exchange it made many more things wrong," the armored man said. "Besides, you're not dead yet."

"Damn it."

The man walked over. His armor made no sound, because it was made of something not metal, but better. The puddle of blood rolled away from the man as if it were a living thing, afraid to stain his boots. He knelt next to Angruvadal and nonchalantly picked up the sword. Surprisingly, the sword didn't punish him for it. The stranger was a handsome man, and as he examined the perfect weapon, a warm smile formed on his face. "Hello, old friend."

"Are you the next bearer?"

He chuckled. "There is no one next. I was the first, and you are the last."

"The last? Have I dishonored it so?"

"On the contrary, you have fulfilled the measure of its creation." Now that he was closer, things seemed clearer. The armor was familiar because the design and color was similar to what the Protectors used, only this was far too smooth, too perfect to have come from the hand of man. It hadn't been forged, but *grown*. The style of the Order's armor was nothing but a poor copy *based* on this, and it had been that way since before the Age of Kings. "Do you know why Angruvadal picked you, Fall?"

"No."

"Me either, but that's what it was always meant to do. I suppose we'll all have to find out together."

"Are you the Forgotten?"

"I've been forgotten by most, but I'm not *the* Forgotten. I'm a ghost of a memory, recorded on a weapon. My name is Ramrowan and you must finish what I started."

Ashok woke up furious with a jagged black shard embedded in his heart. Somehow he knew that it was all that remained of the once great Angruvadal and it hadn't killed him only because it loved him. He could feel it there, almost as if it was molten, purifying him with fire. Reaching up with one shaking hand, he shoved two fingers deep into his chest wound, probing. The shard scorched his fingertips when he found it, and he had to pull his hand away.

He was lying in a puddle of melting ice. The air burned, hot as the Capitol in the summer. He saw Nadan Somsak, revealed as an abomination, screeching at his troops to obey, and he knew that this was not yet done. Struggling to stand, he found that one leg was still pathetically weak, so he dragged it along behind. There was a crossbow bolt sticking out of his stomach. He thought about ripping it free so he'd have something to stab Nadan with, but he couldn't risk tearing out his guts. He didn't have time to shove them back in.

Ashok saw something that would make a passable weapon and scooped it up along the way. Nadan Somsak turned just in time to see that Ashok was still alive, but then Ashok took the antler that had broken off the Somsak's helmet and drove it deep into Nadan's throat. White pus sprayed out. Surprised, Nadan tried to push him away, but Ashok twisted it deeper, rocking the antler back and forth until he found the spine. Ashok pried the vertebrae apart.

Paralyzed, Nadan dropped to his knees. There was fear in his eyes.

Ashok had known fear once, in the river, but never again. "You broke my sword."

Ashok drew back one arm and smashed his fist into the Somsak's face with everything he could muster. He hit him again, and then kept on hitting him. Fat droplets of blood, both red and white, flew into the air as Ashok pounded Nadan's face into meat. An eye ruptured. Sharp teeth sliced into his knuckles, but Ashok kept striking him, following Nadan as he sank to the ground, determined to flatten his skull and beat his brains out.

Every bone in Nadan's face was broken, but Ashok kept beating him until the flesh of the cheeks ripped open. Ashok could see the demon's tongue there, twisting about, an independent creature, a foul parasite, so he quit striking Nadan long enough to take hold of his face, break his jaw open far enough that he could reach inside, then grabbed the thrashing evil bit. It squirmed in his grasp, but he squeezed and *ripped* it out of Nadan's head. The tongue came free with a sick tearing noise.

Ashok stood up, tottering, his injured leg nearly failing him, but he managed to stay upright. The tongue was still in his hand, wiggling about like some grotesque parody of a worm. He moved away from Nadan's twitching body, threw the tongue on the ground, and stomped it flat beneath his boot. It ruptured like a fat slug.

Soaked in blood, the Black Heart glared at the many Somsak watching him along the bridge. "Who else will contend with me? Come and finish it."

The Somsak warriors backed away.

Chapter 51

"Now what do we have here?" Sikasso asked as he strolled over to where his men had secured the source of the strange magic he'd sensed earlier. The villagers had fled in terror as they'd fallen from the sky, giving them a bit of peace in this corner of the village square. The woman was on her knees, with a Lost House wizard holding onto each arm. Bhorlatar was behind her, with the point of his sword pressed against her neck. If her strange powers had any offensive capabilities, it was doubtful she'd be able to use them before Bhorlatar severed her spine.

"Careful, Sikasso, this one's got claws." Bhorlatar gestured toward Vilsaro, who was lying in the mud, throat slashed ear to ear, gurgling, and staring at the sun. There was nothing that could be done for him. "He grabbed her first, but she surprised him. The blade came out of nowhere and damn near took his head off."

That was another valuable wizard lost on this awful, wasteful mission for the Grand Inquisitor. From what Sikasso had seen of the destruction of Angruvadal, he seriously doubted there would be very many fragments left large enough to be worth their effort. He'd never seen a piece of black steel so thoroughly consumed before. Sikasso was feeling very annoyed, but perhaps something could be salvaged from this mess.

Sikasso picked up the knife that had been used on Vilsaro. It was a thin, practical blade, sharp enough to shave with. He walked to the captive woman. "Who are you?" The woman had her head down, hair covering her face, and didn't respond, so he stuck the knife under her chin and lifted. It was either raise her head to face him or get cut. She chose to face him, which was good, because it turned out she was pretty enough that Sikasso would have hated to mar such a nice face. "Tell me your name."

She glared at him. There was rage in this one. "Thera."

"House and caste?"

"None."

"You're no untouchable. You're too tough to be of the first, and workers know how to hide their anger better. Warrior then, and probably thrown out to keep from drawing the attention of the Inquisition when you started to display such a unique talent." Her silent look of disgust told Sikasso that he was close. "Who are you? I'll have it out of you eventually one way or the other."

"Vane, vassal house to Makao, daughter of the warrior caste, but I wasn't thrown out. I left on my own accord during a house war. They think I'm dead, so leave my family out of this."

"You mistake us for Inquisitors. Not even close. We're merely scholars, dedicated to understanding the mysteries."

"Go to hell."

He backhanded her in the face. Then Sikasso glanced around the square, which was still sweltering with unnatural heat. They were surrounded by the bodies of soldiers who'd tried to stop the Black Heart. After Thera's bizarre manifestation, they were being watched by a large group of frightened workers, but they were holding back. The rest of the Somsak raiders all seemed preoccupied by their Thakoor's antics across the square on the other side of the ditch. Sikasso had no idea what those fools had gotten up to after the precious sword had blown up, and he was mostly disappointed he'd wasted such a valuable piece of demon flesh on that idiot, Nadan.

Frustrated, Sikasso turned back to Thera. Her lip was split open and bleeding but she was still giving him a defiant look that was just begging to be sliced off. "I only know of two sources for magic, the ancient and ever-dwindling supply of black steel, and whatever we can wring from the remains of sea demons, yet yours comes from neither. What is your source?"

"I don't know," she muttered. Sikasso put the knife against her cheek. "Really, carve away, you bastard. *I don't know.*"

"Some fool was carrying on about her being a prophet of the old gods while we circled," Bhorlatar said. "That's what her illusion was supposed to be about, I think."

"It wasn't an illusion," Thera said. "The Voice comes from somewhere else and works through me. That's all I know."

Sikasso had been on the ground at the time of the manifestation and he'd clearly heard the voice inside his head. It had been rather impressive. "You have an intriguing power. I believe you're telling the truth." He removed the knife. "Yuval, fly her back to camp and wait for us there. We've got some cleaning up to do here first. There are far too many witnesses."

She struggled against the wizards, but years of magical augmentation had left the men of the Lost House far stronger than they appeared. "Let go of me, or you'll regret this!"

"Doubtful. You'll remain my prisoner until I discover the true source of your power, then afterwards—if you are truly the troublemaking prophet they've been hunting in the south—I'll sell you to the Grand Inquisitor. Perhaps it'll even be enough to make up for this mess...Bhorlatar." He nodded toward his subordinate, who lifted his sword and struck the struggling woman with the pommel hard enough to knock her unconscious. Flying while carrying extra weight was difficult enough without cargo flailing about the whole time too. The wizards let her collapse into the mud so Yuval could change form. You couldn't very well hold onto someone when your arms were turning into wings. That's what feet were for.

"Sikasso, we've got a troublemaker." Bhorlatar pointed with his sword at a thin man who was heading their way. He was dressed as a merchant, but had just picked up a discarded Somsak crossbow and was trying to figure out how to use it against them. "That's the one who was carrying on about her speaking for the old gods. Want me to burn him?"

"I've got him. Save your magic. We still have a village to scrub." With Vilsaro missing his throat, and Yuval carrying the woman back to camp, that meant he, Bhorlatar, and Choval had a lot of work to do. As Sikasso began walking toward the religious fanatic, the area around them darkened as magic was called upon. Yuval was the biggest of them, and in his flying form he seemed huge, with a wingspan that covered a vast portion of the square. His gleaming black talons locked around Thera's arms, and with several mighty beats, he took to the air.

Snap. The fake merchant figured out how to fire the crossbow. Sikasso smiled as the speeding bolt missed Yuval by several feet. "Your aim needs work," Sikasso shouted.

Obviously terrified but determined to stop the abduction of his prophet, the fake merchant picked up another bolt from a dead man's quiver and went about trying to figure out how the hand crank worked on the powerful device. That amused Sikasso to no end. Yuval was already far above the village and searching for a good air current to carry him back to the mountaintops. "Bhorlatar, kill all the hole diggers. Choval, start on the sword swingers, and make sure you secure Ashok's body. As long as the Inquisition thinks he's still alive they'll pay us to keep following him." He started toward the balding man with the crossbow. "I'll catch up."

"Hold on. How's he still alive?" Choval asked, sounding incredulous. Sikasso turned his head to see what his man was talking about. The young wizard was looking toward the bridge, but then he was struck in the chest with a spear thrown across the square so hard that it swept him off his feet and slammed him back into the side of a house. Choval hung there limp, pinned like a butterfly.

"Ashok!" Sikasso bellowed as another of his valuable wizards died. There was no way the Protector should still be alive, but there he was, bloodsoaked and determined, limping across the bridge toward them. The Somsak parted to let Ashok through. "Burn him!" Sikasso shouted at Bhorlatar, as Ashok bent over and picked up a discarded battle axe. "Burn him to ash!"

Bhorlatar was a master of the inferno. No matter how resilient the Protectors' secret rites made their bodies, nothing could survive that kind of fury. Circles of darkness formed around Bhorlatar's outstretched hand as the chunk of demon bone in his fist was consumed. The air around Ashok shimmered with heat waves and the fallen Protector stumbled, clutching at his eyes. The Somsak around him fled, crying about witchcraft, as wood smoked, leather scorched, and cloth caught fire. Ashok cried out in pain as he was engulfed in a sphere of intense heat. Bhorlatar cackled.

This time the fake merchant's aim was true.

Bhorlatar lowered his dark-encircled hand and looked down at the crossbow bolt sticking out of his chest. He seemed surprised by the sudden pain, but not nearly as surprised as when Ashok came out of the faltering fire, covered the distance, and cut off both of Bhorlatar's legs in one swing. The wizard went flipping through the air, screaming.

As he shrugged out of his flaming coat, Ashok limped toward Sikasso.

He was a powerful wizard, possibly one of the greatest in the world, yet when Sikasso looked into Ashok's maddened eyes he saw only his death there. His men were gone. Sikasso was proud, but pragmatic, and knew when it was time to retreat. The Lost House had claimed the girl with the mysterious power. That would do for today.

Taking up one of the demon-bone chunks tied to his belt, Sikasso called upon the unnatural energy inside. Magic was made of tiny bits, invisible to the eye, and as those fled from the bone and into his body, reality changed. Light was vanquished as the bone was consumed, and within the unnatural darkness that existed in the space between, the rules of the physical world no longer applied. His limbs twisted and distorted as the tiniest bits of his flesh were moved and redistributed. Sikasso willed his body into the familiar form of the giant vulture and leapt into the sky.

A few mighty beats of his wings and he was soaring upward, away from the damnable Protector and his—

There was a flash of heat in his left wing, followed immediately by a searing pain.

Ashok had thrown the axe. End over end, it continued past him, but he could no longer follow it into the air. Instead Sikasso spiraled helplessly toward the ground. His left wing was *gone*.

The wizard landed hard in the mud. The magic ruptured and reality flooded back in. As his body and senses returned to normal, Sikasso began to scream as blood pumped from the stump where his arm had been. Panicked, he looked around. A long black wing lay a few feet away, shedding obsidian feathers. It slowly melted into a severed arm and the feathers turned to spatters of blood.

The Protector was coming for him.

Chapter 52

Ashok could barely see through the haze of blood and hate.

"Where have you taken her?"

The wizard weakly held up his remaining hand. "Wait."

Barely slowing, Ashok snatched up another spear from the ground. "*Where?* Where is Thera?"

"Don't. The Grand Inquisitor sent me. You're not allowed—"

"Omand?" That made no sense. He'd obeyed his orders and gone willingly to his punishment. Ashok didn't know this man. "No games, wizard. Where is she?"

"Nowhere you'll ever find her," he snarled as he grabbed for a pouch at his belt. The area around the wizard was consumed by darkness. Ashok hurled the spear into the center of the black, but when it dissipated, the spear was embedded in the dirt where the wizard had been, only his body had turned into a massive pile of swarming insects. The swarm immediately spread outward, flying, scuttling, and burrowing away. Ashok swatted and stomped at them, cursing, but within a few heartbeats the insects had disappeared.

The wizard had escaped.

Ashok sank to the ground. Battered, bleeding, burned, with nothing left to give. The Heart of the Mountain was the only reason he was still alive, and he knew that if he closed his eyes and simply gave up, that would be the end of him.

Ashok held on just out of spite.

Keta appeared, his face swollen and bruised, looking toward the distant peaks where the flying wizard and his prisoner had disappeared from view. "They took the prophet. I tried to stop them...I don't...I don't know what to do."

"Why didn't you tell me who Thera was?"

"The Forgotten said I had to test you—trust you—first. You're still alive. The faithful servant sacrificed was Angruvadal. You're the one...You have to know what to do! What do we do, Ashok?"

"First? Survive..." Keta hadn't noticed that they were being approached by a small crowd of Somsak warriors and Jharlang workers, but Ashok had. There weren't that many, but enough to easily finish Ashok off in the sorry state he was in.

The group stopped, split into two halves, each one nervously eyeing the other. A young warrior, his facial markings only recording a handful of battles, broke off by himself and approached. When he was a few strides away, he stopped and asked, "Is it true? Does the Forgotten truly speak again?"

Ashok had no idea, but Keta boldly stepped forward. "Yes. The old gods have chosen a prophet to speak through, but I'm only the Keeper of Names. The prophet has been taken by these wizards. This is our general." Keta pointed at Ashok. "But we need help to rescue her."

The young warrior looked to his compatriots. There were a few stern nods to give him courage, then he turned back, earnest and imploring, to speak on their behalf. "We want to *remember*."

There were no dreams to trouble his sleep, only a profound sense of loneliness.

"For a man who only wants to die, you're remarkably bad at it."

Ashok woke up on a cot inside a humble dwelling. A large fire was burning in a stone pit. He remembered being taken to a farm somewhere near Jharlang but was unsure how long he'd been out since. Every muscle in his body ached. His skin was raw and stinging and the fire had burned most of his hair off. The simple act of breathing was torture. Worst of all was the contorting pain in his guts from the bolt wound. He noted all of those things and then paid them no further mind.

He was surprised when he saw who it was who'd spoken. Jagdish was sitting on a stool next to the cot. "I must hand it to the Somsak. Despite looking like fools, their surgeons get a lot of practice stitching men back together. The fact you're healing so fast has got the fanatics out there dancing about praising false gods' miracles. Apparently they've elected you general or something. That's an archaic rank no house uses anymore, but I think that's equivalent to a phontho. Not too shabby a promotion from prisoner."

"The Forgotten picked him, not us." Ashok turned his head to see that Keta was standing at the foot of the cot, arms folded, giving Jagdish a disapproving scowl. "I'm sorry, Ashok. I tried to turn him away, but then he threatened to duel me."

"It's all right, Keeper. Jagdish was the warden of my prison. He's an honorable man."

"And these Somsak who've pledged to serve him aren't fanatics. Some of them have been practicing religion in secret. They're faithful who've heeded the call to—"

Ashok cut Keta off. "You're a long way from Cold Stream, Risaldar."

"I found a worker who's got a gift for tracking magic and we followed you. It was quite the journey. I must admit this is the farthest I've ever been from home."

So that was it then. House Vadal had caught their fugitive at last. "I'm assuming you have a legion waiting for me outside. You won't need it. Angruvadal has been destroyed."

"I was told. I truly am sorry. That is a tragedy."

There were almost no memories of the time before the sword. Of his life since, there had been a brief time where Ratul had forced him to live without Angruvadal, and that had driven him to undertake desperate risks to get it back. That made Ashok think of himself and his only friend, huddled together for warmth in an ice cave, two stupid children, too brave for their own good, trying to become real Protectors. Angruvadal had been his constant companion ever since. It was as if he'd lost a part of himself. The ghostly instincts and memories of all of the bearers who'd come before, *gone*. For a people with no belief in life after death, at least the bearers had some measure of immortality, but now they were all lost as well.

"Yes, a tragedy."

"I don't want to be the one to break the news to our House. But we survived twenty years without Angruvadal there to protect us; we will survive more. My brothers will hold. Our house will not fall." Jagdish said "*our* house." Ashok didn't bother to correct him. He lacked the energy to protest. "But I've got no legion at my back. It's just me. Your escape brought even more dishonor to my name. Wizards slaughtered my men and blamed it on you. No unit will have me. I had to send my pregnant wife back to live with her family. Do you have any idea what that's like?"

"My apologies, Risaldar. They were good men. I didn't hurt any of your guards."

"I know that, and after seeing those dead wizards outside, I think they're the same group that attacked Cold Stream and Sutpo Bridge. My tracker, Gutch, found a mark on one and said they're known to magic smugglers as the Lost House, a degenerate lot who are always buying up black steel and demon bits. I intend to find those responsible for killing my men and I'll make sure House Vadal learns the truth. I followed you all this way for the chance. I'll not have my son grow up with the shame of having a dishonorable failure as a father."

"We share a similar goal, warrior. Those wizards took someone very important to us," Keta said. The Keeper looked to Ashok, uncertain. "I know you were somehow being compelled to search for the prophet before, Ashok, and your reasons are your own, but regardless of what you decide to do now, I intend to find Thera."

The wizard had claimed to work for Omand. More than likely, he'd just been a liar, but it forced Ashok to question the strange nature of the Grand Inquisitor's orders. If Omand truly was consorting with forbidden magic for some unknown reason, he would be dealt with, but until then, his word remained legally binding. Ashok had proven to be an imperfect instrument on its behalf, but he still believed in the Law. The judges had declared that his punishment was to *find* and *protect* the prophet, so that was what he would do. "My mission continues, Keeper." Ignoring the pain, Ashok forced himself off the cot. He stood there, swaying, one leg protesting, until the dizziness passed. "*We* will find her."

"Our paths converge once again." Jagdish stroked his beard thoughtfully. "So you're supposedly a general now, and you've gathered a handful of fools who fancy themselves an army. Even a sad army needs officers. I would like to apply."

Keta asked, "What of your wife?"

"She'll appreciate me more when my name is redeemed."

"Helping me may have the opposite effect on your name," Ashok cautioned.

"If not for me, then for the memory of my men, this is a risk I'm willing to take."

Normally, Ashok would have tried to talk an honorable man out of joining with a gang of criminals, but they needed all the help they could get. "I accept, Jagdish. Thank you."

"Then I will serve you until we expose these wizards or the Capitol has us all executed as traitors." Jagdish bowed. It hurt to bend at the waist, but Ashok returned the gesture.

"Wonderful. So our god's army is to be led by men who don't believe in the gods." Keta muttered. "And now we go to rescue a prophet without faith. Brilliant."

"I like these gods of yours, Keta," Jagdish said. "They seem like an amusing bunch . . . So, General, what do you intend to call this little army of yours?"

"The Sons of the Black Sword." They seemed to approve of the choice. Ashok gestured toward the door. "Please, both of you, allow me a moment to collect myself. I'll join you shortly."

Once he was alone, Ashok had to know for sure. All of his wounds had been cleaned, stitched, and bandaged, but there was only one in particular that he was concerned with. He carefully unwound the cloth from his chest until he could peer down and see where he'd been impaled through the heart by Angruvadal's shard. Because it was a black steel wound, it would leave a grisly scar, but the injury was already sealed shut. Ashok could no longer feel the molten metal burning through his chest. It had cooled and solidified. He rested his palm against the wound and could feel the slow, measured heartbeat. There was something cold and hard beneath. *Waiting.*

The Keeper had spoken of the concept many times, but Ashok did not know how to *pray.* The very idea was anathema to his being. He'd always thought of a belief in the Forgotten as a terrible crime, reserved for superstitious malcontents, but there was no denying that he should be dead. Ashok suspected that his life had been miraculously spared because his work was not yet done.

It seemed that even if he was not a believer, Angruvadal had been.

Ashok knelt in front of the fire pit. That seemed as reasonable as anything else. As he looked into the flames, Ashok spoke loudly and clearly, so that there could be no misunderstanding between them.

"Forgotten, if you are real, heed these words. I did not ask you to spare my life. I do not want this. I seek no favor, blessings, or glory. I will do what I believe to be right. That is all. If that is not what you are looking for, then ignite this shard and let me die now, because I serve justice. I have given my oath to protect your prophet, so I will do so or die trying. I warn you now that if your cause is unjust, stay out of my way, because I am Ashok Vadal, and I will make sure even the gods regret crossing me."

The general went to meet his army.

Epilogue

The desert sun beat down on Grand Inquisitor Omand as he sat in a wicker chair along the road between the Capitol and the Inquisitor's Dome, waiting patiently. He'd come alone, without even a slave to hold his umbrella or wave a cooling fan.

Regardless of the season, even the busiest caravans tried not to travel during the hottest part of the day here, but there was a line of men on horseback making their way from the Capitol. If Omand hadn't already been certain who it would be before, the silver armor gleaming in the sun confirmed it. From this distance he couldn't make out too many details, but the riders had far superior vision, some said better than a hawk, so they certainly recognized Omand. The one in the lead broke off and galloped in his direction, his warhorse kicking up a furious plume of fine white dust in its wake.

Omand remained in his chair, comfortable and unafraid, as Lord Protector Devedas approached. For a moment he was concerned that the Protector was just going to run him down, but the horse reared as Devedas pulled on its reins and forced it to stop only a few feet away. Close enough to throw sand on his robes.

"Speak, Inquisitor. Let me hear your voice."

Of course. Just because he was wearing the Grand Inquisitor's mask didn't make him the Grand Inquisitor. It was wise to be suspicious. "Hello, Devedas. Always a pleasure to see you again."

"Omand..." He dipped his head just a bit. "There's no pleasure here."

"Could it be? It appears that all of the stalwart Protectors of the Law are leaving the Capitol."

"We are. The judges have lost confidence in the loyalty of my Order."

"A shame."

"I believe you had something to do with that."

Omand waved one hand dismissively. "My obligation is to protect the governing caste from all who would do it harm. The judges judge, I only provide facts, and the evidence suggested that some Protectors have violated their oaths. If it is any consolation, I believe the vast majority of you to be men of impeccable integrity. My recommendation said as much, yet the Capitol's faith in your Order was still shaken."

"I'm going to personally see to it that faith is restored."

"By killing the traitor Ashok, I take it?"

"I've sworn that I won't return to this city until he's dead. Every last one of us will be pursuing him to the ends of the world." Devedas glanced around the open desert suspiciously. "What a strange turn of events. You just happen to be waiting here as we pass, and you appear to be all alone."

"A happy coincidence," Omand said as he looked across the vast expanse of nothing, as if men of his importance often sat alone in the desert for no reason. "Yes, I am all by myself. Say what you will. There are no ears here except for ours."

"Then you received my message. Speaking of ears, how is your man?"

"Not quite so useful to me horribly disfigured."

Devedas pushed on. "I've been investigating you, Omand Vokkan, and what I've found is most curious. Clandestine meetings with high-status members of every house, bribing archivists to tamper with the histories, and conspiracies to manipulate judges. You've been a busy man, pulling all those strings."

"I must admit, I do enjoy politics."

"You must, since you're planning on overthrowing the government."

"Oh?" That was why he'd placed himself here. Omand had

suspected Devedas was aware of some of his crimes, but he was unsure of which. If Devedas had known that he was behind Ashok's escape, then he probably wouldn't have stopped the horse from trampling him.

"You've mocked the Law enough."

"On the contrary, I'm the Law's fondest supporter. Everything I've done has been to strengthen the Capitol's control of the houses. We both know they have too much autonomy, and such freedom causes disorder. It was a pointless raid that cost your father his ancestor blade, and thus cost you your birthright. I would stop such frivolity."

"So you've distorted history to promote genocide?"

"The non-people are a stumbling block to progress. Religious fanaticism is an infection that can never be cured and it lives on in the tissues of the casteless. Until they are cut away, the infection will continue to spread. You've known this to be true since I told you where to find your old master, Ratul. If this necessary cleansing has the added benefit of making the houses more reliant upon the Capitol, where is the harm?"

"What's to keep me from taking your head right now?" Devedas put one hand on the hilt of his sword.

Omand smiled beneath his mask. As usual, a warlike man underestimated his abilities. Just because he was primarily skilled in rhetoric and manipulation, those quick to violence never realized Omand could crush them like a bug if he felt like it. Luckily, such direct action was seldom necessary. "Calm yourself, Devedas." He'd been observing these Protectors for years, and he knew that Devedas had too much pride in his own achievements to ever be completely devoted to the letter of the Law, and thus could be manipulated. "It would be a shame if something horrible was to happen to that librarian of yours."

The young man's face darkened. "Your clumsy attempt at silencing the archivist was embarrassing."

"Don't waste my time pretending that Rada is just another witness. From the pained expression you're wearing, you thought your relationship was a secret. I truly do see everything that happens in this city. You actually love her. I always thought you were too ambitious for such entanglements. My congratulations. She will make a fine bride once you both decide to end your obligations to your orders, but I tire of dancing around the issue.

I know where you've hidden her. If I die, she dies. If my dark councils are exposed, then she dies. Simple."

Perhaps it wasn't that simple, because Devedas drew his sword.

"*Wait,*" Omand ordered with such force that ripples travelled outward through the sand. Devedas' horse shifted nervously as the ground beneath its hooves moved. Omand held up one fist, indicating he had a chunk of black steel clenched in it, and wouldn't hesitate to use it. "I was a witch hunter long before I was a bureaucrat."

"If you harm her, nothing in the world will stop me from taking your head."

Omand had misjudged the man, and thus picked the incorrect move for this game, but he still had other plays. "Any action against me will be seen by the judges as proof that the Order has been corrupted. The Protectors will be ruined, the members purged, and you will be remembered as the commander who caused it all."

Surprisingly, Devedas laughed. "You truly are the spider like they say! Are people really stupid enough to blunder into your web so easily?"

"Normally, yes." Omand tilted his mask back and studied the Protector with new appreciation. He was smarter than he acted. "I sense you have a different proposal."

"I do." Devedas pointed his sword at Omand's chest. "I suspect you care nothing about the casteless and their false gods except that they're an excuse for you to consolidate power. You want to return to the Age of Kings in all but name. In those days the tribes united to push the demons into the sea. Now you want to do the same thing to the casteless. The events that bring this about are irrelevant, as long as when it is over, you're in control."

"You are more politically astute than I gave you credit for, Devedas. It is truly a shame about your house dying. You would have made a fine Thakoor."

"I'll make a better *king.*"

For once, Omand was the one taken by surprise. "I believe you overestimate my goals."

"Call the office by whatever title you want, governor, minister, I don't care, but you must realize you'll need one. Since I've been investigating your sabotage of the archives, it's given me the opportunity to read up on how things worked in the prior age.

There was usually one man in control, sometimes a figurehead, sometimes not, but if you intend to consolidate power, there must be a single ruler for the people to look to. It can't be you. No one will follow a man who has never shown his face. The first king was chosen because he was the hero who beat the demons. You have found your threat, now you need your hero."

"An interesting proposal...I will take your offer to the councils."

"No, you won't. We both know who runs the web, and I'm sure you've got no shortage of conspirators who each think they're the best man for the job, ready to put a knife in my back. You want the great houses to bow to the Capitol, but whichever of your pet judges you choose to be your figurehead has to come from one of those houses, leaving the rest jealous or suspicious. I have no house."

Omand was impressed by the logic. "Hmmm...Your only loyalty has been to an Order which has been fair and equal to all. You're born of the first caste, but without any of their usual entanglements that entails. The warrior caste would have far more respect for you than any man of the courts. An argument could be made that you would be the best choice." He was practical enough to admit that Devedas also had a charismatic charm and his rugged looks would do well on posters and coins.

"Though I know that's where the power truly lies, I've got no stomach for managing bureaucracies. That's for men like you, Omand. I was born to rule, and that's what I intend to do."

"Very well." This had been a more fruitful meeting than Omand had hoped for. "But what about the destruction of the casteless?"

"Rebellion is coming to all of the houses one way or the other. It's been in the air too long, and recent events will only make it worse. I don't believe in the old foolish superstitions about where the casteless come from, but I think exterminating all of them is unnecessary brutality. Let the rebellious hang, and the rest will fall back into line as usual."

It turned out they were both ambitious, but Devedas still had some measure of humanity. Luckily Omand didn't. "Of course. As long as I reach my political goals I don't care what happens to them. I'm happy to let the obedient casteless live," he lied.

"I intend to crush the rebellion, and when I return, triumphant, we can either be allies or enemies. You will have plenty of time to prepare your people to welcome me back. I believe this may be a long campaign. With Ashok joining the rebels, for once they're actually a threat."

Does he know of my part? Impossible. Only a loyal few knew of Ashok's fabricated orders, and none of them would have talked. "So you believe he has willingly joined the rebels?"

"Ashok was the closest friend I've ever had. I know him better than anyone. There's never been a man born with a greater single-minded devotion to the Law. They say he's without compassion or mercy, but they don't realize Ashok believed he was doing lawbreakers a *favor* by ending them. People think it was because of the sword, but that's not what made Ashok that way. It was his belief, his certainty. He just *is*. So while he was rotting in that cell, pondering on all those who wronged him, if he turned that devotion to something else, some other task, he'd be just as certain, just as merciless, only now there would be no Law to restrain him..." Devedas trailed off, then shook his head sadly. "No, Inquisitor, my Order isn't just searching for him as some political show to satisfy the judges. I have to kill my brother because I know that Ashok is the most dangerous man alive."

For the first time, Omand wondered if he might have inadvertently unleashed something terrible into the world.